Panic rose in Alias. Her body was moving of its own accord, just as it had when she nearly killed Winefiddle. She tried to fight the urge to lunge at the Wyvernspur noble, but without success. Something nearby was burning.

Standing right beside Alias, Akabar felt her stiffen. He noticed the smell of smoke almost immediately. With horror he watched the glove that covered the swordswoman's tattoo blister and burn away. Then he heard Alias snarl, and saw her face contort into a mask of rage.

With murder in her eyes, Alias leaped onto Giogi with a scream, her hands about his throat in an instant. She might have wrung his neck, but she caught sight of a long, sharp knife used to cut pies and cake. She reached for it, but lost her grip on the young man as she did so. Giogi managed to twist away from her, and the swordswoman plunged the pastry blade into the table where he'd been pinned only a moment before.

Alias yanked the blade from the tabletop and drew a fresh bead on her target. Giogi backpedaled furiously. Women screamed and several Wyvernspur menfolk, faced with a mad assassin, fled the area as quickly as possible, leaving the tent sides flapping where they'd torn up the stakes.

Olive, her ode interrupted, her audience gone, moved toward the fight. She helped Akabar up from the ground as she demanded, "Just what does she think she's doing?"

FANTASY ADVENTURE

KATE NOVAK AND JEFF GRUBB

Cover Art
CLYDE CALDWELL

TSR, Inc.
PRODUCTS OF YOUR IMAGINATION™

To my teacher, Ms. Hughes,
because her passion for the truth
has always been inspiring.

To Scott and Gayle,
who care.

AZURE BONDS

This book is protected under the copyright laws of the United States of America. Any reproduction or other unauthorized use of the material or artwork contained herein is prohibited without the express written permission of TSR, Inc.

Distributed to the book trade in the United States by Random House, Inc. and in Canada by Random House of Canada, Ltd.

Distributed in the United Kingdom by TSR UK Ltd.

Distributed to the toy and hobby trade by regional distributors.

FORGOTTEN REALMS, PRODUCTS OF YOUR IMAGINATION and the TSR logo are trademarks owned by TSR, Inc.

First Printing, October, 1988
Printed in the United States of America.
Library of Congress Catalog Card Number: 88-50057

9 8 7 6 5 4 3 2 1

ISBN: 0-88038-612-6

All characters in this book are fictitious. Any resemblance to actual persons, living or dead is purely coincidental.

TSR, Inc.
P.O. Box 756
Lake Geneva, WI 53147
U.S.A.

TSR UK Ltd.
The Mill, Rathmore Road
Cambridge CB14AD
United Kingdom

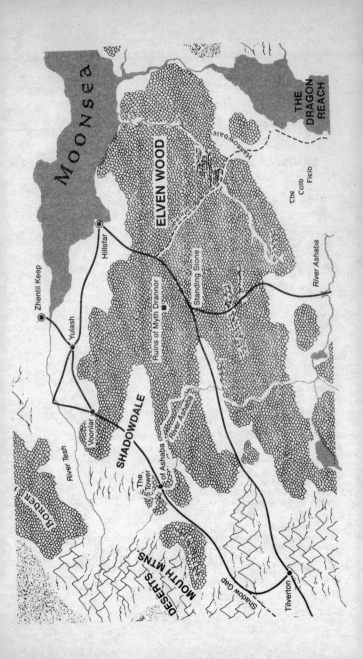

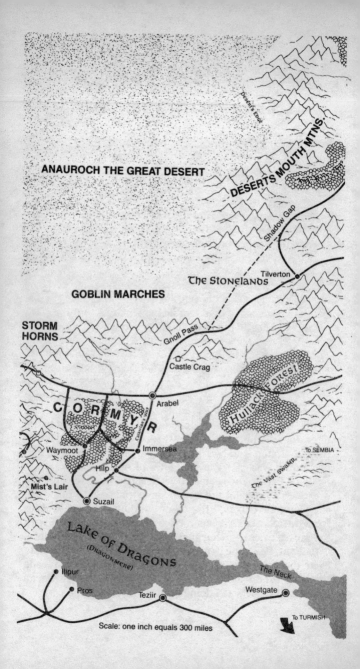

❧ 1 ❧

The Hidden Lady

She woke to the noise of dogs—two distinct barkings beneath her open inn window. A high-pitched yip confronted a deep, throaty growl. Alias lay on the tan-stained cotton sheets and pictured a long-haired puppy cast out from its wealthy owner's household, fending off some huge boxer or Vassan wolfhound.

As with men and other savage races, the show of force was as important to the dogs as force itself. The yipping canine was overmatched, yet its barking went on for what seemed to Alias an eternity. Finally, the dog with the deeper growl reached the end of its patience and snarled savagely. The sound of toppling trash brought Alias fully awake.

She opened her eyes, listening for a dying squeal from the smaller dog, but surprisingly the next thing she heard was a series of deep yelps from the large dog. The sound faded away as the large dog fled from the window.

Alias threw off the light blanket and swung her feet to the floor. She rose and immediately regretted it. Her head felt as though molten lead had been poured behind her eyes, and her mouth was as dry as the sands of Anauroch.

She blinked in the reddish light. Is it dawn or twilight? she wondered. Pressing the heels of her palms into her eyes, she yawned. Through the open window, the sea breezes from the Lake of Dragons wafted into the room, along with the far-off cries of fishermen returning with their catch.

Twilight, then, she decided. She shook her head, trying to clear the cobwebs. Must have slept through the day, she thought. When did I get here? For that matter, where's here? And what was I doing before I came here?

Alias snorted derisively. What she'd been doing was obvious. This wasn't the first time she'd awakened in a strange place after a drunken celebration.

Nonetheless, her surroundings seemed familiar. The inn was built in the same fashion as a hundred others at this end of the Sea of Fallen Stars, and her room held the typical trappings: a bed cobbled together of a mixed pile of wood, topped with a straw tick and sheets that hadn't been aggressively washed in months; a small second-hand dressing table; a single straight-backed chair draped with her armor and clothing; a small rag rug at the foot of the bed; a brass oil lamp chained to the table; a chamber pot; and a single door. The window, inset with colorless circles of crown glass that let in the light of the setting sun, opened inward on side hinges that creaked lightly in the breeze.

Alias got out of bed and padded barefoot to the chair. She furrowed her brows, trying to remember the last few days. There was a sailing trip. Something went wrong and I had to get out of a seaport quickly, she thought.

Random images of lizard men, shadowy swordsmen, and magic-users blurred in her memory. She shrugged. It couldn't have been too important. I wouldn't get drunk if there was trouble, she assured herself.

She reached for her tunic and suddenly realized that this *was* important, that she was in trouble. Serious trouble.

Along the inside of her sword arm, from wrist to elbow, writhed an elaborate tattoo unlike any she had ever seen before. A pattern coiled about five large, distinct symbols was set deep into her flesh, all done in shades of blue.

She held up her arm in the light of the dying sun. The symbols caught the rays and glowed as if they were stained glass lit from behind. She flexed her arm and twisted it back and forth. It wasn't really a tattoo at all, she realized, noting how her skin rippled across the surface of the massive inscriptions, as though they were buried beneath the surface of her flesh.

Engrossed by the symbols, Alias unconsciously sat on the edge of the bed in the fading light. Afraid the symbols might have some hypnotic quality, she studied them with her fingernails pressed into her palms so the pain would distract her from whatever power they might try to exert over her.

The first symbol, at the bend of her arm, was a dagger surrounded by blue fire. The tip of the dagger rested on the second symbol, a trio of interlocking circles. Beneath this was a dot and a squiggle which reminded Alias of an insect's leg. The leg danced above the fourth symbol—an azure hand with a fanged mouth in the center of its palm. The last symbol consisted of three concentric circles, each a more intense blue, so that the centermost circle was the white-blue of a lightning strike and almost unbearable to look at. At the base of her wrist the pattern wound about an empty space, as if a sixth symbol was yet to be added.

Alias cursed, rattling off the names of as many gods as she could immediately think of. When neither Tymora nor Waukeen nor any of the others manifested themselves, she sighed and reached for her gear. She considered bolting out of the room, sword in hand, prepared to smite anyone she could hold responsible. She also considered dropping to her knees and praying for a divine revelation of what she had done to deserve this. Neither action was likely to do her any good, so she settled for getting dressed.

Alias tugged her tunic over her head and stepped into her leather leggings. She frowned at the clothing. Why are these so stiff? I bought them over a year ago. They should be broken in by now. Unless they're replacements, she mused. There was no mistaking the newness of this set of clothing—it even smelled new.

But I don't remember buying any new clothes recently. Is this a spare set I shoved into the bottom of my pack and forgot? she wondered. She looked around for her pack, but it wasn't among her belongings. It might have been stolen, she realized, but then it was equally likely she lost it or even hocked it.

She slipped her shirt of light chain over her head, but decided against attaching the breast, shoulder, arm, and knee plates. She felt a rocking sensation in the pit of her stomach. I know there was a sea trip. Did I get this . . . tattoo before I sailed or after I arrived?

She pulled on her hard-soled boots. The soft leather uppers reached nearly to her knees. She checked for her daggers. Each boot pocket held a slender, balanced wedge of silvered steel. All that remained on the chair was her plate mail and her cloak. Her fire-scorched longsword and the eagle-shaped barrette she used to keep her hair in place lay on the dresser. Worse than her missing pack, there was no money among her belongings, but she was still too concerned about the tattoo to worry about money.

This memory loss and tattoo may be nothing, she tried to tell herself as she reached for the barrette. Holding the silver clasp in her teeth she wound up her long reddish hair and bound it to the back of her head with the barrette. She remembered Ikanamon the Gray Mage telling her about the time he got so drunk and obnoxious that his fellow party members had a vulgar scene involving centaurs tattooed on his backside. Maybe this is just a prank, too, she reassured herself. A clerical cure will get rid of it for me.

The small hairs on the back of her neck rose, and Alias realized that she was being watched. Turning slowly toward the window, she locked gazes with a reptilian creature peering in at her from the alley.

Looking like a cross between a lizard and a troglodyte, the beast's head just reached above the level of the windowsill. His snout was thinner and more refined than the lizard men Alias had fought before, and he had a huge fin which began just between his eyes and continued over the top of his skull. He had no lips, only sharp, disjointed teeth, and his eyes were the yellow of dead things. In his claws he held the smaller of the two dogs Alias had heard earlier. The puppy, unharmed, had short, white hair, not long as Alias had imagined. Both creatures watched her with an intense curiosity, the lizard still as stone, the puppy wagging its tail, with its pink tongue lolling stupidly out of one side of its mouth.

Alias reacted instantly with the practiced grace of an experienced adventuress. She drew one of the daggers from her boot and, with a flick of her tattooed wrist, shot it at her observer. The creature pitched backward without a sound, but the dog fell into the room with a frightened yip. The dagger sank half an inch into the oak window frame.

Grasping her flame-seared sword, Alias flung herself across the room in one fluid motion. When she reached the window, however, the creature was gone and the alleyway empty. The short-haired dog yipped at her feet, rising on its hind legs and placing its front paws halfway up her boots.

"I don't suppose you know anything about this?" she asked the dog. The puppy merely wagged its tail and whimpered.

Alias picked up the small creature, petted it briefly, then dropped it outside the window. The beast barked at her a few times, then began sniffing the rubbish.

* * * * *

"The lady has risen from the dead!" shouted the barkeep in a merry voice as Alias entered the common room. She did not know this particular barkeep, but knew others just like him who ran inns from the Living City to Waterdeep. He was a loud, boisterous man, full of "hail-fellow-well-met" attitudes, favoring adventurers in his trade because the additional gold they usually carried made up for the damage their barroom arguments caused.

A few heads turned to look at her, but there were no familiar faces among them. Alias had decided to wear her armor plate after all. She looked more suited for battle than for a few drinks, but many of the merchants, mercenaries, and townsfolk were similarly armed and armored, so she fit in. Like most of those in the room, Alias wore her weapon at her side. Like all of those doing so, she had the blade's grip tied to its sheath by white cord, fashioned in "peace knot."

She took a table near an interior wall, away from any windows, where she could keep an eye on both doors to the common area, and the barkeep as well. He was a portly, balding man, obviously guilty of sampling his own stock. He took her attention as a request for service, and after a few obligatory passes with a rag over the bar, he filled a large mug from the tap and brought it over to her table. Foam ran down the mug's sides, and beads of water condensed where the rivulets did not run.

"Hair o' the dog what bit you?" offered the barkeep.

"On the house?" asked Alias.

"On the bill," the barkeep replied. "I like to keep things on a cash-and-carry basis. Don't worry, you're still covered."

For the moment Alias was more interested in the blank spaces in her memory than in who was covering her tab. "I was here last night?" she asked.

"Yes, lady."

"Doing?" Alias raised an eyebrow.

"Why, sleeping it off. And it must have been a Hades-raising drunk indeed, for it is the seventh day o' Mirtul." When Alias stared at him blankly, he explained, "You been here since the evening o' the fourth, done nothing but sleep the whole while."

"Did I come alone?"

"Yes. Well, maybe not. May I?" He pointed to the empty seat at the table. Alias nodded, and he lowered his ponderous weight into the chair, which groaned under the load.

"One o' my regulars, Mitcher Trollslayer," he continued, "stumbled over you that evening after the last call. You wuz laid out on my front stoop like a sacrifice to Bane."

The barkeep drew the circle of Tymora on his chest to ward off any trouble uttering the evil name might bring. "Anyway, there you wuz with this sack o' money alongside. I put you up, using the money in the sack to cover your tab. Here it is, too, with only the cost o' the room deducted." From his apron pocket he fished out a small satin sack. "Doesn't count the beer, o' course."

Alias shook the contents from the sack. A small, greenish gem, a couple of Lantan trade bars, some Waterdeep coinage, and a scattering of Cormyrian coins. She shoved a silver falcon at the barkeep. "I don't remember coming here. Someone must have left me. Did you see anyone?"

"I figgered you must have been carousing with a bunch o' mates who, when the effects caught up with you, left you on my doorstep with enough cash to guarantee your comfort. No one told us about you until Mitcher found you on his way out. You wuz alone."

Alias looked at the mug as the foam on top diminished to reveal a watery amber liquid. It smelled worse than the rubbish outside. "Why wouldn't my 'mates' bring me inside?" she asked.

The barkeep shrugged. The mates-leaving-the-lady-on-the-doorstep theory was apparently his favorite, and it was obvious that he had been telling and retelling it over the past few evenings. He was reluctant to change what seemed to him a concise and well-rounded tale.

"No one has asked after me?" Alias pressed.

"Not a one, lady. Perhaps they forgot about you."

"Perhaps. No lizards?"

The barkeep sniffed. "We keep the premises clean. We wuz waiting for you to wake before cleaning your room."

Alias raised a hand. "No lizard-creatures, then? Something that looks like a lizard-creature?"

The barkeep shrugged again. "Perhaps the last brew you had haunted you some. You recall what you wuz drinking?"

"I recall precious little, I fear. I don't even know what town I'm in."

"No mere town, but the gem of Cormyr, the finest city o' the Forest Country. You are in Suzail, lady, home o' His Most Serene and Wise Majesty, Azoun IV."

Alias had a mental map in her head of the region. Cormyr was a growing nation, sitting astride the trade routes from the Sword Coast to the Inner Sea. The name of its ruler struck a responsive chord. *Is he a friend? An enemy? Why can't I remember things?*

"Last question, wise barkeep," she said, holding up another silver orb, "and I will let you go." She turned the hand holding the coin to reveal the inside of her arm and its bright tattoo. "Did I have this when I arrived?"

"Aye, lady," said the barkeep. "It wuz there when we found you. Mitcher said the Witches of Rashemen wear such tattoos, but a Turmishman said he wuz full of bee droppings. There wuz some mutterings, but I put my foot down and, as you see, the sky hasn't fallen on my inn. I considered you a good omen, at that."

"Why?"

"The name of this house. The Hidden Lady."

Alias nodded. Taking this as a dismissal, the barkeep scurried back to his bar, rattling the orbs in his hand as he went.

Alias reviewed what the barkeep had told her. *It makes sense,* she thought. *Adventurers have been known to dump off drunken companions, leaving a tattoo as a reminder. But why these symbols? They mean nothing to me.*

Alias gulped a mouthful of ale, then fought the urge to spit it across the table. The brew tasted like fermented swill. She forced herself to swallow it, wondering if the wretched taste of the beer had been why her unknown benefactors had left her outside and not entered the establishment.

"I hate mysteries," she muttered with annoyance. She toyed with the idea of pitching the nearly full mug at the barkeep, accusing him of poisoning the clientele. When in doubt, she thought, start a brawl.

She pushed the beer away, her attention diverted. The barkeep was talking to a tall man wearing robes of crimson highlighted with thin white stripes and an ivory white cloak with red trim. The barkeep motioned a pudgy hand toward Alias's table, and the man turned to look at her.

His skin was dusky and his hair, a curly brown mane banded with gold cords, hung to his shoulders. He had a moustache, and his beard was cut straight across at the bottom like a coal shovel. His eyes were blue. On his forehead were tattooed three blue dots, and a sapphire was embedded in his left earlobe. Alias recognized him as a southerner and knew the dots marked him as a Turmish scholar of religion, reading, and magic. The earring meant he was married. But she did not recognize the man himself.

Nevertheless, he made his way from the bar to her table. Alias rose as he approached—not from politeness, but to give herself the chance to size him up. He stood several inches taller than Alias—and she was taller than most women and many other men. Beneath his soft, flowing robes, the man had a reasonably sturdy frame. However his muscles did not appear to be trained for battle or hardship, as were her own. He might be a mage, she decided, or a merchant.

"I hope you are well, lady?" His voice had the cultured tone of someone tutored in the local tongue by a scholar.

Alias scowled at his features. "Do I know you, Turmite?"

His expression turned stormy. "No. If you did, you would know our people prefer to be called Turmishmen or Turms."

Alias sat down and motioned him into the seat opposite her. She liked his control in the face of her insult. "You care for my drink? I've lost the desire."

Nodding, the Turmishman took a long pull on the mug. If

it was fermented pig-swill, as Alias suspected, then such drinks were common in the south, she decided, because the stranger seemed to savor his swallow.

"I take it you are the Turmishman who declared I was not a witch?" -

The man nodded and wiped a bit of foam from his moustache. "Your friendly innkeep was too afraid to take you in, and the lout who found you was ready to have you burned. Or at least relieve you of your purse."

"But you knew I was not a witch?"

"I know that the Witches of Rashemen, if they ever leave their frozen climes, know better than to decorate their bodies with tattoos proclaiming their origins."

Alias nodded. "I'm not of that sisterhood." At least as far as I know, she thought inwardly, since I can't swear to what I've been doing for the past week or so.

She hesitated, then asked, "Did you see who brought me here?"

The Turmishman shook his head. "I was at this very table when the northerner left and then came right back in, babbling about a dead witch on the front steps. Everyone here investigated, and I convinced them your glyphs were harmless, though I have no idea what they are. I must confess, to being most curious about them. May I see them again?"

Alias frowned but held out her arm, palm upward, revealing the symbols. In the dim common room they seemed even brighter than before, glowing from within.

The Turmishman looked at them and shook his head, still mystified. "I have never seen the likes of these before. Where are you from?"

"I . . . get around." After another pause she added, "I was born in Westgate, but I ran off and never returned."

"I've seen naught like this in Westgate, and I have traveled the Inner Sea from there to Thay. I must confess, though, I am by no means a sage. May I cast a spell on them?"

Alias involuntarily jerked her arm back. "You a mage?"

The Turmishman grinned, displaying a line of bright white teeth. "Of no small water. I am Akabar Bel Akash of House Akash, mage and merchant. Do not fear. I have no wish to entrap you by magics. I only wish to know if the marking's origin is in magic."

Alias glared across the table at the Turmishman. He was a merchant-mage. One of those greengrocers who dabbled with the art, but probably wasn't skilled enough to cut it as just a sorcerer. Still, he ought to be capable of detecting magic, and he looked sincere. She needed to know more about the tattoo, and here was this Turmishman offering his services for free. She held out her arm. "I am Alias. Magic does not frighten me, but be quick about it."

Akabar Bel Akash leaned over the symbols and began mumbling words quickly and quietly. If the runes on her arm were magical, Alias knew, they would radiate a dim glow.

The merchant-mage chanted, and Alias felt the muscles of her arm writhe beneath her skin as though they were snakes. The symbols danced along her arm as if mocking the Turmishman.

Suddenly, strands of hellish blue light, intense as lightning flashes, shot from the symbols on her arm, illuminating the whole room. The beacons of color crackled along the beams overhead and were reflected off all the bottles and armor in the tavern, turning the surprised faces of every patron in the room to a deathly blue.

Akabar Bel Akash had not been expecting so violent a reaction to his magical inquiry. He toppled backward in surprise, chair and all. His flailing arm caught the half-drained mug of beer and sent it flying across the commons room. The droplets of spilled ale took on the appearance of a cluster of blue fireflies.

Alias caught sight of the barkeep frozen in the blue light. An instant later, the portly man regained his senses and dove like a sounding whale behind the bar. His patrons were a tougher lot; many of them were desperately working loose the peace knots of their weapons.

Grabbing her cloak from the back of her chair, Alias twisted it tight around her arm to muffle the light. The blue glow leaked out of the cloak's edges, and she held the arm close to her body. In an overloud voice she announced, "No problem, no problem! My friend here was just showing me a new magical trick that he hasn't quite learned yet."

Alias quickly circled around the table. She leaned over the tall mage's sprawled form and, to demonstrate that there was nothing wrong, helped pull him to his feet. Already most of the patrons had returned to their drinks, but there was a good deal of scowling and muttering.

Grasping the collar of his white-striped crimson vestments, Alias held Akabar's face close to her own and whispered in the tight voice she reserved to threaten people, "Never, ever, do that again," then added with a hiss, "I should have known better than to trust a greengrocer. I'm going to a real spell-caster to get rid of this tattoo right now. Don't be here when I come back, Turmite!"

With that, she spun and, clutching her cloak-wrapped arm to her belly, strode out of the inn. She caught sight of the barkeep's head surfacing from behind the bar just as she pushed the door open.

Cursing, Alias stormed three blocks before she dared to duck into an alleyway and unwrap the cloak. The symbols on her arm had returned to their normal appearance, if one could consider a tattoo that looked like pieces of translucent glass set beneath the skin normal.

Alias cursed again, this time without venom or passion, and headed toward the Promenade, Suzail's main street, looking for a temple that might still have clerics awake at this hour.

❧ 2 ❧

Winefiddle
and the Assassins

The first two temples she tried, the Shrine of Lliira and the Silent Room, the Temple of Deneir, were locked. Both were posted with identical signs stating they were closed until dawn services.

She passed by the Towers of Good Fortune—the huge temple to Tymora—because it looked too expensive, and the Shrine to Tyr, because it looked too prim and stuffy.

Upon reaching the Shrine of Oghma, Alias glared at the note tacked to the door. She ripped the paper from the tiny nails and let it flutter down the stairs. Pounding on the door with the side of her fist, her assault was answered by a sleepy caretaker who cracked the temple door open all of two inches and peered out at her suspiciously.

"I need a curse removed! Immediately!" she gasped with her best maiden-in-distress voice. The caretaker's look softened, but he shook his head, explaining that the holy mother was out of town arranging a wedding and that they had only acolytes within, new officiates who lacked the power to deal with such things.

"Try Tyr Grimjaws, Miss," he suggested.

Alias backtracked to the Shrine of Tyr the Just only to find her entry barred by two heavily armed guards. "Unless it's life or death," one informed her, "you'll have to wait." Apparently the church of Tyr had hired an adventuring party to deal with a dragon terrorizing the Storm Horn Mountains. The party's dealings with the monster had been anything but successful. The priests of Tyr were all occupied with healing the survivors and resurrecting the bodies of their comrades who had not been incinerated.

Alias was feeling desperate by the time she screwed up her courage to enter the Towers of Good Fortune, the Temple of Tymora. At least there was no sign on its front gates. She jerked on the bellpull incessantly until a priest appeared, yawning but not cross. A corpulent, pasty-faced man, he waddled forward to unbar the gates.

"I must speak with your superior immediately," Alias demanded. "This is an emergency."

The priest bowed as much as his bulk would allow and stood up again, grinning. "Curate Winefiddle at your service. An improbable name for a priest, I know, but we must play the cards we're dealt, right? I'm afraid, lady, that I'm all there is. His worship and the others are helping the minions of Tyr with healing and resurrecting the would-be dragon slayers. Unless, by my superiors, you meant to have a word with Lady Luck herself. It's possible, but very costly, in more ways than one. I wouldn't recommend it."

Alias shook her head. Before the curate could babble anymore, she burst out, "I need a curse removed."

"Now, that does sound serious. Come in." Winefiddle ushered her past the silver-plated altar to Tymora, Lady Luck, and into a private study for an audience. An oil lamp lit the musty chamber. Dark oak cabinets lined the walls. A single, high window framed the night sky. The curate offered her a seat and plopped down into a chair beside her.

"Now, tell me about this curse," he prompted her.

Alias explained how she'd awakened after her unusually long sleep and discovered the tattoo on her arm. At a loss for any other theory, she told him the barkeep's story that she was a drunk left on the doorstep of The Hidden Lady. Then, she related what had happened when the Turmish merchant-mage had cast a spell to detect magic on the tattoo. "I don't remember getting it—the tattoo," she concluded. "I would never have agreed to it, not even drunk. This has to be some sort of stupid prank pulled on me while I was unconscious, but I have no idea who would have done it."

Alias did not bother to mention her hazy memory of the past few weeks—it was too embarrassing—and she omitted the incident with the lizard as inconsequential.

Curate Winefiddle nodded reassuringly, as if Alias had

brought him nothing more troublesome than a kitten with earmites. "No problem," he declared. "There remains only the question of how you would like to arrange payment?"

Alias knew from experience that her coins were an insufficient "offering." She pulled out the only real valuable in her money sack—the small, greenish gem.

Winefiddle accepted the terms with a smile and a nod. "No. Don't put it there," he admonished her before she set it down on the desk. "Very unlucky. Drop it in the poor box as you leave."

Alias nodded. Winefiddle began removing a number of tattered scrolls from a cabinet. "The one advantage to serving an adventurer's goddess," he yawned as he spoke, "is a steady stream of worshippers in need of your special services, worshippers willing to pay in magical items."

The cleric stifled another yawn, and Alias gave him a blank look she bestowed on fools she needed to tolerate. As far as she was concerned, clerics were merely puttering quasi-mages who couldn't cast spells without worrying about converts, theology, relics, and other nonsense. If they weren't so useful when sickness, famine, and war struck, they would probably have died out altogether, Alias decided, taking their gods with them. Perhaps the gods knew that, and that's why they put up with the fools.

Winefiddle pulled bundles of scrolls from the cabinet with all the grace of a fishmonger hoisting salmon. He hummed as he checked their tags. Alias sat there as quietly and patiently as possible, wishing she had stopped at another inn for a pouch of decent rum. Finally, the priest pulled two from the lot that seemed to please him.

Despite Alias's warning of what had happened in The Hidden Lady, Winefiddle wanted to begin with a standard magical detection. He waved aside her objections, insisting, "I need to see this extreme reaction myself. Nothing to be afraid of since we know what to expect this time, right?"

Alias submitted with a grudging sigh. The cleric passed his silver disk of Tymora over her outstretched arm. The words he muttered were different from the Turmish mage's, but the effect was the same. Alias shuddered as the symbols writhed beneath her skin, and she squinted in anticipation of the bright, sapphire radiance which soon lit every corner of the musty study.

Winefiddle's eyebrows disappeared into his low hairline, amazed at the brilliance of the glow. Alias clenched her muscles involuntarily, and the rays swayed about the room like signal beacons, bouncing off the darkened window and the priest's silver holy symbol.

The glow peaked and began to ebb slowly. Winefiddle cleared his throat nervously a few times before he reached for the larger of the two scrolls on the desk. In the blue light he looked less pasty and more powerful, but Alias was beginning to wonder if he knew what he was doing.

"You really think that piece of paper's going to be strong enough?" she asked doubtfully. Maybe I should put this off until morning, she thought. The Shrine of Oghma or the Temple of Deneir might have more competent help.

"This scroll was written by the hand of the Arch-cleric Mzentul himself. It should remove these horrors without delay." He stroked his chin thoughtfully and added, "It being such an old and irreplaceable scroll, perhaps you wouldn't mind, should you come into further funds . . ."

Alias gave an impatient nod, and Winefiddle undid the scroll's leather binding. With one hand on her arm and the other holding the scroll, he began to read.

"Dominus, Deliverus," he intoned. A cold shudder ran down Alias's spine, a feeling quickly overwhelmed by a burning sensation on her forearm. The pain was familiar, but she could not remember why. Is this how the magics felt that put the damned thing here?

The fire on her arm intensified, and she clamped her jaw shut to avoid crying out. She couldn't have been in more pain if molten metal had been poured over her sword arm.

"Ketris, Ogos, Diam—" Winefiddle continued, breathing heavily, his teeth clenched. Alias wondered if he could feel the heat of her arm beneath his hand.

Light beams arced from Alias's arm like water from a fountain, but instead of spilling to the floor, they wrapped around her until she was surrounded by blue light.

Suddenly, she wrenched her arm away from the cleric's grasp and reached down to her boot for her throwing dagger. As if she was in some horrible nightmare her arm moved of its own accord, like a viper she could not control.

The priest had ignored the swordswoman's arm jerking from his grasp. It wasn't really necessary that he hold onto it, and he could not afford to lose his concentration and break off his incantation. "Mistra, Hodah, Mzentil, Coy!" he finished triumphantly.

Winefiddle looked up at his client. She was still bathed in a blue light from the symbols, and her face was a mask of rage. A low, feral snarl issued from her lips. He caught the flash of silver as Alias thrust the knife toward him. With an unexpected dexterity, he shifted sideways.

The weapon sliced through his robes and bit into his flesh, but it was stopped by his lowest rib.

Alias looked down in horror at her hand—it moved with its own volition. Blood from the dagger bubbled and burned as it dripped over the glowing tattoo.

Suddenly, the scroll Winefiddle had been reading burst into flame, its magic used. The curate threw the burning page in Alias's face.

The swordswoman swatted the fiery parchment away, and the priest circled around her. Just as he reached the door, Alias felt an electric pulse run down her right arm. She tried to grab the wrist with her left hand, but she was too late. The arm hurled the dagger at the priest. The weapon whirred past his ear and buried itself in the doorjamb. Yanking the door open so hard that it banged against the wall behind it, the priest fled from the study.

Alias raced after him, no longer in control of any part of her body. She tried to pull the silvered steel weapon from the wood as she passed by, but the blade had buried itself too deep; she abandoned it so as not to lose sight of her prey.

Alias found Winefiddle climbing the steps to the silver altar. She leaped after him and grabbed at the back of the chain around his neck, the chain that held his holy symbol— the silver disk of Tymora. She yanked on it hard, trying to throttle him with it.

Winefiddle lost his balance and tumbled backward down the steps into his assailant, knocking her over as well. The priest's fall was broken by Alias's body, but the swordswoman was not so lucky. The crack her head made on the marble stone echoed through the temple, and the priest's great bulk on top of her forced all the air from her lungs.

When Alias opened her eyes again, she was still lying on the floor. The light on her arm had faded to a very dim glow. Her head was throbbing with unbearable agony. Gods! she thought, as panic gripped her heart. I killed a priest! These hell-spawned markings made me kill a priest! No one will ever believe it wasn't my fault.

She tried to sit up, knowing she had to flee, but the pain in her head made it impossible. Then she heard chanting.

Winefiddle knelt beside her—not dead after all. In the dimness of the temple lamps Alias could see his hands were glowing very slightly. He held them over the wound in his side and then over her forehead. The throbbing subsided.

"How are you feeling?" the curate asked.

"All right, I guess," she muttered, sitting up slowly. She was unable to meet the priest's eyes. "I might have killed you," she whispered.

"Not very likely," Winefiddle replied lightly. "We are in Tymora's temple, and Her luck was with me, not you."

His nonchalance startled Alias. She had to make him understand, even if it didn't matter to him. "It wasn't me, though," she explained. "My arm . . . it took me over somehow."

"Yes. The symbols must have instructions to destroy anyone who would try to remove them, discouraging you from seeking out help. I thought you looked possessed—but it couldn't have been a real possession."

"Why not?"

"An alarm would have gone off if any possessed person approached the altar. You didn't set it off. I don't think you're cursed exactly either, or the scroll I used would have worked. The symbols on your arm are magical, but they aren't just magical. There's some mechanistic component to them that protects them from being exorcised."

"But I have to get them off," Alias insisted. "I can't run around with markings that make me try to kill priests. Who knows what else they might make me do?"

"Indeed," Winefiddle agreed, "but removing them might

prove to be complicated and costly. If it can be done, it would require the power of many clerics and mages, as well as a surgeon. And you would have no guarantee that the markings would let you live through the procedure. It might be easier and safer for you to cut off the arm and retire."

"No!"

"But these markings are very dangerous. You could learn to fight left-handed," Winefiddle suggested.

"I can already do that," Alias declared. "That's not the point. I'm not going to let these things, or whoever put them on me, ruin my life. Besides, suppose they had roots or something that went into my body."

"Well, then, I would advise you to learn all you can about the markings. None of them are familiar to me. Perhaps if you can discover their origins, you can discover who put them on you and get them to remove them for you."

Alias looked down at the blue glyphs. None of them were familiar to her either. Even the Turmishman, Akabar Bel Akash, had found them unusual. "That'll take a sage's service, and sages aren't cheap."

"True," Winefiddle agreed. "However, I happen to know of a very good one who might be willing to exchange his services for yours. His name is Dimswart. He lives about half a day's ride outside of Suzail."

"What kind of services might he be looking for?" Alias asked suspiciously.

"Better to let him explain that," Winefiddle said evasively.

Five minutes later Alias left the temple, a letter of introduction in her pocket, along with the small greenish gem originally intended for Tymora's poor box. She had made a motion toward the box with her hand as she passed it, but the gem remained firmly in her grip. As she had pointed out, sages weren't cheap. Her services might not be sufficient to barter with this Dimswart, she told herself.

As she walked away from the temple, an uneasy suspicion occurred to her that perhaps it wasn't her own frugalness that prompted her to hold onto the gem, but some desire of the sigils not to reward the priest who had tried to help her remove them.

The cobblestone Promenade of Suzail appeared deserted, but as soon as Alias left the temple court a tall figure in rustling crimson-and-white robes stepped from the shadows. He hesitated, uncertain whether he should follow the adventuress or try to discover her business with Tymora. He made for the temple doors.

Then three more figures, dressed in dark leathers, emerged from a dark alley. Ignoring the first figure they trailed after Alias. One last figure followed these three—a figure holding a massive tail over his shoulder.

* * * * *

Alias was in no hurry to return to The Hidden Lady. Three days of sleep had left her quite awake. She wandered down to Suzail's docks. The last of the schooners had shut down for the evening, and only a few firepots from the warehouses lit the water. The sea air rolled into the city, smelling considerably fresher than three-days worth of unlaundered linens.

She ran through a mental list of individuals who might be responsible for having her marked with the symbols and drew a blank. Any enemies she'd made were either ignorant of her name or dead. No friends who were still drawing breath would do something like this. That left someone new—a stranger who had picked her off the street as a suitable vessel for trying out a new piece of magic.

Alias came to the end of the wooden plank sidewalk. The beach spread out in a thin white line to her right. The night sky had grown overcast. Like my life, she thought. She began walking along the shoreline on the sand.

Even if a complete stranger had done this to her, she was still left wondering where and when it had happened. Now that she thought about it, her memory was missing more than just a few weeks. More time than an alcoholic binge could really account for, she decided.

She could recall long-ago adventures quite clearly—like stealing one of the Eyes of Bane from an evil temple in Baldur's Gate with the Adventurers of the Black Hawk, or her earliest sojourns with the Company of the Swanmays.

Her mind went all fuzzy, trying to remember recent

events like the sea trip. And there *was* a sea trip, she insisted to herself, worried that she would forget that as well by the next morning. Was the lizard-creature on the same ship? I think so. Maybe it's the pet of the magician behind this mess.

Alias walked a quarter-mile along the beach before she drew her traitorous arm from beneath her cloak. The pain had dimmed, but the symbols still glowed faintly, like lichen. Cursing did no good, but she cursed anyway. If they can make me attack a priest, what else can they make me do?

If she attacked someone else, she could end up with a bad reputation. No one would hire her as a guard, and there weren't many adventuring companies who'd have anything to do with her. It was one thing to kill people in self-defense or in combat under command of king or church, but if she were to slay some innocent, unarmed person . . .

Alias was lost in her thoughts, absentmindedly digging a half-covered shell from the sand with the side of her boot, so she failed to notice the trio stalking her. The rushing sound of the surf covered the noise of their approach. One hung back and began chanting a spell, while the other two rushed the swordswoman.

The spell-caster's incantation, a high-pitched female voice, inadvertently warned Alias of danger. The swordswoman whirled around and discovered the pair of armed men advancing on her. They carried clubs, but light from the cloud-wrapped moon did not reflect off their black leather armor—armor that was the trademark of a particularly dangerous underworld class.

Assassins! Alias grabbed at the hilt of her sword and nearly jerked herself off her feet before remembering the blade was still tied to its scabbard. The awkward movement pulled her forward so, by dumb luck, she rolled within the swing of the first assailant and away from the second. With one hand she tried to foil the knot at her sword.

Then the spell-caster's magic let loose—a pair of missiles of hissing energy, leaving a wake of glittering dust in their path. The bolts dove at Alias like hunting falcons and caught her in the left shoulder. The arm below that shoulder went dead from the shock, and the force knocked the swordswoman backward on the sand. Ignore the pain, just get the knot, she ordered herself.

Fortunately, the first assailant was an amateur. He rushed forward while his wiser companion circled. Alias brought her leg up hard and connected. The fool dropped his club, clutching himself in pain.

Get the knot, get the knot, her mind chanted as the fingers of her right hand tore frantically at the binding on her sword. Don't think about the spell-caster! Work the knot!

Alias attempted to rise, and the second assailant swung at her from behind, catching her left shoulder again. She rolled with the blow and came up at last with sword in hand. The first assassin had recovered, so that Alias stood on the beach facing both armed assailants, shifting her eyes from one to the other. Worse than that, she could hear the rising chant in the distance of another spell.

The chant died with a sudden muffled scream, and the two assassins half-turned in surprise. Alias lunged, catching the first in the belly. She lost her grip on her sword's hilt as the assassin crumbled to the sand.

The remaining black figure thrust his club like a sword, seeking to catch Alias between the ribs. Alias dodged backward, so the force of his lunge knocked the assassin off balance. She reached to the top of her boot with her good hand and flung a dagger underhand. Her aim was true, and the second assailant fell, hands clawing at the protruding hilt, staining the sand with his blood.

Alias breathed deeply and recovered her weapons. Both men were dead. She rubbed her sore shoulder, feeling the tingling of life returning to it. Then she remembered the spell-caster. Has she fled, or is she waiting in the shadows? Alias moved cautiously in the direction the magic missiles had come from.

The spell-caster lay face down in the sand about twenty yards away, a nasty gash across her back. Bending over her body was the lizard-creature. It's just as ugly in the moonlight as it had been in the dusk, Alias thought. In one paw the creature held an odd-looking blade that had too much steel and not enough grip. The tip of the blade was an oversized diamond shape edged with curved teeth that curled backward. The teeth were bathed in the mage's blood.

Alias raised her own sword into a guard position. The lizard looked up and hissed. Is that a hostile sign? she wondered. She tightened her grip on her own blade. The beast rose from the mage's body. Swordswoman and lizard stood motionless, each waiting for the other to move first.

Finally, the lizard-creature gave a muted snarl as it twisted its odd-shaped blade in its hands, spinning the weapon like a baton once, twice, thrice . . .

And drove it, point first, into the ground at Alias's feet. The creature dropped to one knee beside the grounded blade, head down, offering its bare neck to Alias's weapon.

Alias raised her sword over the creature. I failed to kill the thing this afternoon, she realized, and I'll never have a better chance to deal with it. Putting it out of my misery would be the simplest, most logical thing to do. Four dead bodies on a beach attract no more attention than three.

The lizard remained in its kneeling position, not reaching for its blade. The creature seemed to be holding its breath.

Alias hesitated. You'd think I was a follower of Bhaal, God of Murder. First I try to kill a priest, and now I'm ready to slay a foe who's surrendered. For that matter I don't know that it's a foe. The creature took out the magic-user for me. It's offering me its services like a knight.

Alias tapped the lizard-creature on the shoulder with the flat of the blade. "Okay, you can live." Her voice sounded overloud and pompous. "But one false move and you're dragon bait. Read me? Dra-gon bait."

The creature nodded and pointed to its chest with a long, clawed finger.

Alias rubbed her temples with annoyance. "No, you're not named Dragonbait. If you give me any trouble, you'll *become* dragon bait."

The creature repeated the gesture toward itself.

Alias sighed. "Dragonbait it is, then." She pointed toward herself. "Alias," she said. "Now let's search these bodies and get out of here before the watch arrives."

Dragonbait nodded and, using an overlong thumb-claw, started cutting the strings of the magician's purse.

❦ 3 ❦

Dragonbait
and Dimswart

Dragonbait was like no other creature Alias had ever seen before in all her travels through the Realms. He wasn't a real lizard, at least not of the species she'd helped drive back from the city of Daggerford. As she noted when she'd seen the creature at sunset, his snout was thinner at the tip and more rounded than a lizard-creature's, and he sported a head fin like a troglodyte.

Given time for more leisurely study, she could see many other differences. For one thing, the sharp teeth at the front of his mouth gave way to the peglike molars of a salad eater, and though he walked on his hind legs, his posture was hardly erect. The creature tilted forward some at the hips, balanced by a tail as long again as his torso. With such an odd posture, his head only reached to her shoulder, about five feet high. Finally, the scales that pebbled his hide were so small and smooth he looked as though he were covered in expensive beadwork, like a noblewoman's evening gown.

At any rate, for something more lizardish than human, he was pretty intelligent. At least, that is, the lizard made an excellent servant. Upon their return to The Hidden Lady, he busied himself helping her off with her boots, straightening her room, and fetching food for a late night snack.

"I see you found your lizard," the innkeeper commented cheerily to Alias, upon discovering the five-foot lizard with a cold meat pie and pudding in his paws.

Except for a few catlike hisses, snarls, and mewling sounds, Dragonbait remained mute. If the creature had his own language he did not bother to use it. Alias found she could get him to fetch and carry things on command, but he responded to questions with the blank look of a beast.

She needed to know when she'd first met him, what he knew of her memory loss, and especially what he knew of the tattoo. In frustration and desperation she began shouting questions. Her anger only invoked in the lizard a tilted head and a puzzled expression.

Alias lay back on the bed, defeated. Dragonbait made a sympathetic mewling. Struck with an inspiration, Alias shouted down to the innkeep for an inkpot, quill, and parchment. When the items were brought up, she set them on the table and sat Dragonbait down before them.

The lizard sniffed at the inkpot, and his nostrils flared and closed up in annoyance. He used the quill point to pick clean the spaces between his teeth.

Alias flopped back on her bed, laughing. Lady Luck was playing some cruel joke on her. Here was a creature who might be a key to the fog surrounding her life, and he could explain nothing to her. She leaned back against the headboard and closed her eyes. Dragonbait curled up on the rag rug on the floor at the foot of the bed and wrapped his arms around the curious sword he carried.

Alias feigned sleep for a while, just to be sure her new companion had no plans to give her a second smile, across the throat with his sword. She wasn't really expecting any trouble, but trust was for corpses. She studied the lizard through half-closed eyelids. Asleep, he looked even more innocuous. Like a child, he kept his powerful lower legs pulled up to his stomach. With yellowish claws retracted into his clover-shaped feet, and with his long, muscled tail tucked up between his legs, the tip lying across his eyes, and with his snout resting on the hilt of his sword, Dragonbait reminded Alias of a furless cat curled about its master's shoe.

The sword was as curious as its owner. It looked top-heavy and badly balanced. Forging that diamond-shaped tip, and the jagged teeth curling from it, could not have been easy, and wielding it seemed impossible. Alias wondered how anyone could keep hold of that tiny, one-handed grip. Had she not seen its handiwork on the beach, she would have believed the blade to be ceremonial gear.

Dragonbait had no other belongings, unless she counted the tattered, ill-fitting clothes he wore, no doubt out of modesty, since they certainly couldn't be keeping the creature warm. A torn jerkin covered his chest, and a splotch of ragged cloth knotted at the side hung down from his hips.

What makes me think he's not a she? Granted, there's nothing feminine about his torso, but lizards don't have breasts or need wide hips for birthing, now do they? Alias shook her head. No. He's a male. Some sixth sense made her sure of it.

She looked again at the rags he wore. Aren't lizards supposed to hate the cold? I'll have to find him a cloak, something with a deep hood to hide that snout.

Watching the lizard sleeping at her feet, making plans for his comfort, she could no longer feel threatened by him. But she still could not sleep. Slipping quietly out of the bed, she padded over to the small dressing table where Dragonbait had carefully laid out the booty from their would-be ambushers. Dragonbait gave a snarl in his sleep as she raised the flame on the oil lamp, then he turned over, still resting on his sword.

Some watchdog, Alias thought. She turned back to the scattered assassin equipment and sat down at the table to examine it. The daggers—three from the mage, one from each club-wielding assassin—were quite ordinary. The pair of small vials stoppered with wax were much more interesting. Carefully Alias cracked the top of one, and a rich cinnamon smell wafted up. She quickly restoppered the bottle.

Peranox. A deadly contact poison from the South. Nasty stuff even in the hands of competent assassins, Alias thought. Disaster for first-time bunglers. If the pair had used poisoned daggers instead of clubs, I would be lying dead on the beach instead of them.

Why did they choose clubs to attack? she wondered. Did they want to make my death look like an amateur job? She shook out the sack Dragonbait had cut from the mage. The standard assortment of magical spell-trappings skittered across the wooden desktop—moldy spiderwebs, bits of eyelashes trapped in amber, and dead insects. The only difference, she thought, between a magic-user's pockets and those of a small boy's is that there is less week-old candy in the mage's pockets. After brushing away the debris, Alias found a few coins and a gold ring set with a blue stone.

Something remained stuck in the sack. She shook the bag harder. A talis card fell out onto the desktop, face-down. It bore an insignia of a laughing sun on its back.

Alias pocketed the coins and ring for later inspection and flipped the card over. She drew a sharp breath that caused Dragonbait to start in his sleep.

The card was the Primary of Flames, here represented by a dagger trapped in entwining fire. The card's pattern was twin to the uppermost symbol of Alias's tattoo. Alias felt a twinge from her arm as she compared the two.

She picked up the card and squinted at it. It was home-made. Though the laughing sun was made by an embossing stamp, the rest of the workmanship was pretty shabby. Were the other symbols on my arm from other parts of the deck this card came from? she pondered.

At least that explained the assassins' actions. Alias recalled how clumsily they'd wielded the clubs, as though they were swords. They were unused to the more primitive weapon, but were forced to wield it so as not to harm her accidentally with an edged weapon. They wanted to capture me alive, she concluded. That's why they passed on the poison, too. They must have been keeping the peranox in reserve for anyone who got in their way.

Like a five-foot lizard maybe?

She rose from her seat and, stepping over the soundly snoozing Dragonbait, closed and secured the windows. Windows were open when I woke up this morn—evening. They could have got me then but didn't. Maybe they didn't know where I was until they spotted me on the street. Someone must have left me here to keep me safe. But who?

She fished the ring from her pocket, twisted it, and said quietly, "I wish you'd tell me what in Tartarus is going on," but no djinn issued from the ring to enlighten her, nor did Dragonbait break his rhythmic breathing, sit up, and explain all the mysteries troubling her. Frowning, she tucked the ring back into her pocket.

She lay down on her bed and stared at the ceiling, fingers

laced behind her head.

* * * * *

She was not aware she had fallen asleep until a bell from some temple signaled noon. She opened her eyes to see Dragonbait standing at her bedside with breakfast on a pewter tray—bread and slices of spring fruit with cream.

Alias planned her next move while they shared the meal. "I could rent a horse and ride out to the sage's home in half a day. Save a lot of time," she said to Dragonbait. Even if he didn't understand her, it helped her put her thoughts in order to say them aloud. "But if I purchase a horse and ride it out through the town gate, I might as well hire a loud-mouthed herald to announce my departure. Besides, we have to conserve our meager funds. Sages aren't cheap. And I don't even know if you can ride."

Dragonbait watched her while she spoke exactly as if he understood her.

"And I don't want to leave you behind, do I?"

The lizard stretched his neck forward and tilted his head as though he were confused.

The swordswoman sniffed and laughed. Dragonbait returned to licking the cream out of his bowl.

No, I definitely want to keep him around, she thought. He feels familiar—as though I've traveled with him before. Maybe he was on the sea trip with me. If I lose track of him, he might fade from my memory, too. Besides, I owe him for saving my life last night. Taking him into my service is the least I can do.

After sending the barkeep's daughter out for a cloak to hide her companion's "lizardness," Alias pulled on her boots and rearmored herself. When his cloak arrived, Dragonbait sniffed at it and growled, but when it became clear Alias was not going to let the creature out of the inn in daylight he relented and, seeming every inch the paladin forced to drink with thieves, he slipped on the garment.

The idea of a lizard with vanity amused Alias. She wondered if he was some magical creature, bred to act as combination jester/servant/bodyguard, like something out of a childhood tale. With a shudder, she was reminded of the story of the golem supposedly responsible for the spreading Anauroch desert, a creature ordered to shovel sand into the region and then forgotten by the wizard who gave the order. Why is it I can recall stupid old stories when last ride, last month, much of last year is a blank? Angrily, she shoved the legendary images into the back of her mind.

Their walk out of Suzail was pleasant and uneventful. Alias deliberately set out in the wrong direction and doubled back twice in case anyone had followed her from the inn. Dragonbait proved to be as tireless a hiker as she, and they reached their destination just before dusk.

Dimswart Manor was a sizable farm, an estate just large enough to be considered a suitable "summer home" by a Waterdeep noble. A red-tiled roof set with three chimneys crowned the solid stonework walls of the main house. Alias scowled, knowing that a sage who lived so well would not sell his services cheap.

Despite the gathering gloom, there was a great amount of activity around the house as she approached, as if the grounds were the site of some tremendous siege. Gardeners were trimming hedges and lawns and reorganizing flowerbeds. At the rear of the house, canvasmen were laying out the poles of a huge tent. Dwarvish stoneworkers were arguing heatedly with elvish landscapers over the correct placement of their creations of rock and wood, while a tired-looking gnome tried to mediate between them.

In the midst of the chaos stood a tall, straight-shouldered woman with a sunburst of red hair. She hustled about from worker to worker, consulting with each from rolls of plans tucked under her arms. As Alias approached the house, she could hear the woman shouting for some elves to start hanging lanterns in the newly replanted trees.

Alias pounded on the front door with the hilt of her dagger. She had to knock twice before a parlor maid, loaded down with tapestries, opened the door. "Sorry, but the mistress isn't hiring any more entertainment people."

Alias shoved her boot in the door before the girl could close it. "I've come to see the sage—on personal business."

"The master's very busy. Perhaps you could come—"

Alias stepped into the hall and gripped the girl's shoulder.

She smacked Winefiddle's letter of introduction down on top of the pile of tapestries the servant was carrying. "Give him this. It's from the Temple of Tymora. Urgent."

"Yes, ma'am," the maid nodded, showing a little more courtesy. "Would you take a seat and wait right here, please? I'll send someone to stable your pet."

Alias squeezed the girl's shoulder firmly, and hissed with annoyance, "He's not my pet." Then she sat down on a bench against the wall. Dragonbait sat beside her.

The servant blanched, nodded, and hurried away.

While she waited, Alias scowled at the opulence of her surroundings: an estate full of servants; new, gold-threaded tapestries hung in the hall, undoubtedly replacing the older, less stylish ones carried off by the parlor maid; landscaping that required the services of four separate races; a wedding tent big enough to billet an army, and likely enough food and drink to feed them as well.

No wonder sages aren't cheap. Dimswart should be delighted to see me. How else is he going to help defray all these costs? Whatever happened to ancient, cranky, unmarried sages who preferred pursuing knowledge over wordly goods?

To keep from fidgeting, she studied Dragonbait. He waited more patiently than she did. The lizard sat with his tail over his shoulder, flicking the tip back and forth in front of his face, following it with his eyes.

What is he? she wondered with aggravation. Maybe the sage can shed some light on his origins. Not likely, though. If I've never seen anything like him in all my travels, what chance is there that he's in any of the sage's books?

Despite the obvious chaos of the household, a butler finally arrived to escort her to the sage's study.

If Alias had met Dimswart before her visit to Suzail, she might have ungenerously described his build as chunky. But compared to the innkeep of The Hidden Lady and Winefiddle, the sage appeared broad-shouldered but lean. He rose from his seat by the fire and clasped her extended hand in both his meaty paws.

"Well met, well met," he said, smiling like a halfling with an extra king in the deck. "Sit down here by the fire, and tell me what a humble book-banger can do for a warrioress."

Warrioress? Now there's a title you don't hear every day, Alias thought. It marked Dimswart as a very old-fashioned sort of sage. "It's a little complicated," Alias began.

"We should start with the essentials," Dimswart cut in. "If you will indulge me, I'd like to exercise my skill. Leah, our maid, told me I was to expect a sorceress and her familiar. But this creature—" he nodded toward Dragonbait— "is too large to be a familiar, and few sorcerers carry quite so much steel about their person."

"All I said to your maid," Alias interjected, "was that Dragonbait wasn't a pet."

"Quite," Dimswart agreed, motioning for her to have a seat opposite him. "We are very reclusive out here in the country, though, and Leah, never having seen such a creature, leaped to the conclusion that if it wasn't a pet, it must be a familiar, so you must be a sorceress. You are not. You're a hired sword. From your lack of old scars, I'd say you were either a very new one or a very good one, and you have strange tastes in traveling companions."

Dragonbait cleared his nostrils in a noticeable *hwumpf*, as he stood by the fire, watching the sage.

Dimswart continued. "You're a native of . . . let's see, brown hair with a tinge of red, hazel eyes, strong cheeks, good carriage . . . Westgate, I'd say, though from your fair complexion I'd guess it's been a while since you've lived there."

Alias tried to interrupt, but the smiling sage pressed on.

"Furthermore, you're not some hot-blooded youth looking for information to lead you to riches beyond belief; you have a problem, personal and immediate. A serious problem, otherwise you would never have come to consult with an over-priced, over-educated land-grubber."

Alias spied Winefiddle's letter of introduction lying on the table beside the sage with its seal still intact. "What method do you use, wire under the wax, or do you just hold the letter up to a strong light?"

"You wound my fragile ego, lady. I swear to you I have not yet opened the good curate's letter. I prefer to start afresh. That way nothing can prejudice my reasoning."

Alias shrugged, willing to take the sage at his word—for now, at least.

Dimswart resumed. "You sit at ease, but you keep your right arm beneath a cloak. Hmmmm."

Alias waited for him to give up guessing and let her explain, but after a theatrical beat the man snapped his fingers, saying quickly, "You have a tattoo, or a series of tattoos, that resists all normal magical attempts to cure. They are on your right arm and . . . they are blue, aren't they?"

Alias's brow knit in a puzzled furrow. Winefiddle had shown her the letter before he'd sealed it. There was nothing in it about the color of the tattoo. "How do you know that?" she asked with astonishment—certain he had some sort of trick, but completely unable to guess what it was.

"Good artists never reveal their secrets." Dimswart winked. "But maybe, if we hit it off, I'll let you in on this little one. Now, how about giving me a look at that arm."

Alias, feeling like a much chewed bit of marrowbone, held out her arm in the firelight. The room was warm, and drops of perspiration beaded the skin over the symbols.

"Hmmm," was all Dimswart said for several moments, and he said it several times. He reached for a magnifying glassware and studied the symbols on her arm even more closely. Dragonbait positioned himself behind Alias's chair and tried to see what the sage did. Dimswart raised his head so the lizard could peer once through the glass, watching bemused as Dragonbait pulled back, apparently astonished at the sight of human flesh in such detail.

"A nice piece of work, that," said Dimswart, snapping his magnifier into its case and leaning back in his chair. "The sigils aren't composed of mere pinprick punctures in the flesh like an ordinary tattoo. Each one is made up of tiny runes and patterns packed close together. They appear to have great depth as well, and yet—" the sage kneaded her forearm gently, like a surgeon feeling for a broken bone "—there doesn't seem to be any substance to them. They look as though they are buried beneath your skin. Your flesh above must be invisible, or we could not see the symbols. They also seem to move. All in all, a most fascinating series of illusions. Very artistic. And positively unique. I'd stake my reputation on it. Do they hurt?"

"Not now, no. The tattoo ached some when detect magic spells were cast on it though, and it burned like the Nine Hells when Winefiddle cast a remove curse on it."

"How about when magic is cast on you in general? Like a curative spell?"

Alias thought of the assassin's magic missiles from the previous evening. Fat lot of good the signs did for her then. Why hadn't it flashed into the eyes of her assailants when she really needed it to? "No effect, as far as I know." She shrugged. "I'm really not in the mood to experiment on which spells do what," she added.

"I don't doubt you're not," Dimswart replied sympathetically. "Who have you crossed recently? Any dark lords from deep within the pits of the Nine Hells? Steal any unholy artifacts? Break the hearts of any cavaliers whose older siblings dabble in the dark arts? No?"

Dimswart sat back and pulled a pipe from inside his vest and began stuffing it with tobacco. He leaned toward the fire for a brand, but Dragonbait beat him to it, holding a flaming twig up to the pipe bowl as the sage puffed on the mouthpiece. The sage might have been waited on all his life by scaly servants, his reaction to the lizard was so casual.

"You have him well trained," Dimswart noted. "Where did you get him?"

"We met at the seaside," Alias answered.

Dimswart lapsed into a thoughtful silence, forgetting to puff on his pipe, so that it went out. Finally he asked, "When did you notice this . . . condition?"

"When I woke up last night."

"From a long sleep?"

"Three days, I'm told," Alias admitted. "Though I've slept nearly as long after overindulgences with ale. When I first woke, I thought I'd been drinking, but now I'm not so sure. I have a lot of missing memories, several months worth, and that's unusual for me."

"No doubt, no doubt." Dimswart pulled his pipe from his mouth and leaned toward her. "What's the last thing you remember before you picked up this little token?"

Alias sighed. "I don't really know. I clearly remember leaving my company, the Adventurers of the Black Hawk, on good terms about a year ago. They were going south. I never liked the warm climes, so I took my share and left. Drifted. Light work, you know. Caravan guard, body guard, challenges in bars. When I woke up I had a vague memory of a recent sea voyage—but it's all too hazy. I . . . " Alias halted for moment, trying to pull her memories out of the darkness. "I met Dragonbait last night, but I think I knew him from before." She shook her head. "I just don't remember."

"Does Dragonbait talk?" Dimswart asked.

Alias shook her head. "What about these symbols? You called them signals?"

"Sig-ils," corrected the sage, spreading out the pronunciation. "Sigils are a higher kind of symbol. They're like a signature symbolizing a greater power. Clerics use the ones belonging to their churches. Mages invent their own and protect them, sometimes quite jealously. They aren't really magical, but on a document they carry the authority of their owners, and on any other object they indicate uncontestable ownership of a valuable property."

Alias felt herself growing hot, hotter than could be accounted for by the fire. It was a heat from anger burning within. "I've been branded as someone's slave?"

"Possibly," said Dimswart, "though that's a very special brand. Something that intricate could only have been done with the help of magic—magic that resists its own diminishment. I suspect it's responsible for clouding up your memories. If you knew how you got it, you might be able to remove it. That's probably the way it thinks."

"What do you mean, 'it thinks'? You mean it's alive?"

"Not in the sense that you or I or this polite lizard is, no. But in terms of a magical creation with its own will to survive, given the desires of its creators, yes. Just as an automaton or golem or summoned creature is alive."

Alias slumped in her chair. "So where does that leave me?" This might be more expensive than she had anticipated.

"Quite frankly, it leaves you in trouble," said the sage, pulling on his pipe and finding that it had gone out. He waved away the fresh brand Dragonbait offered. "Unless we find out what those sigils are."

Alias drew her gaze away from the fire and fixed it firmly on the sage. "What will it cost?" she asked. Her look warned she was in no mood to haggle.

"You're not that rich." Dimswart held up a hand. "Yes, I know that, too. You do seem a fairly competent adventuress, however, and I need someone like that at the moment.

"You've undoubtedly noticed the hubbub outside." The sage jerked his thumb toward the study door, and Alias nodded. "My daughter, Gaylyn, is getting married. Last of the brood, thank the gods. I may finally get some peace and quiet. Anyway, her young squire is from a noble family here in Cormyr—the Wyvernspurs of Immersea, some distant relations of the crown. The upshot is, in order to impress these new in-laws, I have to lay out quite a spread indeed, and to that end I've worked wonders: big tent, finest chefs liberated from the crown's kitchens, silver wrought for the occasion, and four clerics for the ceremony. Stuff from which boring songs are written." He gave a cynical laugh.

"I also sent for a bard," he sighed. "No ordinary songster earning meals in a noble's court, but one of the greats. The renowned Olav Ruskettle, from across the Dragon Reach. The caravan Ruskettle was traveling in was attacked by the Storm Horns Dragon. Have you heard about it?"

"I heard that the dragon has chewed up another adventuring company since the caravan."

"Yes. Well, in the caravan with Ruskettle was a merchant who brought me an eyewitness account of the attack. Ruskettle tried to sing the beast into submission, the mark of a great bard. The beast apparently liked the music, but instead of submitting, took Ruskettle in her claws and headed back for her lair. Suzail sent out a group of adventurers in retaliation, but they were, as you said, chewed up. I did, however, manage to obtain from the survivors the location of the monster's lair and a secret 'back door' into it. My question for you is: Will you help a sage who is desperate to avoid breaking his youngest daughter's heart?"

Alias thought for a moment, then asked, "You want the dragon dead?"

"I want the bard, Ruskettle, to play at my daughter's wedding," the sage responded. "Clerics of Suzail want the dragon dead. Deal with them if you want to kill dragons."

Alias shook her head. "I'd rather sneak in, reappropriate your bard, and sneak out. I prefer to leave dragonslaying to those in good standing with their gods."

"It's agreed, then," said the sage. "I'll take time out from the wedding preparations. There are a million-and-one things to do yet, but Leona, my wife, can handle them better than I. Besides, I'll feel more useful helping you find out what those sigils mean. In the meantime, you'll bring me my bard. Let's see that arm."

Dimswart drew Alias over to his desk. He opened up a fat volume to an empty page, and with a pen and astonishing skill, quickly copied the insignias on Alias's sword arm. "None of these are familiar to you?" he asked.

"I've seen one of them on a card carried by assassins who, I believe, intended only to capture me."

"Really? How very interesting. Very interesting."

"Now, where do I find your dragon?"

"The merchant I mentioned before will take you there. He has some interest in helping free this bard as well." The sage called out, "Come on in, Akash," and a figure breezed in— clad in a familiar crimson robe striped with white.

Akabar Bel Akash bowed formally. "We meet again, lady. As I told you, Sir Dimswart, she would leap at the opportunity to aid us." The Turmishman beamed with pleasure.

Alias scowled, first at him, then at the sage. Akabar ignored her glare. Dimswart, having revealed the source of his information, arched his eyebrows like a stage magician demonstrating the trickery behind his feats.

Dragonbait, realizing no one was interested in smoking, blew out the burning brand he'd been playing with and threw it into the fireplace.

❧ 4 ❧

Akabar and the
Back Door

Alias shivered in the damp darkness of the cavern and silently wished the vengeance of Tyr and Tempus down on the heads of Akabar and Dimswart and even Winefiddle for getting her into this predicament. And while they were at it, thrice-damn that mysterious lizard and damn thrice more the demon-spawn who branded her!

The mystical sigils glowed like stained glass on a murky day, illuminating Alias so that she stood out like a beacon in the pitch dark of the cold, dripping cave. When she exhaled, the streams of her breath danced like small azure elementals before her eyes.

At the beginning of her vigil, Alias had kept the treacherous arm with its glowing brands beneath her cloak. She was waiting for the merchant-mage, Akabar, to return from scouting out the passages leading to the dragon's lair. After spending a half-hour huddled in the dark, though, it occurred to her that most dwellers of this cold, wet, limbo would be able to see the heat from her body and smell her above-world scent while she remained blind. Dumb, dumb, dumb, she chided herself and cast aside the cloak. At least now she could see anything that attacked her.

Where is that damned mage? she wondered for the half a hundredth time. Tymora! He could have scouted from here to Sembia by now. How far can this cavern go?

She knew her impatience had little to do with how long the mage was taking. Mostly it had to do with not liking to have to rely on anyone—especially not some greengrocer.

Alias chuckled every time she remembered how, before they'd left Dimswart Manor, Akabar Bel Akash had informed her in that stiff, formal, southern way that House Akash did not sell vegetables. Tymora! He was so naive. He didn't even know he was a greengrocer.

"Riding a wagon along protected trading routes in a guarded merchant caravan doesn't make you an adventurer," she had informed him. "Until you've hiked more than twenty miles a day, slept in a ditch, and eaten something that tried to kill you first, you're not an adventurer. Anyone who isn't an adventurer is a greengrocer."

But the merchant-mage had insisted that he come along and render what assistance was in his power, and Dimswart had insisted she take him with her. What reasons the Turmishman could possibly have for helping to rescue the kidnapped bard, Alias could not imagine. She had deliberately not asked, and Akabar had not volunteered his reasons. He had them, and that was enough.

There was something about Akabar Bel Akash that annoyed her—something that wasn't really his fault, but which she blamed him for nonetheless.

As the three of them, Akabar, Alias, and Dragonbait, began their three-day journey into the mountains—walking because Alias still felt uncomfortable advertising her presence with horses—Akabar had insisted on telling her all about himself—about the fertile land of Turmish, about customs in the south, and about his wives. He had two, and they were shopping for a third co-wife, which was why he was in this savage land in the first place—to earn money for the new partner. He told of his voyage across the pirate-infested Sea of Fallen Stars, the outrageous import taxes he'd had to pay on landing at Saerloon in Sembia, and his profitable detour from Hilp up to Arabel and around the Great Wood of Cormyr. He ended with the disastrous caravan attack by the dragon on the road from Waymoot.

Alias had ground her teeth impatiently. There had been nothing for her to say. She could not remember what she'd been doing or how she got to Cormyr. She had not even been able to answer questions about Dragonbait. The whole trip out she had remained as silent as a stone, angry that anyone had the ability to remember when she could not.

The thing that Akabar described the most was the thing

that distressed Alias the most—his sea voyage. He had begun by discussing Earthspur, the center of the pirate activity dreaded by sailors, its lawless organization of cut-throats, and the well-known bombards that protected it. Then, he had given her a humorous description of the fear-ridden Sembian ship captain continually scanning the horizon for the pirates who, he assured Akabar, were lying in wait for a prize such as his ship. The mage then described all the interesting creatures that made their home in the Inner Sea, followed by an essay on ship life. Yet, despite all this talk, the period around Alias's own sea trip remained as fog-ridden as the port of Ilipur.

Finally, it had occurred to the mage that the swordswoman might have adventures of her own which, though unshared, would make his tales sound dull. Embarrassed and crushed by the weight of her silence, he had slid into an equally solemn mood. It had never occurred to him the frustration he had put her through.

As Alias stood alone in the water-carved cavern, she realized she could not pin down exactly where the borders of her memory loss were. Pieces of her past seemed to have dropped out. Her mind was like a swamp connecting dry land and open water. There was no exact point where murky waters swallowed her memories; islands of certain recollection spotted every time period.

Even worse—without the days, rides, or months of connecting space, the past seemed to belong to someone else, another Alias who stopped, gained the mystic runes, then moved on as another person entirely, bearing the same name. Since she'd awakened in The Hidden Lady, she'd used the battle-skills of the old Alias, skills as finely honed as they were automatic. Although there was some comfort in the fact that she hadn't forgotten her craft, there was something disturbing about the way she felt when she assumed a fighting stance.

Instincts took over. She didn't have time to think and plan. Only react. Like a guardian golem. She remembered Dimswart saying the sigils were alive the way a golem was. Are the brands making me fight, like they made me try to kill Winefiddle? Should I be giving them credit for my ability? She shook off this notion instantly and angrily. I was a good swordswoman before I got these things, she thought, and I'll be a good one long after I've gotten rid of them.

Then the most disturbing idea of all occurred to her. Perhaps I died and was resurrected by someone who decided to take his price out of my hide. Literally. Don't those newly raised from Death's Dominions feel uneasy and disquieted?

More than a few of her companions, after their first visit to the afterlife, chose to retire—to live as farmers, smiths, greengrocers. Speaking of which, she thought with annoyance, where is that damned mage, anyway?

Alias was beginning to consider retreating through the passage back to the outside. Something must have gone wrong for Akabar to take so long to return.

Before she'd made up her mind, the downward passageway brightened and a glowing orb floated up into her cavern. The size of a melon and radiating an orange light, the orb held the image of the merchant-mage's head.

"What kept you, Turmite?" she asked with a sniff.

"I had to wait until the dragon bedded down," replied the mage. His voice was muffled by the effects of his spell, a meld of wizard eye—so he could spy out the territory from the entrance to the tunnel in relative safety—and a special phantasmal force—so he could report his findings back to Alias. "It wouldn't do to have Her Evilness awake when you tried to sneak in. It would spoil our surprise.

"My spell is almost exhausted, and I must leave our mission's completion to you, swordslady. Ahead of you lie a few gentle curves, no serious drops. The ceiling is low about fifty yards ahead, then the passage narrows to shoulder width. It lets out on a ledge above the main cavern floor. Our bard is in a small cage atop a dais on the far side of the cavern." The mage's image began blurring, as if a snowstorm had erupted within the orange sphere. "Spell's wearing off. Anything I should do with your pet?"

"He's not my pe—" Alias began, but Akabar's spell was breaking up too quickly to waste time arguing. "Just keep him from entering the cavern," she ordered. "And don't get him mad at you. The last spell-caster who did didn't live long enough to regret it."

"Gods' luck to you." Akabar's voice sounded a long way off. His image was gone, and the orange sphere was shrinking. "I hope you know what you're doing. You have fought dragons before?"

"This will be my first," she answered quietly, but the sphere was gone and there was no reply from Akabar. I wonder if he heard me, she thought. Better if he didn't.

* * * * *

Five hundred yards behind and somewhat above her, at the cavern entrance overlooking the road from Waymoot to Suzail, Akabar the Turmishman came out of his trance. Dragonbait was still crouched at the mage's feet, watching the cavern entrance intently. The air about them was warm, humming with large bumblebees dotting, diving, and dodging about the mountain daisies.

Akabar sat down and leaned against a rock. He made quick thanks to his southern gods that he was not the one about to face a dragon in its lair. He pulled an apple from his backpack and bit into it. Dragonbait twitched at the sound of the crunch, but the creature did not takes his eyes off the cavern mouth that had swallowed Alias.

* * * * *

Alias continued cautiously along the tunnel Akabar had scouted out for her. The Turmish mage's report had been reasonably accurate in so far as there were no hairpin curves and none of the drops were impassable, but the passage was not so smooth that she looked forward to a possible hasty retreat. The low ceiling didn't bother her, but she was a trifle alarmed at the sound her armor made scraping against the walls when the corridor narrowed. Less frightening, but quite annoying, was having to slosh through the small, icy stream that had carved out the tunnel— something Akabar had failed to note. Too bad I can't shrink into an orange melon and float effortlessly along this passageway, she grumbled to herself.

Still, she was grateful that they had learned of this back door. With any luck, the dragon wasn't aware of it, or at least ignored it as too small to worry about.

A splattering noise warned her that the stream was nearing a considerable drop, and she slowed accordingly. She wrapped her glowing arm back in her cloak to hide her presence from the dragon. She reached the end of the tunnel and stepped out onto the ledge Akabar had mentioned. The stream fell twenty feet or so into a small pool on the cavern floor. Excellent! The waterfall will cover any noise I make climbing down.

Light filtered in from another, larger passage in the side of the cavern. This passage provided the dragon egress from its lair. Holes in the domed ceiling let in more rays of light. At first Alias was glad of the light because it drowned out the dim glow of her sigils, and she unwrapped her arm. Then she noticed the black, cawing birds fluttering in and out of the holes in the ceiling.

Crows! Nine hells! Alias cursed under her breath. Crows were bad luck—not just a sign for the superstitious, but a danger for anyone relying on stealth. One of their raucous cries raised in challenge of her intrusion into their territory would be enough to wake the dead. For the most part, the birds roosted in crannies near the ceiling, though a few circled in the thermals rising from the dragon's body. Since I have no intention of approaching the dragon, there's no reason for them to get excited, she reassured herself.

The great beast itself lay curled catlike. Alias had no doubt that the monster was a light sleeper. She wouldn't be surprised to discover brittle twigs or bells scattered across the main entrance. It was even possible that the dragon was capable of casting magical spell guards to wake her if anyone crossed the threshold into her treasure hold.

And what a hoard that hold held! Even by a dragon's standards the loot was immense. It included not only chests of gold lions and other precious coins, but split bags filled with trade bars, tapestries, and bolts of satin and velvet, marble statues, and bound books. Many of these items were still packed in the wagons that had been picked up and flown here by the monster. The dragon lay between the front entrance and the mounds of shimmering wealth, but nothing blocked Alias's access to the beast's hoard.

If the treasure was enough to start the adventuress sweating with gold fever, the bones were enough to quench that fire. Alias could spot piles of white as large as the treasure itself. Most were the remains of cattle and other large beasts the dragon used for food, but more than a few human skulls gleamed among all that ivory—the remains of adventurers Alias did not intend to join.

Alias leaned against the rock and watched the dragon's massive chest scales rise and fall with the deep breathing of slumber. Akabar's description of the monster had been accurate. The drab rust scales that darkened to a purplish hue toward the belly confirmed that the creature was a female, and her huge size could only come with great age.

The crows danced over the beast's hide, picking at the bugs beneath her scales. Alias realized the crows were actually ravens with wingspans as wide as she was tall. They only looked small, dwarfed by the size of the dragon.

Alias tore her eyes away from her unwitting hostess. No sense in hypnotizing myself with awe, she thought as she peered across the cavern for the bard's cage. She spotted it perched solidly atop an altar carved into the rock. This must have once been a temple, she decided. To what god?

. The body in the cage lay slumped against the bars. Tymora, Alias prayed silently, don't let me be too late. The figure rolled over, apparently in its sleep, and Alias sighed with relief. She prepared to enter the lair.

As quietly as possible, she secured a rope to a stalagmite on the ledge where she stood. She kept herself facing the dragon as much as possible as she climbed down, using only her arm muscles, not daring to push against the wall to break her descent for fear of setting loose rock clattering down. A few ravens spied her and retreated to the roof, but others continued scavenging on the dragon's hide.

Slipping warily between the piles of treasure, Alias checked the ground carefully so she didn't accidentally crunch her foot down on a dry bone and tested her footing lightly so she didn't slip on any loose stacks of coins. She threw off the temptation creeping over her to grab something valuable and flee. She was here for one thing only. Once that had been secured, well . . . maybe on the way out she might manage a few sacks of gold.

She tiptoed up the stairs leading to the altar. The cavern air was filled with the wheeze of the dragon's breathing, the splash of the waterfall, and the occasional croak of a raven. Not until she'd reached the top did Alias take her eyes from the floor and study the cage. It was sloppily lashed but quite sturdy. A small form lay in its center, balled up tightly in a cloak of expensive, gaudy brocade. Alias spied a plait of fire-red hair fastened with a green bow.

Damned mage. He should have checked more closely. This is a little girl, not a bard. I've risked all this for nothing. Ruskettle is no doubt already residing in the dragon's belly, to make room for this new toy.

The swordswoman was so angry that she spun about, intent on leaving that very instant, but she turned back to face the cage. She would rescue the prisoner anyway, not from any sentiment or human kindness, but just for the pleasure of shaking the child in Akabar's face and proving to him what a fool he was. Sliding her sword between the bars, she gently poked the cloaked bundle.

The brocade-wrapped form turned over rapidly, causing the cage to groan slightly where the ropes held its timbers in place. The package opened to reveal not a child, but a small creature dressed in garb that made Akabar's crimson and white robes seem conservative. A creature without footgear, but long, curly red hair on her hands and feet that matched the mop on her head. A halfling! Alias whined silently. And a female halfling at that.

"Rescue at last!" cheered the halfling in a happy whisper.

"Shh!" warned Alias. Why did it have to be a halfling? How come no one mentioned Ruskettle was a halfling? Or even that Ruskettle was a she?

Suddenly, Alias sensed the deadly quiet. The stream spattered on, but the dragon's regular breathing and the crows' occasional caws had stopped. The halfling's eyes widened, transfixed by something behind and above Alias. Something horrible cleared its throat with a cough like a bag of lead coins dropped off a tower.

With a sigh of resignation, Alias turned around slowly.

"Looking for something in particular?" asked the dragon. "Or are we just browsing?"

❦ 5 ❦

Mist

The dragon, though she had not bothered to rise, was no longer balled up like a cute kitten by a fireside. Her front paws curled beneath her bulk, her body rested comfortably below the level of her rear haunches, and her neck curved in a relaxed S-shape. Even seated in this way, her jaws hung twice as far above the ground as Alias's perch on the raised altar, and her reptilian golden eyes looked down from another ten feet higher than that.

From what little Alias could see of her belly, it was a twisted mass of scarred, purple and violet scales. Several of the scars were still fresh and oozing—compliments of the adventuring party that had tried to defeat her but failed.

With those long tendrils hanging down from her chin and face, Alias thought, she looks like a cat. I guess that makes me the mouse. Then the swordswoman noticed, tucked behind the monster's left ear, a raven regarding her with a stare as unblinking as the dragon's—the only one that had not retreated to the ceiling. The dragon's spy.

"Poor dear," rumbled the dragon. "Are you ill-versed in the common tongue? Where do they send these robbers from, anyway? *Asken bey Amnite?* No. You don't look like a southerner. *Cheyeska col Thay?* Not that either. Do you speak any language known to the Sea of Fallen Stars? I detest not knowing where my next meal is coming from."

The dragon's ramblings shook Alias from her trance. The beast had transfixed her with a gaze that would have done a basilisk proud, yet here she was, nattering like some fishmonger's wife. Alias tried to speak several times, until the words found purchase in her throat and she spat out, "I come from Cormyr." For the moment, she added mentally.

"Oh, so you are native flesh," said the dragon, coiling her neck back as if to view Alias in this new light. "How precious. I do hate foreign mystery meat. They put such odd things in their bodies."

Alias blinked hard, fighting the sudden drowsiness that descended on her. First the dragon's gaze, then its rich, rumbling words, seemed to drain the energy from her body, as if the rest she had received earlier in the week had done her no good. This must be what they call dragon-fear, Alias realized. She shook herself out of the lethargy.

"I am no foreigner, but Alias of the Inner Sea, swordsmaster and adventuress," she announced.

"Oh, really?" replied the dragon. "You must forgive me for not knowing anything about you, but I've been so out of touch. I am Mistinarperadnacles Hai Draco. You may call me Mist. And I'll call you . . . supper? Yes, it's about time for a light, early supper. So nice of you to deliver yourself."

The dragon shifted its weight, and Alias saw for the first time the front paws of the beast, huge, three-toed triangles, each corner of the triangles sporting a claw. Further up each foot glinted an opposing dew claw. All the claws were as crimson as fresh blood.

Alias held up her sword with both hands—not to attack, but as a warning gesture. She replied, "You must forgive my unwillingness to serve as your meal, O great and powerful Mistinarperadnacles, but instead I think I will challenge you to the Feint of Honor."

"The Feint of Honor?" Mist echoed the last words with a tone of surprise. Then she chuckled, a sound that echoed like thunder about the cavern. "What can you know about the Feint of Honor, O Supper?"

Alias stepped back until her back was touching the wicker of the cage and replied, "It is the proper name given to the ritual combat of subdual instigated in the most ancient of times by the wisest of dragons."

Mist sniffed, "And I presume you know why?"

"Because, in the most ancient of times, your people fought amongst themselves so fiercely that many promising wyrms died. Indeed, scholars believe you may have wiped yourselves off the face of the land had not the Feint been decreed." Alias pressed her calf against the cage bars in hopes that the halfling would notice the dagger in her boot.

"Yes. True enough." The dragon nodded, settling back on her haunches. "Having heard of this custom, all manner of militia and mercenary have come barrelling into my home and the homes of my brethren, beating on us with the flat of their blades, firing blunt-headed fowling arrows, and generally disturbing our rest until we are forced to destroy them just to regain our composure. A little knowledge is a dangerous thing. It implies a lot of ignorance." Mist twisted her neck so that her jaws were uncomfortably close to Alias's head. "You see, the Feint is a code for dragons. It has nothing to do with you puny, but delicious, mortals."

"Not so, O Mistinarperadnacles. True, many humans may attempt subdual without following the formal codes, and their senses are as *bootless* as a *halfling*. And he who walks in here without sense, walks in here *unarmed*. You are then entirely within your rights to exterminate them as you see fit." Alias felt a pat behind her knee, a signal, she hoped, that the halfling had understood, but she had no sensation of her dagger being slid from her boot. "But you may not with honor deny a challenge properly made—"

"Your speech is oddly accented," said the dragon. "I think you come from beyond Cormyr."

"Unless, of course," Alias continued, "you are a common dragon. Then, of course, you may behave as you will."

Fire flared in Mist's eyes. "And do you know the formal codes, O Supper?"

"I know first to ask the dragon's name if it is not already known," replied Alias.

"Common courtesy, at the very least, common sense as well."

"At this point, I must say you have offended me. You have monopolized the services of this halfling, an offense to art; you have kept her imprisoned in this cage, an offense to humanity; and you have referred to me as Supper, an offense to my honor. For these barbarities, Mistinarperadnacles, red mistress of flame and sunsets, I challenge you!"

"Quite nice," said the dragon. "Your composure does you

credit. You astonish me, young one. This is a custom veiled in antiquity. I don't believe one sage in a hundred could recall the formalities so precisely. Just where did you acquire this knowledge?"

Alias did know the answer to that question. She remembered it, but she did not know how. Instead of trying to answer Mist's questions, she continued with the terms of challenge.

"My weapon will be this single blade." Alias indicated her sword with a nod of her head. "You may use your claws. No biting, no breathing fire, and no magic."

Steam was beginning to rise up from Mist's nostrils, indicating the beast was no longer amused or intrigued, but losing her patience. Alias continued hurriedly, "We fight until the first three hits or until the other surrenders. If I am victor, I demand you free the halfling Ruskettle and allow both of us to leave your lair safe and free."

"What? No demands for a chest of gold or for me to leave this happy land and never to return?" Mist mocked her.

"None," Alias replied flatly. According to the code, the more demands she made, the more compromises she would have to make toward the dragon's terms. If they even came to terms. Steam now poured from Mist in great billows.

She could breathe fire anytime, Alias thought. If her ego and pride don't bind her to the ancient code, I'm dead meat.

"It is a sad state of affairs," Mist growled, "when a dragon cannot use those gifts invested in her by Tiamat. At the very least, I must use my claws and my teeth. We will fight until you are dead or you convince me to surrender. In compensation, if you win, I will grant you a chest of gold. I am a generous spirit, you see."

"Accepted," Alias replied without hesitation.

The dragon reared back, her head raised into the stone dome high above. The raven flapped noisily from her head. Surprised, Mist could only foolishly repeat, "Accepted," thus locking herself into the agreement.

"The code is honored, the pact is made," Alias declared and lunged forward beneath the dragon's chest. She slashed out with her sword, catching the beast just below the forward knee. The blow was not forceful enough to cut into the scales, but it hurt. The dragon roared, and her knee buckled so that she toppled forward. Alias dashed between her hind legs. Careful to avoid the creature's tail, the swordswoman dragged her blade across Mist's purple-plated rump, knocking loose a few half-healed plates.

Mist howled and spun about. Her gleaming eyes seemed to burrow into Alias. "Foul!" she hissed. "You used the sharp side of your blade."

"Our contract did not limit me to the flat of my weapon, wyrm!" Alias shouted, dodging backward to avoid the slash of the triple scythes at the end of the dragon's paw.

"O ho!" Mist cackled, following up her first assault with a thrust from the other front paw. Alias twisted and rolled away as claw tips scored deep into the wall she'd had at her back a moment before. "So you are now a lawyer as well as a fighter!" Mist taunted as she yanked her claw from the rock, causing a small avalanche of stone to topple down.

Alias retreated back among the treasure and bone piles, sparing only a glance for the now-empty cage on the altar. She averted her eyes quickly so as not to alert Mist to the halfling's escape. Have to keep the wyrm's attention on me, Alias thought. Unfortunately, that should be no problem.

Instead of lunging her neck toward the warrior, Mist retreated and rose to her hind legs, unfurling her wings. The leathery folds of flesh caught the subterranean breeze like sails, then fanned the air back in powerful waves toward Alias's corner of the cave.

The last raven retreated to the roof to avoid the assault, but Alias had no way to evade the force of the wind. She was lifted from the ground and buffeted over several large treasure chests. Her rough passage knocked the arm and leg guards off one side of her armor and left her pinned beneath a granite statue of some forgotten Hillsfar noble.

She began squirming out from beneath the stone, but Mist loped forward and laid her chin down on top of the statue. Her fetid breath made Alias gag. Mist's mouth tendrils curled in glee. Alias closed her eyes, certain she was about to have her head bitten off.

"So, little lawyer," Mist hissed, "I can slay you now by fire, for who would know I violated the codes?"

"Well, me for one," came a high-pitched but resonant voice from above. "And you know the old saying—tell a bard, and you tell the world."

Mist whirled around in surprise. The halfling bard stood on the ledge by the opening to Alias's back door. She leaned weakly against the rock wall, but her eyes sparkled with mischief and vengeance. Alias took advantage of Mist's inattention to escape from the embrace of the Hillsfar noble and began to climb up a wagon loaded with treasure.

Ruskettle strummed a chord on her tiny yarting, a miniature guitar with seven catgut strings. "Now let's see, this is spur of the moment, mind, but how about—" The bard began to sing:

> I heard the mighty rush of fire
> From the ledge above the cave.
> The attack of a common coward
> No dragon, just a knave.
> She broke her oath in combat,
> Now shunned by one and all.
> Not even other dragons
> Will have her in their hall.

"Then of course we'll need a chorus for everyone to join in on," Ruskettle continued hurriedly:

> Oh, listen to the story
> Of the scandal of the wyrms.
> Red Mistinarperadnacles,
> Rumored mad and quite infirm.
> With a single belch of fire,
> This fool dragon with no shame,
> Her honor she has vaporized
> Like the Mist that is her name.

Alias cringed at the lyrics' strained meters, but had to admire the singer's nerve. Great clouds of steam filled the dome above Mist's head. The bard hadn't a chance of outrunning the fires that had to be burning inside the wyrm. Instead of escaping, though, Alias noted, she risked her hide to gain time for me to wriggle out of danger.

Goaded forward by the image of a roasted halfling and a failed mission, Alias launched herself from the lid of a large cask toward the dragon's head. She fell short of her mark, but managed to catch a fistful of the tendrils hanging from Mist's chin. Arching her back and kicking her legs like an acrobat, the swordswoman swung herself backward, over the side of the dragon's mouth, past her dripping, exposed teeth, beyond her steaming nostrils, and landed squarely on the bridge of the dragon's nose.

Alias wedged her blade between Mist's eyes, so that the creature's pupils crossed, trying to focus on her foe.

"Match was until surrender," Alias panted, sweat rolling down her face in rivulets. Her exhaustion deepened with her proximity to the dragon's steaming and foul exhalations, yet she tightened her grip on her hilt. "Do you surrender, wyrm, or shall we see how much of your brain I can reach when I plunge my blade into one of your eyes?"

For Alias, the next few moments were frozen in time. Steam rose about her and water splattered to the floor, but the principals of the tableau stood motionless: the dragon considering the value of her eyesight and the length of the warrior's blade, Alias trying to remain perched on the creature's scaly nose, Ruskettle awaiting the outcome, so eager to witness it she would not flee like a sensible person.

Finally Mist hissed, "This time, little lawyer, you win."

"I accept your surrender," Alias replied. She kept her gaze on the creature and her sword over Mist's nose. No blanket of condensing steam poured from the beast's mouth to indicate she had cooled her inner fires.

Mist has no intention of honoring the pact, Alias realized. She wants me dead even more than ever, but she doesn't dare try to kill me unless she can get the tell-tale bard with the same blow. All she has to do is breathe fire once I'm standing beside Ruskettle.

Alias's mind scrambled for a scheme to delay the dragon's attack, hoping that the halfling had enough wits to play along. "I'd like to be let down over there by my friend," the swordswoman said.

"But, of course," Mist replied, her tone full of sugary venom. The dragon kept her head perfectly steady as she swung her neck over to the ledge, anxious that Alias should not slip or lean on the blade and drive it into an eye.

Alias hesitated before she stepped off Mist's snout. Winking at the halfling, she said, "That ring of fire resistance makes you a lot braver than usual, bard."

"What? Oh, yeah. The ring of fire resistance. Well, you know my motto: If you got it, might as well flaunt it. You think I'd have risked singing to a dragon without one?"

Alias leaped from Mist's head to the ledge and sidled behind the halfling, as if to use her tiny body for a shield. The swordswoman's heart pounded as she ordered the dragon, "Now go fetch the chest of gold you promised me."

Mist's eyes narrowed to tiny slits. Steam rose from her nostrils. Tymora, make her believe the ruse! Alias prayed silently. The dragon turned her head away from the ledge and lumbered toward a pile of gold. Alias swallowed hard.

"Why didn't you kill her when you had the chance?" Ruskettle whispered through clenched teeth.

"And fall to my death or get crushed by a dragon in her death throes? No, thank you. That wasn't what I was paid for. Now, let's get out of here."

"What?" the bard asked.

"We're leaving," Alias replied, grabbing a handful of the halfling's cloak. Alias slipped into the passageway leading out of the lair, trying to tug the halfling with her, but Ruskettle jerked herself loose.

"We have to wait for the gold," the bard insisted.

With an exasperated growl, Alias grasped the small woman by her shoulders, pulled her into the passage, and shoved her in the lead.

Their way dimly lit by the runes embedded in Alias's flesh, Alias prodded and pushed at the halfling until they reached the upper cavern where the swordswoman had waited for Akabar's scouting report. Once they reached this point, however, Ruskettle twisted from her grip and dropped angrily to the floor. Alias slipped her sword arm into her cloak before the halfling caught sight of the glow of the sigils.

"Why'd you do that?" the bard demanded. "She was going to get us some gold!"

"Stupidhalfling!" Alias panted, her words running together. "Mist is a red dragon! That makes her as greedy and as untrustworthy as an Amnite merchant! The only thing that stopped her from burning us to cinders was the fear you would escape and tell someone."

"But she believed your story about me having a ring of fire resistance."

"For the moment. But if she had sniffed any jewelry on you when she first kidnapped you, she would have made you take it off. You aren't wearing any rings. Any minute now she's going to remember that, and then—"

Cool air from the outside rushed down the passage. Alias could picture Mist sitting by the ledge, inhaling deeply, smoke from her hidden forges pouring out of her snout.

"Come on!" the swordswoman shouted, picking up the halfling, tucking her under her arm, and running for the surface exit. Ruskettle was unexpectedly heavy, and between the extra weight and having to check her footing, Alias felt as though she were running underwater.

A roar began behind her, a deep rumbling sound. Harsh cries followed—ravens, she realized, caught in the conflagration. Her back grew uncomfortably warm as the dragon's breath chased her down the passage. If she didn't reach the exit quickly, the approaching wall of super-heated air would do her in before the beast's metal-twisting flames even reached her.

The heat grew unbearable, and Alias wondered if she might already be burned so badly that she would die but her muscles and mind didn't know that yet. The halfling was still squirming in her arms as she made a final leap toward the opening in the mountainside, praying to Tymora that she would clear it before the hot air singed her flesh and the fire stripped it from her bones.

The moment Alias cleared the stone passage, Dragonbait's tail snaked out from the right. The powerful muscles in the scaly, green ribbon knocked the swordswoman and her passenger down the slope of greasy grass.

Alias looked back. The opening where she had been only an instant before was now filled with flame and soot. The rock about the cave entrance melted in the heat, twisting and flowing until the passage was sealed shut. Silence settled over the mountainside.

Dragonbait rubbed his mildly scorched tail and gave a

reptilian whimper. Akabar, upon hearing the sound of the dragon's inhalation, had assumed a safer position several paces away from the back door. He now looked down at the soot-blackened women with amusement.

Alias looked down at Ruskettle, and it suddenly dawned on her why the halfling had been so heavy. On her tumble down the hill, the bard had lost, in order, Alias's dagger, two pouches of gold coins, an opal the size of a cockatrice egg, a handful of jade statuettes, a ratty scroll, and a large, ornate book marked with the sigil of Akabar Bel Akash.

For half a score of heartbeats, Alias lay among the flowers of the mountain meadow. She gasped in the thin mountain air, trying to will away the stabbing pain in her chest and the searing agony across her back. She imagined the dragon-heated metal of her chain shirt burning through her jerkin and inwardly cringed.

Dragonbait, having knocked her and the halfling out of the direct path of the dragon's breath, was at her side immediately, his clawlike hands on her shoulders, helping her rise. He smelled heavily of woodsmoke, but his chivalrous aid helped make Alias feel a little better.

Farther down the slope, the halfling was scurrying about, trying to recover the items lost in her tumble. She grabbed one of the leather-bound tomes, but a sandal-clad foot suddenly appeared and held it tight to the ground.

"I believe," Akabar Bel Akash said, "that this particular item is mine."

The halfling gulped. "You were the wizard in the caravan," she piped, wheels visibly turning behind her eyes. "Of course. I brought this from the dragon's lair to . . ." she sighed deeply, ". . . to return to you."

Akabar harumphed and, keeping his foot atop the book, reached over and picked up the age-torn scroll lying near it.

"That's for you, too," the halfling offered, jamming the opal and the jade figures back into her pockets.

Alias had by this time removed her charred cloak and shucked off her chain mail shirt. The cloak was a total loss; the heavy cloth had taken the brunt of the blast. The heat had been enough to fuse portions of her chain into solid lumps along the back and leave the light leather jerkin beneath hard and cracked. The leather must have insulated her back just enough though, for what she could see of her skin there, while pink, was not charred.

Blind Tymora's luck, Alias thought. Her back ached as though she had a sunburn, but no more. She abruptly shouted to the others, "Let's get a move on!"

The newly rescued bard ambled up the hill with the mage. Akabar held his recovered tome pressed tightly under his arm and used his hand to hold open the battered scroll, scanning its contents as he approached Alias.

The halfling planted each foot firmly at shoulder-width, and stuck out her hand toward the swordswoman. "We haven't been properly introduced. Ruskettle is the name, song and merriment the—"

"Not now," hushed Alias. "Look. In about five minutes, ten minutes at most, the red reptile is going to check to be sure we're dead. She'll come lurching out of the cave entrance. It's at least a mile to decent tree cover. . . ."

Dragonbait sniffed the air and growled. The halfling turned to the lizard and offered her still outstretched hand. Dragonbait backed away a step and bared his teeth. Ruskettle hastily lowered her arm.

"If we flee," Alias said, "it's likely we'll be caught in the open and fried." She arched her eyebrows and looked at the mage.

"Any suggestions?"

"Seal her in?" Akabar offered.

"Sure," countered Alias. "Have an avalanche handy?"

"Mayhaps," the Turmishman replied with a grin. He held up the scroll he'd been perusing. It was crammed with tightly calligraphed symbols. "This title says it is a spell to conjure a wall of stone."

Alias's eyes lit up. "Can you cast it?"

The magic-user nodded. "All I need do is use a simple trick to read the magic. That will evoke the powers locked within the text. Of course, it may not work." He spread his hands in a gesture of uncertainty.

"Half a chance is better than none," the warrior insisted. "Let's try it out on the beast's front door. Dragonbait!"

The lizard stopped staring at the halfling and followed the

swordswoman and the mage over the scattered boulders that ringed the mountain. The halfling brought up the rear.

They don't stand on ceremony much here, it occurred to Ruskettle moodily. As she walked, she pocketed her latest acquisitions, a ring and a small vial smelling of cinnamon.

By the time they reached the lair's main entrance, steam was billowing from within. The cavern's front opening was small but still quite wide enough for a dragon to pass through. From somewhere deep within, beyond their sight, a deep, throaty muttering rose and fell.

"Can the dragon use spells?" Akabar asked the halfling, concerned that the beast might have other, hidden talents.

"No. She's just cursing," the halfling explained. "The old girl talks to herself, deciding what she should do, where she should go, who she should eat, and so on. All that stuff."

Alias said grimly, "Can we just seal her in and get out of here before she reaches a decision?"

Akabar held the scroll out at arm's length and began intoning its spell in a low, melodic voice. Every so often, he would glance up at the entrance, then back to the paper.

Alias looked at her sword arm, but the symbols remained inert. Relief was quickly replaced by a sensation of horror as she spotted Ruskettle ambling over the stones directly toward the cavern's mouth.

The small humanoid took up a position some twenty yards from the cavern and cupped her hands before her mouth. She bellowed, or at least shouted as loud as a small creature could, "Heyyy, Misty!"

All at once, the mutterings in the cavern stopped.

Alias held her breath. Akabar looked up and almost scrambled the spell by missing an inflection. He continued to read aloud, though faster than before. Alias looked for Dragonbait, but the lizard was bounding over the rock-strewn hillside toward the halfling.

Ruskettle continued her taunting. "We made it, you big sack of shoe leather! We got out, and I'm going to tell everyone you're an oath-breaker! You jackass-faced salamander!"

Dragonbait was only halfway to the halfling's position when a deep rumbling came from within the mountain, like the sound of an erupting volcano. The mage quickened his verbal pace yet again. Alias was torn between worrying that the mage's speed would spoil the scroll's spell and that the wall created wouldn't be large enough to cover the lair's entrance or strong enough to stop a dragon.

"Oath-breaker, Fight-faker!" brayed the halfling. Twin amber lights appeared far within the cavern, growing larger by the second. They framed a red, open mouth set with swordlike teeth.

"Flame-brain, Lame-brain, Tame-brain, *oooff*—" The halfling's jeers were lost in a sharp exhalation as Dragonbait slammed into her, knocking her down the hillside for the second time in ten minutes.

The rising roar of the oncoming dragon now hurt Alias's ears. Akabar was shouting as well, spitting out the last phrases of the incantation. The scroll itself was being consumed by the force of the magics and was burning bright yellow in the merchant-mage's hands.

Everything broke loose in the span of a breath. Mist's body appeared from the darkness, visible in the sunlight that shone only a little way into the cavern. The dragon was flying low and fast, about to shoot through the small opening, falling upon the party like a hawk among sparrows.

Then there was a great *whooshing* noise, and a huge wall of stone blocked the party's view of the monster. They heard, however, a bone-crushing smash coming from the far side of the wall, and saw the barrier arc outward at its center, trying to contain the force of several tons of wyrm flying at top speed.

When the wall bulged, Alias was sure that the magical mortar would give. Astonishingly, it held, even losing half of the bulge by springing back some. Silence descended on the mountain meadow. Akabar collapsed by the burned remains of the scroll and put his head in his hands.

Ruskettle picked herself off the ground, scowled at the lizard, and shouted down at Alias, "That was hard work. When do we eat?"

⚘ 6 ⚘

Olive and the
Crystal Elemental

For the next few miles, as they wound down the hillside
and into the cover of deeper woods, Alias kept checking
over her shoulder. Despite having sealed Mist in, the
swordswoman half-expected the dragon to dive on them
from the sky, bathing the entire forest in flames. Logic
insisted that Mist had to be at least slightly injured from her
sudden collision, and it would take her at least a day to dig
her way out, but Alias felt more comfortable playing it safe
by assuming that Mist was pursuing them.

The swordswoman made the party turn off the road onto
the first trail into the woods, so it was nearly dusk by the
time they reached the stone circle where she and Akabar
and Dragonbait had spent the night before.

In the setting sunlight, the red hewn rock of the druid circle blazed as though the hillock on which it stood was afire.
According to the map Dimswart had given Alias, this site
had long been abandoned by the clerics of nature, yet the
pines encircling the clearing showed no sign of encroaching
and reclaiming the area. Alias wondered whether the trees
were discouraged by the rocky, frost-cracked soil or
thwarted by some lingering magic.

At any rate, the bare space discouraged her as well. Last
night they had found the clearing too cold to use as a camping site. Twenty feet down the slope under the cover of the
pine branches, on the soft carpet of pine needles, they were
sheltered from the wind and considerably warmer. This
night, the trees would also shelter them from Mist's gaze.
Alias was glad to have good reasons to avoid the stone circle.
The giant columns, set in no detectable order, made her

uncomfortable. She and Dragonbait hurriedly retrieved the party's gear from its hiding place in the hollow at the foot of one of the sandstone rocks.

Akabar was puffing on smoky, sparking pine needles when Alias and the lizard returned to the dark camp under the trees. While Akabar prepared dinner, Alias, wrapped in a cloak from the cache, patrolled the edge of the clearing, occasionally glancing at the bard.

Ruskettle was short, even for a halfling. Not even three feet high. There was nothing childlike about her figure, though. She was in the full bloom of womanhood, with plenty of curves, but she also had a slender waist and none of the plumpness most members of her race had. Her leanness, the muscles of her calves, her deep tan, all indicated to Alias that the bard was an adventuress like herself. Yet, Alias was not prepared to like or trust her at all. The bard hadn't made the slightest effort to help Dragonbait and Akabar set up camp or prepare their meal. Besides, halflings were trouble. Alias had never met an exception to the rule.

She joined the others for dinner, seating herself opposite Ruskettle, still watching her intently.

"I don't know how to thank you properly," the halfling bard mumbled between bites of smoke-cured mutton. "The halflings of the south have a saying: I owe you my life, your belongings are safe with me."

The mutton leg, which might have lasted Alias and Akabar another two days, was quickly disappearing. Ruskettle tossed her long, curly hair over her shoulder and motioned with her clay bowl for another helping of soup, still chewing as though her life depended on it.

Akabar furrowed his eyebrows at the small creature's gluttony, but he ladled out another portion of the hearty gruel, a thick barley stock with bits of salted coney seasoned with herbs from the merchant-mage's copious pockets.

"I can see you're keeping our food safe," Alias joked. "Are you sure it's the musical ability of Olav Ruskettle that is renowned, and not her appetite?"

The bard swallowed and wiped her mouth. "The name's Olive, dear. Olive Ruskettle. Don't worry. Everyone makes that mistake."

"Dimswart said it was Olav," Alias muttered as a tiny fear crept over her. Perhaps she had rescued the wrong person.

"Well, I should know my own name, don't you think? The problem is that some fool clerk made a mistake writing it down once on some official document and ever since I've had to correct people."

"I see," Alias replied suspiciously, wondering whether Mistress Ruskettle wasn't wanted under the name of Olav for something more serious than straining rhymes.

"As for my appetite," Olive Ruskettle explained, washing down a loaf of bread with a long pull on a waterskin, "you should know that that witch of a dragon, while having a civilized appreciation for my musical talents, had a lot to learn about the care and feeding of a halfling. Her own eating habits were anything but regular, and I had a devil of a time convincing her that I could not live on raw venison. Then I discovered that her cooking technique left something to be desired. If you had not come along, my dear," she said shaking her head sadly and patting Alias's boot, "I'm afraid my little bones would have joined those of the heroes littering the floor of the dragon's lair."

As the bard continued to make up for a ride's worth of lost meals, Alias thought of the heroes' bones littering the caverns of Mist. Heroes with all the bravado and lack of sense of the halfling. Alias shook her head remembering the bard's outrageous behavior at the mouth of Mist's lair.

Alias's first adventuring party, the Swanmays, had been like that, all flash and fanfare. One encounter with trolls had taught them the wiser course of stealth and surprise.

She remembered the battle with the trolls clearly, as though it had happened last week. So why can't I remember last week? she thought with frustration. She was so wrapped up in her thoughts that Akabar nudged her.

"I'm sorry, what?" she asked.

"I said, 'Do you think we'll return in time?' For the wedding, I mean."

"We'd better, or all this effort was for nothing," Alias answered, oblivious to the feelings of the halfling.

Olive Ruskettle apparently took no offense. Her mind was also on other things. "As anxious as I am to make my Cormyrian debut, I simply haven't the strength to keep pace with you. I shall have to have a mount."

"I don't care for sore feet and aching muscles any more than you, Mistress Ruskettle," Alias replied. "We walked here for secrecy's sake, but, since we seem to have eluded the dragon, horses sound like an excellent idea. How lucky for us you managed to acquire so much of the dragon's wealth while I was fighting for your freedom and life. We can purchase mounts at the first farm we come to."

Olive moved the mutton bone away from her face long enough to give Alias an unabashed grin. "I assure you, my feet made a bee-line for safety while you so valiantly risked your life to rescue me. My hands would have felt left out if they'd been any less useful, don't you know?" She waved the bone in the direction of the sacks of treasure. "Please, feel free to consider this the party's treasure to be used to cover expenses. Whatever remains should be divided evenly among those who survive our encounters. Even—" she cocked an eyebrow in Akabar's direction "—if some were less useful than others."

Akabar's brow furrowed in astonishment at the woman's nerve. "That is very human of you, small one," he said. "Particularly since that spellbook you pulled from the dragon's lair was my own. Most strange, though, because that book was missing from my wagon since the first day out of Arabel, which was, I believe, where you joined our caravan, several days before the dragon attacked us."

"Most strange, indeed," Olive agreed, returning Akabar's level glare. "But"—her eyes returned to her soup bowl, and she took a gulp of broth before continuing—"these are strange times, so the sages say. Mannish kingdoms war and plot while old gods, long forgotten, stir in their restless sleep." She lifted the soup bowl as if making a toast. "Let's celebrate your good fortune at having your valuable tome returned to you, instead of probing into yet more mysteries." She drained the soup bowl and held it out again. "Is there, perchance, any more soup?"

Akabar drained the last of the pot into Olive's bowl. Olive leaned toward the treasure pile, plucked the magical book from the coins and carvings, and held it out to the wizard as he held out her soup bowl. Both parties gave the other a smile that was less than earnest as the exchange was made.

Akabar inspected his book for signs of damage. Alias reached for a tiny pouch near the treasure pile and loosened the string about its neck.

"Not that," Olive objected. "Those are some of my personal effects." But Alias had already dumped the contents of the pouch on the ground. A collection of keys, picks, and wires glittered in the dirt. A small gold ring rolled toward the fire.

"Oops, sorry," Alias said nonchalantly as Olive snatched the ring from the ground. "You know, that ring looks familiar," she added before the bard had a chance to pocket it.

"Oh, this? I picked it up in the dragon's lair as well."

"I have one just like it. Same blue stone set in gold."

"Maybe you dropped it when you were fighting the dragon," Olive suggested. "Can you prove it's yours?"

Alias regarded the halfling's nervy challenge with considerable amusement.

Olive slipped the ring on her finger. At first it jangled about, too large for her tiny digits, but a moment later it shrank to a perfect fit. "Oooo. It's magic. Was yours magic? What did it do?"

Alias was unable to reply since she had not bothered to experiment with the ring she'd looted from the assassins. But she knew now as well as Akabar just how safe her possessions were in the care of the halfling bard.

Akabar looked up from his books, which he'd been checking for damage. "You had best be cautious with that thing, little one," he warned.

"Nonsense," Olive said with a sniff. "There's no danger as long as you know the right way to deal with these things. All you have to do is hold your hand over your head—" the halfling demonstrated, while Akabar stepped backward and Alias rose to her feet "—and command the ring, 'Show your power to me.' If that doesn't work then there are certain key words you should—"

They never heard the rest of the bard's lecture. Suddenly the ring's power did indeed display itself. Akabar's tome began to glow a soft blue, as did a ring on his finger and the one on Olive's. Alias's sigils outshone them all, emitting blue beams crazily about the pine forest.

"Damn!" the swordswoman shouted, tears brimming in her eyes. She wrapped her cloak tightly around her body, though a blue glow peeked out at the hem and neckline.

"What was that?" Olive gasped, her eyes glued to Alias.

"Detect magic, I imagine," Akabar answered, moving to the swordswoman's side. "You aren't in any pain, I trust?"

"I'm fine," Alias muttered between clenched teeth.

Olive continued to stare at the swordswoman as though she'd grown a second head. "You have a magical arm!"

"Ignore it," Alias muttered.

"But, it's really magical! Incredibly magical! More magical than anything I've ever seen. I'll bet you could have sliced Mist into pieces. Maybe we should go back and try it."

"I said, ignore it!" Alias shouted.

For the next several minutes an embarrassed silence reigned in the camp. Akabar cleaned out the dinner pot and used it to heat water for tea. Olive finished her soup and polished the mutton bone nearly to ivory. Alias clutched her wrapped arm close to her until the sigils' light began to dim.

Dragonbait laid more wood on the fire, and then stepped outside the campsite to stand in the darkness, facing the hilltop, as though he expected danger from that direction.

"So, tell me, mage," the halfling piped up, obviously uncomfortable without chatter about her. "Where did you find your familiar?" She indicated Dragonbait by nodding her head in his direction. "I've seen nothing like him from the Sword Coast all the way south to magical Halruaa."

Alias snapped, "Dragonbait is my companion, Ruskettle, not the mage's familiar. I did not find him. He found me. He has proved more than useful."

"Aye, I've noticed. Especially at pulling halflings out of the fire. I meant no offense, I assure you. It's just that I've never heard of a lizard acting as a manservant before. But then I've never heard of a magical arm before either."

Alias gritted her teeth. If the halfling wasn't going to give her curiosity a rest, it was time to go on the offensive. "You know, I've never heard of a halfling bard before."

"Well, that's easily explained," Olive smiled. "I gained my training in the south; things are very different there."

"I am from the south as well," said Akabar. "And now that the lady mentions it, I have never encountered a bard of the halfling race, either."

"Ah," replied Olive, staring sadly into her empty bowl. "Well, you are from Turmish, I seem to remember."

"Yeees," the mage said, anticipating what was to come.

"Well, I was trained farther south than that."

"Anywhere near Chondath?" Akabar asked.

"Chondath? Yes, just a wee bit farther south than that."

"Sespech?"

"Yes, Sespech. There is a barding college there with a fine teacher who taught me all I know." The halfling flashed Akabar a beaming smile.

"How odd," drawled the mage, tugging at the edge of his beard. "One of my wives comes from Sespech, on the Vilhon Reach, and while she is quite talkative about the merits of her native land, she has never mentioned halfling bards."

"Ohhh. No, no, no, no," corrected Olive. "You're talking about Sespech between the Vilhon and the Nagawater. I was referring to a place much farther south. How far south have your travels taken you?"

"I've traded as far south as Innarlith, on the Lake of Steam," the mage said. The halfling nodded.

"Our company . . ." Alias wrinkled her brow, trying to dredge up memories as bright but as liquid as quicksilver. "Our company fought on the Shining Plains. Yes, that's right, and we traveled through Amn once or twice."

The halfling looked at Alias a moment, confused by her interruption about places farther to the west and outside the realm of the discussion. She shrugged and continued her far-fetched explanation to the mage. "And in Innarlith there were dwarves from the Great Rift?" she asked.

"Yes, from Eartheart," Akabar replied.

"Well," Olive concluded triumphantly, "below the Great Rift, on the Southern Sea, is the land of Luiren. We have a Sespech there, and a Chondath, which are small but bustling towns, the namesakes no doubt of your larger nations. Anyway, in Sespech, the one in Luiren, I was trained, having made a long pilgrimage from Cormyr. I was attempting to return to my homeland when that fool wyrm plucked me from my wagon."

"Dimswart says you came from across the Dragon Reach," Alias said, puzzled.

"No, I come from Cormyr. You see, traveling by boat does not agree with me, so I journeyed to Luiren around the western edge of the Inner Sea. Desiring to see even more of the Realms, I returned from Luiren around the eastern edge of the Inner Sea, through many wild and dangerous lands. I made a name for myself in the nations of Aglarond and Impiltur. I had just entered Procampur when I received Master Dimswart's most generous offer to entertain at his daughter's wedding. And glad I was to come home, Procampur being a stuffy town, too restrictive for an artiste."

Alias and Akabar exchanged glances. Akabar looked frustrated, but Alias had to smile at the halfling's tale. There had to be at least a dozen lies tangled up in her story, but it wasn't worth the trouble proving it. Olive, like any other halfling, would only invent more lies to cover the originals. Better to wait until she accidentally let the truth slip out.

Alias stood up and stretched. "Going to be a cold night. We need more wood." She walked toward the clearing where the moonlight revealed fallen limbs.

"So, what's her story?" Olive whispered to Akabar, jerking her head at Alias's retreating figure.

"Story?" echoed Akabar. "To what are you referring?"

"She has a magical arm!" Ruskettle's voice rose half an octave.

Akabar shrugged. He was taking a lot of pleasure in thwarting the woman's unbearable curiosity.

"Look, mage," Olive sighed. "I owe her. I want to help."

Akabar's feelings softened somewhat. "Not that I believe you for a moment," he said, "but just in case your words are earnest, I will tell you. The glyphs on the lady's arm are magical, not the arm itself. Some unknown power carved them into her flesh, but she cannot remember the event. As a matter of fact, she cannot remember the events of several of the past months. In exchange for the meaning of the glyphs, she has agreed to deliver you safely to Master Dimswart. The best service you can do her is to come along peacefully and perform well at this wedding."

Olive pondered the information for a few minutes, then she speculated aloud, "So anything could have happened during the time she can't remember. She could have been a slave, or a concubine to a powerful sorcerer, or married to a foreign prince—a princess dripping in jewelry."

"Or a wandering swordswoman," added Akabar.

"Or a princess," Olive repeated to herself, "dripping in jewelry, her lover killed, her kingdom usurped, and her memory lost through the fell magics of her enemies."

Akabar shook his head at the bard's wandering fantasy. He was reaching for another log to throw on the fire when a strong wind suddenly rushed down from the hilltop. The pines danced with alarming energy, and sparks from the campfire scattered across the ground. The ground shook, and over the howl of the wind came a malicious laugh that brought both mage and halfling to their feet.

"Alias!" Akabar shouted, dashing toward the clearing.

Olive Ruskettle grabbed a brand from the campfire and rushed after him. If Alias had some wealth, the halfling realized, she could prove profitable to have in one's debt.

* * * * *

While Ruskettle was trying to persuade Akabar Bel Akash to tell her about Alias, the swordswoman was searching for Dragonbait. She'd assumed he had gone off to collect more firewood. If that were the case, Alias thought, he would have returned by now. He kept eyeing the hilltop. I'll bet he's gone to investigate that stone circle.

With a sigh Alias began climbing the hill.

A shadow at the edge of the clearing moved, accompanied by a scrabbling sound. The lightning-blue beams emanating from the sigils had died away, but the cursed patterns still gave off light enough to rival the moon. Alias drew her arm from her cloak and held it up. A large shape by the base of a pine tree, startled by the second light source, scampered down the hill into the darkness. Only a porcupine, peeling tree bark for dinner, O great warrior, Alias mocked herself. But don't worry, you scared it off.

Chuckling, she doubled her pace until she reached the center of the stone circle. The half moon hung overhead like a gold lion coin split apart by looting pirates. In the moonlight, the red stones appeared black and their edges and corners, dulled by the wind and rain, blurred into the darkness. She wondered why more enduring and brighter rock had not been used in the circle's construction. All the druid temples she'd ever visited before had been built of granite, not sandstone, and placed among oaks, not pines.

She jumped on a rock and surveyed the landscape. The tops of the encircling pines stood out against the moonlit sky like triangular crenelations of a castle wall. The original path to the temple was overgrown with brambles which reflected the moonlight. Of Dragonbait there was no sign.

Some parts of the hill dropped away in miniature canyons, and Alias began to worry that perhaps he had slipped or fallen down one of these. She shivered in the cold air. She'd suddenly felt very vulnerable. Like a fool, she'd forgotten her sword. She jumped from the rock and headed down the slope toward the campsite.

A glint of metal on the ground caught her eye. She veered from her intended path and moved toward it. At the foot of a larger than man-sized boulder lay Dragonbait's oddly shaped sword. Alias leaped forward and lifted the gleaming blade off the ground. The weapon's weight astonished her. It felt no heavier than a fencing foil, and its balance was not awkward in the least. It also felt warm to the touch—not just the grip, but the blade as well.

A shadow stirred on the boulder. Alias spun about with Dragonbait's sword raised, keeping the stone to her back, but there was no one there. Slowly, Alias turned back toward the boulder. Then she saw that, unlike all the other rock about the hilltop, this one was clear, like a huge hunk of quartz, and the shadow she'd thought moved across it had really moved *in* it. She pressed her face to the stone.

Thrashing at the heart of the rock, like a fly caught in pinesap, was the lizard's twisting form. "Dragonbait!"

Suddenly, something heavy struck the back of her legs below the knees and she toppled backward, crying out in surprise. A violent wind sprang from nowhere, slapping the pines about the clearing.

She tried to roll away from whatever enemy had felled

her, but something held her ankles fast. She stared at her feet in horror. They were bound in crystalline manacles, and her horror grew into panic as the rock crept farther up her legs in a twisting motion, like a vine climbing a pole.

Using Dragonbait's sword, Alias beat on the stone bonds with fury, not considering what damage she might do to the weapon or even to herself. The blade did not shatter, but cut through the engulfing stone as though it were liquid. Like sap, or syrup, the clear stone oozed back over the hack marks and continued growing faster than she could chop. Soon the stone oozed beneath her legging plates where she could not reach it, miring her tightly in place.

The ground trembled. With a squelching *thulk* a dome of earth rose before her, carrying with it the crystal boulder that imprisoned Dragonbait. Alias looked up in horror and realized that the rounded eruption was a huge, monstrous rock head. Dragonbait's prison rested on top of the head, a lump above its temple. Farther down, two eye-disks glowed a sickening yellow. Below these was a gaping maw smelling of sulfur.

The sound that issued from the mouth sent an ice dagger slicing down Alias's spine. The head laughed, a familiar, hoarse, wheezing laugh. Familiar, she was sure, to her old self, the self whose memory was missing, lost in whatever darkness this monster had sprung from.

A moment later, a great stone arm rose from beneath the earth. The creature's chest rose from its mossy bed as well, dark red earth set with a glowing blue symbol of interlocking rings— just like the set on her arm.

With a sickening lurch, Alias felt herself hoisted above the ground. The stone about her legs proved to be part of the amorphous fist attached to the arm of the monster. The monster held her up to its face. As she swung upside down in the hellish yellow glare of its eyes, she felt her sigils jump and writhe and flare as brightly as they had when Winefiddle had tried to dispel them, until an aura of near blinding blue shone all about her, the monster's head, and the crystal prison holding Dragonbait.

The creature laughed again. Its chortle unnerved her, and she hacked at its fist, its face, its eyes, anything she could reach with Dragonbait's blade. The sword passed through the creature's body; its "flesh" was the consistency of peat, but neither the creature's eyes or voice registered any pain. The hoarse laughter brought a lost memory fluttering across her inner vision, but like a bat in the darkness, she felt it but could not grasp it.

The monster raised her up to its temple and held her against its head so that she stood next to Dragonbait's crystal cell. The lizard gestured to himself, a motion that caught her attention. She took a deep breath in an effort to calm herself while she watched him miming the same motions over and over. First he would raise his hands together over his head, then pound them against the transparent wall of his trap, then slap himself on the forehead.

Huh?

Raise, pound, slap. Raise, pound, slap.

The creature of earth tugged its other arm from the soil. The newly freed fist held a gemlike twin of Dragonbait's prison. The earthen giant brought this second crystal up to where it caught the blue rays from Alias's sigils and scattered them into the dark night. Then the great stone cracked and split along its center. The blue light of her cursed runes revealed a clear, rippling slime within the crystal's open heart. Any moment she would become another bug in amber.

Raise, pound, slap.

Why does Dragonbait keep slapping himself on the head? she wondered.

Dragonbait pointed at her. She slapped herself on the head. He shook his head furiously and pointed at the crystal over his head.

"Not *my* head!" she yelled excitedly, finally understanding. "The creature's head!"

Clenching both her fists about the hilt of Dragonbait's weapon and twisting her body, Alias smashed Dragonbait's sword against the lizard's crystal prison.

Steel screeched on rock, and the force of the blow traveled up Alias's arm, leaving it numb. The crystal split like an eggshell, and Dragonbait spilled out of the jagged hole, followed by a mucky ooze that poured down the monster's face.

The monster shrieked, a baneful cry that carried leagues on the wind and seemed to set off a gale that bent large pines and snapped their heavy branches. A moan issued from the earth, echoed by the rocks of the stone circle, and then the huge beast's shoulders slumped and began to flow back into the ground.

Patting her hand gently, Dragonbait took his sword from her numbed grip. He slashed at the rock hand that held her, and the stone flowed away from her legs like sand. They were free, but there was a forty foot drop from the monster's head to the ground, and Alias was reluctant to make the leap.

She spotted Olive Ruskettle below, throwing daggers at the behemoth. The halfling's weapons buried themselves in the monster's chest. The tiny blades couldn't possibly hurt the monster more than a bee sting would harm a human warrior, yet the monster cried out again like a feral child.

More goo oozed from the shattered crystal on the monster's head. The wound was undoubtedly mortal, but Alias worried now that she and Dragonbait might be crushed by the monster's death throes. Dragonbait tugged on Alias's arm and forced her to half-leap, half-slide to the rock monster's shoulders.

Akabar's voice rose in a chant, and a lance of rainbow light struck the creature in the chest above the dimming rune of interlocking circles. The rainbow broke into a thousand small motes, spreading across the creature in a dancing, swirling pattern.

With one arm about Alias's waist, Dragonbait began climbing down the monster's back, using his hand and foot claws to keep his grip. Dragonbait jumped the last ten feet just as Akabar's magic consumed the creature's torso and slid up its head and arms. The moon shone through the stone wherever the rainbow light covered it.

The creature gave one last plaintive groan and faded into the night. Even the torn earth where it had risen fell neatly back into place. Akabar and Olive ran toward Alias, shouting victory cries. Behind her, she smelled the woodsmoke scent that seemed to cling to the lizard. A clawed hand squeezed her numbed shoulder gently, and Alias felt warmth flow into the limb. Dragonbait looked up at her, and she felt sure there was concern in his eyes, though they looked as dead yellow as ever. The lizard drew back as the halfling and the mage reached Alias's side.

"Did you see?" Olive asked. "While this one was struggling to remember his spell," she jerked her head in Akabar's direction, "I wounded it to the quick with two daggers to its heart. My aim was never better. What was it, anyway?"

Akabar looked down at the bard in disbelief. "Perhaps later you would care to hone your abilities by throwing at the side of a barn," he suggested dryly. "That was some type of earth elemental, though not one of the standard breed normally called up by magic-users. Perhaps it was from the Plane of Minerals, which abuts the Earthen Plane. At any rate, it was a conjured creature, or my dispel magic chant would not have worked on it."

He turned to address Alias. "I'm sorry I cast my spell before you could finish climbing down, but I judged you were safer falling than being crushed beneath the monster."

"Quite right," Alias answered, nodding her head, though she was obviously preoccupied with some other thought.

"Someone summoned something that big just to capture you?" Olive gasped. "You must be someone important."

Akabar turned to study Dragonbait, who sat on a rock, studying his blade in the moonlight. The lizard-creature ran a clawed thumb along the edge and growled like a cat. "It seems you've nicked his blade," Akabar said to Alias, pointing to the lizard. Dragonbait pulled something from his belt pouch. Alias watched as Dragonbait began sliding a whetstone along the steel edge.

"He seems more worried about his weapon's condition than yours," the halfling sniffed.

"Quite right," Alias repeated. She shivered. Pulling her cloak about her, she headed back down the hill to the campfire. Her head still echoed with the stone creature's hoarse laughter. Familiar, she thought, familiar as an old friend. Familiar as death.

❧ 7 ❧

The Wedding Reception

In the backyard of Dimswart Manor, two days journey from the mountains, in the countryside near Suzail, laughter and the clink of fine crystal filled the wedding tent. Now and then the multi-colored cloth walls shivered as some high-spirited child ran into the slender, black vloon wood rods supporting the sides. The white roof wafted alarmingly each time some tired or drunken soul leaned against the huge center pole that supported the tent roof.

Alias and Akabar had arrived late the previous night, mud-spattered and exhausted, but with a famous bard on the pony between them. Dragonbait loped along behind them since he refused to ride. Fortunately, he'd had no trouble keeping up with the group.

The lady of the house welcomed them with as much hospitality as she could, considering her home was already full of visitors, all certain of their supreme importance in the scheme of things. Small but comfortable rooms were found for the adventurers in the servant's wing.

Their hostess insisted they attend the wedding, though it was obvious to Alias that she did so only because it would be awkward to ask them to leave. Gratitude for the service they'd just rendered was the last thing on Lady Leona's mind. She had given Alias the distinct impression that, in her opinion, fighting a dragon was a snap compared to planning a wedding for three hundred people.

More suitable attire was found for the female guest—a sky-blue strapless gown with leggings and a capelet. One accessory had been added, a pair of arm-length, fingerless gloves, no doubt supplied to cover up her "affliction."

Alias was uncomfortable in the gown, despite the good fit and excellent cloth. She felt naked without her armor, and she kept tripping over the skirt. *You'd think I'd never worn a dress in my life,* she chided herself the third time she'd neglected to lift the hem and stepped on it. *After all, I wasn't born in armor.*

As far as her unreliable memory could recollect, she had worn dresses before becoming an adventurer. Even after she took up the sword, she'd risked teasing from the male members of her party and allowed herself the luxury of a more feminine wardrobe while she stayed in town.

That thought reminded her of her purpose in remaining here. Dimswart had uncovered information on the sigils, but wouldn't have time to review it with her until after the wedding. She scanned the crowd anxiously for the father of the bride, hoping that he might have a moment to give her some clue, something that would make the wait, in this warm tent full of frivolous people, bearable.

Dimswart was mingling through the crowd, looking as jolly as a trader who has deceived the tax collector. When Alias spotted him, he was lending a friendly ear to a gathering of his daughter's friends, no doubt hearing a saintly version of the bride's last night of freedom. Shrieks and giggles emanating from the bride's quarters had kept Alias awake into the small hours of the morning. Yet, the bride looked fresh as morning, and though she was important enough to warrant a seat, she would not stay in it. Instead, she roamed the tent and the lawn in her white gown, with the crest of her upswept hair bobbing like peacock feathers.

Nothing holding that girl up but the stays in her bodice, and nothing keeping her moving but nervous energy, Alias thought. The bride, Gaylyn, had greeted everyone, even taken a moment to thank Alias for all her help. It was doubtful she knew exactly what Alias had done, since she'd greeted many people with the same platitude, but she seemed in earnest. *She'd go far in court,* Alias decided, *even without help from her new in-laws.*

The groom, Lord Frefford Wyvernspur, towed along by his new bride, sparkled almost as brilliantly, dressed in the green and gold of his family, the Wyvernspurs of Immersea.

The wedding was the social event of the season and, in a spirit of festive goodwill, the imported nobility bumped elbows against the local *hoi palloi*. His Majesty, Azoun IV, remained in court in Suzail on the advice of the court wizard, Vangerdahast. However, a number of lesser Cormyrian lords and ladies were present to benefit from meetings and conversations with the heads of rising Suzail merchant households and local freeman leaders.

Alias caught a glimpse of swirling crimson and white on the far side of the tent. Akabar's head poked above the press of shorter Cormyrians. Tired of being a stranger among so many, she decided that even the foreigner's company would be preferable to standing alone. Elbowing her way through the crowd, she caught fragments of conversation.

"Well, if you ask me," said one bass voice, "they should have had a cleric of Ilmater there. God of endurance, suffering, and perseverance."

Alias gave a derisive snort. Considering the confusion caused by having four clerics at the marriage ceremony, a fifth might just have helped start a jihad. The swordswoman recalled the moment when both the bishop of Chauntea and the patron of Oghma stepped forward at the same time to offer the blessing. For seven heartbeats the priest and priestess stood, staring stonily at each other until the male bishop bowed deeply and surrendered the floor.

"If you must know," a disconnected whisper confided, "we dressed in blackface and wrote filthy slogans on the side of the citadel. Horrible, horrible things about Princess Tanalasta and a centaur."

A strong political statement, Alias thought sarcastically.

"Go ahead, Giogi," a slurred female voice encouraged some unseen gentleman. "Do your impression of His Majesty. Giogi does the most on-target imitation, you can just close your eyes and picture the old stuffed codger. You know that line he always uses, 'Let me state, O people of Cormyr, my people.' Everyone says that even Azoun himself would do a double take. Pleeease, Giogi."

Yes, please, Giogi, the swordswoman begged silently. Anything to keep the woman from whining.

"No, you're quite wrong," a gravelly male voice replied in a different conversation. "The problems in the Moonshaes are completely local. The rise of their goddess has nothing to do with the tenets of Chauntea's faith."

Alias shook her head incredulously at the speaker's arrogant assurance. As a traveled adventurer she knew better. No problem was ever completely local; problems rippled through the Realms from shore to shore. Now where did I hear that line before? she wondered.

"Lady Alias?" a familiar voice addressed her. "I trust you're having a fine time?"

Alias turned and blinked twice to accustom her eyes to the shadowed side of the tent. Dimswart stood, his comrade-in-ale, the priest Winefiddle, right behind. Each held a foaming mug of beer.

"Yes, yes I am," Alias replied politely, brushing a loose strand of hair from her face. "I was just trying to cross the room, but it's like wading through soft sand." She could not meet the eyes of the cleric. In addition to trying to kill him, she had also cheated his church of his fee.

But Winefiddle smiled absently at her, and the sage nodded in blank agreement. Their faces were both more flushed than the heat in the tent warranted, and they swayed from side to side, bumping into each other.

Giving her elbow a little fatherly squeeze, Dimswart bellowed over the noise, "We'll talk about your little problem just as soon as Leona and I get the children off. That way I'll get out of the clean-up." He laughed, and some of the ale sloshed from his mug. "Have you eaten? Had a mug?"

Alias shook her head, and Winefiddle pressed his flagon into her hands. "Hardly touched," he slurred.

Alias smiled nervously and, not wishing to give the curate any further cause for offense, took a swig. The ale was as vile as The Hidden Lady's.

"No more, thanks," Alias said, passing the mug back to Winefiddle. "I think I'd better keep keep my wits about me."

The curate shrugged and took a long, hearty draught. Alias excused herself and plunged back into the crowd in the direction she'd last seen Akabar's head. She spotted Olive Ruskettle seated on a small bench in front of the wedding table, leaning low over her yarting as she tuned it so she could hear the strings over the noise of the crowd.

Alias's attention was drawn away to Akabar, who was watching something with great amusement. Empty crystal cups rose and fell above the heads of the crowd in an ever increasing number. How odd. I would have thought jugglers too common for Lady Leona, Alias puzzled.

"Higher taxes will be the death of me," complained a voice in the milling crowd.

"A lovely couple," an elderly woman declared. "I wonder if he's told her about his second cousin. The one who went quite mad and became an adventurer, you remember?"

"Oh, go ahead, Giogi," wheedled the slurred female voice Alias recognized from earlier. "Just once. He really does sound just like King Azoun."

Finally, Alias squeezed between the multi-hued bodies and stood beside Akabar. Upon spying the juggler though, she growled with annoyance. Dragonbait lay on the ground dressed in fool's motley, tossing and catching seven pieces of Lady Leona's crystal with all four feet and his tail. Akabar was just tossing an eighth cup into the fray.

The clear hemisphere landed in the lizard's right front claw and scribed a complicated journey behind its mates from right front to left rear to right rear to left front to tail, and finally bounced up in a high arc by the tail to land again in the right front claw. Already an admiring crowd had gathered, allowing the lizard more open space in the mob than anyone else had received.

"What's he doing here?" Alias hissed to Akabar.

"It's called juggling. Don't you have that in the north?" The mage grinned as he added a cup to the bobbing glassware.

"I can see that," Alias replied, beginning to lose her patience. "Why?"

Akabar shrugged. "Some northern women assumed he was a pet and began tossing him food. In their excitement, they began bombarding him, actually. Rather than appear impolite he began juggling what he couldn't eat. I thought it would be easier and cleaner to toss cups than fruit salad."

"But he's not supposed to be here," Alias insisted through clenched teeth. "I told him to stay in my room."

Suddenly, Lady Leona broke through the crowd, and the

party-goers went deathly quiet. The noisiest members of the group turned away hastily to engage themselves in the more civilized pastime of conversation.

The mother of the bride gave a polite but firm cough, such as a god might make on the last day's dawning. Dragonbait lost his concentration, and eight cups tumbled to the grass. The ninth cup bounced off his nose, and he looked up sheepishly at Lady Leona.

Dimswart's wife glared at Alias. "If you are quite through with your pet, I would like to signal for the professional entertainment to begin."

"He's not my . . ." began Alias, but Lady Leona swirled about and headed for the wedding party's table. The crowd parted for her as a rank of archers breaks at the arrival of a formation of lancers.

Alias hustled the lizard to his feet. "Where did you get that ridiculous getup?" she asked, tugging on the silk motley.

Dragonbait smiled and spun about so she could see the whole outfit. Little bells attached to the costume jangled.

Alias sighed. "Pick up the cups," she ordered, pointing to the crystal on the ground.

With exaggerated care the lizard obeyed, stacking the glittering hemispheres on the table with the punch bowl.

Lady Leona's voice rang out from the wedding table. "Attention, everyone. Lords and ladies." The tent quieted to a low hum, and the mother of the bride continued. "I am very pleased to introduce Olive Ruskettle, master bard and songsmith. Mistress Ruskettle has composed an ode to commemorate the joining of our two families."

Polite applause followed, and then people were still again.

Alias decided to take advantage of the temporary emptiness of the doorway to escort Dragonbait back to their room. She grabbed a handful of the baggy motley and began tugging him away from the crowd. Whimpering slightly, he pointed at Olive.

"I think he wants to hear the bard sing," Akabar said.

Alias sighed in resignation.

Dragonbait folded his arms and tilted his head, the very archetype of a music connoisseur. Except for being a lizard.

Ruskettle began strumming the yarting. The opening

chords sounded to Alias like those the bard had used to taunt the dragon three days ago.

Though the halfling sang well and her tune was catchy, conversations continued about the edges of the tent, out of earshot of the hostess.

Alias caught the words of a nasal voice. "As I said to Sir Rafner, taxes. Raise taxes."

"She seems awfully short for a bard," remarked one of the bride's girlfriends, "but I wouldn't know good music if it attacked me in the dark."

"Not much, just fourteen or fifteen mugs," a drunken voice insisted from the ale table.

"Giogi, do it for me, please?"

For gods' sake, Giogi, Alias thought, would you just get it over with?

Giogioni Wyvernspur sighed. Minda would not quit asking him to repeat the imitation until he complied. He should never have done it for her in the first place. Giogi was not a young man of much sense, but he had enough to realize that his cousin Freffie's wedding reception was not the sort of place one did imitations of one's sovereign king. His only hope lay in getting it over with quickly and quietly.

Alias heard a young man's voice reply, "All right."

"Hooray, Giogi!" the woman cheered.

"Finally," Alias mumbled.

"Let me gather myself," Giogi said. Then his voice changed, becoming deeper, huskier, masking the squeakiness of youth and taking on a mountain lander's burr.

"My Cormytes. My People. As your king, as King Azoun, and as King Azoun IV, I must say that the need to raise your taxes is a result of the direct depravations of . . ." The voice dropped to a whisper. "Vangy, who is being depraved this time?"

Alias's breath quickened. She focused her attention on Giogi's altered voice. To her, the rest of the chatter died away, leaving only the husky tone. A powerfully sinister feeling swept over her, leaving her dizzy. The crowd was suffocating her. Her arm began to ache miserably. Nearby she heard a growl.

Panic rose in Alias. Her body was moving of its own

accord, just as it had when she nearly killed Winefiddle. She tried to hold herself still, fight the urge to lunge at the Wyvernspur noble, but without success. Far off she heard women screaming and men shouting. Something nearby was burning.

Standing right beside Alias, Akabar felt her stiffen. He noticed the smell of smoke almost immediately. With horror he watched the glove that covered her tattoos blister and burn away. Then he heard Alias snarl like a dog, and saw her face contort into a mask of rage.

Dragonbait turned to look at her in confusion. When Akabar laid a hand on her left arm to offer his assistance, she shoved both man and beast away with unbelievable strength, propelling herself in the opposite direction. With murder in her eyes, Alias leaped onto Giogi.

She landed on top of him with a scream, her hands about his throat in an instant. She might have wrung his neck, but she caught sight of a long, sharp knife used to cut pies and cake. She reached for it, but lost her grip on the young man as she did so. Giogi managed to twist away from her, and she plunged the pastry blade into the table where he'd been pinned only a moment before.

"I say, I wasn't that bad," the green-and-gold-clad noble sputtered. "I didn't want to do it, really. It's just that Minda kept begging me, you know?"

Alias yanked the blade from the tabletop and drew a fresh bead on her target. Giogi backpedaled furiously. Women screamed and several Wyvernspur menfolk, seeing their kin beseiged, shouted a battle cry and moved in on the attacker. Alias kept them all at bay with the knife. One cocky fellow got too close and received a slash across his cheek to show for it.

Several of the groom's relatives, faced with a mad assassin, fled the area as quickly as possible, leaving the tent sides flapping where they'd torn up the stakes.

Olive, her ode interrupted, her audience gone, moved toward the fight. She helped Akabar up from the ground as she demanded, "Just what does she think she's doing?"

"I think the sigils," Akabar explained in a whisper, "are trying to make her kill that man because he sounds like the king of Cormyr."

Olive glanced over at Giogi, who was now crawling along the ground. "But he doesn't look anything like Azoun."

"The sigils don't know that," Akabar pointed out, wracking his brain for some way to put the warrior woman out of commission without injuring her too severely.

A northerner of huge girth tried tackling her from behind. Alias pivoted, jammed an elbow into the man's belly, and backhanded him in the face with the handle of the knife. Bleeding from the nose, the man fell into the crowd.

Having lost her target, Alias's eyes swept through the tent. She spotted Giogi cowering beneath the punch table. She dove for him just as he managed to scramble to the other side.

Dimswart, realizing that it would not look good if one of his clients murdered one of his new in-laws, grabbed Akabar's shoulder. "Do something," he demanded.

Akabar nodded his head, but he hadn't prepared any magical spells that would be useful at a wedding celebration-turned-brawl.

Olive seized control of the situation by grabbing Dragonbait. "We have to stop her!"

The lizard cocked his head in confusion.

In a flash of inspiration Akabar cried, "Stop her, before she gets hurt!"

Dragonbait nodded. Dodging the confused, fleeing guests, he tackled the central pole of the tent. The huge beam slid across the grass, pulling the walls up and the roof down. Stakes ripped from the ground, and the pole toppled over with a thud, bringing acres of tent down and putting an end to the pandemonium with a great *whoosh*.

❧ 8 ❧

The Sigils

Akabar was one of the first to emerge from under the cloth, his red and white silk robes only slightly stained with grass. He immediately scanned the area for Alias's figure, but his view of the grounds was blocked by the growing throng of refugees. He waited by the edge of the collapsed structure, assisting others to their feet and hoping the swordswoman would appear.

When Giogi emerged from beneath the tent, he kept crawling until he bumped into the knees of a dowager Wyvernspur.

"Giogioni, you are a fool," the lady declared. "This civil unrest is a direct consequence of your open disrespect for our sovereign. I've warned you time and again that you were courting disaster."

"Yes, Aunt Dorath."

"Get off your knees, you idiot."

"Yes, Aunt Dorath."

The bride and groom and their attendants rolled out from the tent, giggling hysterically. Lady Leona emerged near Dragonbait, looking less than amused. Upon seeing whose scaly hand had helped her rise, the woman jerked her arm back while blasting the Turmishman with a withering glare. She looked about impatiently for Sir Dimswart.

When the sage finally appeared, empty mug in hand, Leona drew him aside. In quiet but threatening tones she declared, "I will not have Gaylyn's wedding day ruined. I am taking our guests into the garden to continue with the celebration. You must deal with this . . . situation."

Spying Olive Ruskettle, who was smoothing out her bulging pockets as best she could, Leona made her way to the bard and escorted her to the garden.

Dimswart turned to Akabar. "Your adventuress has caused a great deal of trouble." His voice was even, but his upraised eyebrows made his point.

"If you could have spared fifteen minutes from testing ale this morning," Akabar said in equally polite tones, "and not kept her waiting, this would not have happened."

"You forget she is my hireling," Dimswart said. "I am not hers."

"In the south we say the gods bless all duties faithfully performed. Alias has accomplished her task, while you have yet to complete your end of the bargain."

Dimswart grimaced but accepted the chastisement with good grace. Like many sages, he liked to consider himself a man of the people. It wasn't in him to behave haughtily. "That's still no reason to start a brawl at my daughter's wedding," he replied with a sniff.

"It was not her, I believe, but the sigils."

"Really?" Dimswart's scholarly curiosity was peaked.

Akabar described how Alias's glove had burned just prior to the attack.

"Fascinating," the sage muttered. "Where did she go?"

A handful of servants rolled back the tent, revealing a few more guests, but no Alias. The refreshment tables stood on the bare lawn like the skeletal remains of some huge beast. The ale keg was immediately carried off to the garden, followed by the punch bowl and tables to hold them. The food was a little crushed, but already reserves were being carried from the kitchen.

Akabar spotted Dragonbait circling the beaten grass where the tent had stood, emitting interrogative whines.

"He sounds confused," Dimswart commented.

Akabar went to the lizard. "We'll find her, don't worry."

Dragonbait gave him a distressed look and issued a sort of chirp.

"You look in her room," he ordered the lizard. "I'll search the stable."

Their search of the house and grounds came up empty. Akabar found Dragonbait on the lawn, staring off at the horizon.

"We'll have to try the roads," the mage said. "I need to study my spells. You pack and ready the horses."

An hour later, Akabar, dressed for traveling, cornered Dimswart, demanding Alias's information.

With a shrug the sage ushered him into his study and reviewed what he had discovered about the sigils on the swordswoman's arm.

"Where will you search?" Dimswart asked Akabar when they'd finished.

"I'm not certain," the mage answered. "There's a good chance she's gone back to Suzail, since that's where we first met. But if she's gone in another direction . . . " His voice trailed off, and he shrugged his shoulders.

"Why are you bothering, Akash? She's nothing to do with you. You just met the woman."

"She needs help. Isn't that reason enough?"

"A lot of people in the Realms need help. That doesn't usually get them the attention of wealthy Turmish merchants. House Akash probably wouldn't think too highly of you galloping off after some northern warrioress."

That was true enough, Akabar knew. House Akash, his first wife's firm and its partner, Kasim, his second wife's business, would probably never understand. He shrugged again. "The dragon destroyed my inventory. I have no other duties in this region."

"Any other merchant would cut his losses and head home while he still could," Dimswart pointed out. "But not you. You've got it bad, haven't you, my friend?"

Akabar stiffened angrily.

"Adventure-lust," Dimswart sighed. "Not content to remain a greengrocer, are you?"

No, I'm not, Akabar realized. How is it this northerner understands me better than I understood myself?

"You could have picked an easier quest to begin with," Dimswart continued. "This woman, these sigils, are very dangerous. They represent very evil powers."

"You have a saying up north, do you not, concerning the number of times opportunity knocks. Besides, I like her."

"No reason why you shouldn't. She's talented, headstrong,

arrogant. The two of you have so much in common."

Akabar grinned. "All the things upon which my friendship with you is based. *Amarast*, Master Dimswart."

"*Amarast*, Akash."

Dragonbait was waiting in the stables with the three horses they had bought after freeing Olive Ruskettle. He left Olive's mount, a pony she had named High Roll, behind for the halfling. Akabar had named the first horse, a white stallion, Windove, in honor of its speed. The pack horse, a black gelding, they jokingly called Lightning because it was the only mount docile enough to allow Dragonbait's touch. Alias had chosen a purebred chestnut for herself. "That one's a real lady killer," she had said when they bought it.

"Lady Killer," Akabar whispered as he patted Alias's horse before mounting Windove. He shuddered, wondering if the chestnut's name hadn't been a bad omen.

He and Dragonbait walked the horses out of the stable and away from Dimswart Manor. The mage led them toward the main road to Suzail. Dragonbait, still dressed in motley, snuffled and snorted in the road's dust. Akabar had just mounted when he caught the sound of short legs trotting toward them. A shrill voice blew over the hill.

"Akabar, you charlatan, wait up! You're likely to get hurt traveling out here alone!"

"If we double time it," the mage said to Dragonbait without looking back, "we can probably lose her in the dust."

Upon hearing the halfling's voice, however, Dragonbait's face broke out in a grin and he halted, keeping a firm grip on Lightning's reins. Since the pack horse held most of Akabar's belongings, the merchant-mage had no choice but to wait, too, as Olive Ruskettle came charging over the hill, bouncing up and down on her pony.

"You can't leave yet," Akabar said. "The celebration is supposed to last until midnight."

"Look," Olive said, "I've done my three sets. If I don't put my foot down, that Leona woman will have me singing till I lose my voice. They don't pay me enough to lose my voice."

"They won't pay you at all if you don't give them satisfaction."

"Show's what you know, clod. I'm an artiste. I get paid in

advance. Now, which way do you think our lady's heading?"

Akabar scowled. He wondered if it were really true that someone as supposedly wise as Dimswart had paid Ruskettle in advance, yet it seemed impossible that the woman would leave without what was owed her—and not just to help Alias. Akabar remembered the way she'd smoothed her pockets after crawling from under the tent. Even if she hasn't been paid, he realized, she's already picked up her share of the wedding loot.

Akabar's fists clenched in frustration, but there was nothing he could do. "We are going to look for her in Suzail. It's only a half day from here, and she knows the city."

"Ah, Suzail, gem of Cormyr, home of his most serene and wise marshmallowness, Azoun IV. Think she's going after the king after practicing on that Wyvernspur buffoon?"

Akabar scowled. "Your disrespect for your own lawful king is appalling."

Olive laughed. "Down south your leaders behead people for that sort of talk, don't they? We halflings have a saying: If you take your leaders too seriously, they're going to start taking themselves too seriously. Azoun's all right, for a human. But he is a marshmallow. He let his pet wizard keep him at court today, didn't he?"

"Perhaps the mage Vangerdahast had some idea of the danger there," Akabar said.

"Which leaves my original question. Do you think our madwoman's going to try something foolish in Suzail?"

"I fail to see what interest you have in the matter."

"I already told you, I owe her. I pay my debts."

"With whose money, I wonder?"

The halfling gave the mage a sly smile, unruffled by his distrust. From what Olive had seen, Alias did not rely on him for advice, and it was Alias who interested her. The halfling had no doubt the attractive warrior and her magical arm would lead to a fortune. And even if the swordswoman didn't, she would make a good subject for a song.

As they traveled south, Akabar remained buried deep in his own thoughts, trying to make up contingency plans should they discover Alias was not in Suzail, or worse, that she was, as Olive had suggested, attempting to assassinate

King Azoun. Dragonbait loped along beside the pony High Roll, with the bells from his jester's costume jangling. Olive chattered away to the lizard about all the celebrations she'd played at. Akabar wished she *had* lost her voice singing.

At dusk, three hours later, Dragonbait suddenly stopped moving. He tilted his head and placed his hand over his chest. Then, he moved on down the road with more energy.

"Think he's picked up her scent?" the bard asked.

Akabar studied Dragonbait. "He senses something."

They arrived in Suzail shortly after dark. Without hesitation Dragonbait led them right to The Hidden Lady and into the tavern room. Akabar wondered if the lizard could sense Alias's presence, or if, like a dog, he simply expected her to be there. Whatever the case, there she was.

She sat in a booth at the back. The hem of her blue gown was dirty and tattered. Her legs were drawn up to her chest in a tight ball, and her head lay on her knees. She was crooning a love song, explaining the tears of Selune—the mysterious glittering shards that followed the moon's path. In all her travels, the bard had heard neither the haunting lyrics nor the lovely melody, marred somewhat by the swordswoman's sniffling and drunken timing.

A toppled mug oozed thick mead over the oak table in front of Alias. She took no notice of the group as they approached—until Akabar's height blocked out the light from the hanging lamp that illuminated her table. She stirred herself and, with some effort, raised her head to look up at the trio. Her eyes were rimmed with red.

"Go 'way," she croaked.

"Are you all right?" Akabar asked.

"It's a shame you had to leave," Ruskettle chirped up. "I thought I might not survive the crush of people when the tent fell, but it was all for the best. Imagine trying to sing to three hundred people in there. The party got much better after we moved. Everyone said so."

Dragonbait looked at Alias with his head cocked, making a soft mewling noise. The bells on his jester's hat jingled when he moved his head.

Again Alias told them, "Go away," but her voice was much softer.

The barkeep came to the booth. "Did you want company, lady?" he asked protectively.

When Alias did not reply, the barkeep asked the others what they were having.

Dragonbait pointed to the overturned mug of mead. Akabar ordered white wine.

"I'll have a Red Rum Swirl," Ruskettle said.

"Never met one," the barkeep answered.

"How 'bout a Dragon's Bite?" the bard asked.

"What's that when it's at home?" the barkeep asked.

"All right. A Yeti's Breath. You must know that one."

The barkeep shook his head.

The halfling sighed. "Rivengut then."

"Sorry, all out. Don't get much call for it so's I don't order much of it."

"I'll have a Black Boar then."

"I'll see what I can do."

Before the man could walk away, the southern mage took his arm gently and whispered, "How many has she had?"

The barkeep held up two fingers.

"Two? Just two?" Akabar mouthed.

The bartender shrugged his shoulders, unable to explain Alias's intoxication.

Akabar slid into the booth next to Olive. Dragonbait perched on the stool at the end of the table. "Would you like another drink?" the mage asked Alias.

"They can't make good liquor in this god-forsaken hellhole," said the woman warrior, not raising her head.

"I'll say," agreed the halfling, "Imagine not knowing how to make a Yeti's Breath. Now there's a drink with . . . um." Olive grew silent under Akabar's glare.

Dragonbait reached over and placed his hand on Alias's shoulder. She tried to shrug it off at first, but when the lizard gave a little worried chirp she let the hand remain.

The barkeep brought their drinks and another mead for Alias.

"Perhaps a tray of food would be in order," Akabar suggested.

"Great idea," Olive agreed. "I'm starving. Would you like to hear the ode to the couple?" she asked Alias. "Since you didn't get to hear all of it before. They made me repeat it three times afterward. Everyone was so impressed by it."

"Not now," Akabar answered quietly, elbowing the bard.

Ruskettle frowned and guzzled her drink. She set her glass back down on the table and took a deep breath. "Hey! That wasn't a Black Boar. Barkeep!"

"It happened again, just like the last time," Alias said softly, her voice cracking on the final word. "I should have known it was coming. I remember my arm hurt. I didn't want to lunge at that poor fool or grab that knife, but I wasn't in control. It was like a nightmare. Then the tent fell. I ducked out before anyone else and took off.

"I couldn't stop myself from running. Whatever was controlling me would have made me run until I dropped, but I caught a ride into Suzail on a farmer's wagon. When I remembered the information Dimswart had for me, I tried to jump off and go back, but I couldn't move. It wasn't until twilight that I was free to do as I choose. I came here. I didn't know where else to go." She put her head down again on her knees, and her lean form shook with sobbing.

Dragonbait pulled the hair back from her face and tucked it behind her ear. He stroked her head gently. Ruskettle waved her empty glass, trying to attract the barkeep's attention, but finally settled for stealing Alias's untouched mug of mead.

Akabar stared at the table until the warrior had calmed down. Then he asked, "So, was it the sigils that made you drink yourself into a stupor?"

Alias's head snapped up, and she glared at the mage. "Listen, Turmite, you don't know what it's like to not remember anything. To not know if you're going to forget even more things. To not know who you're going to attack next. First a priest, then a Cormyrian noble—"

Olive, whose mind had been occupied with memorizing snatches of the song Alias had been singing when they arrived, looked up suddenly, asking, "Did you say a priest?"

"Didn't Akabar tell you?" Alias retorted icily. "I tried to kill the priest who attempted to remove this curse. But it wasn't a curse, it's a thing alive in me."

"The thing, not you, tried to kill the priest," Akabar corrected.

"What difference does it make? I can't get rid of it. It's not going to let me go back to Dimswart to get the information he found for me. Gods! I'm lucky it didn't make me kill Dimswart."

"Maybe this thing was keeping you from the scene of the crime, so to speak," Akabar suggested. "Unless it can make you deaf, I hardly see how it can prevent you from learning Dimswart's information."

"What?"

"I brought Dimswart's information."

Ruskettle's ears perked up, and the bells on Dragonbait's cap jingled again as he tilted his head with interest.

"Well?" Alias prompted.

"First, I want you to promise me something."

"I don't have to promise you anything. This is my information. I earned it."

"True. But who knows what might happen if you try to return to the sage's manor to ask for it."

Alias snarled at the mage. "You desert snake—"

"All I want," Akabar interjected, "is for you to let me accompany you on your quest to remove this thing."

"Are you crazy?" Alias hissed. "Don't I have enough trouble without dragging my frien—complete strangers in on it."

"Who better to drag in it than frien—complete strangers?" Akabar smiled, then he lifted his head proudly. "Besides, I still owe you a debt of honor for helping me to recover my spell book."

Yes, Alias realized, even if he wasn't so anxious to prove he isn't a greengrocer, he'd help me because he's the type who takes debts of honor seriously. "I'm not exactly socially acceptable these days," Alias pointed out weakly.

"As a rule, men of my nationality are not invited to many parties in the north," Akabar replied with a shrug.

While Akabar was insinuating himself into Alias's quest, Olive was frantically trying to make up her mind. People who tried to kill priests weren't, as a rule, to be trusted, she argued with herself. But it would make such a fascinating addition to the song. Better make it a lay. Or maybe even a book. *The Magic Arm Chronicles,* as told by Olive Ruskettle.

All thoughts of danger faded before the imaginary promise of gold and fame. Besides, Olive told herself, I have to find out the rest of that song about the tears of Selune.

"Hang on," the halfling interrupted. "If anyone owes this swordswoman a debt of gratitude, it's me. She saved my life. If you take this one along," Olive said to Alias, jerking her head toward Akabar, "you're going to need someone to keep him out of trouble. A fast thinker."

The corner of Alias's mouth twitched in amusement. She had no illusions about Olive. Pure greed motivated her. Still, the halfling's debt was even greater than Akabar's. It was likely she'd prove more hindrance than help, but at least she was an experienced traveler.

"My journey may prove perilous," Alias warned, hoping to discourage the small woman.

Olive shrugged. "As the halflings in Luiren say, 'From perils come pearls and power.' I've seen my share of danger."

"And more than your share of pearls, I'll warrant," Akabar muttered under his breath.

Alias looked at Dragonbait. "I don't suppose you'll be leaving my side either."

The lizard tilted his head with a jingle.

Something inside Alias's chest grabbed her heart. She had an uncomfortable suspicion the lizard wouldn't know what to do if he wasn't serving her.

Alias sighed. "All right. You can help, but remember—I tried to talk you out of it." She turned to Akabar. "Now what did Dimswart tell you?"

The mage pulled a small package from a pocket. He unknotted the yellow cord that bound it and flipped away its leather wrapping. Within lay five copper plates.

"Flaming dagger," said the mage, laying the first plate on the table. A flaming dagger sigil was etched into the soft metal surface, and beneath it in neat, delicate letters of Thorass, was a paragraph of explanation. "Interlocking rings, mouth in a palm, three concentric circles, and a squiggle that looks like an insect leg." Akabar laid down a corresponding copper with each description. "Which would you like me to cover first?" he asked Alias.

Alias pointed to the plate with the flaming dagger. "The

assassins who attacked me carried a card with this design."

Nodding, Akabar stacked the five plates together with the dagger on top. "The symbol is derived from a Talis deck. In Turmish, we use the suit of birds, but here in the north it has been converted to the suit of daggers. In either case, the suit represents money and theft of the same. The symbol was adopted by a small group of thieves and assassins in Westgate that calls itself the Redeemer's Guild, but the group is more commonly known as the Fire Knives—from its calling card.

"The Fire Knives are not native to Westgate, but came originally from Cormyr where they ran a very profitable operation. Until, that is, they incurred the wrath of His Royal Majesty, Azoun IV. He broke their charter, executed their leaders, and sent the rest packing across the Lake of Dragons. They set up shop anew in Westgate, with the permission of the local crime lords, the Night Masks. Naturally, they have no love for Cormyr, its king, or its people."

"Do any of them carry their symbol as a brand or tattoo?" Alias asked.

Akabar shook his head. "It has never been reported that they do. Of course, your attack on someone who sounded just like King Azoun was the sort of thing they desire. Somehow, they might have ensorceled you to do so."

"Then why did they attack me the other night?"

"Perhaps they thought you discovered their plan and would warn His Majesty," the halfling guessed.

"No," Alias said. "I had no idea I was going to do something like I did. Besides, they went to a lot of trouble to capture, not kill me."

"Perhaps they were planning on delivering you to the king's court," Akabar mused. "You know, Azoun might have come to the wedding. His mage, Vangerdahast, advised him against it. At least, that was the rumor I heard."

"It's just coincidence that I ended up at Dimswart's," Alias replied.

Akabar shrugged. "Perhaps. But if Azoun had attended—"

"I'd have tried to kill him instead of that fool Wyvernspur."

"Not a chance," Olive said. "Vangerdahast goes everywhere with His Marshmallowness. He would have fried you with a lightning bolt before you got within an arm's length."

"I don't think this conjecture will get us very far," Akabar said, confused. "Shall I continue with the other sigils?"

Alias nodded, and Akabar held up the card bearing the sign of three rings, each interlocked with the other two. "The trinity of rings is pretty common as well. It was used by several trading houses about the Inner Sea until the Year of Dust, over two centuries ago, when it was taken up as a banner by a pirate gang in Earthspur. After a few years new pirate leaders toppled the old and adopted a new banner.

"Since then the circles have been used as a signature mark for a notable Cormyrian portrait artist, as a stamp for a Procampurian silversmith, and the sign of an alehouse in Yhaunn in Sembia. The alehouse, by the way, was fireballed fifty years ago by a wizard because their symbol happened to be his sigil. He claimed the exclusive right to use it. He was a pompous northerner known as Zrie Prakis."

"I knew some fell wizard had to be involved," muttered Alias.

Akabar held up a finger to continue. "Prakis protected his mark religiously, seeking out any others who used it and destroying those who would not give it up. It's a mark of his success that the symbol is now considered unlucky among many taverns, silversmiths, and artists. However, Zrie Prakis was supposed to have died in a magical battle some forty years ago, somewhere near Westgate."

"Someone must have made a mistake," Olive pointed out. "After all, when two mages are fighting, no one in their right mind gets close enough to tell who's winning. This was the symbol on the crystal elemental that attacked us in the stone circle, isn't it?"

Alias nodded, remembering how the sigil had blazed from the monster's chest.

"Anyway," Akabar concluded, "Master Dimswart got a cleric to do a divination for him. The exact question was: Does Zrie Prakis, whose symbol was the triple rings, still live? The answer was: No."

"Well, I'm not a work of art or a silver dinner service," Alias said. "That leaves me branded by a defunct pirate gang or an alehouse. Neither very likely candidates."

Akabar, though tempted, did not disagree with her about the alehouse. He held up the next copper plate engraved with the insect leg-shaped squiggle. "The sorceress who destroyed Zrie Prakis was named Cassana of Westgate. This happens to be her sigil. To the best of Dimswart's knowledge, Cassana still makes her abode in Westgate. She's reputed to be fairly powerful, but she's extremely reclusive. No one's seen her for years. She's not dead, but she must be getting on in years."

"Maybe this Prakis fellow had an apprentice," Olive suggested. "The apprentice is greedy for power, see, and he teams up with his master's enemy, this Cassana, and tells her how to defeat him. Then, when Cassana kills Prakis, the apprentice takes his master's sigil."

Akabar's eyes narrowed into slits. "Your expertise on the workings of betrayal is quite interesting."

Olive smiled sweetly. "Over the years I've made a study of all the evil you humans perpetrate on one another."

Alias's head began to throb. Anxious to get this discussion over with, she pulled out the next copper plate, but the writing blurred before her eyes. She held the plate up to Akabar. "What about this mouth in the hand?" she asked.

"Dimswart found this most curious," answered the mage, running his fingers along the engraved fangs in the mouth. "This is a holy symbol—or the unholy symbol, rather—of a cult that has been dead for a thousand years or more. They worshipped Moander the Darkbringer. He, she, or it—the texts keep changing the pronoun over time—had a huge temple complex in the days of Myth Drannor, the elven kingdom, and was a continual menace to the forest peoples. Eventually, the elves burned the complex to the ground, slaying all its priests and banishing the god-thing from the Realms.

"The town of Yulash was built on the site of the complex, but Yulash has itself long since been turned to rubble. Hillsfar and Zhentil Keep are continually battling over its strategic location. Dimswart gave me the name of another sage who may know more, but he warned me that getting an appointment with this person may prove to be a problem."

Alias held up the last copper plate. The blue upon blue

bull's-eye was represented on sheet metal by three concentric rings, its deepening shades of color not represented at all, but described in the upper right hand corner. Nothing was written below the sigil. Alias looked up at Akabar, her eyebrows raised.

The mage shifted nervously. "Dimswart has seen naught like this in his travels or his books. He thinks it's something new, perhaps an up-and-coming power. Note that the two magic-user's sigils are grouped together, but this sigil follows the marking of a dead and banished god."

"So Dimswart thinks it may be another cult," said Alias. She picked up her now empty mug and stared into it. The halfling studied the ceiling beams.

"Actually, that was my own observation," Akabar replied. "Balancing the sigils seemed logical to me, but . . ."

"But we may not be dealing with balanced or logical people," Alias concluded for him.

Akabar nodded. "The evidence that the Fire Knives are involved is pretty incontrovertible. The attack of the summoned earth elemental would seem to indicate that some mage is definitely at work here as well. The pattern circling the symbols is common throughout nations of the Inner Sea, symbolizing unions or contracts. Ivy and rose vines are generally used for weddings, dragons for royal charters . . ."

"Serpents for evil pacts," Alias added in reference to the serpentine pattern that wound around the runes on her arm.

"What about the sixth party?" Olive asked.

"What sixth party?" Akabar demanded.

Alias held out her arm, wondering herself what Olive was talking about.

The bard pointed to the swordswoman's wrist, where the serpentine pattern that linked the five sigils wound about an empty space.

"There's nothing there, you fool," Akabar snorted.

"Not yet, there isn't," Olive said. "Maybe Alias escaped before they got around to adding it, or maybe they're waiting for a sixth member to pay up their dues. Maybe a sigil's going to grow there."

Alias shivered and curled her arms back around her

knees.

Akabar tried giving the bard a kick on the ankle to shut her up, but the little woman's feet swung too far off the floor for him to reach.

"As much as I'd hate to slander a patron," Olive continued, "I think you need better advice than Dimswart's given you."

Alias was inclined to agree. "Where'd this other sage live, the one Dimswart recommended?" she asked Akabar.

"Shadowdale. That's rather far off though," the mage pointed out. "It would be simpler to investigate Westgate first."

The barkeep came to their table and wordlessly unloaded a platter of sandwiches and fresh drinks.

"Shadowdale is on the way to Yulash," Alias said.

"But it makes more sense to head for Westgate," Akabar argued. "The Fire—" he looked up at the barkeep "—two of the five guilty parties work out of Westgate. Another one died there." He smiled at the barkeep. "Thank you. That should do nicely for some time," he said, dismissing the man. "We can reach Westgate by ship in two or three days. If we can discover nothing there, then a trek to the north would make more sense."

Alias remained silent, feeling nauseated at the sight of food. With a last paternal glance toward the swordswoman, the barkeep left the table and returned to his other duties.

Olive picked up the five copper plates and began idly shuffling them. Her little hands moved the pieces with amazing dexterity.

Annoyed, Akabar reached over and lifted the sigil engravings from the halfling's palm. He rewrapped and tied them and handed the bundle to Alias. "So, shall I arrange passage for the morning?"

"I'm almost positive I came to Suzail by boat," she mused.

"By ship," Akabar corrected.

"Couldn't we travel to High Horn and circle around the Lake of Dragons?" Olive suggested. "The roads to Westgate are pretty good."

Akabar remembered the little woman had claimed to dislike sea journeys.

"We're going to Yulash," Alias said quietly.

"What?" both the bard and the mage demanded in unison.

"Suppose I came to Suzail from Westgate," Alias whispered, "fleeing from whoever did this to me—the Fire Knives or this Cassana person. Instinct tells me to avoid Westgate. I don't know why—I can't remember. Maybe I was there and tried taking care of someone else the Fire Knives don't care for—then I could be wanted by the law, as well as by the underworld. Besides, I don't want to take on two enemies at once. I've already waltzed into one dragon's lair this month. I don't intend to do it again for at least another year. In Yulash, as far as we know, I have only one enemy. Also, this master sage you mentioned is on the road to Yulash. We may get more information from him."

"But the temple in Yulash is destroyed," Akabar objected. "Yulash is in the hands of the Zhentarim, and they're not . . . decent people. It is too dangerous."

Alias frowned. "Look, Akash, whose quest is this, anyway? You want to accompany me, you can come with me to Yulash. If you're afraid, you can go to Westgate without me, or better yet, just go home and forget about me."

Akabar colored. Whether he was more angry that Alias would not take his sage counsel or embarrassed that his honor and courage had been called into question, Olive could not tell for sure. She chimed in, "If this sage in Shadowdale can help, we may not even have to go to Yulash."

Alias turned to glare at the halfling. "I'm going to Yulash," she hissed. "I leave in the morning!" With that, she rose from the table, staggered two feet, and passed out on the wooden floor.

"Better make that late morning," Akabar sighed. He rose to settle accounts with the barkeep while Dragonbait and Ruskettle hauled the fallen warrior to her room.

❧ 9 ❧

Trek Through Cormyr

It was almost noon when the party left Suzail. Akabar had spent the morning purchasing supplies. His was the easy job.

Olive and Dragonbait had the dubious honor of tumbling Alias out of bed so she could lead them to Yulash. The swordswoman cursed them both feebly. When they finally got her to sit, she threw up. Finally, they got her cleaned up and dressed. She moaned all the while and wept some, too.

"To hear her complain," Olive sniffed, "you'd think she was a fifteen-year-old debutante suffering from her first drunk. Is she always like this?" she asked Dragonbait.

The lizard made no sound or gesture in reply.

The halfling looked about the room for another bottle of liquor. According to the barkeep, the swordswoman had had only two mugs of mead. Granted, it was good, potent stuff and the barkeep's mugs were a generous size, but that couldn't possibly be enough to leave a seasoned warrior so incapacitated, Olive decided. Yet, there was no sign of alcohol in any of Alias's belongings.

Olive remembered her aunt who would go into a crying jag after a single glass of wine. It wasn't the booze, her mother had explained to her, it was the feeling in her heart when she drank. The halfling wondered how anyone could be so depressed. Alias had her health, gold in her purse, she wasn't love-struck over anyone, and this afternoon she'd be three steps ahead of the law on open road. Who could ask for more? Humans! Go figure. Olive sighed and ran a cool, damp rag about Alias's face.

By the time a scowling Alias stumbled out of the inn, her

hood up to shade her eyes against the bright sunlight, Akabar was waiting with the party's horses and pony saddled and packed.

If Alias had any appreciation for Akabar's efforts and skills as a quartermaster, she didn't bother to note it aloud. "I have to make a stop somewhere," she whispered, nudging Lady Killer into motion. The others followed her to the Towers of Good Fortune.

"Wait here," she ordered. The mage and the halfling remained mounted as she entered the temple to Tymora. Dragonbait scratched Lightning's muzzle thoughtfully.

Alias kept her hood up even in the dim light of the church. There were three priests and about twenty people seated in the congregation hall, some whispering, others praying silently. She knew it was unlikely Winefiddle had returned so soon from Dimswart's, but she really didn't want to run into him in case he had.

So she stood near the doorway, studying the carving of Lady Luck in front of the altar. The image of Tymora had short hair, tousled like Alias's. The goddess's figure was more boyish, but no more muscled than the swordswoman's. The sideways shift of her eyes and the half-grin gave her a crafty look Alias had noted a few times on Olive's face. Halflings, she remembered, worshipped an image of Tymora that resembled a halfling female. Alias tried to remember the last time she'd grinned that way.

All I've had lately, she thought, is bad luck. I don't even believe in luck. What am I doing here? At her elbow was the poor box where she was supposed to have left the green gem the night Winefiddle had tried to remove the runes on her arm, the night she'd try to kill him.

Personally, she addressed the goddess in her thoughts. If someone tried to kill one of my priests and then cheated me out of what they owed me and then came back and tried to make it up to me by paying me even more, I don't think I'd feel any better disposed toward them.

From her purse she drew out the opal Olive had liberated from Mist's lair. The huge gem felt warm and smooth in her palm. She dropped it into the poor box. Just in case you aren't like me, she thought. She turned about and left the temple.

Alias just didn't have the energy to lay a false trail out of the city. She led her party through the east gate which led directly to the road north. She rode along without a sound.

Wracking his brain for something to say that might make her feel even a tiny bit better, Akabar came up with, "I had noticed, as regards liquid refreshment, that the emphasis north of the Inner Sea is on strength as opposed to flavor. It is no doubt a common thing for a person to be caught unawares by the power of the beverages served here—"

The mage soon regretted having said anything. Alias made no reply, but, even worse, the bard launched into a defense of the drinks of the northern Realms. Her comparison of a Delayed Blast with a Flaming Gullet did nothing to disprove Akabar's original point, and only served to turn the swordswoman a more distressing shade of green.

Akabar remained as quiet as Alias after that, but Olive continued chattering to Dragonbait for some time. When she got tired of talking to the mute creature, she sang. She was on the thirteenth verse of her fifth ballad when Alias finally spoke.

"Olive, please, try to show some consideration for the dying," the warrior whispered.

"Oh. I'm sorry, Alias. Are you still feeling poorly?"

"I meant you."

"But, I feel fine," the halfling replied in confusion.

"If you don't shut up, I'm going to have to kill you. Then you won't feel fine at all."

The bard gulped and remained silent for about half a mile. Finally, though, she dropped back some ways from the party so she could continue humming softly without incurring the swordswoman's wrath. Dragonbait slowed down to join her, perhaps out of pity, though Akabar suspected the lizard really was a music lover.

"Cheerful people are so depressing," Alias muttered.

The mage smiled, and they rode on in silence.

After a good night's rest at an inn in Hilp, Alias seemed fully recovered. As they progressed northward, Alias kept a watchful eye on Dragonbait, who loped along beside the horses. She'd admonished him to let her know if they went too fast. The lizard had responded by running around the horses with a curious bouncing gait and then turning three cartwheels.

Alias even tolerated the halfling's prattle and went so far as to try teaching the bard a ballad she claimed to have learned from a Harper.

"Not a Harper!" Olive gasped, obviously impressed.

Alias nodded.

"I don't understand," Akabar said. "What is so special about playing the harp?"

Olive shook her head and sighed.

"Up north," Alias explained, "one who plays the harp is a harpist. A Harper is something rather different."

"What then?" the mage asked.

"Well, they're usually bards or rangers, though sometimes they ask other adventurers to join them. They . . . " Alias hesitated. It would sound so banal to say it aloud. "They work for good things," she answered quickly and then launched into the ballad for Olive.

Akabar mused over Alias's words. He now recalled having heard a story or two about these Harper people, but he had not paid much attention. They were supposed to be a mysterious, powerful bunch, but Alias's reaction interested him more. The woman had seemed flustered when giving her explanation.

He listened now to her singing. Her voice was better than the bard's. It had a clear, lilting quality. The song she sang was better than any of Olive's, too. Like the song she'd sung about the tears of Selune, two nights ago in The Hidden Lady, the lyrics were haunting. They told of the Fall of Myth Drannor, the splendid elven city, now a ruin in the woods.

The song caused Akabar to begin speculating on Alias's lost past. Only now his speculations were even wilder than Olive's had been. Suppose she was more than just a mercenary. Certainly evil things were after her. Had she, to put it in her own words, "worked for good things" so well that she was considered a threat? Had she been enchanted with those fell runes on her arm so that she would do some evil and thereby destroy her reputation?

"You know," Olive said after she'd managed to pluck out

the melody to Alias's song on her yarting, "I've often wondered how one gets to be a Harper. Do you volunteer for a position, or do you have to be asked?"

Alias shrugged. "I've no idea." Inwardly she smiled, trying to picture the powerful and righteous Harpers accepting the help of a greedy, arrogant pickpocket of a halfling with pretensions to bardhood. Alias felt too good at the moment, however, to destroy Olive's grandiose illusions.

They skirted the countryside about the city of Immersea, ancestral home of the Wyvernspurs, and made camp at dusk beside the road. Rain drizzled the entire next day, and they traveled mostly in silence.

They reached Arabel by nightfall. The inns were crowded with merchants and adventurers all taking advantage of the city's shelter. Alias's group had to settle for a remote inn by the city wall, but they were grateful to have shelter from the rain.

Alias found the noise and light and driving rain strangely comforting. The violence of the elements made her own inner turmoil seem mild in comparison. Her rage at being branded and used faded somewhat, humbled by the anger of the sky.

The next morning dawned bright and clear.

"I estimate it will take us two rides to reach Yulash," Alias said before they set out.

"Not possible," Akabar disagreed. "The distance is much greater than that."

"Two rides if the weather holds good and no disasters hit us."

"It will take at least twenty days," Akabar said.

"Isn't that what I just said?" Alias snapped.

"Not at all. You said it would be only two rides. An impossibility, even for a very strong horse."

Olive started giggling. "He thinks you mean a ride, not a ride."

"Huh?" both mage and warrior asked at once.

"A ride up north," Olive explained to Akabar, "is ten days."

"No man can ride for more than two or three days without becoming exhausted," Akabar insisted.

"Forget it," Alias said. "Twenty days. We're going to spend

the next six camping at night. I don't want to risk any trouble from the soldiers at Castle Crag, the north Cormyrian outpost," she explained to Akabar. "We'll skirt around it."

She outlined the rest of their route as they traveled. Once through Gnoll Pass, she planned to leave the main road, which detoured east through Tilverton and, instead, travel along a ranger's path, which led straight through the Stonelands to Shadow Gap. Olive was indignant at missing the sights of Tilverton, which boasted an inn of some renown, but Alias was adamant.

Olive sulked quietly, which was more nerve-racking than her constant chatter. Finally, Alias began describing the North Gate Inn, which lay at the top of Shadow Gap. She painted so rosy a picture that Olive began to look forward to seeing the mountain resort.

The pattern of the next several days—riding, setting up camp, dinner (prepared with surprising skill by Akabar), breaking camp—repeated over and over, restored Alias's confidence. This was the life she knew best—although a few saddlesores and aching muscles told her that she'd spent a lot of the time lost to her memory taking things too easy. Singing songs with Olive on horseback by day and lying beneath the stars at night gave Alias a feeling of contentment that had too long been missing. The sigils on her arms retreated in importance, becoming no more a threat to her and those around her than mosquito bites.

Stranger still, the farther north and away from the shores of the Inner Sea they traveled, the more cheerful Alias began to feel. Akabar was sorry to leave the green woods and fields of Cormyr, but the winds whipping across the stony soil of the vast plain north of the Storm Horns delighted Alias. She would face into the wind and smile, as though it blew away all her miseries. Despite the fact that they had to veer off the trail or cower in undergrowth occasionally to avoid parties of orcs and goblins, the warrior grew steadily calmer.

Alias's new tranquility even prompted her one evening to apologize to Akabar as they stood watch together. She'd begun to feel guilty about the way she'd shamed him into following her north.

Akabar, too proud to show himself offended by so small a thing, shrugged off her apology, but Alias persisted in trying to explain her reasoning.

"I know you're a wise man," she said, waving aside the protests his modesty compelled him to make. "Fools don't get to be mages, and all your reasons for going to Westgate were good ones. But when you've been an adventurer for as long as I have, you begin to think with your gut. I had a gut feeling that Westgate was a mistake. Poking around in Yulash feels more like the right thing to do."

Akabar didn't know what to say. He was afraid to spoil her newfound peace of mind by speaking his own. Secretly, he was afraid the sigils were maneuvering the swordswoman toward Yulash. Once the site of a temple to great evil, it remained a place of unquestionable danger.

"You've also been very kind, helping me through a bad time and accompanying me. I've never led a party before. Usually, I traveled with bands who debated and voted on their plans. Anyway, I just wanted you to know that I didn't take your advice lightly, and I won't in the future, should you, well, give me any more."

Her sincerity left Akabar speechless for several moments. Finally, he managed to say, "You honor me with your trust."

It was a ritual Turmish saying. Strangely enough, Alias knew the proper reply. "Your honor is my own."

They were silent for a while, until Akabar could no longer resist his curiosity. "Do you remember ever having visited Turmish?" he asked.

Alias shook her head. "No, I don't remember."

The next evening, their fifth out of Arabel, they camped at the base of the foothills of Shadow Gap, the high pass between the southern extension of the Desertsmouth Mountains.

❧ 10 ❧

Giogioni Wyvernspur

Giogioni Wyvernspur, sitting in the muddy road, cursed his bad luck. After all the misfortunes that befell me at Cousin Freffie's wedding, he complained to himself, you'd think it was time for a little sunshine to fall into my life. But no. I've got a cloud of Tymora's blackest luck following me.

"Daisyeye, come back here!" he shouted as he picked himself off the ground and tried, as best he could, to brush the wet mud from his velvet britches. "That's the problem with really good horses—they spook so damned easily."

The mare that had thrown him was now out of sight, having galloped around a bend in the country road.

"If it isn't one thing, it's another," Giogi muttered. He began to relate his adventure aloud, rehearsing it for his chums. "First I made a fool of myself at Minda's behest and did that silly imitation of Azoun. This caused the bard's lovely but quite mad sell-sword to attack me with a cake knife. Then Darol seized the opportunity to make himself look like a hero in front of Minda and got himself slashed across the face. Minda positively swooned with admiration when she saw his scar, and she gave the scurrilous cove permission to accompany her carriage to Suzail.

"Naturally, I considered I might play up to Minda's sympathies as well. After all, I was the one the lady in blue tried to assassinate. I'm not completely witless. I knew this was not a good time to visit court. Aunt Doroth is a horrible gossip and just a little too palsy with His Majesty's pet wizard, Vangerdahast. And if Aunt Doroth doesn't let the whole sordid affair leak out, you can bet Darol will find a way to let His Majesty know all about my remarkable impersonation.

"So while everyone is riding off to the capitol, I'm forced to travel back to Immersea, all alone, on horseback. Though I must say that Dimswart fellow was quite decent, putting me up for an extra two days until I recovered from my shock. I left early in the morning, traveling up the road to Waymoot. I was thanking Chauntea for the nice weather when Daisyeye reared up on her hind quarters and galloped up the road, leaving me in the mud."

Suddenly realizing that if he didn't catch Daisyeye in a hurry he'd never reach Waymoot by nightfall and would be forced to stay in some roadside inn, or worse, a farmer's bed, Giogi set off after his mount. He hummed what he called "that catchy little number" written by that Ruskettle woman for Freffie and Gaylyn. Rounding the curve in the road, he noticed a clicking noise.

"Is that you, Daisyeye? You naughty girl. Whatever possessed you to run off like—" Giogioni halted in his tracks, his words constricting in his throat. Very cautiously, he took a step backward, then another.

"Just where do you think you're going?" an imperious voice demanded.

The young Wyvernspur froze, unable to answer the red dragon who had addressed him. Quite aside from the shock of discovering poor Daisyeye serving as the red dragon's entree—quite a shock since there was blood oozing all over the cobblestone, and Daisyeye's eyes remained open in death as though accusing him of something—he couldn't get over the size of the monster. A single one of its paws could block traffic along the road, and Daisyeye looked like a chicken leg next to the beast's maw.

"Well?" the dragon asked.

"I-I-I—"

"Oh dear, a stutterer," the dragon sighed. "Try to relax. The words will come out more easily."

"—don't want to disturb your meal. I'll just be moving on. Don't mind me," Giogioni gasped.

The dragon swished its big russet tail around so that the scaly appendage made a curl about Giogioni, blocking all avenues of escape. "You've been so kind to provide me with lunch," the monster said, swallowing another gobbet of

Daisyeye's haunch, "the least I can do is offer you a lift."

"Oh, that's very kind, but I wouldn't want to trouble you any." Giogioni took another step backward.

"Freeze!" the dragon ordered.

Giogioni froze.

"What's your name?"

"Giogioni Wyvernspur. Ah, everyone calls me Giogi."

"How quaint." The dragon sliced off the straps to Daisyeye's saddle with a single claw and shoved it over to Giogioni's feet. "Have a seat."

Giogioni collapsed onto the saddle, feeling a little green. *I never realized that such a pretty horse could look so awful with her middle slit open,* he thought, reaching down into his saddlebag and pulling out the flask of Rivengut he always kept there. *Thank Oghma,* he prayed silently, *it was more than half full.*

"D-d-do you mind if I pour myself a drink?" he asked the dragon.

"Be my guest."

Giogioni took a long, hard pull on the flask of liquor. "If I might ask, what shall I call you?"

"Mist."

"Is that all?"

"That's all," the beast snapped and went back to rasping her tongue along Daisyeye's ribs.

Giogioni took another swig of Rivengut. If he was going to be dessert, he decided, he didn't want to feel it. He wondered idly if he would be served *en flambe,* so to speak.

"I heard you singing," Mist said when there was nothing left of Daisyeye but shattered bones. "Catchy little tune."

"Yes, something composed by that new bard, Olive Rus— oh, gods!" The man gulped. "You're *that* Mist."

Suspicious, Mist cocked an eybrow and asked, "Just what did Mistress Ruskettle have to say about me?"

"Nothing, nothing. Er—just that she was your prison— uh—guest."

"She still traveling with that tramp, Alias of Westgate?"

"The red-headed sword-sell, er, I mean, sell-sword? Maybe. If she could find—um, I have no idea."

Mist grinned from ear to ear—not an attractive sight with

parts of Daisyeye still caught between her teeth. She rested a claw on Giogioni's shoulder. "We musn't have any secrets, my dear boy."

"I don't know, really I don't. She went a little crazy at the wedding, this Alias person, that is, and then she ran off."

"Which way did Ruskettle go?" Mist asked.

Giogioni gulped. Only a cad would betray that cute little bard. He was determined not to be a cad.

A little steam escaped from Mist's nostrils, but enough Wyvernspur blood—and Rivengut—pumped through Giogioni's veins to give him the courage to keep silent.

"Very well," the dragon sighed. "If that's the way it has to be." She slipped a claw through the back of the man's shirt and lifted him from the ground.

"Oh, gods!" he gasped, sure he was about to follow Daisyeye into heaven. Instead of swallowing him, though, the dragon lifted him up, beat her massive wings, and took off from the ground.

Mist spiraled up over the Cormyrian countryside. When she reached a cruising altitude of one thousand feet she barked, "Look down, Giogi."

"No, please! I'm not very good with heights."

"You'll be an expert on them in a moment, for all of eight seconds—at which time you'll hit the ground rather hard—unless you tell me which way Ruskettle went."

"Suzail!" Giogioni gasped. "She headed toward Suzail! On a small pony named High Roll."

"Such a nice boy. I knew we could come to an understanding. Now, I need a message taken to King Azoun."

"Oh. I'd be happy to, but there's just a teensy problem. You see, at the moment, I'm not very welcome in court. I wouldn't be the best person to represent your interests."

"That's too bad, Giogi," Mist said. "If you can't help me out, I don't have any more use for you, and if I don't have any more use for you, I may as well just drop you here."

"No! No. I'll do it. Anything. Just don't drop me, please!"

Mist smiled, and dove toward the earth.

* * * * *

Azoun IV focused his telescope at a point west of the city

walls, on the Fields of the Dead. "What cheek," he muttered. The dragon, Mist, had taken up a post on Suzail's burial ground, outside the gates of the city, but near enough to be seen by any of the populace who cared to swarm on top of the walls. And swarm they did, too intrigued by the preening wild beast to fear for their lives. No work would get done in the city until the monster left.

"If only we still had the Seventh Division in the city," His Majesty sighed.

Vangerdahast spoke from the doorway, where he awaited reports from his own network of spies. "I assure you, Your Highness, that Tilverton's need of them was greater than our own. Besides, Lord Giogioni said that she would fly off only if attacked, and then her offer will be rescinded."

"It would have to be a sudden, single deathblow. I don't suppose any foolhardy adventurers have come forward, offering their services?" Azoun turned from the window to address his court wizard.

Vangerdahast shook his head. "The wyrm has chosen her ground too well. There is no cover for a sneak attack, and she will leave before sunset, so we cannot use the darkness to any advantage. Mist is too wise to fly over the city and set off the magical wards protecting it."

"Well, I don't like this. Dealing with a creature like that goes against my grain."

"Her offer is quite generous, Your Highness, if she keeps her word and departs the area forever. In addition to making the merchant caravan routes safe again, there are livestock and Your Highness's own hunting grounds to consider, both of which Mist has seriously depleted of late."

"I can't believe I'm hearing this from you, Vangy. Naturally I'd expect the merchants to jump at the chance of ridding us of the dragon at the price of a human sacrifice. I, however, must consider the safety of all my people, even some poor, little adventuress."

"This Alias claimed to be from Westgate, Your Highness," Vangerdahast said, already putting her in the past tense.

"Even worse. How would it look to the outside world, foreign traders and travelers, if I simply turned over one of their own just to rid my realm of a dragon?"

"If it please Your Highness, there is something more you should know about this poor, little adventuress. Something to indicate a more sinister nature."

Azoun tapped his foot impatiently. "Well?"

"Perhaps you should hear it from a firsthand witness," Vangerdahast suggested, nodding toward the young man who stood in a corner, working hard at steadying his nerves with large snifters of brandy.

"Giogioni!" Azoun snapped. "What do you know about this Alias of Westgate?"

"Me?" Giogioni squeaked, turning toward Azoun.

"You," the wizard insisted. "It would be best if His Highness heard it in your own words."

"I suppose so," Giogioni whispered, though he didn't suppose so at all.

"Spit it out, boy," Azoun ordered.

"She was at the wedding, Freffie's, uh, Lord Frefford's. She attacked me. Tried to kill me. Would have succeeded, too, if the crowd hadn't gotten in her way."

"What was this lady killer doing at the wedding of Lord Frefford and Sage Dimswart's daughter?" Azoun asked.

"Dimswart said he was doing some research for her because she was under some curse," Giogioni blurted.

"Dimswart would have to come up with an excuse," Vangerdahast said.

Azoun wrinkled his brow in confusion. "Why would this woman try to kill you?"

"She thought I was you," Giogioni answered with a gulp.

"What nonsense. You don't look anything like me."

"No, Your Highness," Giogioni agreed.

"He does, however, do a remarkable impression of Your Highness's voice," Vangerdahast explained.

"He does? You do?"

Giogioni nodded weakly.

"Well, let's hear it," Azoun said.

Giogioni's jaw dropped, and his face went pale.

"Come on, boy," Azoun prompted him.

"If you please, Your Highness," the Wyvernspur nobleman gulped, "I would rather n—"

"That's an order!"

Giogioni gulped. "M-m-my Cormytes," he began. "My people, as your king, as King Azoun, and as King Azoun IV, I must say that the need to raise your taxes is a result of the depravations of-of-of th-this d-dragon."

"I don't sound like that," Azoun said, scowling.

"With respect, Your Highness," Vangerdahast intervened, "you do."

"I don't stutter like that," Azoun objected.

"No, Your Highness. Lord Giogioni's stutter is a consequence of the shock he's had. Ordinarily, his impression of you would be much better. Apparently, he was giving a performance at the wedding when he was attacked."

"But he still doesn't look like me."

"No, but perhaps this Alias woman thought you were in disguise. You have been known to travel *incognito*. Any good assassin would know that. If she did indeed come from Westgate, there can be little question exactly who sent her."

"No," Azoun agreed, remembering the numerous threats made by the Fire Knives when he banished them from his kingdom. Their new headquarters was in Westgate.

There was a knock on the tower room door, and Vangerdahast left to answer it.

Azoun looked at Giogioni, who swayed slightly. Wyvernspur blood must be getting thin for one little dragon to upset him so, the king thought. "Better sit down, boy," he said kindly. "Not there, that's my chair," Azoun corrected him before the young man sank onto His Majesty's own royal, purple cushion.

Vangerdahast returned to the conference table. In his wake was a portly, balding man in a tavernkeeper's apron.

"Who's this?" Azoun asked.

The man bowed his head. "Phocius Green, Your Highness. Owner of the inn and tavern The Hidden Lady."

Azoun shot a questioning glance over the barkeep's head to Vangerdahast.

"The woman Alias stayed several evenings in The Hidden Lady," the wizard explained.

"Oh. You came to tell us about her?" Azoun asked the barkeep.

"Begging Your Majesty's pardon, but I was summoned."

"Oh?" Azoun looked surprised.

Vangerdahast explained further. "Since I have been unable to track this Alias woman by magical means, a suspicious circumstance in and of itself, I summoned Goodman Green here. I knew the woman had stayed at his inn, because one of Your Majesty's citizens reported her last week to the town guard. Apparently, he thought she was a Rashemen witch."

"Mitcher Trollslayer," the barkeep muttered.

"What made the man think that?" Azoun asked.

"She was branded with a bizarre tattoo," the wizard explained. "A member of the Council of Mages went to the inn to register her, but the woman was unconscious, so the councilman let her be."

"Please, Your Highness," the barkeep interrupted. "She was no witch, just a sell-sword. She came in with so much iron on her she wouldn't've been able to cast a light even if she were magic."

"Where is she now?" His Majesty asked.

The barkeep shrugged. "She left nearly a ride ago, Your Highness."

"When exactly?" Vangerdahast asked.

The barkeep thought for a moment. "The fifteenth, Your Lordship."

"Eight days. Do you know which way she was heading?" the wizard asked.

The barkeep stiffened. He turned to address his answer to the king. "Please, Your Highness, you aren't going to tell the dragon where she is, are you? She hasn't done any harm. She's just an adventuress with some bad luck."

"What makes you think she has something to do with the dragon?" Azoun asked.

"Well, she fought it, now didn't she?" the barkeep said. "Freed Olive Ruskettle, the famous bard. The bard herself told me."

"That's right," Giogioni piped up from his chair. "She told us all about it at the wedding party. Ruskettle told us, that is. Wonderful bard."

Having confirmed the barkeep's story, Giogi went back to slurping His Majesty's brandy and humming snatches of

Ruskettle's wedding song.

"Did you know about that, Vangy?" Azoun asked.

The royal wizard colored slightly. "No, Your Highness."

Azoun turned to the barkeep. "For the time being we need to know where this Alias is. She may be nothing more than a sell-sword, but she could be something much more dangerous. We must know all about her. Now, which way was she heading?"

The barkeep sighed. "She and the bard and the Turmish mage said something about going to Westgate, then they said something about going to Yulash."

"Yulash?" Azoun exclaimed. "How bizarre."

"The two towns are in opposite directions," the wizard pointed out. "Which way did they decide to go?"

The barkeep thought for a moment again. He remembered the Turmish mage listing all the reasons for going to Westgate. The barkeep was a loyal subject to his king, but he didn't quite trust the wizard Vangerdahast. To him, Alias would always be the hidden lady and hence, like the name of his inn, good luck. She had looked so miserable the last night she'd stayed at his hostel. The barkeep was not keen on turning her over to the undoubtedly less than tender ministrations of the royal wizard.

"The lady wanted to go to Yulash," he told Vangerdahast.

"Thank you for your cooperation, Goodman Green," the wizard replied. "You may leave now."

The barkeep bowed his head to the king and left the tower room. Vangerdahast's eyes followed him thoughtfully.

"I don't know many assassins who rescue bards in distress," Azoun said to his wizard.

"But many make deals with dragons, Your Highness, and as is the way with their kind, they often cheat on their agreements. The dragon might only be interested in collecting an unpaid debt."

"But why would the bard lie about her rescue?"

"This Olive Ruskettle is a halfling. She may not be a bard."

Giogioni rose from his chair. "Now, hold on just a moment," he said. "She's a fine bard. What gives you the right to slander people just because they're short?"

Vangerdahast fixed the noble with a cold stare.

"Well, I thought she was good," Giogioni muttered, sitting back down.

King Azoun struggled with his conscience and his reason. On one hand, if this woman were an assassin, he wasn't troubled by letting the dragon take care of her. On the other hand, if she were some innocent victim of a curse, he wasn't going to sleep well that night. Still, it was a long road to Yulash. The dragon might not find her, he reasoned, and Alias had defeated it once already. Ridding Cormyr of a dragon was no small accomplishment for a king.

He nodded his assent to Vangerdahast's plan.

"Lord Giogioni," the wizard said. "Upon receiving the dragon's promise to leave and never return to Cormyr, you will inform the creature that Alias of Westgate left Suzail eight days ago. To the best of your knowledge, the adventuress was headed toward Yulash."

Giogioni rose to his feet with a sigh, bowed his head, and left on his mission.

"Perhaps now that he's served as Your Majesty's messenger, he might consider rendering you some other service."

"Such as?"

"Investigating Westgate," the wizard suggested.

Azoun's brow furrowed in anger. "You mean that barkeep was lying! Why didn't you tell me?"

Vangerdahast shook his head. "No, Goodman Green was telling the truth, though perhaps not all of it. The woman and her companions were seen leaving by the Eastgate, which leads to the road north."

"So, why send Giogi to Westgate?"

"The barkeep may have been mistaken. Alias could make it to Yulash and back to Westgate without the dragon finding her. Someone who knows her appearance and holds your interests to heart should be sent there, just in case."

Azoun nodded. He turned back to the window and peered over the western wall again. "You remember, Vangy, when I was your pupil and you used to give me those tests in ethics?"

"Yes, Your Highness."

"I always hated them. Still do."

"Only now, Your Highness," Vangerdahast replied softly, "they are no longer tests."

❧ 11 ❧

Shadow Gap

Whenever Alias saw Shadow Gap she thought of some weary titan dragging his axe behind him as he stepped over the hills. At least that was how she imagined the creation of the steep-sided, steep-sloped gorge that split the mountains in two.

No more than an hour of noon sunlight ever reached the floor of the pass. At all other times, it remained in the shadow of the mountains, hence its name.

The gap was barren, save for a scattering of short, scrubby bushes. The road through it wound upward in an interminable series of hairpin curves and ascending switchbacks, resembling a dry wash. Alias had passed through the gap as a caravan guard many times and remembered how, in the spring, water followed the same course down the hill as the merchant wagons.

Heavily laden wagons draped with thick rugs and waterproof slickers would rumble up the gorge at a snail's pace. The lord merchants urged the drivers on, while mercenary sell-swords watched the cliffs for ambush. Occasionally, a procession of pilgrims on foot interrupted the flow, oblivious to the bustling world around them. More rarely a wizard's wagon, with lumber sprouting fresh, spring leaves, clattered through the vale on ancient wheels, pulled by oxen, gorgons, or more fantastic beasts.

Today, all that was absent, banished as if by magic. The vale was emptier than a tax collector's Yule party. The only sound the travelers heard was the clopping of the horse hooves beneath them. Alias wondered what could have halted the trade so completely. A war, perhaps, or rumor of one. But she'd heard nothing of that sort in Cormyr, and the Cormyrians were not, as a rule, insular.

Akabar, having never passed through the gap before, rode at the head of the party as if nothing was amiss. Behind him, Olive found the stillness jarring. Dragonbait hissed once, never a good sign, and Alias caught a whiff of something that smelled like ham. She furrowed her brow in puzzlement and sniffed again. Nothing. Must have imagined it, she thought, but she made sure that her longsword was loose in its scabbard and her knives were handy.

Something croaked her name, harsh and low, and she came up with a dagger in hand. The others seemed not to hear the voice.

Did the wind carry it to her ears alone? Or did sorcery? she wondered, remembering the attack at the abandoned druid's circle, where the wind had drowned out her cries for help.

The swordswoman reigned in her horse behind the others and listened. The sound came again, a harsh, dying croak that called her name, this time from one of the scrub bushes on Alias's left.

Spotting Alias behind them, Olive harrumphed.

Akabar called back, "Alias? Are—"

Suddenly, the bush near Alias rustled and exploded in a flurry of feathers.

Old reflexes took over, and Alias felt like some mechanical toy. She aimed, snapped her wrist back, and flicked her knife forward, loosing the dagger.

The spinning weapon struck the bird, a huge raven, at the base of its left wing and stuck there. A smaller creature would have been skewered, but the raven took to the air with the blade embedded in its flesh—the dagger's gold-wrapped hilt jutting out and flashing in the sun.

Hissing, Dragonbait drew his sword.

"Lee-as, Lee-as, Lee-as," the bird shrieked as it rose straight up, spun, and flapped in an ungainly manner toward the nearest cliff wall, taking Alias's weapon with it.

The woman warrior shook her head angrily. The unnatural silence had unsettled her, and her little flash of paranoia had cost her a good throwing dagger.

"I thought it was something more dangerous than a blasted bird," Alias said, rejoining the group. "I thought it was calling my name." Then she laughed, one of the first deep-hearted laughs she'd permitted herself in gods knew how long.

"It was only a robberwing," the mage said, surprised by her reaction. "They're quite common on the southern shores of the Inner Sea. I thought they were well-known in the north, too. They take shiny objects on occasion, but otherwise they're harmless."

"In Waterdeep," chimed in the halfling, "a corrupt lord trained a flock of robberwings to steal for him."

"Natives of Waterdeep," replied the mage, "have all sorts of odd ways to pass the time . . . when they aren't counting their money."

"Robberwings are considered an ill omen in Thay," Olive added.

Dragonbait hissed again. His dead, yellow eyes glared at the cliff where the raven had disappeared.

Alias's laughter subsided. "It's all right, Dragonbait," she said, patting him on the back. "I know it was just a raven." She turned to the others. "It's just that I was expecting . . . a dragon. Or a harpy. Or at least a nest of blood-sucking stirges. I feel a little foolish at having lost a weapon to . . . just a bird."

"A lost weapon's like a lost meal," said the halfling, wheeling around on her pony. "Replaceable, but you have to know where to look. Speaking of which, are we going to sit here until dark or press on to this marvelous inn of yours?"

"We press on," Alias said.

"Thank heavens," the bard said, kicking her pony past Akabar's stallion. "Great adventure can wait. Hark, I hear something calling my name, too." She held her hand up to her ear. "It's a warm bed and something else . . . a hot meal, one not spiced to within an inch of my life."

Ruskettle peeked out from under her wide-brimmed hat to catch Akabar's reaction, but his face remained impassive. Five nights before, Olive had complained about the mage's cooking and announced that, if Akabar didn't go easier on the pepper, she'd be forced to take a hand in the cooking herself. Since then, she had continued to complain about the spicing, but had yet to lift a finger to help prepare meals.

The halfling set her pony in a trot. Akabar followed, looking regal on his white mount. Dragonbait waited for Alias to pass him, then brought up the rear, still watching the cliffside warily.

"Don't worry," Alias told him. "I can get another dagger when we reach Shadowdale."

Dragonbait did not look away from the cliffs for a long time.

Olive's dreams of a warm bed and a less-seasoned meal were shattered when they topped the last set of switchbacks. Instead of a charming house and a warm, welcoming cup of mulled wine, they found the remains of a great hall, its massive timbers blackened by flame, its stone floor littered with slate from the collapsed roof.

"Don't tell me, let me guess," Olive snapped angrily. "This place has gone downhill somewhat since you last visited it."

"Obviously, the clientele has changed," Akabar said dryly, gingerly poking his foot through the rubble. He, too, had been looking forward to a comfortable bed.

"Nine circles of Hell," Alias muttered. Above the shattered roof, the last rays of the evening sun were playing against the eastern cliff, turning it as red as blood.

"There are no bodies," Akabar pointed out, "and the fire damage looks several months old, so I don't think there can be much danger. As to comforts, there's still some roof left in that corner and the firepit is serviceable. Shall we stay or ride on?"

Alias sighed. "We may as well stay."

Inwardly, she was thankful for the mage's calm assessment. She had been looking forward to collapsing in the inn, and her disappointed muscles revolted at the thought of riding any farther.

Akabar nodded. "Stay it is."

"I say we should go," Olive objected vehemently. "There's still daylight left, and we can be a few miles beyond this place when whatever did this comes back."

"As I said—this damage occurred some time ago," the mage argued.

"Increasing the likelihood that whatever caused it will return," retorted the bard.

"There are no bodies," Akabar insisted.

"That's even worse," Olive cried, her voice growing shrill. "It just proves that whatever did this burns or swallows people whole, probably vomiting up their bones in its lair. Look!" Ruskettle lifted up a very large, heavy, two-handed sword. "Not even the owner of this sword could defend himself." She dropped the blade in disgust.

"Or—" Alias interrupted, "—or it proves that this was just an ordinary fire—an accident—and everyone got out in time or other humans buried the corpses. Try not to overreact, Olive."

"Me?" Olive squeaked. "You're the one who tried to skewer a robberwing for calling out your name. If it were just an ordinary fire, why didn't they rebuild the inn? Why isn't anyone using the pass?"

Alias shrugged. "They'd have to import the building materials, and that would take a few months. I'm sure we simply went through the pass on a slow day." She knew her last comment was improbable, but she also knew she'd feel foolish giving in to the halfling's anxieties.

"Ha! This is just the kind of place you tell children about to keep them from straying into the woods."

Alias reached under her stallion to unbuckle the saddle straps. "Well, Olive," she said, lifting the saddle from her horse, "just be sure you don't stray too far, then."

Olive growled in frustration and left to tend to her pony.

Dragonbait, who was snuffling over a pile of timbers, snarled once.

"See!" Olive turned excitedly. "Even Dragonbait votes we should go."

Alias laughed. "He's more likely snarling at a garden spider. Besides, Dragonbait doesn't get a vote. He can't talk. He barely understands what we're saying."

"He understands well enough when it really matters," Olive muttered.

"Pardon?"

"I said, we could be halfway down the gap, away from this place before night fell."

"Then we'd have to eat a cold supper," the mage teased.

That was food for thought to the halfling. In the end, she decided safety was more important than comfort. "It wouldn't matter, you'd only add too much spice anyway."

"Perhaps you should show me how to do it properly."

"I wouldn't dream of depriving you of the joy of figuring it out for yourself," Olive replied. "Besides, I have a more important job this evening." She drew out a set of pasteboard cards from a jacket pocket.

"Oh? And what job is that?" Alias asked with a smile.

"Teaching your lizard to vote," the halfling announced, grabbing Dragonbait firmly by the arm and hustling him to a far corner of the ruins.

"You keep an eye on Olive, Dragonbait," Alias called. "Don't let her wander into the woods."

Akabar started the fire, using pieces of charred wood from the inn. The mage struck a spark off his flint onto some wool and soon had a small blaze going. Alias squatted on her haunches and blew into the flames, spreading them among the drier tinder until the heavier kindling caught.

Akabar pulled out a pan, some cooking utensils, and a package of meat from a saddle bag. "Lamb, I think." Carving the meat into strips, he added, "We're going to have to start hunting soon."

"I know," Alias sighed, staring into the flames. "If I hadn't been such a frightened ninny and had hit that bird square on, I'd still have my dagger and we'd be eating fresh meat tonight."

"Your aim can't always be perfect," he said.

"Why not?"

The mage laughed. He poured a splash of oil into the cooking pan and balanced it on two large logs which straddled the fire. "You're only human."

"What's that got to do with it?"

"Why is perfection so important?" he asked her.

"Why is being alive important?" she returned. "One miss too many and I could end up someone else's supper."

"You lead a hard life."

"It's worth it," the swordswoman insisted.

"Why?"

Alias shrugged. "The feeling of being free, I guess."

"Free of needing others?"

Alias did not reply. She fished a brush from her saddle bag and walked over to where Lady Killer stood munching the stiff mountain grass.

The mage smiled as he watched her grooming the pure-bred stallion. If she took that brush to her own hair, he thought, she would look as well bred. Akabar believed he understood why she spent her affection on the horse. The creature would never betray her, it didn't really need her, and it didn't ask questions. Rather like her other companion, the lizard.

He shook off the pity he felt for her, knowing that if she saw it, she would go for his throat. The oil in the pan spat, and the mage added the strips of lamb.

The mountain air was chill. Before long, Alias returned to the fire to warm her hands.

"Do you think a dragon may have caused this damage?" Akabar asked. The thought had been preying on his mind, but he had not wanted to appear nervous.

"No," Alias replied. "A dragon wouldn't leave things so neat. It'd burrow through the stones on the floor, looking for treasure. The damage was probably caused by an ordinary fire. Unless two mages decided to fight it out here with heavy magic."

"I was just wondering," the mage explained as he covered a pan of boiling broth and millet, "because you said Mist had ravens as familiars. This is the height of the trading season. It is unusual, is it not, for this route to be so deserted?"

"Yes," Alias admitted. "But it might have nothing to do with the inn's destruction. Trade routes go out of fashion for other reasons than monsters. Sometimes it's just the rumor of monsters, put out by secret societies to discourage competition. Wars. Too little grain to trade. Import taxes and tolls. You know more about trading. What do you think?"

"I think something is wrong, but it may or may not concern . . . us."

"You mean me, of course. And my affliction."

"Have there been any problems?" the mage asked.

"Not since the wedding."

Alias watched as Akabar lifted the lid from the pan and crushed a fistful of dried peppers over the steaming grain, letting most of it settle in a quarter of the pan.

"I take it that's Olive's portion," Alias noted, smiling.

The mage grinned fiendishly. "The vengeance of wizards and cooks can be subtle but terrible. Each day I add another quarter fistful. Eventually Mistress Ruskettle will help prepare a meal, or her tongue will fall out of her head."

"More likely, you'll run out of spices."

Akabar chuckled.

Alias looked over to the far corner of the ruined inn, where Olive sat cross-legged before Dragonbait. The bard held a card in front of the lizard and said something Alias could not hear. Dragonbait looked at the card with a deadpan stare, then abruptly plucked it out of her hand and started to nibble on the edge.

"The halfling has less chance for success than a fat school priest trying to convert kobolds," Alias said with a smirk.

"You remind me of my younger wife. What she cannot see, she will not believe. When I return, she'll sit and count the money I bring home, but she'll laugh in disbelief at the wondrous things I tell her about the north country."

"She'll be laughing pretty hard about this troupe," Alias predicted.

"Perhaps when you have finished your quest you might accompany me back to Alaghon, where my wives base our business."

His tone was light, but Alias felt something underlying it, something deeper that he struggled to keep from surfacing. "I hope that wasn't an invitation to join your little harem, Turmite." She intended the remark to sound like a sneer, but it became more of a question.

Akabar sighed inwardly; he'd made her shy away again. He forced a smile he did not feel. "The invitation was only for a traveling companion, not a future bedmate. I hoped to prove to my wives that women of the north wield dangerous weapons and travel where they please. You need not fear my desires. Turmish women keep their mates so enraptured with their amorous abilities that foreign women pall by comparison."

"I see," Alias replied, looking down into the fire to keep her grin from showing.

"Besides," continued Akabar, "as I've explained once, they have veto power over co-wives. They would never approve of you joining the family. You're much too hot-tempered, and my older wife is offended by the smell of damp wool."

Alias laughed and threw the horse brush at him. "You smell like damp wool, too, Turmite." She gave a tug on his cloak.

Akabar shrugged. "Yes, but my wives cannot veto me."

Olive and Dragonbait joined them at the fireside, the only warmth and light for miles now that the sun had set. The lizard carried wood for the fire. The bard was all smiles.

"I've done it," Olive declared.

"Done what?" Akabar asked, tasting his concoction.

"Taught Dragonbait to speak to us," the bard said. Fixing Alias with a reproachful stare, she added, "It's surprising no one thought of it before."

"So, let's hear what he says," Alias said, holding out a piece of flat trailbread for Akabar to spread with the meat and grain mixture.

"It doesn't work like that," the bard explained. She pulled out a deck of Talis cards from her pocket. "He doesn't speak any tongue I recognize, but he can understand us. Watch." Ruskettle leafed through the cards, pulling out two.

"The Holed Plate, Primary of Stones, means yes," Olive said. "The Flaming Dagger, no. He picked that one himself."

"I wonder why," Alias smirked.

"I ask him a question and he can give the answer. Watch." She turned back to the creature and, smiling like a maiden aunt, Alias thought, she asked, "Dragonbait, are you a lizard?"

The lizard-creature held up the Holed Plate indicating yes.

"Are you hungry?" Olive asked in the same cheerful tone.

Dragonbait held up the same card. Another yes.

"Should we stay in this haunted place?" Olive demanded, suddenly stern, pointing to the burned rafters.

Dragonbait lifted the Flaming Dagger card.

Olive turned back to face the swordswoman and mage. "You see. You've held this poor creature, virtually as a bond-servant, for weeks now without even trying to communicate with him. I reached his mind in a single session." Olive shook her head sadly. "I wonder why you humans are running the world at all."

Alias studied Dragonbait curiously. She had tried to communicate with him back at The Hidden Lady without success. Why did I give up so soon? she wondered, but she knew the answer to that. Dragonbait seemed to understand what she wanted without her even having to ask, and besides, he'd offered her his sword, which made her his leader. Still . . . is it possible that I didn't want to know anything he could tell me? She felt more than a little annoyed with herself.

Akabar polished off his supper and licked his fingers. "Congratulations," he said to Olive, handing her a folded meat and millet sandwich filled from the far side of the skillet. "May I try?"

"Of course," the halfling replied, relinquishing her seat beside the lizard. "Answers told, mysteries revealed."

Akabar sat in front of the lizard, frowning in deep concentration. "Dragonbait," he asked, "can you understand me?"

The lizard held up the Flaming Dagger. No.

"Well," the mage said, "at least he's honest." With a smile he asked, "Is the halfling a perfect fool?"

Dragonbait lifted up the Holed Plate. Yes.

Alias giggled.

Akabar screwed his face into a scowl. "Would you mind very much if we threw her on the fire for kindling?"

The Flaming Dagger. No.

Akabar burst into laughter. "Idiot bard! You've trained him to show the *yes* card when you smile and the *no* card when you frown. He's a quick study, but there are trained monkeys in Calisham who know that trick. Now, eat your dinner before it gets cold." He and Alias turned back to the pan for second helpings.

"The way you spice food, it could melt steel for hours," the halfling grumbled. Before she took a bite of the peppery mixture, she glared at Dragonbait, saying, "I bet you're proud of yourself, lizard."

Dragonbait held up the Holed Plate, cocked his head at the halfling, and a strange clicking sound came through his stubby teeth. Olive felt certain he was laughing at her.

❧ 12 ❧

The Dream
and the Kalmari

The evening sky over Shadow Gap was overcast except in the far south, where a few stars glittered between the mantle of clouds and the horizon. Alias exhaled slowly, watching the vapor from her breath rise and drift away in the cool mountain air. Despite the chill, she was quite comfortable. Akabar had not stinted on warm clothing and blankets for their trip north.

On second watch, Alias looked over at Akabar, who lay under only one wool cover, and his arms over that. Gently, she dropped a fur hide over him from chin to knees. In no time he pushed most of it aside, and his arms, clad only in his flimsy robe, once again lay exposed to the cold air.

Either he's got some magic trick to keep warm, or he carries the heat of the southern sun inside him, Alias thought.

Olive, under the pretext of keeping the extra bedding dry and safe from marauding beasts, slept on top of most of them. In sleep she looked deceptively childlike and innocent, the swordswoman thought. But Akabar, with his beard and the sun-wrinkles about his eyes, looked older.

Alias studied the sleeping Dragonbait, trying to decide if he looked older or younger. He slept as peacefully as a child, yet even with his tail drawn up between his legs and curled beneath his head, the power of his warrior's frame was apparent. Alias wondered if he didn't sleep, as the saying went, the sleep of the righteous, untroubled by his dreams because he lived up to his own standard of goodness.

He was neither a slow riser nor one to awaken with a start. Whenever she awakened him, he opened his eyes curiously, smiled that toothy grin, and gave a pleasant chirp. The few times the party had shifted camp in the middle of the night to avoid being stumbled upon by goblins and orcs, Alias had discovered the lizard already awake, lying very still, sniffing the air, his hand wrapped around the hilt of his sword.

She wrapped one of her own blankets about the lizard's shoulders, a custom she'd adopted from her travels with the Company of the Swanmays. She'd missed the sisterly concern the seven members, all women, had had for one another, but she hadn't felt comfortable enough among the strangers with whom she now traveled to perform so intimate a gesture . . . until tonight.

She thought very hard about Dragonbait, about all he'd done for her, all she knew about him, all the things she felt about him. He was the least human of her companions, he couldn't talk to her, and she had little idea what went through his mind, yet Dragonbait was the only member of the party she trusted completely. Regardless of what Olive had said about failing to communicate with him, she knew that the two of them, lizard and swordswoman, had an understanding.

"You're not my bondservant, are you?" Alias whispered to the sleeping lizard. "You're my brother."

She'd never really had any siblings, at least as far as she knew. Her mother, an uncommunicative fisherman's widow, had never told her of any, and when her mother died, just after Alias reached her teens, no long-lost relatives appeared at her wake. The following year Alias ran off to avoid being bonded to a decent but unimaginative weaver. It wasn't until she had insinuated herself into the Swanmays that she felt any kinship to anyone. The Swanmays had relished the risks and beauty of the open wilderness as much as she did. Just remembering them now made her throat tighten with emotion.

Yet, the feeling she had for Dragonbait, one she was certain he shared, could not possibly be based on mutual interests. As far as she knew, they had none. His behavior toward her was most definitely the tender protectiveness of a brother. Oddly enough, Alias realized that she felt the same way about him. And the strength of that feeling without, as she perceived, any logical foundation, was what made her so certain there was no one closer to her in all the world.

Despite the admission of her feelings for the lizard, she was no closer to remembering anything about their past association than before.

Her relationship with Olive was as clear as glass. Alias knew she could trust the halfling to look after the halfling first, the party's possessions second, and everyone else probably not at all. Though the bard had shown one flash of bravado in Mist's lair, taunting the dragon long enough for Alias to get back on her feet, bravado was not the same as courage, and had nothing at all to do with heroism. Alias realized that Olive would weigh every risk against how much treasure she estimated lay at the end of Alias's quest.

Akabar was a little more complicated. He was on a quest of his own to prove to himself that he was more than a Turmish merchant. Eager to collect his own adventures to relate to his profiteering wives and, Alias conjectured, probably anxious to keep from returning so soon to a family with little tolerance for such nonsense as adventures. Alias was certain that if he hadn't stumbled across her case, he'd have found some other adventurer to lavish his attentions on. She felt she could trust him not to deceive her, but she wasn't going to count on him to lay down his life for her. She knew the mage possibly had one other reason for accompanying her, but he had been wise enough to deny it, so she wasn't going to dwell on it.

She wasn't aware she was falling asleep, but when the wreckage of the inn began to shimmer and reform into the building she remembered from years ago, she knew she'd drifted into some dream. Angrily she tried to shake herself awake, frightened that her dereliction of duty would bring great harm to the party, but she had no success.

The inn took on an increasing solidity. First, the thick timber walls returned, their joints sealed with dabbed mud. Doors and tables and chairs and the bar seemed to rise from the ground. Without moving, Alias found herself seated at a small table by the firepit.

Alerted by the groaning beams above, Alias looked up.

Overhead, the charred timbers grew whole, the drooping section of ceiling that had survived the fire straightened. Planed boards crisscrossed the timbers and, though she could not see them, Alias heard the clatter of pottery shingles as they multiplied across the boards outside. Chains began to snake downward from iron hooks which sprouted from the main timbers. The ends of the chains blossomed into gourd-shaped lamps, burning oil from small wicks.

The flame in the firepit flared into a roaring blaze, and the North Gate Inn began filling with customers, though they did not enter by the door. Alias heard them first, the mutter and roar of many people speaking all around her. She fixed her attention on a booth in the corner where she heard an argument, but all she could see were shadows.

Of course, I might not be dreaming, Alias considered. This could all be some fantastic illusion. But the noise would have wakened the others, and they would still be here sleeping beside me. No, this was a dream, she concluded.

Suddenly there was a tremendous clatter to her right. Her head turned in time to witness a burly man berating a small servant girl for spilling wine down the copious cleavage of his female companion. As the youngster protested her innocence, the man stood up and loomed over her. He was twice her height, but Alias caught the glint of sharp steel as the servant reached into her apron pocket.

A loud roar came from the corner booth again, and she turned her attention back to it. No longer occupied by shadows, it was filled with people of depth and color. A tired cleric and a young fighter argued some fine religious point. The cleric insisted that *Tempos* was a corruption of the southern *Tempus*, and that *Tempus* was the correct pronunciation. This supposition seemed to madden the fighter, a northern barbarian on his manhood journey, no doubt. His face, already quite red from several drinks, flushed even darker. He was preparing his argument by reaching his right hand over his left shoulder to grasp the lion-headed hilt of the massive sword strapped to his back.

Alias wondered which of the two arguments would be the first to cause a room-clearing brawl.

"Neither," answered a pleasant voice. Alias started at the

reply. A young man stood beside her table, holding two crystal glasses in one hand and a dusty bottle in the other. He sat in the chair beside her, setting the items he carried on the table. "But devastation will arrive shortly," he assured her with a lopsided grin and a wink. Alias would have judged him to be not yet twenty, but his suave manner belied her estimate. He wiped off the bottle and extracted the cork with an expert ease.

The youth's blond hair hung loose about his shoulders and glistened in the firelight. He had what the members of the Swanmays would agree was a well-formed figure, yet his blue eyes reflected the firelight back in pinpoints of red. As attractive as Alias found him, he made her quite nervous. She felt as if she were waiting for someone in the dream, but this man was not that person.

"I took the liberty of ordering a wine special. I know you'll like it." He smiled as he poured copper-colored liquid into both glasses.

"How do you know what's going to happen?" Alias asked.

"We all have our little curses," he whispered, running a finger down her right arm along the brands. They tingled, an entirely new sensation. "My curse is that I'm required to read the script before the play begins." He held up his glass and waited for her to do the same. "In a few minutes the plot will pick up. Plenty of time to finish your drink."

Alias lifted the delicate crystal by the stem and allowed her host to clink his own against it. "To drama," he said.

Alias sniffed the beverage warily, afraid to discover yet another Cormyrian mixture unsuited to her tastes. Instead, a pleasant, tangy scent wafted to her nostrils. She took a sip and then, without thinking, drained the glass. The sharp, sweet taste of mountain berries clung to her lips, and the alcohol coursed through her body like a shock. Her face warmed immediately, as if she stood in bright sunshine, and the aching muscles of her back relaxed. It wasn't just the only good thing she'd tasted in a long time. She had a strong suspicion it would be the best thing she would ever taste.

"Which of these incidents is responsible for the fire?" Alias asked the young man as he refilled their glasses.

"Neither," the man said. He nodded toward the burly man

and his buxom companion. The servant girl had convinced the man at knife point to return to his seat and stop fussing. She tossed the woman a dingy towel and left them.

"Labor troubles are quite common this far north," the youth told her. "Every potscrubber dreams of becoming a petty lord, inspired by the few who, with luck and reckless-ness, have done so. The situation here in Shadow Gap is, of course, exacerbated by the minute population, making not just good help, but any help at all hard to find."

"And the loud barbarian and cleric?" Alias asked, turning to discover the reaction of the other patrons when the fight-er pulled out his weapon, but both were engaged in drain-ing large mugs of ale.

"They're old friends from way back. They've had this argument at least a hundred times before in this very place, and in as many other inns."

"So, what did cause the fire? Does it have anything to do with why the pass is deserted?"

"Patience, my dear, patience," her drinking companion chided. He raised her glass to her mouth and tilted the ambrosial liquid so that it flowed past her lips. Alias grasped the stem and swallowed until the entire draught was con-sumed. A greater heat washed over her, and she slipped off her cape.

"You know what your problem is?" the man asked.

"No, what?" She reached for the wine bottle and poured herself a third glass.

"You aren't used to acquiring information slowly, listening to people explain things in their own way, experiencing life as it comes. You expect someone to just pour everything you want to know into you, as though it were a bottle of wine." He raised the wine bottle and filled his glass again. "Ah!" he said with glee, his eyes fixed on the doorway. "Finally, a principal actor."

Alias turned. The man was not the one she was waiting for either. A small man, he was dressed like a merchant, with a purple robe gathered at his waist and a fat, over-stuffed hat with a long, swan feather plume on his head.

The small man climbed upon a low, stone platform oppo-site the fire pit, waved a parchment scroll over his head, and shouted "Silence!"

Half the conversations died out, but a few scattered patrons continued chattering. The quieted persons turned their attention to the merchant. Assured of at least a partial audience, the man unrolled his scroll and began to read.

"Hear, all and sundry, the words of the Iron Throne." The last words caught the attention of those who had ignored him. Silence blanketed the room.

The herald paused for effect. Alias frowned. The eyes of the young man beside her twinkled merrily. "The Iron Throne," her companion explained in a hushed whisper without taking his eyes from the speaker, "is a young trading organization, just beginning to compete with the better established merchant houses. Their favorite strategies include force, treachery, and magic."

The herald read on. "The Iron Throne is much concerned with the growing violence in the north, violence fed by the arms merchants who line their own pockets at the expense of others."

"The Iron Throne should know, their pockets bulge, too!" a heckler called out, followed by a spattering of applause.

The herald's eyes narrowed. "Hence, the Iron Throne pronounces an anathema upon the warmongering merchants and will close Shadow Gap for thirty days."

Boos and catcalls followed.

"It would take four divisions of mercenaries, at least, to hold this pass," Alias commented.

"You think so?" the young man replied with a laugh. "Wait and see, shall we?"

"All those within Shadow Gap will be allowed to leave, but they may carry no weapons of war. Thus will the Iron Throne demonstrate its ability to keep peace in the region," the herald concluded.

"Bull spittle!" shouted the barbarian in the corner booth, rising drunkenly to his feet. "The Iron Throne is shipping weapons by the cartloads to goblins and maggots from Zhentil Keep! They just want to keep the Dales light in armaments for their Zhentarim masters! It will take more than a proclamation-spouting toady to keep us from aiding the free people of the north."

The herald glared malevolently at the barbarian.

Sensing some unseen power, the cleric tried to pull his friend back to his side, but the barbarian strode over to the herald. The warrior towered above the smaller man, even though the herald stood on the raised platform. He yanked the parchment scroll out of the herald's hand and shredded it, tossing the pieces in the herald's face. "Send that message back to the Iron Throne."

"You needn't worry about safe delivery of your master's weapons to his contact in Daggerdale," the herald hissed. "The contact is already dead, a victim of his own penchant for violence."

The barbarian drew in a shocked breath. "You killed Brenjer, you murdering swine! I'll show you violence!" He drew his two-handed sword, swung the massive blade over his head, and struck the herald in the forehead.

The steel sliced through its target down to the waist with the same ease and sound it would make ripping through taut canvas.

Alias gasped, for the body of the herald did not gush blood or fall to the floor, as would a carcass of meat. Instead, two ragged shards of purple cloth drifted to the floor and a black mist rose from them, forming into the shape of an inverted tear drop above the barbarian.

Two unblinking, yellow eyes glowed within the cloud of dark vapor. Beneath the eyes a huge gap parted, revealing rows upon rows of needle-sharp teeth. From this maw came the sound of a thousand snakes hissing in a stone room.

"A kalmari," the youth whispered to Alias. "They're native to the lands of Thay, used by the Red Wizards and their allies. Some speculate they are relatives to intellect devourers. Remarkable, isn't it?"

Alias, intent on watching the barbarian deal with the monster, did not reply. The barbarian passed his sword through the mist, but his blow did no more damage than it would to smoke. The kalmari gave a rattling laugh, then distended its jaws so its mouth made up more than half its body. The creature fell forward over the man and swallowed him in a single gulp, broadsword and all.

For a moment there was silence while the inn's occupants

struggled to comprehend what had happened. Then the room erupted with a clatter of toppled chairs and tables and shuffling feet as the inhabitants sought escape.

Clerics and mages intoned the words of half a dozen spells and wardings as they backed away from the beast.

The kalmari tilted its head back and spit out the barbarian's sword, its blade propelled upward in a twisting ribbon of flame. The sword flew into the upper rafters and stuck there, imbedded to the hilt. The flames spread across the ceiling, engulfing the rafters in a white heat.

The kalmari smiled, a wide grin that stretched three-quarters of the way around its body. The smile lasted only a moment before a battery of offensive spells struck—bolts of lightning and flame and radiant blue daggers of magic missile. Alias felt her right arm ache and, looking down, saw that her own runes glowed.

She tried to rise, intent on aiding in the battle any way she could, but the youth beside her placed his hand over the sigils on her forearm and, with the lightest of pressure, held her trapped against the table.

"You'll get your chance," he grinned mysteriously. "What's your hurry?"

The fires spread with unnatural speed, and soon the entire area, save for where Alias and her companion sat, was engulfed in flame. Through the dancing flames Alias could see the kalmari swallowing a mage whole, then belching up another burst of burning ichor.

Yet Alias felt no heat. A moment later, the flames, the kalmari, and its opponents diminished to shadows against the walls of the common room. Then, even the shadows vanished. The inn around her was whole and sturdy, unaffected by the fire, but nearly barren of inhabitants.

Still seated beside the youth, Alias spotted a solitary figure at a table across the room. The figure's features were completely concealed by a cloak and a hood. This is the one I've been waiting for, she told herself with certainty. But now she was reluctant to make the meeting.

The young man drained the last of his wine and rose to leave.

"Wait!" Alias insisted, grabbing his arm. She wanted to say,

"Don't leave me alone with that one," but she knew her words would not influence him. So instead she asked, "When did this happen?"

"While you were still hunting halfling-stealing dragons west of Suzail."

Surprised that she got him to answer so easily, she pressed her interrogation further. "Where is the kalmari?"

"Still at large, defending the area for its masters."

"How does one ward against it?"

"It fears only the mark of its maker."

"How is it defeated?"

"The kalmari cannot eat anything twice."

"What does it have to do with me?"

"Enough," a woman's voice whispered.

Alias shivered and turned to look at the figure seated across the room. All about the inn was fog.

The woman's voice cut sharply through the rising vapor. "You've gone too far, Nameless. You are dismissed."

"But she asked a question," the youth objected. "I want to answer all her questions."

"You have stalled our interview long enough. I will answer this question for her. The creature is, after all, mine."

There was something very familiar about the sharp, feminine voice, and Alias felt her right arm throb. When she stood, her senses began to spin. She cursed the wine silently and turned to accuse the youth of getting her drunk, but he was already gone, swallowed in the dream mist.

"Well?" Alias demanded, trying to appear undaunted as the figure rose and drifted, like a ghost, toward her.

"The kalmari is a meager demonstration of my power," the woman said, making a sweeping gesture with her right hand, palm up. Her features remained concealed in the shadows of the hood, but Alias noted that her left arm was in a sling. "It's just something I had out on loan to the Iron Throne, who wished to demonstrate their power. Many will think twice before crossing the will of the Iron Throne."

"But what does this have to do with me?" Alias repeated. She stood only an arm's length from the woman. Alias realized she could easily reach out and yank back the woman's hood to reveal her face. Perhaps, Alias hoped, if I can recognize the face, it will help to explain my lost memory or the tattoo on my arm. Yet, why do my instincts hold me back, tell me to flee fast and far? Is she a lich or a medusa?

"Why, the kalmari is another of my creatures," the woman laughed. "I was going to station it here to watch for you. The Iron Crown's fee only sweetened the pot."

"Another one of your creatures," Alias repeated, certain she had gained a new insight. "Like the crystal elemental?"

The woman snorted derisively. "Please. You insult me, my dear. Such a heavy-handed, clumsy thing. My creations have always been elegant."

"Then what other creature did you mean?" Alias asked.

"Why, I meant you, my child. You're one of my creatures. Of course, I must share you with the others, but I will always think of you as my own." The woman held out her good arm in a beckoning gesture, as a mother would welcome a prodigal daughter. Very slowly and sweetly she said, "Come back to Westgate, Puppet. We're your masters. You need us, and we want you back."

Alias's breathing came fast and heavy. "I'm my own master," she shouted angrily, "not anyone's puppet." With a sudden movement she jerked the hood from the woman's face.

She looked into her own face.

Alias screamed in her dream and woke with a start. The camp was back to normal. She sat near a dying fire in a roofless hostel. It was only a dream, she told herself over and over. She wondered how long she'd been asleep.

Only a dream, she thought again. Though a very bad dream. When was the last time I dreamed like that?

Never, the answer came from the back of her mind. You never dream like that. Ever.

The dream had to be magically influenced, Alias decided, and the woman in the dream had to be Cassana, the Westgate sorceress who branded me with one of these sigils. Why did she look like me?

Alias closed her eyes and concentrated on the woman in the dream. She didn't look exactly like me, Alias realized. The woman looked older. Perhaps she is a long-lost relative no one ever told me about. Who's Nameless, then?

Alias stood and stretched by the fire's dying embers. Her

thoughts remained fuzzy, and she had a difficult time concentrating on details. Am I still sleepy, she wondered, or is it possible I'm drunk on dream wine?

Then she heard a noise that set her hackles rising, a noise from her dream—the sound of a thousand hissing snakes in a stone room. The sound of a kalmari.

She whirled about, scanning the boundaries of the campsite, but the darkness defeated her eyes. She glanced over the campsite. Dragonbait lay curled like a cat. Olive snuggled in a nest of blankets. Akabar—there was only darkness where Akabar should have been.

Something in the darkness glittered, and Alias recognized the rows of needle-sharp teeth. Only then was she able to make out the silhouette of the beast. From the tear-drop shape extended a dark, prehensile tail. The creature's shadow shifted just enough for Alias to make out Akabar's sleeping figure. The kalmari wrapped its tail about him and began lifting the mage to its gaping maw. Muttering in his sleep, the Turmishman struggled feebly, trying to kick off the blanket entangling his legs, but he did not awaken.

With a shout, Alias leaped forward. Her movement was sloppy and awkward. Damn dream wine! I'm not sober, she realized as she accidentally kicked the sleeping Olive. The kalmari, still hovering with its tail firmly wrapped about the mage, fixed its unblinking, yellow eyes on the warrior.

Alias drew her sword but she hesitated, remembering that the barbarian's two-handed weapon hadn't even bloodied the monster. If the dream was true, her weapon was useless. But if the dream was true and the kalmari was indeed one of Cassana's creatures, then according to Nameless, it could be warded off with the sorceress's sigil on Alias's arm. If Nameless had been telling the truth. . . .

Frustrated with all the uncertainties, the swordswoman stopped analyzing the situation. Still holding her sword, she raised her branded arm over her head, wrist forward. Her arm felt heavy and sluggish, as though a solid gold shield were strapped to it. Damn wine! she thought. She gritted her teeth and kept the arm up. A brilliant, blue light shot from the sigils, illuminating the campsite and making the black, smoky form of the kalmari easier to discern.

Lacking the eyelids to blink in the strong light, the kalmari's elongated pupils narrowed to slits, and the creature floated backward the length of a sword. Its grip on Akabar was still firm, however, and it held its tail forward, using the mage as a shield.

I can keep the creature back, Alias thought grimly, but how do I get it to drop Akabar?

In her dream she had asked Nameless how to defeat the kalmari. He had told her, but the details of the dream were already drifting from her memory. Alias struggled to remember his words.

He hadn't told me what to do exactly. He'd said something about what the kalmari couldn't do. It couldn't eat something. It couldn't eat something twice. What nonsense! Alias thought. If you've eaten something, you can't eat it again, can you? Unless you're the kind of creature that regurgitates the bones of your victims.

Behind her came a high-pitched curse from Olive. "What in the burning lake is that?"

Ignoring the halfling, Alias lunged at the monster, slicing her blade through the extremity that entrapped the still unconscious Turmishman. The monster's hissing increased in pitch and volume. It was not Alias's sword that troubled it, though.

The closer she got to Cassana's creature, the brighter her brands blazed. Annoyed by the intense light or perhaps, as Nameless had said, afraid of its mistress's sigil, the kalmari retreated farther, though it did not appear ready to flee.

Alias's eyes roamed across the floor, looking for remains of the northern warrior or other travelers already consumed by the kalmari. Finding nothing to feed the creature, she lunged again, plunging her sword into one of the monster's eyes. Again, the beast moved away from the light of her arm, but showed no damage from her sword.

Sword. The barbarian's sword! The kalmari had spit out the barbarian's sword. A sword with a lion-headed hilt, just like the one Olive had plucked from the ruins.

The adventuress shot quick glances over her shoulder, her eyes scanning the rubble-strewn floor. Nothing. Alias cursed silently. It had been there before. What could have happened to it? Or who—

"Olive!" she shouted. "You found a sword with a lion's head grip in the ruins earlier."

"I vaguely recall something of that nature," the halfling answered.

"You must have it, damn it! Give it to me!"

"Really," the halfling huffed. "I was going to give it to you later as a surprise."

"I don't want to hear any excuses, just go get it!" Alias screamed.

"But it's on the other side of the wall—on the other side of the monster!" Olive squeaked. "Why can't you get it?"

"If I move away, it's liable to eat Akabar. It can't touch me, but if it asked for dessert I'd be inclined to serve you to it. Understand?"

Ruskettle muttered something that sounded like cursing in an un'nown language, but she nevertheless moved to Alias's ' swinging wide around the edges of the destroyed hostel and the kalmari.

Alias moved to her left, too, keeping the arc of her circle smaller so that she remained between the monster and the halfling. Then Dragonbait was at her left shoulder, fully awake, his sword at the ready. The sigils bathed them both in an eerie blue radiance. With Dragonbait clearing a path for her through the rubble, the swordswoman managed to back the kalmari into the corner of the hostel that still stood. Alias suspected the wall would prove no impediment to the monster's retreat, but perhaps it couldn't pass through the wooden beams without letting go of the mage.

There was a scrambling noise from the edge of the wall behind the kalmari. The kalmari's hissing grew louder and more threatening. It twisted ever so slightly, keeping one eye on the two warriors, while turning the other on the halfling pawing at the rubble not twenty feet away.

Alias's throat constricted in fear. Olive seemed to take forever pulling out the massive blade. The weapon stood taller than the halfling, and she could barely lift it. To Alias's horror, the kalmari turned both eyes on Olive. At that moment the halfling looked up and froze.

"Olive! Use the sword!" Alias shouted. "Use it to defend

yourself!"

Alias moved to her right, hoping to force the monster to turn its eyes from the bard, but the leaden feeling in her arm seemed to spread over her entire body, and she tripped over a fallen roof beam and sprawled across the floor.

Her body's heaviness persisted; her attempts to rise were met with failure. She felt not just drunk, but as though she'd been drugged. It was an effort just to raise her head to watch the kalmari close in on the bard. "Set the sword like a spear!" she cried.

Olive snapped out of her shock and raised the sword. Perhaps she'd only caught the last few words of Alias's command, or maybe she had some halfling-berserker blood in her, but Olive did not remain standing still, waiting for the monster to impale itself on the weapon. Instead, she charged the creature, holding the sword like a spear. Astonishingly, it looked to Alias as if Olive might succeed in skewering the monster—until the halfling slipped on a pile of broken roof shingles. The sword flew from her hands, and the bard crashed to the floor beneath the kalmari.

The kalmari smiled so broadly that Alias could see its grin from behind. The creature made the same rattling laugh as in her dream. Alias had a clear view of Olive's terrified face as the halfling looked into the throat of the kalmari—about to become an hors d'oeuvre before Akabar's main entree.

A blur of dark green shot across Alias's vision as, with one continuous motion, Dragonbait dashed toward the barbarian's sword, lifted it, leaped toward the kalmari, and plunged the weapon in the monster's back. The sword dug into the kalmari's form with a satisfying *thuck*. Dragonbait had to jerk the weapon out before he could strike again.

The kalmari made a high-pitched whine Alias hoped was a scream. Turning away from the halfing, the creature dropped the mage. Dragonbait swung again, this time striking the monster above its eyes, and the kalmari whined again, lashing out with its tail. With lightning reflexes, the lizard-warrior met the strike with the sword, severing the appendage. The monster whined again, now at an unbearable pitch, and came at Dragonbait, mouth first, obviously intent on swallowing the scaly warrior. Dragonbait threw the sword, point first, into the monster's maw.

The kalmari's smoky body disintegrated into a dozen tiny motes of darkness, which in turn ruptured into smaller fractions, like a drop of oil shaken in water. The bits of darkness were blown away on the night breeze. The barbarian's sword clattered to the floor of the devastated inn.

Shards of light pricked at Alias's vision and then faded. Her head dropped to the floor, and she allowed the darkness of unconsciousness to take her.

Through it all Akabar had remained asleep, snoring softly.

* * * * *

Alias awoke to the sound of Olive and Akabar arguing. By the sun's position, she could tell it was late morning. She felt a little hungover, and it took her a moment to remember the wine Nameless had helped her guzzle.

"Your story is most amusing, little one," the Turmishman was saying to Olive, "but just not probable. My dreams were pleasant and my sleep uninterrupted. I would have been awake in an instant if the events you described had truly occurred."

"I tell you, this thing was huge and black and had more fangs than you have hairs in your beard. Its mouth opened so wide—" Olive flung her arms out as far as they would stretch "—that it could have swallowed itself."

Akabar laughed. "It sounds to me as though perhaps my cooking was *mer a lammer* for you," the mage commented, using an expression in his native tongue. "Much and too much," he translated for the halfling.

Alias shook the last bits of sleep from her head. "Olive's telling you the truth, Akabar. Hard to credit, I'll admit, but she wasn't the only witness to the attack."

The grin disappeared from Akabar's face. "Why did it strike at me first, I wonder."

"Maybe you looked the tastiest," Olive suggested.

"The creature was a kalmari, impervious to normal attacks," Alias said. "It probably recognized you as a mage, and hence the greatest threat."

Then Alias remembered what Cassana had said in her dream. "I have reason to believe that it was waiting here for me," she added, "and that it belonged to one of the wizards who branded me. When I got close to it, the sigils began to glow again, something that also happened in the presence of the crystal elemental. Perhaps my foes have judged you too useful to me and have decided to have you removed. A demonstration to prove the futility of defiance."

"A kalmari," Akabar mused, no longer puzzled. "Yes, such things can hold a man in slumber. How did you defeat it?"

"Chopped it with a sword it had already swallowed."

"Ah, yes," the southerner nodded. "They cannot digest steel, so they spit it out. They can be poisoned by the very secretions that they've left on the blade."

"You've fought one before?" Alias asked.

"No," Akabar admitted. "I have read of them. They are a horror attributed to the Red Wizards of Thay, I believe."

Alias nodded.

"Even with a regorged weapon, it could not have been an easy battle. However did you manage?" he asked Olive.

Alias smiled. No doubt the bard had exaggerated her role in the destruction of the monster.

Olive looked down at her furry hands. "I got some help from Dragonbait."

"Where is Dragonbait, anyway?" Alias asked.

"I noticed him climbing that hill," Akabar said, pointing to the western slope looming over the top of the pass. "He was carrying a monstrous sword."

"Hmmm. You two start breaking camp," the adventureress ordered. "I'll fetch him, and we'll be off. I'm not inclined to hang around here."

Climbing toward the western slope, Alias heard Akabar chiding Olive. "Why didn't you tell me it was a kalmari instead of babbling on about a big, black, fang-toothed thing?"

Catching the sound of soft, whistling tones, Alias followed them to a spring-fed pool, where she found Dragonbait. The lizard had made a set of bird pipes, and the tune he twisted out of them, while sad and plaintive, was also exultant, a cry of loss and pain spun into beautiful music. Somehow Alias knew it was made to honor a fallen hero.

She sat beside the lizard and waited for him to finish. A

long, low mound of dirt stretched before him. When he was finished, he lay the pipes, very gently, on top of the newly turned earth and bowed his head silently.

A bird twittered in some distant glade. The air smelled of roses. Dragonbait finally looked up at her and smiled. Not really a happy smile, but a bittersweet one, though Alias doubted anyone but she could tell the difference.

"That the sword?" she asked, pointing at the thin grave.

Dragonbait nodded.

Alias sighed. "It could be magical. We could use a weapon like that."

Dragonbait shook his head, though Alias could not tell if he was denying the sword's possible enchantment or their need for such a thing.

"Someone else will only dig it up," she argued, though her own heart wasn't really in it.

Dragonbait shook his head again.

Alias sighed. "Okay. We'll leave it as a memorial. Come on now. We've already lost half a day, and we're tempting untrustworthy gods by staying here any longer." She patted the lizard's arm as she rose. His tightly knit scales reminded her of warm jewels, dry and smooth.

As she turned to make her way down the slope, it occurred to her that Dragonbait couldn't have known about the sword's owner. Unless he had the ability to sense an object's past or he had read her mind or . . . Alias halted in mid-step and turned around. "Did you dream the same dream?"

The lizard cocked his head as if he didn't understand.

"Never mind," she said, realizing that, though they did communicate with one another in a fashion, some questions were just too complicated for her to convey. "Just finish up here. We'll be waiting at the camp."

Dragonbait remained at the grave for a few moments, then rose and followed his lady out of the glade. The birds picked up his pipe-song and carried it throughout Shadow Gap, south into the Stonelands and north into the Dales.

❧ 13 ❧

Shadowdale

After inspecting his maps Akabar had assumed that Alias had overestimated the time it would take to reach Yulash. Her experience of the roads north, however, proved more accurate than the parchment image of the land he had purchased in Suzail. On his map, the road from Shadow Gap to Shadowdale passed through clear terrain, but in reality the land was quite different.

The route twisted out of Shadow Gap, and approaching the dalelands it climbed and descended numerous hillocks. Akabar found the land pleasing to the eye. Sheltered from the Great Desert by mountains, the Dales were nothing at all like the barren Stonelands to the south of Shadow Gap. The hills were lush with greenery and wildflowers.

On the third afternoon outside of Shadow Gap, a storm lost them half a day's travel. As they cowered in a vale beneath their waxed tarps, the sheet of black water falling from the sky was broken only by flashes of lightning.

The next day the rain continued, but with only half the ferocity. Horses, supplies, and clothing drenched, they took a quick vote. They decided to push on to Shadowdale rather than sleeping on wet ground again, even if it meant riding all through the day and night. Dragonbait abstained.

With the coming of night, the rain let up, but the moon and stars remained hidden behind dark clouds. They all shivered with damp and fatigue, but they pressed on. Just as the dawn light began to highlight ominous purple clouds with red streaks, they crossed the ancient bridge spanning the Ashaba River and looked out over Shadowdale.

The town of Shadowdale was the southern entrance to

the region of Shadowdale. Olive rambled on about the myriad legendary adventurers who had come from Shadowdale or had made it their base or who had retired there. She had never been there herself, she admitted, but Shadowdale was mentioned in more ballads, lays, and drinking songs than any other city in all the Realms.

As they passed the Tower of Ashaba, Olive tugged excitedly on the mage's robes, insisting he take in the sight of the off-center spire with its landing decks for aerial mounts.

Alias rode on without stopping, too tired to take in the sights. She had been here before, and the only sight that interested her now was a bed in The Old Skull, Shadowdale's inn.

Still, it was a relief to find the city standing and not a burned out shell. She hadn't been back for seven years, ever since the Swanmays had disbanded, but she had many fond memories of the town.

As they'd crossed the river, she'd spotted two new temples. Otherwise, nothing had changed since the time when the Swanmays had rescued Alias from servitude in Westgate and smuggled her north.

Alias had been the youngest of the seven women who made up the Swanmays, and a thumb-fingered fighter. If not for the shielding of the other members of the company, she would have been skewered in her first battle. But she'd grown into a seasoned swordswoman within three seasons, while the company earned its living guarding caravans through the Elven Wood.

The group had broken up over a foolish argument concerning a worthless man, and each member had gone her separate way. Alias found that she still cared enough about them all to wonder what had become of them.

Naturally, Alias had been closest to Kith, since they'd been closest in age. Kith had been a very beautiful young girl—so lovely she'd made Alias feel awkward and plain. Kith had been like a sister to her though. They'd even pricked their thumbs and become blood-sisters. Alias used to plait Kith's long, silky, chestnut hair and Kith had taught Alias to read and write. Kith had received her magical training in Shadowdale, from the river witch Sylune.

Maybe I'll visit Sylune before we leave here, Alias thought. If she can tell me her former pupil's whereabouts, I might look Kith up after I put this sigil mess behind me. It feels wonderful to remember something so fully. I can remember it as clearly as though I'm reading it from a book. I only left the Black Hawks a year ago, but their faces and names are fuzzy. Somehow, though, returning to Shadowdale has brought back all my memories of the Swanmays.

"An excellent reason to visit here, even if it weren't on the way to Yulash," Alias muttered.

"I beg your pardon?" Akabar asked, pulling his horse up alongside Lady Killer. Olive, on High Roll, and Dragonbait, leading Lightning, clomped far behind.

"Nothing," Alias replied. Just for a while she wanted to keep to herself the joy of these clear memories. Akabar could not possibly understand, and Alias didn't want the memories belittled by someone else's indifference.

The Old Skull had not changed a bit. The stalwart building of timber and stone still rose three stories high, its upper levels lined with windows.

The smell of smoke mixed with damp clay and fresh-baked bread attracted Alias's attention to the building next to the inn. She remembered it was the shop of Meira Lulhannon, a potter and baker. Funny, Alias thought. I don't remember noticing the smell before. Not that it's unpleasant, but still, you'd think it would stick in my mind.

The Old Skull's innkeep was Jhaele Silvermane, a pleasant, motherly woman who had joined the Swanmays for more than one evening of strong tales and stronger drink. Alias remembered that when she'd last visited the inn, Jhaele's son had grown sons, so Jhaele had to be at least in her late fifties by now. Her hair was grayer and the lines around her eyes deeper, but otherwise she looked just as Alias remembered.

If Jhaele recognized Alias she gave no sign. Alias, for her part, did not feel up to rehashing the good old days until she'd had ten hours of sleep and had cleaned herself up. So, from beneath her sopping hood, she asked if the Green Room, the Onyx, and Warm Fires were available. In The Old Skull, each room was decorated differently and given individual names, a custom that had, unfortunately, died out in more civilized and overpopulated regions like Cormyr.

Jhaele informed her that all three rooms were vacant and ready for guests. She gave Alias a curious look as she led the party to the third floor, no doubt wondering if she was a previous patron.

Olive grumbled about the inordinate number of stairs in human buildings. Even Dragonbait puffed and growled some. Alias didn't care, though. To her mind they'd rented the best rooms in the house.

Alias claimed Warm Fires, a room with three separate hearths, all blazing merrily. Akabar choose the Onyx, with its white carvings. Ruskettle sniffed at the wilderness scenes on the tapestries that completely covered the walls of the Green Room.

"This will do in a pinch," she declared, sprawling out on the bright yellow bedspread, and promptly falling asleep.

"Her room has no windows," Akabar noted to Alias as he closed her door. "Keeping an eye on her comings and goings will be that much easier."

"You don't say? That's just the reason the leader of my first adventuring group always reserved this room," Alias explained. "We had two sleight-of-hand artistes."

Akabar grinned. "If I'm not here when you wake, I'll probably be speaking with the sage Dimswart recommended."

"Fine." Alias nodded sleepily.

"Pleasant dreams," he wished her.

"Pleasdream," Alias mumbled, closing her door.

With Dragonbait already curled before the largest hearth, snoring deeply, Alias stripped off her clothes, wrapped the bed coverings around herself, and crawled onto the goose down mattress. She was awake only long enough to note the rain had started again, a steady drizzle which lulled her to sleep within minutes.

* * * * *

When Alias awoke, the rain had stopped and the sun was low in the western sky. She rose leisurely, stretching and yawning and wriggling between the warm sheets, luxuriating in what nine silver pieces a night could buy.

Finally, Alias sat up and looked around. Her clothes were spread before the blazing hearths. Dragonbait's doing, Alias realized, but where'd he taken himself to? she wondered.

The warrior yawned, stretched, and padded across the room, collecting what she would wear. From two floors below came the rythmic thumping of people dancing. The locals had already begun their evening festivities.

She pulled on her leggings, stiff from drying. Instead of an ordinary tunic, she chose from her pack a new robe, something made from wool dyed a turquoise color. Its long sleeves tied around her wrists, hiding her arms completely. Tonight she would forget her problems for a few hours if she could.

Dragonbait had already polished and dried her armor, but she was sick of wearing it. Tonight she would forget her profession, too. She wouldn't even bring her sword, not even peacebonded. She didn't need it for feasting, drinking, singing, or dancing. Besides, she was known in Shadowdale. No one here was an enemy.

She slid her remaining dagger in a boot sheath—only because daggers could be used in games, she told herself. She made a mental note to purchase another, to replace the lost one, but promptly forgot that, too. Akabar will remember, she thought with a grin.

Alias knocked on the mage's door. There was no answer, so she went down to the taproom alone. Olive was already there, holding court for a roomful of locals. Dragonbait sat at her feet. The halfling held her hands to her mouth, fingers spread and curled in imitation of fangs and then opened her arms wide. Alias realized she was recounting her battle with the kalmari.

A sudden anxiety swept over the swordswoman. The foolish halfling might babble about the sigils. It hadn't occurred to Alias to forbid the bard to mention them. Stupid, stupid, stupid! she scolded herself. Did she think she could rely on Olive's halfling sense of propriety?

Tonight of all nights she did not want to be identified as a marked woman, a magnet for danger.

"Your friend spins quite a tale," a mellow voice beside her commented. "How much of it is true?"

Alias turned toward the speaker. He was an attractive man, clean-shaven, well-dressed, with the lean body of a fighter. The only ornament he wore was a ring of red metal, inlaid with three silver crescents wrapped in blue flames. He had the smooth polish of the Dale's nobility, polite, but not stuffy, yet Alias could detect a trace of a western accent. He almost, but not quite, lost the "h" when he said the word "how." He's from Waterdeep, Alias thought.

"Depends on what she's saying," Alias replied with a smile. "And how many drinks she's had, of course."

"Of course." The man smiled back. "She says Shadow Gap is clear of the Iron Throne's monster. If that's true, the people of the Dales owe you thanks."

"Oh?" Alias said. "Olive hasn't explained how she alone defeated the monster with nothing but her quick wits and magical voice?"

A charming grin spread over the man's face. "No," he answered, "she admitted to relying as well on her prowess with a broadsword that once belonged to a barbarian god, a holy artifact of Tempus, or so we have been given to understand. Under the constant reminders of the creature at her feet, we have elicited a confession that you and the creature had some part in the affair as well."

Alias smiled fondly at Dragonbait. *Always where he's needed most, which right now happens to be keeping an eye on the halfling.*

"I get the feeling," the man continued, "that besides making the halfling share the credit, there's something specific the lizard-thing's keeping the halfling from mentioning. Her chatter is the usual bard tales about adventurers, red dragons, elementals, and royal weddings, but in every episode there is some point where the creature nudges her and she changes course, so to speak."

Alias had to force herself to remain calm. "We all have our little secrets, um . . . you haven't told me your name," she said.

"Mourngrym. Mourngrym Amcathra."

"Alias."

Mourngrym bowed his head. "On behalf of the people of the Dales, I thank you for ridding us of a fell beast."

"Your thanks are graciously accepted," Alias answered, bowing her own head modestly. Inwardly, however, she felt guilty. The kalmari was in the gap partly because of her. But she couldn't bring herself to spoil the one little moment of glory due her by confessing the truth.

Something about Mourngrym's official tone made Alias wonder just who he was. "Are you one of Lord Doust's men?" she asked.

Mourngrym smiled. "I had that honor until last year, when the good cleric retired. Not that he was too old for the job, but he wanted to spend more time with his family. He lives in Arabel now."

"Oh." Alias hadn't heard about that. Why hadn't she heard about that? Something that important happening, in such an important place, it should have been talked about for months. She had to have known. It must have been lost with the memories of the last year. "Who is lord of Shadowdale now?"

"Me," Mourngrym said, grinning.

Alias blushed deeply.

"I'm sorry," he said softly. "I thought you knew. If there is anything you need, I'm sure we can provide it. In thanks."

She had the lord of Shadowdale offering her whatever she needed, and all she could think of was her lost dagger. She wasn't going to bother him with something that small.

Someone struck up a reel on a songhorn, accompanied by the rhythmic thumping of a tantan. "How about a dance partner?" Alias asked shyly.

Mourngrym's grin widened. He rose, offered Alias his arm, and led her to the center of the floor.

The reel was fast and lively, and Alias loved every minute of it. Mourngrym was a fine dancer, and it had been a long time since Alias had done something so frivolous. When it was over her partner led her to a chair.

"Not as easy as swinging a sword, is it? What will you have Alias, ale or wine?" Mourngrym signalled the waiter.

"Wine, please," Alias panted. "I must have danced that reel a dozen times a night when I was younger. Of course, I wasn't so lucky in my partners back then. There used to be a dearth of gentlemen in this inn, and Kith and I always had to dance with each other."

"Kith?" Mourngrym asked.

"She was our mage," Alias explained. "Long ago I was with the Company of the Swanmays. We guarded caravans through the Elven Wood. We used to winter here."

The waiter stood at Mourngrym's elbow. "Ale for me, Turko, wine for the lady. Swanmays," he repeated as Turko hurried off. "Yes, *Elminster's Tales* mention them. Six women, all fairly hot-tempered, if I remember correctly."

"Seven," Alias corrected. "I was the youngest."

"Wasn't the youngest a mage?" asked Mourngrym.

"That was Kith," said Alias. "She was half a year my elder. She studied under Sylune for a short while."

"Yes, the witch mentioned her once," smiled Mourngrym. "Not too favorably, as I recall, but spellcasters are a temperamental bunch."

"Speaking of temperamental spellcasters, have you seen the other member of my party?"

"The Turmishman?" Mourngrym asked. "Aye, he came down late this afternoon and paid a lad a gold eagle to ask Elminster for an audience. He waited until about an hour ago, when Elminster's reply came back. The message was—and I quote Elminster's words—'Hie thy backside to my outer office and await there on my pleasure.' So your spellcaster is probably pacing the tower floor right now."

The waiter returned with their drinks.

"Good fortune," Mourngrym toasted, raising his mug.

"Good fortune," Alias agreed before she sipped the cold, pink liquid. She'd come to the conclusion that part of her curse involved not being able to enjoy ale. After her dream in Shadow Gap, she'd decided to try wine instead. The drink the waiter brought her was nowhere near as pleasant as the wine in her dream, but it was at least palatable and, with any luck, not so potent.

"Poor Akabar," Alias said. "Elminster must be this local master sage he was so anxious to talk to. Akabar is so responsible, he'll miss out on all the fun. I hope he isn't wasting his time. Is this Elminster any good?"

Mourngrym nearly choked on his ale. "Elminster? You used to winter here and you've never heard of Elminster the sage?"

Alias shook her head. "That was over seven years ago. I take it Elminster is someone new."

"Only as new as the Sunset Peaks and twice as craggy," the lord of Shadowdale replied, giving her a strange look. "He's been here forever. He's the wisest man in the Realms. He's the reason most people come to Shadowdale, though he doesn't usually hire his services out anymore."

Damn, damn, damn, damn! Alias thought. I've gone and spoiled everything again. How could I remember so much about this town, and not remember someone so important?

Alias lowered her eyes. "I'm afraid I have trouble remembering things sometimes," she explained.

"Well, as you said, that was seven years ago. You were young, and young people don't often take much note of old sages and their ilk," Mourngrym answered kindly.

The songhorn began another melody accompanied by Olive on her yarting.

"I remember this song, though," Alias declared. It was an elvish tune, but its lyrics were in the common tongue. It was about the Standing Stone, the monument erected to commemorate the pact made between the dalesmen and the elves of the wood over thirteen centuries ago.

Determined to put the awkward moment behind her, Alias began to sing, her voice clear and strong. The taproom patrons turned from the musicians to the swordswoman. Alias shifted her glance from one face to the other, catching the eyes of her audience, making them feel as if she sang for them. She spotted Dragonbait smiling at her, keeping rhythm with the end of his tail. The only eyes she did not catch were Olive's. The bard bent over her yarting strings, apparently too intent on her fingerings to look up.

When she finished, the room burst into applause. Alias blushed and turned back to the table. What could have possessed me to show off like that? she wondered. She had always kept as low a profile as possible in towns. Now she was behaving like a child. For a moment she thought of the runes, but there was no tell-tale heat or light coming through her sleeve.

The songhorn player came up to her table. "Excuse me,

my lord. Lady," he addressed Alias, "do you think maybe, if you have time, you might give me the words to that song? They were just wonderful. Did you write them yourself?"

"No. I learned that song here, to that melody. You've never heard the lyrics before?"

The musician shook his head. "No, lady. I learned the tune from an elf, but he told me it had no words."

"But I learned it here," Alias insisted.

"Sometimes these old songs get lost if they aren't written down," Mourngrym said. "Isn't that right, Han?"

"Yes, my lord," the musician agreed.

"I thought it was a common song in the dalelands," Alias said, growing a little frustrated.

"It will be soon, lady, if you tell me the words. With your permission, I'll sing it from here to Harrowdale."

"I'll write them down later," Alias promised the musician, "and leave them with Jhaele before I go."

"Thank you, lady." The young man smiled. "Excuse me," he said, bowed to Alias, and went back to his stool to play more sets with Olive.

Alias looked up and spotted Jhaele just then. "Would you excuse me, Your Lordship? There's someone I'd like to say hello to."

"Certainly," Mourngrym said, nodding. He watched Alias walk over to the innkeep, and then he turned to focus his attention on the musicians. The swordswoman was acceptable, he decided, a little addled maybe, but nice. From experience, though, he knew it wouldn't hurt to keep an eye on the halfling.

Alias went up to the bar, smiling at Jhaele. The woman smiled back, but still gave no sign of recognition, so Alias asked her, "Jhaele, do you remember the Company of the Swanmay?"

"Yes, I do." The innkeep's smile spread further across her worn features. "They were hell-raisers, that lot."

"How many were there?"

"Well, let's see. The two fighters, a pair of thieves, a cleric, and Kith, the would-be mage. Six in all. All women."

"You don't remember me?"

Jhaele stared at Alias for a long moment. "No, I'm sorry,

lady. I can't say that I do. The Swanmays would sometimes pick up strays, but none of them stayed in my memory, I'm afraid. I won't forget you now, though. Your song was wonderful. I'm honored you sang it in my taproom."

"But, Jhaele, you taught me that song," Alias insisted.

Jhaele laughed. "You must have me mistaken for another, lady. I can't sing a note. Never could."

Alias opened her mouth to laugh, thinking Jhaele was teasing her, but the sincerity in the innkeeper's face unsettled her. She blushed and fled through the door to the kitchen. Jhaele looked after her, but the swordswoman ran out the side door into the night.

"Something eating at that one," Jhaele muttered and returned to her chores at the bar.

The sun had just slipped behind the distant Desertsmouth Mountains, and the sky was a deep, dark blue. The night air was cold, but Alias was too furious to notice as she strode hastily away from The Old Skull eastward down the road toward the common and the river.

"This doesn't make any sense," she growled. "I wasn't some stray the Swanmays picked up! I was a member! For three seasons!"

It was one thing for this new lord, Mourngrym, to forget the tale of the Swanmays, but Alias had wintered twice in The Old Skull. She and Kith and Belinda had spent at least a hundred evenings in Jhaele Silvermane's company. The innkeep had mulled wine especially for them and taught them bawdy songs about men in general and certain male adventurers in particular. And Jhaele had taught her the song about the Standing Stone.

"How could she forget me?" Alias whispered angrily. Her throat constricted as tears welled in her eyes. She gulped uncomfortably for air.

How can you blame Jhaele, when you don't even remember Elminster? her conscience said. To hear Mourngrym describe him, you'd think this sage was a town landmark. I could not possibly have missed noticing him in a town as small as Shadowdale. And even if I had, according to Mourngrym I should have heard about him from people in the outside world. He's supposed to be famous.

Maybe, she thought, Mourngrym was exaggerating the sage's renown. Anyway, Mourngrym hadn't been here seven years ago either, so how could he know for sure if Elminster was around then? Maybe these *Elminster's Tales* that Mourngrym mentioned weren't all that accurate. How could this Elminster mention the Swanmays and not mention me? How dare he forget me?

Having passed the dozen or so buildings in the heart of town, and exhausted by her tirade, Alias considered going back to the inn to sleep. Secretly, she hoped that when she woke up she would discover the disappointments of the evening had all been part of another bad dream. That's about as likely as my tattoo disappearing in the morning, she taunted herself. She walked on.

She passed Tulba the weaver's house. Next to it was a small, well-beaten path leading up to the side of the grassy rise known as the Old Skull. She could just barely make out a dilapidated sign by the path. It was marked with an upturned crescent with a ball hovering between its horns.

Alias stepped onto the path to inspect the sign more closely. Below the symbol, in the common tongue, was written, "No Trespassing. Violators should notify next of kin. Have a pleasant day. —Elminster."

Alias's eyes traveled the length of the path up to the hillock, where it ended at a ramshackle building perched awkwardly on the side of the rise. It was a sort of tower, but so many additions were built against it, cluttered with further additions leaning against or built on top of them, that it was hard to pick out the original structure. However, a spire of solid stone reached at least three stories higher than all the more recent constructions. Thick vines of flowering kudzu covered the tower and additions.

Alias remembered every other building she had passed, from Lulhannon's pottery to the weaver's, but the path and the sign and the building were a blank. Alias had never seen them before. Ever. Not once in the thousand times she'd traveled this road. It was possible to miss a sage—he might have stayed inside all winter to protect himself from the cold—but she couldn't have missed this building.

The path could have been beaten hard in a year, the sign

could have weathered to look that old in seven years, but the building was ancient. Kudzu grew like crazy, but it would have taken centuries for its vines to grow so thick and high.

Maybe there were more trees here before, blocking the view, Alias mused. But then, wouldn't I have seen it from the top of Old Skull? I scrambled up there often enough with Kith.

With a surge of excitement, Alias began to wonder if Cassana and company wanted her to forget Elminster for a good reason. Maybe he could tell her more about her sigils than Dimswart. With a new determination, ignoring the sign, she strode up the path, planning to join Akabar as he waited on Elminster's arrival.

Reaching the building, she knocked loudly. She waited several minutes but there was no reply, even though lights could clearly be seen glittering in the upper windows of the tower. Certain that someone was within, Alias called out, "Hello," and knocked again even louder. A shadow went across one of the windows. Several minutes passed, but still no one answered her or came to let her in.

With just a trace of embarrassment, Alias tried the doorknob, but it would not turn. She tried other doors, and even a window, but found them all held fast. With a huff she spun about and marched back down the footpath.

At the road she turned east and walked down the left-hand fork of the road that followed the River Ashaba south. "I'm going to find someone who remembers me," she declared. "Sylune will remember me. She didn't know me well, but she never forgets anyone."

In her haste she was oblivious to the shouting that came from the tower behind her.

❧ 14 ❧

The Scribe
and the Old Man

"What do you mean, more forms?" Akabar bellowed, finally losing his temper. Secretly he hoped that his shouts would gain the attention of someone besides the bureaucratic fool of a scribe who stood before him—someone with the insight to understand the importance of his problem, someone who would rescue him from this morass of paperwork. Someone like Elminster.

"Well, ummm, here," Lhaeo the scribe said and pointed to a place on a form Akabar had completed over an hour ago. He blinked at the southern mage through a strange set of thick lenses wrapped in wire which perched precariously on his nose. "Here, where you mentioned that you have more than one wife, you should have gone to line twenty-three and listed all your wives' mothers' names, instead of line twenty-two, where you listed your first wife's mother's name. That error is going to require a special schedule HL, in order to keep our files straight."

"Files?" shrieked Akabar. "Look around you!" he demanded. "Does it look as if anything has been filed here in the last millennium?"

The question was purely rhetorical. The scribe's outer office, which also served as a waiting room for those seeking audience with the great Elminster, was a firetrap waiting for a spark. Parchment scrolls, leatherbound tomes, sheaves of loose leaves of paper, empty folders clearly labeled *Important* or *Confidential*, and bark textbooks stained with berry ink, and chalk dust lay on every available horizontal surface or leaned against a vertical surface. Colored streamers, on which were scrawled the most exotic letters, hung from the ceiling.

Besides the gray slate used to write temporary messages, such as *Attend Azoun's Coronation* and *Warn Myth Drannor of Attack,* there were stone and clay tablets and sheets of soft metals to hold more permanent messages, the ones to be handed down through history— *Pick Up Laundry* and *Pay Lhaeo.*

All this, of course, was a tribute to Lhaeo's ability to intimidate adventurers and keep them from disturbing Elminster. Akabar sensed this to some extent. At least, he could not believe that anyone, including Lhaeo, really gave a bat's dropping for what he wrote down. His perception was that Lhaeo's forms were some sort of test of his patience or intelligence or desperation. If he just stuck it out long enough, he was certain, Lhaeo would finally recognize his worthiness as a candidate and remind his master that a southern mage waited in the outer office.

However, Akabar had been waiting five hours—three at the inn and two in this dismal, cramped room. His patience was spent, his intelligence exhausted on figuring out the ridiculous forms. Desperation was his final strategy. He considered dashing from the room to the tower, but without Lhaeo's guidance through the maze of halls and doors and rooms, he wasn't sure he could find it. Even if I did find the stairs, Akabar mused, I have no guarantee that Elminster is in the tower.

Lheao shrugged. "You must understand, Elminster is a very busy man. This is the only way we have of determining if a problem is truly important enough to warrant interrupting his already overcrowded schedule."

"Just what size dragon does it take to land in this room to merit the sage's attention?"

"Oh, Elminster doesn't consult with dragons," Lhaeo assured the mage. "Consults on dragons, perhaps, but not with them. The sage is very, very busy, and he does not, as a rule, waste his time with dragons. That's what adventurers are for. And if, um, when you get in to see him, I would advise you to mention dragons as little as possible."

"Look," Akabar said, "I understand that the sage is busy. When I got his message to hurry over, I assumed he would see me on his dinner break or something."

"Dinner break?" The scribe used a delicate finger to push the wire rims around the lenses higher up his nose. "I don't think Elminster has taken a dinner break since, let's see . . . umm . . . this is the Year of the Prince, then that makes it . . ." Lhaeo consulted a calendar.

"Does anyone ever make it past this blizzard of parchment?" Akabar growled.

"Well," Lhaeo sat and thought for half a moment. "There was a delegation from the Forest of Anauroch."

"Anauroch is a desert, not a forest," Akabar said.

"Well, now it is, yes."

"Was that supposed to be a joke?" Akabar snapped.

"Am I laughing?" the scribe asked, looking at Akabar over the rim of his glasses.

"No."

"Then it couldn't be a joke, could it?"

"Look," said Akabar, "I realize the sage can't spare time for everyone. I wouldn't bother him with a petty problem. I'm a mage of no small water. Another member of the sage community, Master Dimswart of Suzail, was unable to handle all the complexities of my case. He recommended I see Elminster. I traveled all this way to do so."

"Oh!" Lhaeo exclaimed, his eyes lighting up behind the thick lenses. "You're a referral! Well, then we need to start again with a different set of forms. One moment, I'll get them." The scribe put his hand in a drawer and drew out a bird's nest of shredded paper. "No, this can't be them. They must be in that other cabinet."

Akabar counted to ten.

Far below, someone knocked on a door, but in his search for the referral forms, Lhaeo ignored it.

"Here we go," the scribe announced. "Last copy, too, so we need to fill out an acquisition memo to file with the local merchants for the next shipment of parchment." The referral form passed dangerously close to a candle flame. "Ooooh, singed it a little, but, uh, we can just, yes, we can just make out an addendum form to explain that the singed parchment was my fault."

From below, someone knocked again, only louder.

"Isn't someone going to answer that?" Akabar asked.

"Well, no."

"Why not?"

"It's way after business hours. We're closed."

"But, I'm here," Akabar said, then nearly bit off his tongue.

"So you are. We'll need another form for that. Nocturnal visitors."

The knocking stopped.

"Now, please, include as much information on the sage Dimswart as you can recall. What you asked him on this line, what he answered on this one, what he didn't tell you on this one. Any reasons you may have to believe he may have been incorrect on this line."

Akabar dipped a quill in the inkpot and began again. He wished he'd brought Alias along. Broadswords had such a nice, satisfying way of cutting through red tape. It wasn't until a minute later, upon discovering there was a form to fill out because Alias, not he, was the sage's real client, that Akabar lost his temper again and renewed his loud verbal assault on the sage's scribe.

* * * * *

Sylune's hut was atop a low rise overlooking the road and the River Ashaba. Alias remembered the dwelling as small but comfortable, covered with vines, with smoke always drifting from a chimney for a cooking fire. She remembered Sylune as a radiantly beautiful woman with shining silver hair. Kith had told her that Sylune was at least a century old but kept young with her magics. Alias had always suspected that Kith planned to use her power toward the same goal, improving and maintaining her looks.

The thought put a smile on her face that disappeared as Alias topped the rise. Illuminated by moonlight, Sylune's hut was nothing but rubble, its timbers and stone shattered and scattered along the hilltop. A rocky stump, once the fireplace, was the only indication that a dwelling had once stood there.

"Bhaal's breath," Alias cursed as she walked through the remains of the hut. The damage had occurred years ago. Her boots struck an occasional flagstone, but the majority of the floor had long since disappeared beneath grass and creepers.

The hairs rose on the back of the swordswoman's neck, and she realized Shadowdale was no safer a haven for her than Shadow Gap had been. She immediately regretted leaving her sword in her room. Then she thought, what difference does it make? The sword was useful against the assassins, but it could never have cut through the crystal elemental the way Dragonbait's did, and only the barbarian's sword could have defeated the kalmari.

Reason told her to flee back to the inn and the safety of her companions, but feelings of pain and anger overwhelmed her and made her fey. I'm sick of retreating, she thought. I want a fight.

"This is as good a place as any," Alias muttered. Her voice rose in volume and pitch. "First, there's the old ruin—an abandoned or burned-out shell. Darkness all around. The stage is set." She began shouting. "What are you waiting for, O mighty masters? Here's where the nasty, creeping horror lurches out at me, isn't it?"

She laughed. "What's the matter? Can't make up your minds what to send this time? How 'bout a beholder, all round with flashing eyes? Oh, no, wait! I've got it! Send a mind flayer or, better yet, an intellect devourer! It'll starve, you know, because you're driving me crazy!"

Her raging bellows carried across the Ashaba.

"Show yourselves, you cowards!" she shrieked, losing all control of her anger. "I'll teach you to make a puppet out of me! Come on, attack me! I dare you!"

"Well, I don't want to," a reedy voice answered her from the fireplace. "But if ye don't stop shouting, I will."

Alias whirled around, but all she could see in the dark was a shadow near the ruined stump of the hearth. She instantly came to her senses and reached down to grab the dagger from her boot.

"I'm . . . sorry," she whispered, still crouching, ready to cast the blade if the shadow made any sudden moves. It appeared to be an ordinary man, but then the kalmari had looked like an ordinary merchant in her dream until it was ripped asunder and the deadly cloud rose from its shell. "I thought I was alone up here."

"Talk to thyself often, do ye?"

"Well, I mean, I thought someone might be listening. Someone far off—hopefully."

"Keep shouting like that," said the shadow, "and ye'll bring the entire dale up here. I was about to lay a watch-fire. Do ye care to help me tend it?"

Without waiting for an answer, the figure turned away from her and knelt by the hearth. Alias stood up straight, and the tension she'd felt eased as the cool metal hilt of the dagger warmed in her palm. The figure by the hearth hummed an aimless tune while piling the logs and tinder together. There was a spark, then a second flash, and the dry tinder went up, casting a circle of light and warmth from the center of the ruined hut.

Illuminated, the shadow transformed into a beanpole of a man, dressed in weatherbeaten and stained brown robes. His gray beard was stringy and unkempt, and his hood was thrown back to reveal a balding pate which gleamed red from the flames of the fire. He seemed nothing more than an elderly, crotchety goatherd.

"If ye aren't going to take advantage of the warmth," the old man said, "at least come into the light so I can see ye use that dagger."

Alias stepped into the firelight, feeling foolish for having been caught raging at fate, but even more foolish for having threatened an old man. She sat down crosslegged before the hearth.

"I'm looking for the river witch Sylune," she explained.

The old man sat down facing her and leaned his back against the broken fireplace wall. He pulled a ball of tobacco from a pocket and used his thumb to shove it into a thick, clay pipe. He looked at her thoughtfully. "She's dead," he said quietly.

"What?"

"She's dead," repeated the old man. "Deceased. Here no more. People die. Even here." He lit the pipe with the end of a burning twig.

"How?" Alias whispered. The news hit her like a blow to the gut. She had never been close to Kith's mentor, but everywhere she went, anytime she felt close to getting some answers, her efforts were thwarted. I'd been counting on Sylune more than I realized, she thought.

"She died battling a dragon," the old man explained. "A flight of 'em descended on the region a couple winters back. They destroyed a bunch a' towns. One of 'em took advantage of Elminster bein' out of the country. When this dragon attacked Shadowdale, Sylune was the only power around. She didn't stand a chance, but she had this staff."

Alias realized that the old man meant a magical staff, a staff of power.

"She broke it across the critter's nose, and everything went up in a pillar of flame—the dragon, the staff, and Sylune. It happened right across the way there." The old man pointed to the other side of the river.

By the moonlight, Alias's eyes could just pick out the naked, burned-out area of the woods. "Damn," she whispered softly.

"Aye."

There was silence between them for a while. Then the old man spoke again. "I heard thy singing at Jhaele's," he said. "I never thought I'd hear that old song again."

"You know it?" Alias's head snapped up.

"I heard it once."

"Where?"

"Ye tell me first," the old man insisted, "where ye learned it."

"I learned it from Jhaele," Alias said.

The old man laughed. "Jhaele! Impossible. The woman's tone deaf."

Alias shrugged. "She doesn't remember teaching me, but she did. I know she did," she said vehemently.

The old man peered at Alias through half-closed eyes, considering her answer. Finally he asked, "Do ye know any other good, old songs? One about the moon maybe?" He pointed to the bright sphere. "And the lights that follow it?"

"*The Tears of Selune*," Alias said.

"It's a love song, isn't it?" the old man asked.

"Yes," Alias answered. "About how the goddess of the moon weeps because her lover, the sun, is always on the other side of the world."

"That's the one. Where'd ye learn it?"

"You want me to sing it?" she asked.

"That's not what I asked, now, is it?"

"No."

"Well?" the old man prompted.

Alias did not answer. He'd laughed when she said Jhaele had taught her the song about the Standing Stone. If she told him she'd learned *The Tears of Selune* from a Harper, he probably wouldn't believe that either.

As though he were reading her mind, the old man asked, "Do ye think ye learned it from a Harper maybe?"

It was Alias's turn to stare at him.

"Your short friend, the bard, was singing a song about Myth Drannor. She said a Harper had taught it to her."

Alias snorted. "Sounds like Olive."

"You sayin' she didn't learn it from a Harper?"

"She learned it from me," Alias said.

"Which leaves the question—where did ye learn these songs?"

"A Harper," she admitted.

"I thought so," the old man said smugly. "What was this Harper's name?"

Alias thought very hard, but she drew a complete blank. "I don't know," she whispered.

"I thought not," the old man said.

"No, you don't understand. I'm telling you the truth. I just don't always remember things."

"Oh, I understand, all right. More than ye know. I believe ye. Ye learned the song from a Harper, but he never told ye his name."

"That's not possible," Alias said, wracking her brain for memories of the Harper. "We were close. . . ." Her voice trailed off. She could not even remember the Harper's face, let alone where or how they had met. "He was a Harper," she insisted.

"He was," the old man echoed.

Warmed by the fire, Alias pushed her sleeves up to her elbows without thinking.

"An interesting tattoo you have there," the old man said,

nodding at her right arm.

Alias was about to pull her sleeve back down, but the old man snatched her wrist and pulled her arm toward him. The firelight flickered over the blue sigils. The markings remained still for the moment; they could almost pass as a normal tattoo. Yet, Alias felt uncomfortable revealing the sigils to strangers. "It's not mine," she said.

"Oh. Ye just rented it for the month of Mirtul?" the old man joked.

"Someone put it on me without my permission," Alias explained. "I must have been drunk." She shrugged.

The graybeard raised his eyebrows and squinted. "Nice work, nice work, indeed. I've seen naught like it. They aren't very nice symbols, are they?"

"What would you know about them?" Alias asked, trying to yank her arm back, but the old man's grip was surprisingly firm.

He tapped the sigil at the crook of her arm. "Flame Daggers," he muttered.

"Fire Knives," Alias corrected.

"Oh, right. Right. They're a guild of Thieves and Assassins from Cormyr. Young Azoun sent 'em packing. They operate out of a warehouse in Westgate now."

Surprised by the old man's knowledge, Alias quit struggling and let her arm rest in his grip.

"And the two below," she prompted him.

He snorted. "What do I look like? A sage?" he retorted.

"Well, yes, kind of," Alias said.

The old man chuckled. "Ye can't live in a town as small as this one without pickin' up stuff. Elminster's always out advisin' on the lambin' and the hayin', always tellin' stories. He could tell ye what these were without blinkin'."

"We've never met," Alias replied with a sniff.

"I suppose not. He doesn't care much for adventurers."

"Oh. I suppose he prefers greengrocers," Alias retorted.

"Greengrocers?"

"Townfolk. Farmers. Traders. People more interested in profit than adventure."

The old man chuckled again. "They've got land and a town to show for it. What have ye got?"

Alias had never thought about that before. She had some gold, but it would be gone before long. If she'd actually got a chest full of treasure from Mist, she could have bought herself some property. But then she'd be a greengrocer, too, and she had no intention of retiring, ever. All she wanted to do was travel freely throughout the Realms.

"My memories," she answered, but she knew that wasn't saying much, at least not in her case.

The old man grinned. "Ye are smarter than ye look." He tapped her wrist where the snake pattern wound about empty space. "There's nothing in this place."

"I got lucky, escaped before they finished, I think."

"Ye think so, do ye? Maybe."

"Do you know the other sigils?" Alias asked.

The old man was quiet for so long Alias thought he had drifted off to sleep. He let her arm slip from his grasp. Suddenly, he said, "Zrie and Cassana!"

Alias started. The old fool couldn't be just a goatherd and know that, unless . . . unless Olive had managed to babble something in the bar before Dragonbait could stop her.

"What do you know about them?" she asked.

"It's an old story, one that happened before ye were born—quite a scandalous one." The old man clucked his tongue and poked at the fire with a stick, sending sparks and flames flying.

"Well?" prompted Alias.

"A deep subject, that," the old man teased.

"The story," Alias insisted.

"Oh, the story of Zrie Prakis and Cassana?" the graybeard asked. "It's quite common, ye know."

"I've never heard it," Alias said. "They didn't know the story in Cormyr."

"Oh, Cormyr," the old man muttered. "Well, they wouldn't. But around here, in the Dales and in Sembia, I think everyone knows the tale. They turned it into an opera in the Living City. It's a long-winded piece where one character tells another to be quiet in a long, screaming five minute speech, and the other replies he'll be quiet in another long, loud five minute speech. Absurd thing, opera."

"The story," Alias whined.

The old man clucked disapprovingly. "Not the patient type, are ye? Ye know, if ye just sit quiet and listen, ye'll learn a lot more than if ye poke at people all the time."

Alias remembered that Nameless had said something very similar. It was true. She wanted the information poured into her. She didn't like the game of asking questions and then having to listen to all the roundabout replies people gave her. "Please," she asked.

The old man sniffed. "I ought to make you travel to the Living City and listen to the opera."

Alias glowered.

"Very well. I suppose that I'd better make it the short version before ye explode, hmm? Ye wouldn't appreciate the poetry of the tale, or the subplots of the opera, would ye? I'll cut to the heart of the matter.

"Zrie and Cassana met when they were both magelings. They fell in love, pledged their eternal faithfulness. Then they parted. In one version of the story their masters send them to the opposite ends of the Inner Sea for their journeyman quests. In another version, one of them lands in the ethereal plane and it takes him or her years to return. In the opera Cassana is kidnapped by pirates.

"Anyway, they each grow vain, proud, haughty, and very powerful. When they meet again, somewhere in the south, they end up burying their love for one another in an argument over who is the most powerful. They duel over it, and Zrie loses big. Cassana kills him. Not real tragic, considering what a mean-spirited cuss he was, but Cassana feels remorse over slaying her first and true love. Being, by this time, a basically sick, depraved person herself, Cassana packs Zrie's charred bones in a glass sarcophagus that she keeps by her bedside for the rest of her life."

The old man was silent for several moments. "That's all?" Alias asked.

"Of course, that's all," the old man snapped. "I didn't want to get ye all hot and bothered by going into too many details. In the opera ye've got to sit through a description of every pearl on Cassana's gown when Zrie first meets her. I don't imagine ye're much interested either in the story's symbolism or the implications it makes about the nature of power and evil, are ye?"

"No," Alias admitted.

"Then what's your problem?"

Alias shrugged. "Nothing. I was just hoping it would shed some light on how I got these things." She held up her arm to indicate the sigils.

"Ye could always go to the Living City and catch the opera."

"No, thanks."

"Do ye wish to hear the story about Moander?" the old man asked.

Alias looked up, startled. He did know a lot. He wasn't simply some old goatherd. To recognize most of the sigils on her arm he had to be some sort of wise man or mage. Probably an ex-adventurer himself. "I thought the elves banished him from the Realms," she said.

"They wish," the old man snickered. "No. The best the elves could do was use powerful enchantments to lock Moander up deep beneath the ruins of his temple in Yulash. They wiped out his priests and priestesses, hoping the god's power in this world would shrink to nothing if he was starved of worship."

"Did he?"

The old man shrugged. "Probably not. A lot of Moander's worshipers survived and fled south, where they resurrected the priesthood. Every now and then Zhentil Keep or Hillsfar forces—whichever one happens to be squatting in the ruins of Yulash at the time—come across a party of Moander worshipers trying to release their god. They're usually executed as looters, but they keep trying. There was this prophesy, see, about a non-born child freeing the Darkbringer—that's what they call Moander. The priests of Moander have tried to force the event, no need to go into the gory details about how they try and get non-born children, but so far they've all failed. Non-born child—mean anything to ye?"

Alias shook her head. "No. I remember being born."

The old man laughed as though she had said something funny.

Alias asked, "You know anything about this last one?" She

pointed to the blue-on-blue-on-blue bull's eye between Moander's symbol and the blank space at her wrist.

"It's a new one on me."

"That's just great," Alias muttered. She shoved the shavings of the twig into the fire, wiped her dagger clean, and sheathed it. "I knew the other ones already. This is the one I have to find out about."

"Why?"

"Because I don't know anything about it," Alias said, exasperated.

"Ye think it will make a big difference in thy life?"

"It might," she insisted.

"If I were ye, I'd work on the assumption that it is big and evil."

"Kind of broad assumptions."

"No broader than the one ye've obviously made about the sixth space by your wrist," the old man said.

"It's empty," Alias objected.

"There's nothing worse than nothing."

Reminded of her missing memories, Alias could not disagree. "You've been some help. Can I pay you something?" she asked, uncertain whether she would offend his pride.

"All ye have to show for thy adventuring life are thy memories," he reminded her. "Were ye planning to pay me in those?"

Alias smiled. "I have some gold."

"I don't need gold. Suppose I asked ye to never sing again. Ever. Would ye do that?"

"That bad, am I?" she joked.

"I'm serious."

Alias looked into the old man's eyes. He held her gaze without blinking.

"This is about those songs, isn't it? You didn't tell me— Who did you hear them from?"

"Probably from the same person ye did."

"A Harper?" Alias asked.

The old man nodded.

"What was his name?"

The old man did not answer.

"Tell me his name." Alias lunged forward and shook the

man by the shoulders. "Say his name."

A slow grin crept over the old man's mouth. "Why don't ye say it?" he asked.

"Because I don't remember it!" she shouted, shaking him with every word.

The old man put his hand up to her cheek and stroked it gently. "I'm sorry," he said.

Alias took a deep breath and released the old man. She slid out of his reach. "It's not your fault," she answered. "I just forget things sometimes. I'm sorry I shook you. I don't know what came over me."

"Not remembering makes ye angry?"

Alias hesitated. It didn't make her angry. She looked into the old man's eyes. "It makes me frightened, and that makes me angry."

"A terrible curse, not remembering," he whispered.

Alias shrugged. "Could be worse. Could have forgotten my own name."

"What's that?" the old man asked.

"Alias."

"Unusual name."

"It's pretty common in Westgate," Alias said.

"Is it, now?" The old man chuckled.

"Why won't you tell me the Harper's name?" Alias asked.

"I'm an old man. . . ." His voice trailed off.

"Are you saying you forgot it, too?"

Her companion did not reply.

"You won't lie about it, will you. You haven't forgotten. Why won't you tell me?"

"Harpers are a secret organization."

"You've taken some sort of oath?"

"I can't tell ye," the old man said. "I'm sorry."

Alias sighed.

"If I told ye about the sigil ye don't know, would ye agree not to sing?"

"You do know it!" Alias growled.

The old man shook his head. "No. But I might be able to find out. Would ye pay me what I ask?"

Alias tilted her head in puzzlement. It was a stupid request, but she had to consider if the information were worth the price. It might help her keep a step ahead of Cassana, Fire Knives, and company if she could discover the last secret partner. And, after all, she was a swordswoman, not a damned bard. Olive might be a little disappointed if she stopped teaching her songs, but no one else would care.

Except me, she thought. Singing has consoled me when I grieved and brought me joy and pleasure when times were better. Everyone sang. Even people with no talent for it. Nine circles of Hell! Even orcs sang. How could anyone ask anyone else to give that up? Why? It isn't my singing the old man objects to, she realized, but the songs themselves. But they're good songs. Everyone likes them. A Harper taught them to me.

Suddenly, the old man made Alias nervous. She slid farther away from him and rose to her feet. "I won't!" she answered. "They're good songs! They deserve to be sung! How can you ask such a thing? It's cruel, wicked, evil!" She backed away from the fire, turned, and fled down the path.

The path lay in the hill's moonshadow. Alias had a difficult time picking out the trail. She sunk her right foot into a chuckhole filled with water. She lost her balance and came down hard on her left knee, her body sprawled across the wet, muddy ground.

She heard a chuckle on the path behind her. She could see her own shadow in the soft, glowing light coming up behind her. Then a hand reached down under her arm and lifted her to her feet. It was the old man's left hand. In his right he held a yellow crystal that illuminated the area around them evenly, without the annoying flicker of a lamp.

"Are ye all right?" he asked.

Alias yanked away from her rescuer without replying. Her right ankle ached some, but she did not think it was a serious sprain.

"Ye'd better take this," the old man suggested. "It's a finder's stone. Help's the lost find their way." He held the glowing crystal out toward her. His features, lit from below, looked sinister.

I ought to give him a shove and run off again, she thought, but she couldn't resist the temptation to ask, "How much is it gonna cost me?"

"Mourngrym thought we should help out supplyin' ye, in thanks for takin' care of the monster in the gap. Just doin' my bit."

At the mention of Mourngrym's name, Alias felt a little calmer. The lord of Shadowdale had been gracious, and, well, normal, even if some of his citizens were a little strange. She reached out with her sword arm. The blue sigils reflected back the light, but remained still. She took that as an indication the stone wasn't some harmful magic, like the crystal elemental or the kalmari. She took the stone from the old man's hand.

She looked up at the old man and held his eyes for a dozen heartbeats. "Why?" she whispered.

"Try to remember this, Alias," he said, "good and evil aren't always." He turned about and began climbing back up the hill.

"Aren't always what?" Alias called after him.

"Good and evil," he called back.

Alias watched until his retreating form disappeared into the darkness. She had no idea what he meant, but she was grateful for the light.

"Thank you," she whispered. Then she jumped. She thought she heard the old man whisper, "Ye're welcome, Alias," right in her ear. Only a freak breeze and my imagination, she tried to assure herself. Even so, she scurried down the path and headed back to town, tired of the night's adventuring.

* * * * *

Back atop the hillock that once held the hut of the river witch Sylune, the old man used a stick of charred wood to sketch out Alias's five sigils on one of the flagstones. He tapped the unknown one with his stick and frowned.

"Why is it," he muttered, "that the years seem to fly by, but the nights seem to last forever?"

❧ 15 ❧

Olive's Deal and Dragonbait's Secret

It was long past midnight when Olive weaved her way to bed. The local merchants had been thankful for the figurative nose-tweaking Ruskettle and her companions had given the Iron Throne by destroying the kalmari, and they showed their appreciation in the form of several kegs of Jhaele's finest ale.

It was no Luiren Rivengut, Olive thought, but still a potent brew. With Akabar off kissing up to some high sage, her high-and-mighty ladyship disappearing into the night, and the lizard watching everything mutely from a corner, someone had to accept all the congratulations and free brew being passed around.

Actually, Olive had a dim recollection of Alias returning to the inn. At the time, the bard had feared the sell-sword might resume her foray into musical entertainment, but Alias had simply hurried to her room.

The trouble with humans, thought the halfling as she rested on the second story landing, is that they're no fun at parties.

She glared at the stairs she had yet to climb. And their buildings are the wrong size, she added. No doubt her ladyship thinks it amusing making me climb steps that come up to my knees.

Olive wondered if some servant would carry her up to her room if she pretended to pass out. More likely, she realized, they'd call out her ladyship or her pet lizard to dispose of my body. It doesn't matter, anyway. I'd never willingly suffer the indignity of being carried by a human. It's bad enough putting up with the pats on her head. Some day,

Olive knew, she'd take a bite out of one of those hands—. when she could afford to be considered a "tempermental" artist.

"Happy thoughts, Olive-girl," she muttered to herself. That was her motto when living among humans. No matter how patronizing or cruel or stupid they are, she told herself, keep a smile plastered to your face. Tonight wasn't too hard. This celebration, she realized, was the group's first tangible reward since they rescued me from the dragon.

Olive ordinarily would have considered herself a fool for offering to share the loot she'd secreted from the red's lair, but the halfling had been grateful to Alias for her rescue. She'd even forgiven the sell-sword for lugging her around like a sack of potatos as they made their escape.

For a foolish human, Olive thought, her ladyship sure knew what made dragons tick. Olive shivered at the thought that, were it not for Alias, she would still be a prisoner beneath the Storm Horns, wasting away until she was too feeble to sing. Then the dragon would make a light meal of her, an appetizer before a hearty meal of a herd of cattle or a brace of villagers.

This thought distressed Olive so badly that she craved the comfort of a late snack. However, the thought of all those stairs deterred her from raiding the kitchen.

She scrambled up the remaining stairs quickly, to get them over with, then zigzagged down the long corridor to the Green Room. She was sober enough, however, to notice the bits of shaved wood on the floor before the door.

Olive had put the wood shavings between the door and the jamb at halfling waist-level, where a human was unlikely to spot them fluttering to the floor should they open the door. In her mind rose the image of someone malicious pawing through her things, looking for treasure.

The halfling knew that the mage hadn't come back yet and the lizard was still sitting by the taproom hearth. Could it be her high-and-mightiness? Olive wondered. Or an outsider?

Olive turned the knob slowly and eased the door open a crack. With her eye to the opening, she could see the human-sized overstuffed chair and tea table that stood opposite the bed. A single, tallow taper illuminated the room, affording Olive a sight to warm the chilliest of halfling hearts. A small figure seated in the chair was counting and recounting high stacks of thin, glittering, silverish coins.

"Ahem," Olive coughed politely.

The small, seated figure looked up. An inhumanly wide grin spread across his childish face. He was a male halfling dressed in the robes of a southerner.

"Excellent," her guest said. "I wondered how long it would be before you stopped taking bows and decided to retire for the evening."

"An artist never tires of her audience," Olive replied as she entered the room, scanning it for other intruders. There was no one else. "Though, alas, the opposite is often true," she added.

"But there are audiences, and there are audiences."

"True enough. But that is a discussion for another day. Who now graces my presence with this display of breaking and entering?"

The little figure slid from the chair and took a moment to smooth his robes. Then, he thrust out a hand and said, "Call me Phalse."

Olive closed the door behind her and stepped forward. She gave Phalse's hand a single, brief squeeze, as was the custom among halflings. "False what?" she asked.

"Just Phalse will suffice for now," the intruder answered, smiling smugly.

He had the most peculiar eyes, Olive noted. Dark blue where the whites should have been, sky blue irises and pupils the blue-white of hot iron. It must be some trick of the candlelight, she decided.

"You are Olive Ruskettle, companion to the warrior Alias?"

"We're traveling in the same direction," Olive corrected, hoisting herself onto the mattress and perching on the edge. Phalse hopped back into the chair and leaned back against the cushions with his legs stretched out across the seat.

"And your destination is . . . ?"

"I'll know when I get there," Olive replied. "Bards need to travel, to gain information, pass on tales."

"I see," Phalse said. "I think I have a tale for you." Carefully, he pushed a single stack of coins across the tea table in Olive's direction.

The bard kept her eyes on the coins. From the bed, she could see they were not silver, but platinum. Keeping her voice as level as she could, she said, "I'm always interested in tales."

"I thought you might be," said the other halfling, flashing another wide grin, a grin too wide for a human and almost too wide for a halfling. "It's a tale about two people who were traveling in the same direction. One was a woman, the other a human female."

"Is this woman a bard?" Olive asked.

"If it makes a suitable story," Phalse replied, pushing another stack of coins toward Olive.

"This human female had done something horrible. She was a very sick human female—she carried a curse, you see, a curse which could not easily be removed. Fortunately, certain powers were seeking to capture and imprison her until such time as a cure might be found for her.

"Unfortunately, part of this human female's curse was that she deliberately avoided these powers. As a matter of fact, this human female killed all the agents sent to bring her back to those who would help her. Of course, the woman who was a bard knew nothing of this; she did not realize what peril she was in."

A third stack of platinum joined the first two.

"Horrors," Olive said, her voice still even, her eyes still glued to the money on the tea table. "What could this woman who was a bard possibly do when she found out these things? I take it this human female was much, much bigger and stronger than the woman who was a bard?"

"True," Phalse said, "but according to the tale a helpful stranger approached the woman and offered her a ring set with a yellow stone." He twisted his wrist and revealed a golden band set with a large, jagged crystal.

"Nice palm," Olive complimented. "I almost didn't see it. What does this tale say is the ring's power?"

"The tale doesn't say, exactly. Only that the stranger offers it to the woman who is a bard as a token of appreciation from these powers, should she agree to continue traveling in the human female's direction and keep an eye on her."

"I fail to see why any woman, bard or no, would hang around a human female if she were so powerful and posed such a threat. Would this human female have a short, dragon guardian and a human mage for companions?"

"It would make a good tale," Phalse agreed.

"Personally, were I this woman," Olive said, "I would seek to put great distance between me and the human female in question, having been warned that she poses such a danger. What could possibly encourage the woman in your tale to remain near this dangerous human female?"

"Well, for one thing, this woman wanted to do the right thing and help these powers find this human female before she did anymore horrible things. This woman who was a bard was brave and clever enough to manage it."

Phalse shoved his remaining stacks of coins toward the others. One of the stacks toppled, and the slender coins bounced and rolled about the floor in a mercantile dance. Phalse did not interrupt their ringing, clattering music. He simply continued to smile.

As Olive watched the spilled coins, her mind raced toward a decision. She had no reason to doubt this "tale" was not a true one, and several incidents supported it. Alias had, by her own admission, attempted to murder a priest and later, right before Olive's very eyes, tried to assassinate a Cormyrian nobleman. Who knows what else she had done? Olive thought. The tale would explain why Alias chose to travel north to Yulash and avoid Westgate, as well.

If her ladyship's road leads to imprisonment and not treasure, Olive realized, this would be a good time to begin saving for the inevitable rainy day. Besides, the sell-sword knows a lot of interesting songs. Naturally, we'll have to come to a parting of the ways in the future. She sings just a little too well, and she sings for free—very unprofessional. I have enough problems without adding competition from my own bodyguard to the list.

"If I'm to wear this ring myself," the bard said, "I have to know what it's for. I'm no fool."

"The ring will let these powers know your location at all

times, so they won't lose track of the human female's trail. Then these powers can all close in on her at once, making her capture a little less . . . messy."

"Is that all?"

"That is sufficient. For the moment."

"If these powers are so powerful, why don't they just use scrying magic to keep track of her?"

"Alas, something very peculiar about the woman prevents them or anyone else from doing so."

"How'd you—um—this stranger know where to look for her to offer the woman bard this ring then?"

"The human woman is known to frequent certain haunts. These were staked out by various agents, including the humble stranger."

"Couldn't they plant the ring on the human female?" Olive asked.

"No," Phalse explained. "It must be carried by a halfl—by the woman who was a bard."

"What makes this humble stranger so certain that the woman who's a bard won't accept his offer and then throw away the ring and leave the company of this dangerous human female?"

"In that case, she could easily be found by scrying magic, and she would be dealt with . . . accordingly."

"The woman who was a bard might develop doubts about the humble stranger's motives and throw away the ring and remain in the company of the human female."

"In that case, eventually, the powers seeking out the human female will find some other way of tracking her. Then the woman who is a bard will realize she should have kept her end of the bargain. Alas, by then it may be too late, since the servants these powers might have to employ to capture the human female are neither gentle nor kindly beings. And the humble stranger would not be inclined to intervene on behalf of the woman who was a bard to ensure her safety." Phalse's smile was now as wide as a cat's, revealing a mouth full of sharpened teeth.

"You're not a halfling," Olive said, a note of surprise escaping into her otherwise steady speech.

"Dear Olive, I am as much a halfling as you are a bard."

Phalse's smile spread until it almost split his head.

Olive gave Phalse a blank stare.

"Oh, I realize that everyone you've run into so far assumes that a halfling bard is merely one of those wonderful things they have never experienced, but the well-traveled will always recognize you for a charlatan."

"I can sing, play, and compose original verse," Olive replied, her tone quite chill. "It seems to me, therefore, that the burden of proof lies on my detractors. Threats of slander are ill-advised, especially here in Shadowdale where I already enjoy the gratitude of the population."

Phalse bowed his head in acknowledgement. "Bard or no," he said, still smiling that frighteningly large smile, "you are a halfling, and I have never seen a halfling walk away from a table full of coins."

Olive did not reply immediately. She would like to turn down Phalse's offer, just to replace that grin with a look of astonishment. People did not endear themselves to her by suggesting she did not take her art seriously. But the platinum coins were so beautiful. Not only their color and size and shape and the ringing sound they made, but the sheer number of them. Enough to wash your hands in, as her mother would say.

Olive sighed. "You are a good judge of halflings."

"I'm sure you know the saying—a halfling will never sell her own mother into slavery. Not—"

"—when she can be rented at a greater profit," Olive said sourly, beating the pseudo-halfling to the punchline. She hated that joke.

Phalse interpreted her knowledge of the saying as agreement. "Do we have a deal?"

Olive gave herself a moment to brood over the offer. As far as she could see, it would bring her no harm. Phalse's friends would take care of the sell-sword long before she caught on to Olive's treachery.

The halfling would miss the warrior. She'd have to get Alias to teach her as many songs as possible before Phalse's friends caught up with her, but then the songs would be Olive's. The unpleasant scene tonight, where Alias had swept the halfling's audience away and then returned it like a plate full of meat cut up for a child, would never happen again.

She'd miss traveling with this particular set of companions, too. They were the first adventurers who hadn't forced her into the role of cook. But who knew? Maybe Akabar would come out of this unscathed and she would travel with him to the south.

Olive had no doubt that Phalse's friends would succeed. And Dragonbait would probably lose his life defending Alias, though gods knew why. Olive didn't see that her decision made too much difference in the long run. She was, at worst, only hastening Alias's capture.

"I find your tale most interesting. Well worth the price. Leave the ring. And the coins. The woman who is a bard will stay with the human female."

* * * * *

Akabar awoke with a stiff back from having spent an uncomfortable night in an overstuffed armchair. The morning light illuminated dancing dust motes in Lhaeo's office. The scribe sat at the desk, still scribbling on parchment, just as he had been when Akabar dropped off last night.

Akabar yawned and stretched. "Noble scribe, I don't suppose the sage is awake yet?"

"Oh my," Lhaeo said as he looked up at the Turmishman with a startled expression. "He's been here and gone. He rises early, when he does go to bed."

"What!" Akabar shouted. "You mean he's left?"

"Oh, yes, definitely. He's gone on an extended tour of the planes. You just missed him."

"Why didn't you wake me?"

"Well," the scribe replied matter-of-factly, peering over the rim of his wire-framed lenses, "I didn't have the proper form."

The door nearly snapped off its hinges as Akabar yanked it open and threw it against the wall. But, like many wizard-built things, its fragile appearance was deceptive. It had survived many men angrier than the mage and would survive many more in the future.

Lhaeo made a reproving *tch-tch* sound as the Turmishman stalked away from the building without closing the door behind him. With a wave of his quill pen, he closed the door quietly, and the scribe returned to his work.

Akabar stalked down the hill, cursing vehemently. He reached into the tongues of Calimshan and Thay to find the right invectives, pronouncing them all on the head of the Sage of Shadowdale. The availability, and hence usefulness, of any sage always seemed to be in inverse proportion to his learning. Dimswart had not exactly been a genius, but he had been a pleasant host and a useful resource. Elminster must be the most learned sage in the Realms, Akabar concluded, owing to the fact that no one could ever talk to him!

As he passed the warning sign at beginning of the path leading to Elminster's, Akabar heard a voice coming from behind the weaver's shop. Its tone was low and serious. Akabar would have ignored it, mired as he was in frustration and anger, but he caught the words, "Alias, the warrior woman."

He froze in his tracks. He could not have been mistaken. The voice was unknown to Akabar, who prided himself on his recognition of voices as a way of remembering customers. The speaker's voice was succinct enough for that phrase to carry over the high hedge. It was probably only a townsman reporting the story of how Alias had cleared the kalmari from the gap, but Akabar, his curiosity aroused, was overcome with the urge to peek through the hedge and see the speaker.

As Akabar crept up to the hedge, the scent of freshly baked bread wafted over him, setting his stomach rumbling and reminding him that he hadn't eaten for over twelve hours. Then he heard the same voice say, "I think ye will find ye are mistaken," then pause, then say, "I did not mean to question thy discernment—" then pause again. This led Akabar to the conclusion that there was a second speaker who spoke too softly to be heard by any but the first speaker. When the mage finally discovered a break in the greenery, that was not what he saw.

The first speaker was a tall man, taller than Akabar, and thin, with expressive hands withered with age. He wore a cloak with the hood pulled up, and his back was to the hedge, so Akabar would not have been able to identify him even if he had known him. But the person the hooded one spoke with was known to Akabar. It was Dragonbait.

The lizard knelt on a bench beside a vat of water he must have commandeered for a washbasin. He held a fluffy, brown towel up to his chest.

The hooded one stood opposite him on the other side of the vat. He asked Dragonbait a question, but all Akabar caught were the last words—"remain here?"

What puzzled Akabar, besides the lizard traveling down the road to wash, was that the hooded one stood before the lizard, still and attentive as though he were listening to the creature. Yet Dragonbait remained mute. The scent of roses from some garden caused the Turmishman's nose to twitch irritably. He held his fingers up to his nostrils hoping to stifle the sneeze he felt coming on.

"I can offer ye much," the hooded one said. Then his words grew more quiet. But the last one was clear to Akabar—*home*.

Dragonbait whistled, not with his lips as a human would, but from the back of his throat. It was really only a wheezing cry, but it conveyed the same sense of awe a human whistle would have.

"Once they're removed, ye'll be completely free," the hooded one continued, pointing to the towel Dragonbait clutched to his chest.

Dragonbait dropped the towel on the bench.

Akabar gasped, fortunately not loudly enough to give himself away. There on Dragonbait's chest was a snaking pattern entwining sigils by now quite familiar to the Turmishman. In the same bright blue colors, the same symbols Alias wore on her arm were imbedded into the lizard's green scales!

Only the shape of the lizard's tattoo was different. While the sigils on Alias's arm lay in a straight line, those on Dragonbait's chest were arranged at the points of a hexagram. At the top-most point, the joining snake pattern wound about an empty space. Clockwise from that lay the Flame Knives marking; then the interlocking circles once so aggressively defended by Zrie Prakis; at the bottom, Cassana's squiggle; then Moander's unholy symbol; and finally the unknown bull's eye sigil.

Akabar's mind raced. Is this the bond that keeps the lizard so close to Alias? If she knows of it, why hasn't she told me? Of course she doesn't know it. The lizard has kept it a secret from her. That's why he's come all the way down here to wash. No doubt he is afraid of losing her trust if he reveals that he too is branded. Is he truly just a benign companion helping her evade her enemies or is he one of the enemies' servants helping to track her?

Akabar caught one last phrase spoken by the hooded one. "Sure ye will not accompany me?" he asked.

Dragonbait hissed and shook his head.

"Ye've chosen the hardest path. I'd wish ye Tymora's grace, but I don't believe in it." The hooded one turned to leave.

Hastily, Akabar leaped back to the path and began walking toward the road to conceal his eavesdropping. But when the Turmishman rounded the hedge, the hooded one had vanished and Dragonbait's back was turned as he pulled on a shirt of kelly green cotton.

Confused by the hooded one's disappearance, but anxious to see Dragonbait's reaction to his own sudden appearance, Akabar called out cheerfully, "Dragonbait? What are you doing here?" as though he'd just spotted the lizard.

Dragonbait wheeled about and went into a defensive crouch. Startled, Akabar fell back a step. Hardly the behavior of an innocent creature, the mage thought. Aloud, he chided the lizard, "Jumpy this morning, aren't we? I just got through at the sage's. Are the others at the inn?"

Dragonbait glared at him suspiciously and nodded curtly.

"Well, you had better come back there with me then." The lizard continued to glare at him.

"Can't have you dawdling about people's backyards," the Turmishman joked. He felt as though he were addressing a wall, and a hostile wall at that. Dragonbait's gaze was like a snake's, unblinking and unwavering.

Finally, the lizard turned and snatched up his towel and cloak from the bench by the water vat. Akabar could tell something long and stiff was wrapped in the cloak.

Undoubtedly the creature's sword. Dragonbait pushed past the mage without a sign or sound and headed down the road toward the inn.

As he followed Dragonbait through the town, Akabar marveled at the creature's rudeness. In Alias's presence, he was always the polite, servile clown. Perhaps he really is an arrogant servant of some sinister power, Akabar thought. His conversation with the hooded one must have upset him greatly. He's dropped his guard and revealed himself.

If he told Alias of Dragonbait's behavior, with no one else to substantiate his words, would the swordswoman believe him? Probably not. Alias was very attached to the lizard. She felt safe with him.

Which left Akabar to decide whether or not to tell the swordswoman of the markings on her scaly follower's chest. Trying to get the creature to remove his shirt to prove it would no doubt prove painful and perhaps even violent. And was no guarantee of Alias's reaction. It was possible that she would perceive the lizard keeping his markings hidden from her as an act of betrayal, but it was more likely that she would feel even more attached to him, believing him to be a fellow victim. Were Akabar to try to convince her otherwise, she would no doubt accuse him of jealousy or paranoia.

No, he would be better off waiting, keeping a close watch on the lizard until he could discover some incontrovertible proof of the creature's guilt. But would it be too late by then? he wondered.

As he reached The Old Skull, Akabar remembered he had one other subject which required some consideration— his meeting with the sage. Alias, intent on reaching Yulash, had not really shown any interest in the mage's self-appointed mission to the sage of Shadowdale, but it would not have slipped her mind. She would ask about it. In the face of his uselessness the evening Dragonbait had destroyed the kalmari, the Turmishman was loath to confess his failure to gain an audience with Elminster.

* * * * *

The hooded one flipped down his shadowy cowl and

shook out the full, gray beard that he had kept tucked within it. "Surely our guest hasn't given up waiting on my pleasure so soon," he joked.

Lhaeo looked up and shrugged. "For a magic-user he seemed a bit impatient."

"Takes all types," Elminster commented sagely as he threw his cloak over the chair Akabar had only recently vacated. He sat down and stretched out his long legs.

"Did you discover what you needed to know?" Lhaeo asked.

"I have all the pieces of the puzzle and I have put them all together. But the picture makes no sense."

"Oh?" Lhaeo said, a little surprised.

"I may have to make that journey to the other planes after all."

"Shall I begin packing?" Lhaeo asked.

"Not just yet," the sage replied. "There's a good chance the puzzle may just throw itself on the fire." But a rare ache crept over his bones and he knew he was wrong. "In the meantime, maybe ye'd better dig some of the old Harper scrolls out of the vault."

Lhaeo nodded and slipped out of the office jangling a set of great iron keys. Elminster retired to his study to research a single puzzle piece.

Back at The Old Skull, oblivious to the sage's concern, the four adventurers tended to their own business.

Akabar worried about the meaning of the sigil he had been unable to trace and considered how to trap Dragonbait into betraying himself.

The lizard kept his own council and told no one of his plans.

Olive counted the platinum coins four more times, finally tucking them neatly into the pockets of her backpack.

Alias slept the morning away, and when she awoke in the early afternoon on the last day of Mirtul, she felt refreshed and peaceful.

♣ 16 ♣

Run Aground

Giogioni Wyvernspur, suddenly aware of his duty to posterity, began the first entry in his journal, despite the inconvenience of the rocking boat. With a stick of soft lead he scrawled:

The last day of Mirtul has dawned fair and bright, and the Dragonmere's southern coastline is now in sight. The trip across the lake from Suzail has been a pain in the britches. The ship, on which that cad Vangerdahast has seen fit to book passage for me, is no larger than a festhall and a good deal less clean. A violent storm last night threatened to capsize this vessel, and consequently dinner was not served. But all that hardship is behind me. We will dock tonight in Teziir and proceed to Westgate in the morning, traveling along the coast, with land in sight at all times, thank Tymora.

This business of being a royal envoy might not be so bad, Giogi thought as he closed his journal. All he had to do was carry a letter from Azoun to a member of Westgate's ruling council, find out if they knew anything about this Alias person, and then keep an eye out for her in case she showed up within the next two months—all at the crown's expense.

As he stood at the upper deck's railing, the Wyvernspur noble could pick out snatches of the conversation the captain was having with Teziir's harbormaster. Something about an increase in the docking fee—another ten gold pieces was owed. A reasonable sum for making it to land, Giogi thought, but the ship's captain had another opinion.

"Outrageous! I won't suffer such extortion. I'll bring her in without your help. See if I don't!"

Somewhere astern, on the lower deck, a high-pitched voice asked another passenger, "Penurious, our captain, or merely recalcitrant?"

Giogi turned toward the sound of the voice. *Funny, I didn't notice any halflings aboard before.*

The passenger the halfling had addressed was a lady cloaked from head to toe. When Giogi saw her face he froze. The halfling was male, completely unfamiliar, but the woman's face—he couldn't be mistaken. *It was her!*

"Why, Master Phalse," the lady smiled. "If I had known you were traveling on the same vessel, I might have forsaken dinner with the captain for your company."

"Dinner with the captain, dinner with me, while poor Zrie is left alone in Westgate. You can be so cruel, Lady Cassana. You know he falls to pieces without you."

So, Giogi thought, *Alias isn't her real name, after all.*

The Lady Cassana laughed with cruel amusement. "He needs the reminder occasionally. What are you doing here? I didn't notice you board."

"That's because I only just popped in. I thought I might accompany you. How's your arm?"

The lady frowned. "How did you know about that?"

"My master's been scrying you to be safe. There was a blur as the One approached your bird form. When she passed by we noted the dagger in your wing."

Cassana shrugged. "All healed when I polymorphed back to my own body."

"Well, our condolences on the failure of your mission."

The lady snarled. "The beast sleeps with his damned sword, so I could only use the subtlest of magics lest I alerted him to my presence and he dispelled my attacks. My creature would not approach him, branded as he is. I almost had the mage and the thief, but Puppet managed to shake me off in time to raise an alarm."

"Well, there will be other opportunities," the halfling replied, shrugging.

"We were lucky she had the brands checked for magic, or we might still be searching all compass points. But it was a fluke she had it done again near Zrie's old rock garden, and a fluke that my creature spotted her in the gap. Don't you think it's time your master got involved in this?"

"There is no need when he has such efficient, clever helpers as myself."

"Oh? And what have you done lately to earn such praise?"

"Planted a tracking device in the One's, or as you would say, Puppet's, party. A device strong enough to be detected despite the enchantment of misdirection about her."

"Planted with the thief, I presume."

Phalse nodded.

"But, how did you find the party?" Cassana asked.

"Upon interrogating Nameless I learned of a peculiar desire he had to sing in Shadowdale. Like father, like daughter. I kept watch on the town. As soon as my scrying power became blurred, I knew the One must have arrived. Sneaking in was a bit perilous—the town is heavily warded against my kind, but nothing I couldn't handle. Now, aren't you glad I didn't let you kill poor, foolish Nameless?"

Cassana smiled slyly. "I suppose I am." From her pocket she drew out a small serpent. The reptile tried unsucessfully to slither from the woman's grasp.

"You took him with you?" The halfling sounded surprised.

"He proved quite useful in holding Puppet's attention. He really is a remarkable storyteller." Cassana slipped the snake back into her pocket.

Giogioni withdrew hastily from the railing. It isn't possible, he thought. She's supposed to be heading to Yulash. Something has gone very wrong. She's here, discussing the most sinister-sounding things. Using magical attacks against branded people, threatening to kill someone's father, and turning humans into snakes. Instead of a sell-sword named Alias, now she's a sorceress called Cassana. Giogi didn't know what to make of it all, but his duty was clear. The woman had to be placed under arrest.

The sailors were all too busy dropping lines overboard and calling out numbers, so the Wyvernspur noble made his way toward the captain. "Excuse me, sir, but there is a woman aboard your ship who is wanted by the Cormyrian authorities. A very dangerous woman."

"Ten!" a sailor shouted from the port bow.

The captain seemed not to see Giogi. His eyes were fixed on the port, his hands clenched about the ship's wheel.

Giogi stepped closer, whispering confidentially. "Why, not sixteen days ago she tried to assassinate a very important Cormyrian official."

"Eight," shouted another sailor from the starboard bow.

"The fourteenth of Mirtul to be more exact," Giogi said.

"Nine," the first sailor called out.

"We all thought she'd gone north to Yulash, which is over six hundred miles away, but," Giogi gave a nervous laugh, "I just saw her on the lower deck."

"Seven," called out the sailor on the starboard bow.

"It doesn't seem possible. I mean, it would take nearly two rides, twenty days, for her to get back here that quickly, but maybe she never went there to begin with, don't you see."

"Five." This last came from the starboard bow.

"Five!" the captain shouted. "Nine Hells!" He twisted the wheel furiously, but it was too late.

Giogi felt the deck rise in a most peculiar fashion. It began sloping rather steeply down to the stern and remained that way. "I say! Have we hit a shoal or something?"

The captain glared at him with murder in his eyes. "Strike the sails!" he shouted.

The ship's first officer approached with his evaluation. "It's no good, sir. We've grounded too far. Have to wait for a change of wind to shift us."

The ship listed perilously to starboard, and Giogi was forced to grab the wheel to keep from slipping on the deck. A peculiar cracking noise came from the housing beneath.

The first officer looked at the captain with alarm in his eyes.

"Prepare to disembark the passengers, Master Roberts. Start with this one." The captain jabbed Giogioni Wyvernspur with his index finger.

"That's most thoughtful, Captain," Giogi said. "I say, but I can wait for the woman and children first. Wyvernspurs know their duty when they see it."

"Sir," the captain said. "You can disembark now in the long-boat, or you can walk the plank."

Giogioni found himself lowered in the longboat. He'd been too busy fretting over his baggage as the other passengers were loaded in beside him, so it came as quite a shock to look up and find himself staring into her eyes.

Giogioni gasped, "You!"

"I beg your pardon," Cassana said. "Have we met?"

Giogi gulped. This close up he realized he'd made a mistake. This was not the lovely, mad sell-sword Alias. The woman seated opposite him was too old. Her hair was the wrong shade. Her flesh was soft and unmuscled.

"Excuse me," he mumbled. "I mistook you for someone else."

"Attractive men need never apologize for mistaking me for someone else. Provided they never mistake me again. I am Cassana of Westgate." Cassana squeezed the Wyvernspur noble's knee in a suggestive manner.

Flustered, Giogi tried to explain further. "I meant—that is, you look just like her, except older. I swear you could be her mother, er, older sister."

Cassana's eyes narrowed, and Giogi kicked himself mentally for violating a sacred rule about never telling women how old they really looked.

"This woman I look like," Cassana whispered. "Tell me about her."

Giogi gulped again. Oh, gods! Suppose she is her mother? "Well, she's like you. Very pretty. With red hair and green eyes. She's a sell-sword though, not a lady like you."

Cassana laughed. "So tell me, who are you and how did you come to know this sell-sword who looks like me?"

All the while they were being rowed to land, Cassana tried to pump information from Giogioni. He explained he'd met Alias at a wedding, that she was merely a passing acquaintance, but this did not satisfy the woman with the strange resemblance to his attacker. Unwilling to reveal the truth, Giogi began to invent details of an imaginary conversation he held with the sell-sword. Remembering Alias had rescued Olive Ruskettle, he said they had discussed music.

He grew increasingly uncomfortable in Cassana's presence. She moved alarmingly close to him and insisted on arranging his alternate travel plans to Westgate. She's just the type of woman Aunt Dorath is always warning me about, Giogi realized. Not that I need any warning—with my sixth sense when it comes to danger.

He was very tempted to ask what had happened to the halfling he had seen her with earlier, but he realized just in time that that might give away what he had overheard.

He found the answer to his question soon enough. As they rowed up to the dock, the halfling reached a hand down to help Cassana up the ladder lowered to the longboat.

"There's another boat to Westgate pulling out in an hour. I've arranged passage," Giogi heard the halfling say.

Fervently Giogi prayed Cassana would forget him in a rush to get to her next ship, but he saw her whispering something to the halfling. Phalse looked down at the Wyvernspur noble with curiosity.

If I know anything at all, Giogi thought, I know that going with that woman and halfling would be a serious mistake. I need a distraction. Something to take their mind off of me, before I end up in the sorceress's pocket.

Giogi handed up his gear and climbed the ladder. Cassana did not even have a chance to introduce her companion before Giogi shrieked. "Oooh! Keep it away!"

"My dear Giogioni, what is wrong?"

Giogi pointed a shaky finger at a pile of crates on the dock. "A snake. A huge snake." He spread his hands out the tiny distance of two hand spans to be sure his exaggeration was not mistaken. "It crawled into that pile of boxes. I don't mean to be such a ninny, but a snake swallowed my Aunt Dorath's pet land urchin once. It was horrible."

Phalse was no longer paying attention to the young Cormyte. He was too busy searching through the crates for what he had been led to assume was the snake Cassana had kept trapped in her pocket. The sorceress, however, instinctively checked her pocket first, but that moment of inattention was all Giogioni needed.

Scooping up his baggage, he fled from the dock into the city of Teziir, desperately searching for a horse, a coach, or any quick means of escape from this den of foreign villainy.

❧ 17 ❧

Brunch in Shadowdale and the Trek North

"Well, that's a switch," Alias muttered as she drew back the curtains to let daylight into her room. Dragonbait lay by the fireside, snoozing away. She was awake before him. Of course, he'd been up late last night keeping an eye on Olive, and he had walked, not ridden, from Cormyr.

He must need rest very badly, she thought, more than the rest of us. And he's done the most to earn it, too. Still, she couldn't help wondering mischievously what he would think and feel and do if she were gone when he awoke.

When she'd returned to The Old Skull the night before, he'd been standing near the door of the inn, obviously torn between keeping an eye on the halfling and leaving to find the swordswoman. She had offered to stay in the taproom with Olive so that he could retire, but he had shaken his head in refusal. Alias, feeling worn from their forced march and with her ankle throbbing from her trip in the darkness, had accepted his gallantry gratefully and gone to bed herself. She had no idea what time he'd come up to sleep.

Now she felt just a touch guilty. She crept about quietly as she dressed. Another pang assaulted her conscience as she sat on the bed, pulling on her boots. Dragonbait always slept on the floor. It had never occurred to her to rent him his own room; she'd always assumed he would want to stay near her. She might at least have asked for something with an extra bed for him. "I'll make it all up to you. Somehow," she whispered to the sleeping lizard as she slipped out of the room and very gently pulled the door closed.

The taproom was empty when Alias came down the stairs, but Jhaele popped her head out of the kitchen to wish her a good day and ask if she'd slept well.

"Very well, thank you," Alias assured her. "Do you have any idea where my friends have gone?"

"Did you try their rooms, lady?" Jhaele asked. "I would have thought they'd all still be sleeping."

"Oh. No, I just assumed they'd be up and about by now."

Jhaele shook her head. "Mistress Ruskettle didn't retire until the very small hours, and she drank a good deal of bottled sleep, if you catch my meaning. And your Mister Akash was out all night. Didn't come home until after dawn. Same with the lizard-creature. He sat by the fire until morning, slipped upstairs for a minute, then left the inn for about an hour and returned with Master Akash."

Alias ordered breakfast, then took a seat at a table. She stared around the room, feeling a little sad. Everything here was so familiar (except of course the new lord, Mourngrym, and the elusive Elminster), and it hurt that no one remembered her. Last night, however, she'd come to the conclusion that that was part of her curse. Besides making her forget things, the azure brands made other people forget her. Both conditions were bound up in the same spell.

Akabar came down the stairs just as Jhaele was bringing in a tray loaded with waffles, ham, fruit, and tea. "I'll whip up more of the same," the innkeep offered.

Alias nodded and pulled out a chair for her companion.

"I understand your meeting with the wise Elminster kept you out all night," she said. "How'd it go?"

Akabar smiled weakly. "It was all right, I suppose."

"And?" Alias prompted. "What did he have to say?"

"Say?" Akabar echoed.

Something in his manner made Alias suspicious. "Something bad?" she whispered after Jhaele had laid out extra tableware for Akabar and left.

Akabar shook his head. "I waited half the night to see him, and I came away with nothing more than what we learned from Dimswart back in Suzail."

"Did he mention the lay of Zrie Prakis and Cassana?"

Akabar made a noncommittal noise as he poured syrup over some waffles.

"Did he?" Alias asked, taking the syrup from him.

"Did he what?" Akabar grumbled, feigning listlessness.

"Did he tell you about the lay of Zrie Prakis and Cassana?"

"No, he didn't," Akabar answered and promptly stuffed his mouth with waffles to give himself time to think. What was he going to do? So far, all his answers had been the truth. He had waited half the night for Elminster and longer. He had not learned anything new, and Elminster had not told him about any lay. He could not keep up the ambiguous and vague answers much longer, though. He would either have to admit his failure or lie to her.

He had thought that, when the time came, one action or the other would come easily to him, but they did not. He had been little help protecting Alias, rather the reverse, needing her to rescue him from the kalmari. Now his role as information-gatherer had completely collapsed. His pride could not cope with the admission of his own uselessness.

Yet, surprisingly, the alternative—lying to her—did not come any easier. In his dealings as a merchant, Akabar could stretch the truth with a skill that would make Olive Ruskettle's head swim, but that skill did not extend to deceiving women. He had never been able to lie to his wives either, even though it might have made some of his nights a little less tumultuous.

"What's the lay of Zrie Prakis and Cassana?" a shrill voice chirped. Olive climbed into a chair and promptly popped one of Alias's strawberries into her mouth.

"Apparently," Alias explained, "they were lovers before they went at each other in the duel that killed Zrie Prakis."

"Ooo. You humans are such fascinating people. Did Cassana throw herself off a cliff in remorse?" Olive asked, using an extra fork to swipe a large piece of one of Alias's waffles.

Alias shook her head. "No. She did keep his bones, though. By her bedside as a keepsake."

"Yuck," the halfling muttered as she chewed.

"Definitely. I'm surprised Elminster didn't mention it. It's supposed to be a common story up north. There's even supposed to be an opera about it."

"Perhaps Elminster is not a big opera-lover," Akabar sniffed and stuffed more waffle into his mouth.

"I don't blame him," the bard said. "I've heard that people

commit murders at operas, and no one notices because everyone on stage is bellowing at the top of his lungs."

"I don't see how this story about the mages helps us any," Akabar said.

"It doesn't, really," Alias admitted, "but I just wanted to show that you're not the only one able to get information. I pick up bits here and there."

Inwardly injured by the swordswoman's remark and encouraged by the presence of the halfling, Akabar somehow found the strength to invent a meeting with Elminster.

"I got nothing from this supposedly renowned sage but the standard material we already know. He might have looked it all up in the same book Dimswart used. He had no idea what the last sigil was, either. His reputation is overrated. It must be based on past victories. I only hope when I'm that decrepit and befuddled, I'll have a profitable business in the hands of my daughters and not have to rely on gulling foolish adventurers."

"Elminster was decrepit and befuddled?" Alias asked, remembering Mourngrym's description of the sage as the wisest in the Realms. Still, perhaps Mourngrym's standards weren't up to those of Cormyr or the lands farther south. She had harbored one odd idea, however, so she had to ask, "What did he look like?"

"He looked like a spider," lied the Turmishman, leaning over the table and speaking in a low voice. He had to be carried about from room to room. His hands were shriveled into useless sticks, so that he had to be dressed and fed by his manservant. I know. I watched him eat. It was most unpleasant."

Alias pondered the mage's description while she sipped her tea. She had suspected her goatherd to be Elminster, though he had tried to lead her away from that idea. Powerful, famous people often traveled around dressed as commoners, at least in lays and songs. But if the sage was chair-ridden, her goatherd had to be someone else.

That didn't mean she valued the old man's advice any less, and she certainly appreciated his finder's stone, kept safely tucked away in her boot top. It made her feel a lot less nervous, knowing he had been just a wise, old man. Had Elmin-

ster himself taken such an interest in her singing, she'd
know she was in more trouble than she could handle.

Jhaele brought out another breakfast tray and unloaded
the contents onto their table.

"Pass the strawberries," Olive demanded, dumping the
contents of the fruit bowl on top of another grilled cake and
handing the empty bowl back to Akabar, who put it aside
without noticing. He was nearly holding his breath, afraid
Alias might make some comment about Elminster that
Jhaele would hear and contradict, belying his story.

"I need to do some shopping," Alias announced, draining
her tea cup. "Would you mind very much taking care of the
food provisioning?" she asked the Turmishman.

"Not at all," Akabar assured her, forcing a smile to his lips.
That's all he felt good for lately, buying the groceries from
other greengrocers like himself.

Alias rose from the table and went over to knock on the
kitchen door. Jhaele handed her another tray.

"I'm taking this up to Dragonbait," she explained to the
others.

"Why? Is he sick?" Olive asked.

"No. I just thought he deserved breakfast in bed for a
change."

Akabar tried not to look too anxious when he asked,
"When are we leaving here?" The sooner they were gone
from Shadowdale, the sooner his lie about Elminster would
be safe from revelation. Also, it would be easier to keep an
eye on the lizard when they were on the road.

"About two hours. There's a way station up the road
about ten miles. I'd like to reach it by nightfall."

"Anything I can do?" Olive asked offhandedly.

"Keep out of trouble," Alias suggested.

"I might manage that," the halfling said with a prim nod.

Dragonbait was still asleep when Alias returned to the
room. She set the tray down by his nose. He inhaled before
he opened his eyes.

"Hungry, sleepy-head?"

The lizard sat up and smiled. His cloak fell away as he
broke off some waffle and popped it in his mouth.

The scent of lemon wafted about the room. Aren't we too

far north for lemon trees to bloom? Alias wondered.

She began packing up her clothes. The turquoise wool tunic lay across a chair. Last night it had been mud-spattered from her fall. Now it was mysteriously laundered and dried. She gathered it up in her hands and went to sit beside Dragonbait.

"Look, you've got to stop doing things like this."

Dragonbait tilted his head and made a chirping noise.

"Don't give me that I-don't-understand look," Alias said. "I don't care if you tease Olive, but I know you understand me. I want you to stop this servant routine. You're not my servant. You're . . . my traveling companion. I know I'm lazy about looking after my things sometimes, but you'll spoil me if you keep this up. I know how useful you are. You don't have to keep proving it to me. Do you understand?"

Dragonbait met her gaze with his unblinking yellow eyes. He nodded.

"All right, then. Better finish your breakfast. We're leaving in a few hours. I'm going to the smithy to have the kinks ground out of my blade. You can bring your sword down too if you want."

Suddenly anxious to leave for the open road, Alias hurried to finish packing. While the lizard polished off his meal, she wrote out the words to the Standing Stone song and left them for Jhaele to give to the songhorn player.

No one in town would let them pay for supplies or services. Mourngrym had passed the word that bills were to be submitted to the tower. Alias was glad she hadn't assigned the halfling any shopping tasks. Who knew what the bard would pick up on the town's tab? For herself, Alias picked up a new dagger and shield from the smithy and had him sharpen her blade.

Dragonbait looked a little anxious about turning his own bizarre weapon over to the craftsmen, but the man reassured him with the special care he took handling the sword before he began working on it.

They left town four hours before sunset. A few townsfolk bid them farewell as they traveled along the road, but Alias caught no glimpse of her goatherd.

* * * * *

The weather held fair and warm, and no extraordinary encounters marred their travels. A singularly stupid troll attacked Dragonbait on watch their second night out from Shadowdale, but when the rest of the party woke up the troll was burning merrily on the fire. The next day, they lost several hours in the Elven Wood, hiding uncomfortably in a damp cave to avoid a large party of orcs.

Their stay in the town of Voonlar was cut short when a sheriff's deputy's purse was found in Olive's room at the inn. Rather than arrest them, the deputy accepted an apology accompanied by the return of all his gold, thrice what could have possibly fit in the leather pouch. They also had to agree to leave town immediately. Alias was ready to throttle the halfling, but Olive argued her innocence so vehemently that the swordswoman believed her.

More than the loss of a night in clean sheets troubled Alias. There were rumors of a war to the east, and she hadn't had any time to confirm them.

They camped outside of town and continued toward Yulash in the morning. Twice that day the shadow of some great, flying beast crossed the sun, causing all the horses to panic and rear on their hind legs.

Still, Alias remained unperturbed. She felt that "they," the people who had branded her, had given up. There were no more disturbing dreams or giant monsters or assassins in black. The swordswoman was willing to bet that the kalmari in Shadow Gap had been their last card. I've passed out of their range, she assured herself. Only Moander is up here, and he's been locked up beneath Yulash.

By twilight they were in sight of the great mound on which the city of Yulash stood. The single hill sloped gently, resembling a giant shield lying face-up on the plain. According to Olive, once upon a time an individual standing in the highest citadel atop the crown of the hill could see the smoke rise from the dark furnaces of Zhentil Keep, and the fog roll off the shores of the Moonsea.

"One of the merchants in Shadowdale told me that the Yulashians could have seen the glow of fire when dragons destroyed Phlan, except they were being destroyed by dragons themselves at the time. A horde of them came down on the Dales two years back," Olive explained. "Destroyed one of Shadowdale's high-muckety witches."

"Sylune," Alias snapped.

"Yes. That was her name. Anyway, the dragons left Phlan and Yulash in ruins, killed all the rulers and mages, and scattered the commoners."

"Now Zhentil Keep forces occupy the rubble," Akabar reminded them. "Its altitude makes it a strategic location."

As the darkness settled, they could see there were fires on Yulash mound, punctuated by flashes of fireball and other magical flames.

"The war is at Yulash." Alias spat with annoyance.

"Hillsfar forces trying to take it away from the Zhentil Keep army stationed there," Akabar guessed.

The next day they traveled more cautiously as they passed great, burned stretches of overgrown fields, untended orchards completely shattered by lightning, and ridges of ground torn up by the claws of great beasts.

When piles of rusted weapons and rotted carrion began to dot the side of the roads, they dismounted and walked beside the horses and pony to calm them and to avoid presenting themselves as targets.

They could have ridden into Yulash before sunset if it had been a more peaceful season. Instead, they camped a quarter mile away, using an overturned wagon to shelter them from view of the forces defending and attacking the town's main citadel. Even if they could get closer without being hit by a stray arrow or magic spell, they could be caught by an army and executed as spies.

They were close enough to hear metal clashing on metal as some of the combatants met in swordplay, commands barked out by captains, cheers from men who'd just managed to kill someone or something, and cries of horror from men who had seen their last battle.

After dark, a great, glowing whirlwind spun around the top of the mound, igniting members of the attacking force. As their bodies scattered down the slope, they looked to Alias, from a distance, like sparkling seeds falling away from a flaming dandelion.

"Well, it certainly is more amusing to watch than your standard campfire," Olive commented. "Though it lacks a certain warmth."

They hadn't dared light their own campfire for fear of being discovered by a foraging patrol, so after a cold dinner, the four adventurers sat huddled against the overturned wagon as the night air grew more and more chill. Olive shivered, wrapped beneath her own cloak and two of Akabar's. The mage affected a pose of calm unconcern, but Alias caught him blowing into his cupped hands, trying to keep them warm. Dragonbait kept peering around the side of the wagon, fascinated by Yulash mound. The horses, tethered nearby behind the one remaining wall of an ancient farmer's cottage, whickered uncomfortably. Dragonbait echoed the sound, though whether he was trying to comfort them or agreeing with them Alias could not tell.

In the soft glow of the finder's stone, Alias could not escape the halfling's accusatory stare or Akabar's expectant one. "When I led us up here, I had no idea the area would be so unsettled." Each intermittent flash from the city's ruins drew her attention. I feel like a moth, she thought, trying to get into a lantern, beating against the glass. Somewhere in that maze of ruins lies the answer to my curse—I'm sure of it.

"I had assumed the city would be firmly in the hands of one side or the other. Then we could use the same trick we used in the dragon's lair. Akabar would scout ahead with his wizard eye trick, Olive would accompany me to help with locks, traps, and other tricky parts, and Dragonbait would remain behind with the gear."

Olive muttered something about "thief's tricks," and Dragonbait scowled, but Alias ignored them both. "However," she continued, "that was all assuming we only had to elude a sleepy city guard. With two active forces looking for enemy troops, our chances of sneaking in unnoticed are . . ." she hesitated, trying not to sound falsely optimistic.

"Slim," Akabar suggested.

"Try nil," Olive retorted. "Humans. Always fighting over who gets the better view."

"They don't battle over it just because it's the only major terrain between the forest and the river," Akabar lectured. "Remember, it sits on the route south from Zhentil Keep. If Hillsfar should take and hold the city, they would effectively blockade Zhentil Keep's bulk trade."

"And there's probably more gold and treasure left in the wreckage, in hidden cellars and dungeons, than in the active mines of the dwarves," Alias added.

Olive perked up a little, cheered by the thought of treasure. Dragonbait stood and walked over to the horses to stroke Lightning. All the while the lizard's eyes remained fixed on the glowing hill.

Akabar followed the lizard.

"Where are you going?" Alias called to him.

"To help Dragonbait with the horses."

"You've been fussing over him ever since we left Shadowdale," the warrior noted. "Helping him fetch wood, keeping watch with him. He can take care of himself." She tugged on the mage's robes until he was forced to sit back down beside her. "Now, what do you think our chances would be if we contacted one side or the other to make a deal?"

Trying not to appear too distracted with keeping an eye on Dragonbait, Akabar said, "If you do, contact Hillsfar. Their ruler, I've heard, is a merchant-mage like myself. His name is Maalthir. If one of these forces is indeed his, it will include a company of his prize mercenaries, the Red Plumes. We need only look for their banner."

"Yes, then we'll have found the Red Death," Olive growled. "That's what Maalthir's mercenaries are called among my people. Under his orders, they carried out a campaign to purge Hillsfar of thieves. Human thieves could hide, but all halflings were thieves, as far as Maalthir's Red Death was concerned. They drove every halfling from the city in the middle of the night, forced them to leave their valuables behind, didn't even give them a chance to sell the land or shops they owned.

"As distasteful as Hillsfar's policies might be, you can hardly expect us to deal with the baby-slaying Keepers. I've heard that they plight their troth with succubi, eat the brains of elves, and worship gods so black they make Moander seem nice. Their names are feared as far south as my native land. And the council who rules them, the Zhentarim, are twice as dark as the Keepers."

"I didn't suggest we deal with the Keepers," Olive replied. "I was only reporting on the firsthand news I have about the Hillsfar government. I have no reason to expect better of the Zhentil Keep soldiery. They're all human, too, at least mostly, I'm told. You must realize, though, that all the accusations you've made against Zhentil Keep are the standard lies told about any successful city by its jealous enemies."

"There are too many stories told of the Zhentarim for them all to be lies. As a bard you must know stories of their methods—how they secretly support orcs so they will attack any who oppose the Zhentarim's will."

"And as a bard," Olive said, "I have the ability to separate the grain from the dross."

"Gold," corrected Akabar. "Gold from dross. Grain from chaff."

Alias sighed and stood up. The mage and the bard could argue until Yulash was dust. She strode over to watch the battle with Dragonbait. As the finder's stone illuminated their mounts, she could see the beasts stood alone. She poked her head around the wall, but the lizard was not there. She went back to the wagon and peeked around that, but he wasn't there either.

Olive was continuing her testimony on the cruelty of the Hillsfar people, while Akabar was trying to interrupt her with some point about the evil of the Zhentarim.

Made impatient with a sudden attack of anxiety, Alias snapped at both of them. "Listen to yourselves. You're not disagreeing with each other, you're just arguing for the sake of arguing. Can't you see something's wrong?"

"What is it?" Akabar asked.

"Dragonbait's gone," she whispered.

"Gone where?" Akabar asked, glancing around their campsite while cursing himself for not keeping an eye on the potentially treacherous lizard.

"Just gone," Alias said. A particularly bright flash filled the sky, and thunder rumbled all about them. The swordswoman peered across the momentarily illuminated open fields, but she could not pick out the lizard's figure.

"Perhaps you better stay down," Akabar suggested.

"He's disappeared," Alias whispered, still standing.

"He's probably only out looking for firewood or something," Olive suggested.

"We haven't got a fire," Akabar growled.

"Maybe he decided we should have one," Olive retorted.

If I hadn't been such a fool, Akabar berated himself, arguing with the halfling and allowing myself to be distracted from watching the lizard, this wouldn't have happened. Who knows what sort of betrayal I've let us in for now?

"Or he could be out filching us a nice, hot, ten-course meal, with wine," Olive continued brightly.

Alias scowled. She noticed Akabar frowning as well. She hadn't realized he cared for Dragonbait as much as she.

Should I tell her about the lizard's brands, Akabar debated. I can't prove it now, and it still might not make her doubt him. No, better just to watch for him.

Alias stared at the city. The crackling of the fires and magics burning there pulled at her like a siren's call. Olive could be right. But suppose he's scouting out the territory to prove he should not be left behind? It was one thing to leave him guarding the equipment or even to have him fighting at her side, but imagining him out there, alone, unable to call for help, not even if he were injured. . . . Alias moaned softly, feeling suddenly miserable.

"He'll come back," Olive said again. "He always does."

The night grew even colder, and eventually, as the combatants on the hill wearied and let their fires and magics die out, it grew darker, too. Olive was a snoring lump in a bundle of furs, Akabar a motionless mannequin in his colored robes and one blanket. Alias shivered in her only cloak, but she could not stay wrapped in her blankets. She spent her watch pacing and staring into the darkness, waiting for Dragonbait to return. She did not bother to wake Olive, but continued to watch past her turn.

But Dragonbait still did not return.

A few pins of light from watchfires in the city pricked at Alias's eyes. He's there, was all she could think. He went into the city without me.

Like I planned to do to him, she added. Again she felt the draw of the city, an ache to learn the mystery within.

Her heart prompted her to look in Yulash, but her head insisted she had no proof that he was there. He could be anywhere. He might have been captured by the Keepers or the Red Plumes. That thought made her more anxious. As far as she knew, both Akabar and Olive had been right in their claims of Hillsfar and Zhentil Keep atrocities.

Actually, Alias couldn't think of any army that would let a creature as blatantly non-human as Dragonbait pass unchallenged. They'd try to capture or kill him immediately. Probably kill, Alias admitted, because he'd put up a fight.

She was ready to wake the mage and bard and set out immediately when another thought made her hesitate. If he's wandering out on the plains, lost, but finds his way back to an empty camp, he'll think we've been captured. Someone has to stay, she decided. But Akabar looked so concerned by the lizard's disappearance, Alias knew he would insist on accompanying her, and Olive would not stand for being left behind, believing there was treasure to be had in the city.

She hovered uncertainly over the two sleeping forms for several moments, trying to make up her mind. Going alone would only perpetuate the lizard's folly, but she could not help herself. She bent down over Akabar's pack and dug out a stick of charcoal and his map. On the back she wrote: "Looking for D. Wait here."

She lay the parchment by Akabar's head. Then, after slipping the finder's stone in her boot, she picked up her shield and sword and walked away. Her steps drew her toward the great mound city.

* * * * *

Akabar's eyes snapped open the moment Alias opened his pack.

The mage had cast a magic mouth enchantment on his earring to tell him if Dragonbait returned, and at first he thought that was what had awakened him, but when the piece of jewelry repeated its magical warning, whispering, "Someone's in your pack," he realized his mistake.

After the earlier disappearance of his magical tome, back when the halfling had joined his caravan, the mage had decided that it would not be squandering his power to use it to protect his property, even from a fellow traveler. Still, he wondered at Ruskettle's nerve and dishonor.

He lay perfectly still, focusing on his baggage through the slits of his eyelids, but the figure rooting through his belongings was too big to be Ruskettle. It couldn't be Dragonbait; his other magic mouth spell would have warned him.

When the figure straightened, Akabar nearly gasped and sat up in surprise. It was Alias. She scrawled something hastily on his map and then took a step toward him.

Akabar closed his eyes. He almost held his breath, but caught himself in time and began feigning the shallow breathing of a sleeper. Through his eyelids, he could sense the stone's light on his face and then sense it move away. He peeked through one eye. Alias took up her sword and shield and left the camp.

Slowly, Akabar rose and looked out across the plains. He caught a flash of moonlight glinting off of Alias's polished shoulder-plates. She was headed toward Yulash.

He spied the map. He picked it up and tilted it until the letters could be read by Selune's light.

Wait here, indeed! thought the mage, tossing the map onto his sleeping blanket with a deep frown. She lugs us all the way up here and when things get really dangerous, when she could use our help, she abandons us to chase after that lizard—who's probably reporting us to his hidden masters, setting up a trap for her to walk into.

His first impulse was to chase after the warrior woman and convince her to return, use force if necessary to keep her from marching into Yulash. He would tell her it was smarter to wait for daylight. But he knew in his heart that once the sun had risen, he would only try to convince her that the nightfall might be a better time after all.

She would never hesitate to go searching for the creature she thinks is a friend, while I, Akabar Bel Akash, mage of no small water, cower behind an overturned merchant's wagon. I am more greengrocer than master mage, the Turmishman thought, ashamed of his fear.

He could wake the halfling, and they could follow Alias together. Olive would have no trouble making up her mind what to do, Akabar realized. You could call her anything except late to looting. Still, taking the halfling did not seem particularly wise. As the old Amnite saying went, when matters are bad, think how much worse they could get if halflings were involved. Akabar didn't want to put her in any risk of running into the Red Plumes.

Standing with his face toward the waning moon, Akabar began to intone a spell. The deep, rich words rolled off his tongue as his right hand sliced through the air. In it, he held a bit of his own eyelash embedded in a resin of tree gum. At the end of the evocation, his left hand came down hard on the tree gum. The sticky pellet flared a bright blue, consumed by mystical energy.

Akabar held his hands up in the moonlight and watched them go transparent, as though they were sculptures of ice. Then they vanished completely. His vision blurred for a moment, then the world refocused for him. He could see normally, save that when he looked down at himself there was nothing to see but a pair of depressions in the grass.

The parchment map rose from the ground, hovered for a moment, then settled next to the sleeping halfling. What Alias had written could apply to both of them.

Then he used his long legs to stride toward Yulash in the wake of the swordswoman. Nothing but a wave of bent grass blades marked his invisible passing.

❧ 18 ❧

Yulash

A fog began to roll in across the plains minutes after Alias left the campsite. The swordswoman was uncertain whether she should thank Tymora for the weather or not. On one hand, it would make spotting Dragonbait more difficult, but on the other hand, it would cover her approach to the mound. The soft glow of her tattoo was enough illumination to see the ground beneath her feet.

Their camp had only been a quarter of a mile to the base of the hill, but it was another quarter mile climb up to the wall. Alias avoided the roads into the city; there were plenty of footpaths up the slope, and she knew they'd be less patrolled. Twice she thought she heard someone following her and she waited on the path, hoping maybe it was Dragonbait tracking her scent, but no one appeared. The third time she backtracked quickly, thinking perhaps she was being stalked by a sentry, but still she discovered no one.

Halfway up the hill, Alias emerged from the fog. She turned to survey the plains. There was nothing to see though; all below her was whiteness. Yulash was an island in the clouds. She climbed farther up the slope.

The great walls that once ringed the cities were breached in more than a dozen places. She avoided the larger, more easily navigated breaks on the assumption that they would be guarded. She chose a hole that afforded her shoulder plates enough space to slip through.

The wreckage of the town spread out before her in all directions. Occasionally a section of wall remained braced by a door or corner, but there wasn't a rooftop to be seen on any of the old buildings. Ahead and a little to the east stood the fortifications of the old citadel, rebuilt by the Zhentil Keep soldiers trying to hold the region. A campfire blazed in that direction, so Alias moved off to the western section of the city.

A scraping noise came from back by the hole she had used to enter the city. She whirled around, blade ready, expecting some assassin, wishing it were Dragonbait, but there was no one there. Just loose rubble, she thought, disgusted with her nervousness. She continued west.

Rather than walk in the streets, Alias picked her way over the razed walls. Anything that might have survived the dragon invasions, human armies, and looters had been carried off long ago. If there was treasure to be found in the city, it was well-hidden.

There was a jiggling of horse-rigging in the streets, and Alias crouched behind the wall. A single rider approached. He held his reins in one hand and a hooded lantern in the other. Enough light leaked from his lantern that Alias could see he wore a scarlet cloak and a silver helmet with a single plume jutting from the top, also scarlet.

As she watched the rider pass, something across the street caught Alias's eye. Reflecting the rider's lantern light, lying in the rubble, was a familiar symbol—a fanged mouth gaping in the palm of a hand.

Moander, at last, Alias thought with glee. A third stroke of luck. Tymora must be favoring her. She crept out from behind the wall, ready to dodge back into the shadows if the horse so much as nickered. The horse and rider continued down the street, eyes forward, oblivious to her presence.

Alias scurried across the street, but when she reached the broken stone there was nothing there. Was her mind playing tricks on her? A mossy smell assailed her nostrils. She peered into the darkness, searching for its source.

The pile of rubble where she stood was part of a ring of collapsed wall. Within the toppled stone was a broad pit. At first, Alias thought it must just be the cellar of some collapsed building, but the darkness within the center was so complete that she realized it must be a very deep hole. She spotted a narrow staircase winding around the edge of the hole's interior. On the wall by the first few steps was another hand glowing blue.

The glow of her tattoo was insufficient to illuminate the stairs so Alias risked pulling out the finder's stone. Its light seemed dimmer here, illuminating no more than four or five extra steps, but that was enough for Alias to make out a set of tracks preceding her into the pit, tracks made by something with three-toed feet, separated by a single groove, made by the heavy tail of a lizard.

What do you know? Alias thought. The finder's stone did help me find someone who was lost. She began her descent into the pit. Each step felt as if she were pushing against water, as if something were resisting her entry. The stairs were steep as well as narrow, and the rim of the pit soon rose over her head and swallowed her.

With total darkness around her, the yellow glow of the stone seemed to grow brighter, but Alias no longer needed it. An azure aura sprang from beneath her right sleeve. Alias hesitated and wondered if she were walking into a trap. Of course, her arm was going to glow as she got nearer Moander's temple, just as it had glowed in the presence of Cassana's kalmari and the crystal elemental. She didn't know what she had to worry about. Moander was locked up. According to the goatherd in Shadowdale, only someone unborn could free the ancient god.

Since she knew she'd been born—she could remember the day quite clearly: the snoring of her mother, the cooing of the midwife, being sniffed at by the house cats—she had no fear she might accidentally unleash one of the evil elements responsible for her mutilation and lost memory.

Alias could now discern pungent, all-too-human smells. The pit was used as a midden. The stench grew more powerful the deeper she went. The steps grew damp and slick, and pockets of muck and slime collected in the depressions worn into the stairs by a millennium of visitors. Bits of green goo dripped from one step to the next.

A stone bounced down from above, followed by a shower of small rocks. Alias looked up, expecting to see someone tossing a bucket of something foul over the rim of the pit, but only the dark sky hung over the darker hole.

A stray soldier idly investigating the city, Alias guessed,

and continued her descent until she came to a wide, stone-work platform ringed with rubble. The staircase ended, though the pit continued down. The finder's stone was unable to light the bottom of the stinking darkness. Alias doubted if even the moon could do so were it to shine directly in. There was no trace of Moander's sigil.

Alias studied Dragonbait's tracks. The three-toed imprints wandered about the muck-covered platform, to the beginning of the blocked stairs, to the edge of the platform, to the wall of the pit, but there was no trace of them after that.

He wouldn't have jumped over the edge, Alias puzzled. She lifted the finder's stone and investigated the slime-encrusted walls. There was a faint vertical shadow from a line of moss buckled against more moss. The line continued above her head, running horizontally and then back down. It was a door, recently opened and closed.

Reluctantly, Alias ran her fingers along the slimy moss and lichen, feeling for a catch to push, pull, or slide. In the center of the door, at waist level, she discovered a hole. Mindful of finger guillotine traps set against intruders, she poked her smallest finger into the hole.

No blade sliced at her digit, but a stinging charge of energy ran up her arm. Her runes writhed and danced, but caused her no pain. From behind the stone wall came the clattering of lock mechanisms tumbling and falling.

When the azure sigils were still again, though still glowing, Alias withdrew her finger and stepped back. The hidden door swung out silently. A foot thick, it pivoted on an unseen post.

Beyond the doorway, the smell of fresh waste and muck gave way to the older decay of ancient paper and bones. Warm, dry air blew from the passage. The walls were carved with tiny, intricate, flowing designs. They reminded Alias more of the tree sculptures grown and shaped by elves than of something wrought of dead stone.

Then she saw the three-toed footprints on the dusty floor. The curiosity that had beckoned her this far now tried to drive her forward like a fire forcing wild animals through the woods. She was sure that not only Dragonbait, but the answers to all her questions lay at the end of the mysterious passage before her.

She wanted to rush right in, but her adventurer's sense of caution asserted itself just in time. Stepping back on the platform, Alias grabbed a large, wedge-shaped rock from the pile of rubble and slipped its smaller edge beneath the door. She found several others like it and shoved them beneath the door as well. Then she shifted a pile of rocks to the edge of the door frame.

Satisfied with her precautions, she entered the passage. About six paces down the corridor, she felt a stone beneath her foot shift nearly an imperceptible amount. Behind her, the door jerked a hand's span but was held fast by the rocks. Something mechanical whined a high-pitched plea. The whining grew louder as though the trap were crying out desperately to fulfill its only purpose in life. Within a minute, the whine dropped in pitch and then was silent. The door was still. Smiling to herself and feeling smug, Alias continued down the corridor.

Her mood was soon quelled by the walls around her. They were carved with horrible bas reliefs interspersed with lines and lines of engravings of archaic runes. The carved figures depicted heroes suffering deadly tortures at the hands of leering humanoids, torn apart by chaotic beasts, and fried, frozen, dissolved, and poisoned by dragons and beholders and other deadly creatures.

The ugliness of the walls seemed to go on forever and, with each twisting and widening of the passageway, the scenes grew larger as well as more obscene and gory.

Alias felt a growing revulsion which turned her stomach sour and tightened her throat. She kept her eyes forward and tried not to look at the walls anymore.

The passage widened further one last time before ending abruptly in a wall twenty feet ahead. This wall was completely different from the disturbingly carved stone passages Alias had come through. Constructed of blue glazed brick, it was bound together with a red-tinged mortar. Down the center of the mortar work were great gouges, as if a giant claw had been scratching at it. At the base of the wall lay the crumbled figure of Dragonbait.

The swordswoman rushed forward and knelt at the lizard's head, laying the finder's stone on the ground.

"Dragonbait! Are you all right?" she asked. She'd whispered the words, but the corridor caught and amplified them so that her echo boomed back at her.

As Alias knelt beside him, the lizard turned his head to look up at her. The change in him was horrifying. He was completely emaciated. His scaly flesh hung about his frame as if his muscles had been eaten away by months of starvation. Wear and exhaustion were etched deep into the lines of his face. His tongue lolled out the side of his mouth, and he panted heavily in the dusty air. His eyes, normally a dead, yellow color, now looked even worse—their clear sparkle had turned to a murky gray.

A deep, violet perfume rose from his body, something Alias had never noticed before. Forgetting he could not really answer, she asked, "What happened to you?"

The lizard pointed his finger back down the way they'd both come, and he tried to push her away from him in that direction, but his shove was far too feeble to budge her. A low snarl escaped his lipless mouth.

Alias stood up. "All right, I'm going," she agreed, understanding his signals perfectly. "But not without you. Come on, I'll help you up."

Dragonbait pulled heavily on her arm and rose to his feet. His legs looked too spindly to support his weight. He leaned on his sword like an old man with a cane.

What could have done this to him? Alias wondered. She felt reluctant to leave without exploring this place, but she was too frightened by the lizard's condition to delay getting help for him. Maybe, she thought, I can find a cleric to heal him in one of the army camps.

Then she noticed that many of the backward-curved teeth at the end of his sword were damaged—chipped off or curled askew. Realizing the sword had caused the scratches in the brick wall, she joked, "If you wanted a slegehammer for a weapon, you should have asked back in Shadowdale."

Dragonbait tugged on her arm, anxious to hurry away.

Alias had never seen him frightened before, but she had no wish to meet whatever had done this to him either. She stooped to retrieve the finder's stone.

As she stood up with the goatherd's gift, Alias felt a throbbing curiosity about the blue and red wall. She reached out to stroke the blue-glazed bricks with her fingertips.

The wall glowed. For a single pulse of a human heart, the bricks shimmered and then became translucent. From behind the wall, a bright blue light shone, silhouetting the lines of red mortar and turning the passage where Alias stood an eerie aqua. Then the bricks returned to normal and the light faded.

Alias stood, staring at the wall in amazement. It was some moments before she became aware of the writhing sensation on her arm. The sigils were wriggling and twisting like maggots nesting in her flesh, and the unholy sign of Moander seemed the most vibrant. The fingers of the hand appeared to clench and flex, while the mouth in the palm snapped its fanged teeth open and closed.

Fascinated, Alias reached out to stroke the wall again. Dragonbait's hand snatched at her wrist and pulled her back. Then some pain forced him to release her and clutch at his chest. He fell forward, his sword clattering to the stone floor, making a ringing noise down the passageway.

"Dragonbait! What's wrong?" Alias gasped, kneeling again beside him. Then she saw it—a bright, blue light, pouring out between the weave of the lizard's shirt, escaping even through the flesh of his hands held over his chest.

"Gods!" the warrior whispered. "No. It can't be." She shook the lizard by the shoulders, dropping the finder's stone to the floor. "What's on your chest?" she demanded.

Dragonbait took a deep breath and held his head up. He untied the fastenings that held his shirt closed.

Alias gasped. The same sigils. In a different shape, but the same sigils. The same blue, gemlike, writhing, azure-lit brands. The scales over the pattern were translucent just as the flesh covering the pattern on Alias's right arm was.

"Why? Why didn't you tell me? Are you one of their pets, too?" she growled angrily.

Dragonbait met her angry eyes with his own, but there was neither shame nor triumph in his look, only sadness. Now he smelled to Alias of roses. It brought to her mind the morning in Shadow Gap when he'd buried the barbarian's sword. The sword he'd used to destroy the kalmari.

"Oh, Dragonbait. I'm sorry," she whispered. Of course he wasn't an enemy or a traitor. He was her friend and probably another victim like her. That had to be the reason she felt such a kinship with him.

"Why didn't you tell me?" she whispered gently, reaching up with her right hand to touch the markings that scarred his body. Energy crackled through her fingertips and over the lizard's chest. Dragonbait drew a deep breath. The lines smoothed from his face, his shoulders straightened, and his eyes widened in surprise.

Alias gasped and drew back her hand, uncertain what she had just experienced. She didn't feel any weaker, so she didn't think Dragonbait had sucked the energy from her. But she couldn't possibly have healed him. She had no training as a cleric. Could the sigils know how to help someone else branded the same way? It didn't seem likely, but Dragonbait's awful condition had been corrected by the mere touch of her hand.

Dragonbait retied his shirt fastenings and stood up easily. Shouldering his sword, he offered her his arm. Alias accepted it with a smile and used it to balance herself as she rose to her feet. The warrior woman shifted her sword to her left hand as she reached down to scoop up the finder's stone.

Alias gasped. Her fingers reached of their own volition, not for the light, but for the wall. She broke out in a sweat in her effort to pull her hand away from the blue bricks. She hadn't actually felt the wall this time; her hand seemed to pass through it as though it were an illusion. The wall reacted in the same extraordinary way it had before.

Again, the bricks seemed to go clear and the passageway was bathed in blue light. The effect lasted a few moments longer this time. The sigils on her arm grew brighter.

Dragonbait knocked her to the ground, away from the blockade, and whatever lay on the other side, beckoning her hand to turn traitor to her body. Dragonbait stood over her, his muscles taut, ready to keep her from reaching out for the wall again. The smell of violets wafted from his body even more strongly now, and Alias wondered if that was the scent of his sweat or his fear.

Out of nowhere came the chant of a magical spell, and a sparkling dart slammed into Dragonbait's body. The lizard was propelled backward into the brick wall.

Alias gasped again. The wall remained solid and unaffected by contact with the lizard's body. She leaped up and spun about, sword raised to defend against the attacker.

"Akabar! Have you taken leave of your senses?"

The mage stood in the passageway, his invisibility negated by the casting of the magic missile he'd used on the lizard. He had had a lot of trouble coming down the staircase in the dark. He had turned the corner into this passage just in time to watch the lizard send Alias sprawling across the floor. "Are you blind, woman?" the mage snapped. "He just attacked you."

"You fool! He was trying to help me—"

"No. He's one of them! And I can prove it!" Akabar shouted, leaping toward the lizard with his dagger drawn.

Dragonbait could have responded by raising his sword and letting the mage skewer himself, but instead, he held his arms out to grapple with him. Akabar was no weakling, and the lizard discovered too late that the Turmishman would not be so easy to shove away. Akabar slashed at the lizard's shirt, ripping the ties so the garment fell open.

"Stop it!" Alias shouted. She dropped her sword and rushed forward to pry Akabar loose from the lizard. The two males shifted their weight, and Alias stumbled. All three fell toward the wall, but while Akabar's and Dragonbait's shoulders hit the barrier with a thud, Alias's hand and wrist plunged right through the brick and mortar. Only the lizard's body kept her from falling in farther.

The bricks went transparent yet again and the hellish, blue light that filled the passage from the other side of the wall caused the sigils on her arm to perform an entirely new trick. They replicated miniature illusory copies of themselves which slipped from her flesh. The little daggers, rings, fanged palms, and the rest circled about her arm like angry hornets. Alias tried to pull her arm from the wall, but it was mired fast, just as her legs had been trapped by the crystal elemental. "No!" she screamed. "I'm stuck!"

Dragonbait, squished between her and the wall, let his

sword drop and tried pushing her shoulders away.

"No good," Alias groaned. "You're pulling my arm from its socket."

Brought to a more reasonable state of mind by the new crisis, Akabar ceased struggling with the lizard. "How did you do that?" he asked, amazed at her ability to pass through the wall.

"It's not me, you stupid Turmite. It's the arm. That's why Dragonbait pushed me away from the wall. He must have known there was danger."

"He might have planned all this," Akabar insisted. "To help capture you. He's branded the same as you."

"Tell me something I don't know," Alias snarled. "Like how to get my arm out of this wall!"

"Try pushing forward a little and then jerking back," the mage suggested.

Alias pressed forward up to her elbow, covering all the sigils, but she could not pull back a fraction of an inch. "Great," she growled. "Now I'm stuck worse." Instinctively she put her foot up to the wall to use it as leverage to pull herself out, but the foot slipped through the brickwork as well, all the way to her knee.

"Any more bright ideas, Akash?"

Despite his awkward position, Dragonbait remained pressed against the wall, rather than risk losing Alias. Pulled closer to him, Alias could smell the scent of roses again, mixed with the odor of violets. Suddenly, it came to her—the rose smell always was present when he was sad. He was mourning her already. "Don't give up on me yet, chum," she whispered to him.

Dragonbait tried to smile, but it was meant for her benefit, not one he felt. She was in too much danger.

Akabar ran his fingers along the wall. He tapped on the brick and scratched at the mortar with his dagger. "This is the most unusual brick I've ever seen," he murmured. "But the grouting is common enough. Mortar mixed with gorgon blood, or something similar. It's used to block the passage of beasts that can walk through walls."

"Well, I can't walk through walls. Why isn't it stopping me?" Alias said through gritted teeth. Dots of perspiration formed at her brow.

"Precisely. It wasn't made to stop people. That's what the brick is for, I presume."

"The brick's not stopping me either!" Alias shouted. "Akabar, stop jabbering and do something!"

"All right, already." The mage ran nervous fingers through his hair. "I'm going to try to dispel the magic they must have cast on the wall while the mortar hardened. It was undoubtedly cast by a more powerful mage than I, but if the spell dates back as far as the destruction of the temple, it may have decayed some over the centuries."

"Cut the lecture. Just do it."

Akabar stepped back and spread his arms out so as to encompass the entire wall in his field of disenchantment. He began preparing to cast his spell.

Alias shrieked and began squirming furiously. Akabar had never heard Alias make such a noise before. The sound completely broke his concentration. Fortunately, he had not yet begun his spell, so it was not ruined and wasted.

"What's wrong?" he shouted crossly.

"There's something," Alias cried, her features distorted with terror. She gulped air far too quickly. "Something on the other side. It's got my arm."

What could terrorize a woman who's stood up to dragons, earthly titans, and man-eating kalmari? Akabar wondered as he peered at the wall. The blue light had dimmed considerably. All the mage could make out beyond the translucent bricks was a vast shadow.

As he watched, the warrior woman's body lurched forward, dragged deeper into the wall by her arm. Now she was embedded to her right shoulder plate.

"Oh, gods," Alias whined. "Gods, gods, gods, gods," she moaned over and over, as though she were pleading with heaven.

"Hold her tight, Dragonbait," Akabar barked. "I'm going to try to dispel now."

Akabar resumed his stance and began to intone his spell. The rise and fall of his voice became an eerie melody superimposed over the warrior's panicked, repetitious rhythm.

Dragonbait strained between the trapped warrior and

the wall. Even if his restored strength proved sufficient to counter the slow, steady force that sucked her through the barrier, Alias feared they might only end up tearing her in half. Equally bad was the possibility she would end up the instrument that crushed the life from the lizard before he was willing to sacrifice her.

Akabar finished his disenchantment spell by unlacing his fingers with a flourish to scatter the magical energies across the surface of the wall. Sun-yellow motes sparkled toward the wall, which was now the dark blue shade of a sky about to rain.

The motes struck the wall and hissed like sparks falling into water. The blue light grew even dimmer as the bricks grew opaque. Alias managed to pull her leg completely free and her arm came out up to her elbow. The half with sigils still remained buried.

Dragonbait, unprepared for the success of Akabar's spell, was dislodged from his position between Alias's trapped foot and arm, and he stumbled to the floor. He scrambled to his feet, grabbing her about the knees, but the entity on the other side gained the advantage with a sudden tug.

Alias gave one last inhuman scream before her boots slid from the lizard's grasp and she fell through the wall like sand in an hourglass.

The wall went completely opaque, and the sigils on Dragonbait's chest ceased radiating light. The lizard and mage were left alone, bathed in the now-feeble, yellow glow of the finder's stone.

Dragonbait picked up the glowing crystal and struggled to his feet. Tears streamed down the lizard's cheeks.

Akabar stared at the wall in disbelief. He ran up to it and pounded on it with his fists. "Give her back!" he screamed. The string of curses he began issuing rang down the corridors and echoed back, drowning out the ones he finished with. The wall remained smooth and hard. If Dragonbait's sword had only managed to scratch its surface, Akabar's bare hands weren't going to bring it down.

"You!" the mage growled, turning to the lizard. "This is your fault." He hurled his words like a mad monk throwing shurikens. They spun with poisonous, deadly precision, unconcerned whether or not they caused harm. "She came here after you. You should have held on to her. You lost her. We could have saved her, and you lost her. What kind of accursed beast are you? Who pulls your strings?"

With each accusation, the mage took a step toward the exhausted, grieving lizard until he had backed him against the wall and was standing over him nose to muzzle. Akabar screeched at the top of his lungs, "Answer me or, I swear, I'll wear your hide as sandals!" He reached down to grab the creature by the shoulders.

He never got the chance. Dragonbait used the finder's stone to smack the mage on the side of the head. The Turmishman staggered back and stumbled over the lizard's sword.

Dragonbait walked up to the mage and bent over him to retrieve his sword. Standing, he snarled down on him. His unblinking lizard eyes narrowed as the mage began to intone a short, deadly spell.

The Turmishman's spell and the lizard's leap to attack him were both interrupted when the ground shifted beneath them. Akabar forgot his spell and Dragonbait sprawled across the floor. They both looked back at the wall. The blue glazing from the bricks began to crack and flake away.

The lizard rolled away from the cascading shards of brickwork while the mage crab-crawled backward, keeping his eyes on the destruction. The glazing sloughed completely off, the brick beneath crumbled to dust. The red-colored mortar remained suspended in air for a moment and then crashed to the floor in a cloud of dust.

In the light of the finder's stone, it looked to Akabar as if a second wall stood just beyond the first, only this wall was composed of garbage, rotted plants, and turned earth. And bound in the center of the wall was Alias, her eyes closed, her body still. Her arms and legs were pinioned beneath coverings of moss and moist plant roots. Beneath the wet lichen covering her right arm, the runes pulsed like an evil, blue heart.

Akabar cried out, but Alias did not stir. She was unconscious. Just above the warrior woman's head, in the garbage wall, a human eye opened. Then, to the left of Alias's head, a feline eye opened, followed by a third eye above that, as large, milky, and deep as a dragon's. A fanged mouth opened to the right of Alias's right hand. A sharp hyena bark filled the room.

Tendrils shot out from the base of the wall-thing, and with these it began to drag itself forward, a rotting juggernaut. More tendrils oozed from slime-dripping pores, wet and thick tendrils, ending in mouths filled with sharp fangs.

The mage scrambled through the spells he had memorized. All he could think to try was another magic missile. He was struggling to calm himself so that he could begin chanting when a scaly arm grabbed the collar of his robe and dragged him down the passage and around the bend.

Akabar jerked away from the lizard's claws and knocked his arm away. "Was this your plan, beast," he spat, "to sacrifice her to that thing?"

Dragonbait's face twisted into a deep scowl, and Akabar thought the lizard was going to hit him again. Instead, he pointed around the corner, back toward the living wall.

It had become a wave of pungent rot. Fresh green shoots sprouted over it, and it moved with surprising speed, already having lumbered over the spot where Akabar had been standing only a moment before. New taproots shot out every second, and brownish slime oozed from beneath its flowing bottom. Alias remained asleep, entranced, trapped against its leading edge.

"So, you've saved me," Akabar shrugged. "How do we get Alias back?"

Dragonbait scowled again and pointed up.

Akabar had no better plan, so he allowed himself to be tugged back through the passages, looking behind every few yards to see if the wall of slime was still following them.

It was. The wall lumbered along like a mastodon, its bulk filling the corridor, oozing into different shapes to fit the narrower corridors. Its multiple mouths were babbling now, each inhuman throat finding its voice, wheezing through rotted pipes too long ignored.

The mage and the lizard finally reached the secret door from the stairs into the garbage midden. The stench of human waste was strong, but fresher and more alive than the dead-rot that followed them. The door had resumed whining, trying to overcome the rocks Alias had jammed in its path.

Dragonbait began kicking the stones away.

"No!" Akabar shouted, trying to push him away. "You can't do that! She'll be trapped in there with that thing!"

The lizard shoved him across the platform toward the stairs and kicked the last stone from the door's path.

The mossy barrier slammed shut.

"What have you done?" Akabar screamed.

Suddenly, Akabar gasped, breathless. Sharp pains laced through his chest like needles running beneath his skin. His lungs labored for air.

Dragonbait pointed upward and began climbing the stairs.

"Damn you!" the mage shouted up the steps from the platform. "I may be a greengrocer, but I know better than to abandon a friend! I'll die before I abandon her to that thing, you coward."

Directly behind him, the wall with the secret door exploded and the great, oozing mass surged into the pit. The stone platform began to collapse under its great weight, but the corruption cascaded downward still babbling from innumerable mouths. Now, the squealing cries were chanting in chorus.

In voices ranging from frog piping to deep, resonant tongues as ancient as the great elven forests, the word repeated over and over was *Moander.*

The Turmish mage blanched and fled up the stairs.

❧ 19 ❧

Moander's Resurrection and Mist's Return

Dragonbait was waiting for Akabar halfway up the stairs. The lizard's breathing was fast, but nowhere near as labored as the mage's. Akabar staggered up the stairs with his hands clutching his chest. The pain there had changed from sharp needle pricks to a deep, crushing sensation. His face was drenched with sweat. His shoulder and back ached.

"Why?" he gasped, his furor burned out by the fire in his lungs, "why did you let her die?"

Dragonbait made a quick dismissive shake of his head such as an adult might use to warn an overbearing child. Then, noticing the perspiration dripping down the Turmishman's anguished face, the lizard reached out to take his shoulder.

Akabar retreated from his grasp. "No," he insisted. "You go ahead. I can't run. Muscle cramp," he lied. "If it climbs up the walls, maybe I can slow it, maybe have a chance still to free her. Go!"

The mage collapsed in a heap on the stairs.

Dragonbait slipped past Akabar a few steps lower and knelt to get a better look at him. He put the finder's stone down beside him and reached out with both clawed hands. He laid his palms and fingers over the slime-spattered robe covering Akabar's chest.

The smell of woodsmoke enveloped them. A small aura of light flared around the reptile's claws. Nowhere but in the blackness of this pit would Akabar have been able to see the light the lizard generated. A feeling of warmth and relief spread out from Akabar's torso.

Akabar stood and the pain in his chest, back, and shoulder was gone. He stared at the lizard in confusion.

"Who in Gehenna *are* you? *What* are you?"

But Dragonbait's attention was fixed on the pit. He stared over the edge of the staircase into the earth's depths. Akabar tried to adjust his eyes to the darkness to see what held the lizard's gaze. A bright, blue light shimmered in the depths. At first, Akabar thought it might be the moon reflected in water, but the sky above the pit was dark.

"Alias!" he whispered excitedly. "She might still be alive. Look, the light's coming closer."

The light was indeed approaching them, the blue light shed by the sigils on the warrior woman's arm, but it was not Alias propelling herself upward. The bottom of the pit, a mass of rot and oozing garbage, was rising up the shaft. Alias was just a tiny human figure pinned to the muck.

Dragonbait pointed up the stairs and nudged Akabar to climb in front of him. The mage nodded and ascended without further argument or complaint. When he reached the top, he was only mildly winded. The pain had not reasserted itself with the exertion of the climb. He turned around to check on the lizard's progress up the stairs.

Having judged the speed of the monster to be less than their own, Dragonbait now took his time, turning back often to study it. Is he some sort of tribal shaman? Akabar wondered. What other secrets has he kept hidden?

Akabar peered back down the pit. Far below, the oozing mass that had kidnapped Alias was still crawling up the sides of the midden. It rose like lava in a volcano and had already regained the height of the ruined platform. The titanic effort of hauling its vast bulk did not seem to tire it. If anything, it seemed to be moving faster now.

"Don't move, mooncalf," a strange, rough voice ordered. Then it shouted, "Captain!"

Akabar looked up from the pit. Ten feet away, a single soldier was sitting on the pile of rubble about the midden. He was wrapped in a faded red robe, and a red-plumed helmet lay beside him, next to an overful bucket of kitchen waste. He held a loaded crossbow aimed at Akabar's chest.

Dragonbait's head rose over the rim of the pit. He ducked

back quickly, but it was already too late.

"No good, pigeon," the soldier barked toward the pit. "Bring your carcass over the side, or we'll push your buddy in."

Akabar watched Dragonbait shove the finder's stone into his shirt and sheathe his sword across his back, though the soldier did not have his line of sight and could not have noticed. The lizard scrambled over the edge with both his hands held out before him. He positioned his body between Akabar and the crossbow.

The mage had always assumed that in the event of Alias's inability to take charge, he would be the next leader. Obviously, Dragonbait did not agree. He took responsibility for their safety and put himself at the greatest risk.

The captain and four more fighters strode through the ruins toward the midden. Two carried lanterns and handheld crossbows. The rest were armed with short swords, drawn and ready.

"I got me some looters," their captor announced. "Or maybe spies," he added. By the brightening of his face, Akabar could see that this thought had just entered the man's head. The glee it brought him indicated that there was a bounty paid on spies.

Akabar looked to Dragonbait. Leader or not, he would need an interpreter. He stepped forward to stand beside the lizard as the captain approached. Dragonbait stood motionless, but Akabar could sense the lizard's tension. The fragrance of violets wafted from his body. The mage could smell his own sweat. Dragonbait glanced meaningfully at the pit and back at Akabar, raising his scaly brows. If he could stall the soldiers, they would soon be too busy dealing with an ancient god to bother with two stray adventurers.

"I am no looter, but a mage of no small water," Akabar announced to the captain. "I have important information for the commander of your unit."

"No small water," mimicked the crossbowman who'd discovered them.

"Sounds like a southerner," one of the other soldiers said.

"Don't like southerners," the first one said. "They lie and stink."

The Red Plumes captain held up his hand, silencing everyone. "Who are you, and what is your information?" he asked Akabar.

Akabar could not keep from glancing at the pit. Using the lumbering garbage pile of a god as a diversion would not work if Moander engulfed them before engaging the Red Plumes. "Let us go to your camp, where I will tell you," he said, trying to keep his voice steady.

"You'll tell me here and now," replied the captain, "or your bodies will be lying at the bottom of the pit."

The bottom of the pit may be here any minute, the mage thought nervously. Aloud he said, "There is something very dangerous in this pit. A threat to you and everyone else in this city. It climbs out even as we speak. You must fetch fire, oil, and powerful mages, quickly. We might still repel it."

The captain chuckled. "Our mages are asleep, southerner, resting after a powerful contention with the forces of Zhentil Keep. It would not be worth your life or mine to roust them. Your story sounds to me like a looter's tale, but it will not help you escape the noose. We have firm laws against looters. But I'm sure you know that."

"No," Akabar replied. "I do not." He looked around at the ruined city. "I wasn't even aware there was anything worth looting in this pile of rubble."

"I'll bet," the captain said, smiling with amusement at Akabar's cool denial. "However, ignorance of the law is no excuse. The Hillsfar Red Plumes are here at the request of the Yulash government in Hillsfar. On their behalf, we are authorized to hang all looters. No exceptions."

"I can understand that," Akabar said. "Please," he pleaded, "let us move away from the edge of this pit."

The captain surveyed the mage and the lizard. For the first time that evening, Akabar missed the presence of the glib-tongued Ruskettle. By now, the dratted halfling could probably have convinced the captain to organize a full alert, the mage mused, were she here and not snoring away at camp. He wondered if he would ever have another chance to scold her for her laziness.

Finally, the captain made up his mind. He motioned permission for Dragonbait and Akabar to move away from the pit. The crossbowmen kept their weapons leveled on the prisoners. The captain, having apparently sensed and caught Akabar's and Dragonbait's nervousness, moved away from the pit first, though he tried to appear calm and unperturbed as he leaned on his weapon. The other two men rested their swords on their shoulders.

The two adventurers moved cautiously through the rubble, away from the edge of the pit, until they stood with their backs against a half-toppled wall.

"Try again, looter," the captain ordered. "I'm sure you can come up with a better story than a pit fiend."

Why is it one's friends will believe one's lies, but one's enemies are incapable of recognizing the truth when one speaks it? Akabar pondered. He knew better than to backtrack. "Sir," he said urgently, "as one civilized man to another, I assure you, there is indeed a horrible creature in that pit, no mere fiend, but an ancient god."

"I've heard of you 'civilized Southerners'," their discoverer said, "you're baby-killers, every man-jack of you. Worship gods darker than those who squat at the Keep."

Either bards are spreading the tales about baby-killers in every society, Akabar thought, or they're neglecting their duty to disabuse people of these absurd notions.

The captain, not quite as obtuse and single-minded as his subordinates, gave an order to a crossbowman. "Soldier, take a look down the pit. The rest of you, watch this pair. If they so much as sneeze, skewer them."

The crossbowman climbed over the rubble to peer down into the pit. "Looks fine to me," he insisted, holding the lantern over his head. "Kinda full. We're going to have to find another dump soon. Hey, there's a body in there, a wo—"

The crossbowman never had a chance to finish his sentence. A slimy tendril whipped up over the edge of the pit, wrapped around the man's neck, and yanked him over the edge. The sickening crack of shattering bones followed.

The monster crested the rim of the pit and then rose above it. It had used the slimy refuse of the midden to increase its size and its stench was overpowering. But more hideous were the thousand singing mouths, some pitched gratingly high, others grindingly low, some smaller than a babe's, a few the size of a dragon's maw, all lined with gleaming, sharp fangs. In the center of the mass facing them, clustered around the immobile form of Alias, a set of mismatched eyes scanned the soldiers.

"Fire!" the captain shouted, flinging his own lantern at the beast. The glass shattered and the burning oil spread out over the rotting decay. It smoldered briefly, but the waste that made up the creature's body was too wet to ignite. Crossbow bolts disappeared into the garbage, but did not seem to cause much damage, except for puncturing an eye. Three more eyes opened around the injured eye, staring cross-eyed at the thick, green ichor oozing from it, then turned their attention to the fighters.

The mound of rot and refuse towered over its attackers. Wet tendrils, as thick as broomsticks, dripping with mire, lashed out from the body and struck three of the soldiers, including the captain. They were all dragged screaming into a different large, open maw, feet first. The Abomination bit each man in half before swallowing.

Dragonbait clutched at Akabar's robes, pulling him toward the city wall. Akabar tore loose from the lizard and planted his feet firm. "Look," he said, unable to tear his gaze from the horror that was Moander, "I'm sorry about what I said before. You were only doing what you thought best. Now you have to go get Ruskettle. Go get help—Elminster or Dimswart. The Harpers—anyone you can find. This is more than we can handle. I have to stay and try to free Alias."

Dragonbait shook his head.

"It's no use arguing. I'm not leaving. There's no sense in both of us risking our lives. Someone has to warn the world." Akabar did not bother to consider that Dragonbait had no voice to raise such an alarm. He shoved the lizard toward the city wall and moved toward the battle, circling to keep in sight the "face" of Moander that held Alias.

Dragonbait loped from the pit. He stopped a short distance away and turned to watch the battle.

The Abomination of Moander, singing its name, tore through the ruins, overrunning the camp of the Red Plumes. Akabar screwed his eyes shut and muttered, fast and furious, the opening lines of the spell.

When he opened them, the beast had turned back toward the pit to clean up the stray humans it had left behind. It was almost on top of him, its fanged mouths smiling and the eyes that clustered about Alias all fixed on his body. Akabar aimed his spell square on those eyes.

A pool of light blossomed across the god's "face." The eyes turned a blind, milky white or shut tightly to shield themselves from the brightness cast over them. Akabar grabbed a tendril and hauled himself up the hulking body.

When he reached Alias's side, he drew his dagger. He began hacking furiously at the roots which bound her to the monster. The blinding light would not last long, and he did not stand a chance once an eye spotted him.

There was movement along the garbage hulk. Akabar looked down to discover the source of the disturbance. Dragonbait was using the jagged teeth of his sword to saw through the thicker tentacles entrapping Alias.

Annoyed but not surprised, Akabar shouted, "You should have followed my orders." Dragonbait finally got one of Alias's legs free and moved up to work on the restraints about her arm, but he suspected he was fighting a losing battle. Tendrils were regrowing already, and Akabar had to slash them back, keeping him from making any progress toward liberating the swordswoman.

An eye opened near Akabar's hand. He stabbed it and it shut up, tearing yellow ichor. Below him, a large branch, as thick as a boa constrictor, reached for Dragonbait. Shouting a warning, the mage launched himself over Alias's body and kicked the lizard to the ground. The tendril caught the mage's wrist and snaked up his arm. At its tip was a venomous-looking flower shaped like a great, yellow hand that groped blindly toward the mage's head.

Dragonbait watched in shocked horror. Akabar shouted, "Run, damn you, run!" before the foul blossom curled over his face. Akabar was dragged into the heart of the pulsing mass. Tendrils grew over Alias's body.

Dragonbait fled toward the city wall. The heaving monstrosity shambled after him, swords and half-eaten bodies stuck out at all angles from the boundaries of its oozing flesh. There was no sign of the mage. The light Akabar had cast was fading, and only the hot blue glow from the warrior woman's buried arm revealed her position.

Diving through a hole in the city wall, the lizard curled himself into a tight ball and rolled down the slope of the mound with reckless speed. A shower of brownish vines and tendrils shot out after him but fell short of their mark. Shouts came from the far side of the wall—more mercenaries alerted to the Abomination's presence. The whine of missiles, ordinary and magical, reached Dragonbait's ears.

The lizard stood up and dashed down the mound. At the bottom, he turned to check on the monster. The city wall, already weakened from years of abuse, began to give under the pressure of the god's bulk. Part of its body oozed over the wall, crushing beneath what it could not push aside.

Dragonbait turned again and ran toward their camp, chased by the shrieks of the soldiers dying in the city. He did not weep for Akabar; all his tears had been spent on Alias, and he had no time to make more.

* * * * *

Olive Ruskettle turned in her sleep and moaned softly. A shadow passed through her usual dreams of wealth and fame and food and wine. Phalse's face appeared briefly, his head split by that unhalfling-like grin, followed by a recurring nightmare—her abduction by Mist. Panicked horses neighed over the rushing sound of the dragon's wings. The dream was so real that Olive's sleeping form curled into a tight ball and pulled the covers over her head.

Then something poked at her, a swift, sharp shove. Alias, Olive guessed, demanding that I take my turn at watch.

"Go 'way," Olive grumbled, clutching the covers more tightly about her. "It's the lizard's turn. Let me have five more minutes. Tops."

"Five more minutes," an agreeable voice rumbled. "Then I will fry you where you sleep."

Olive's eyes shot open. Very slowly, she turned over to find herself looking square in the steaming face of the not-so-honorable Mistinarperadnacles.

"Boogers," the halfling whispered. She scanned the campsite for the others.

There was no sign of them. They were gone—all three of them. Dead already? Olive puzzled. Without a fight?

The tethers of the horses had been pulled up, but the twisted, half-eaten form of the purebred chestnut, Lady Killer, lay not far away.

The dragon followed her gaze. "Yes," Mist purred, "I had a wee bit to nosh before waking you. I get so crabby trying to talk to people on an empty stomach. The temptation to eat them wears on my nerves, you see." Steam poured from the creature's nostrils, engulfing the halfling.

Olive coughed back a breath of the noxious vapor.

"Now," the she-dragon demanded, "where is the lawyer?"

"Lawyer?" Olive squeaked, trying to gain her mental footing. How could the others leave me like this, unguarded, in so much danger? Of all the inconsiderate behavior!

"The woman who knows the old ways," said the dragon. "The warrior. I understand she travels with a pet mage and a lizard-creature."

Olive's heart leaped. They were still alive! Somewhere. They can rescue me! Aloud she said, "Gee, they were here a little while ago. Maybe they—" Her hand fell on Akabar's parchment map. Squinting in the moonlight, she could just make out writing on the back, but not what it said. Cautiously, explaining her every move to Mist in detail to avoid any sudden incinerations, the halfling drew out and lit a candle from her pack. She read the message to herself.

"A clue?" Mist asked hopefully.

"Yes," the halfling nodded. "See?" She held the map up to the dragon's left eye.

"And what does it say?" Mist inquired.

"You don't read Common?" Olive asked meekly, afraid of offending the vain beast.

"I prefer the more visual arts," the lumbering creature said with a defensive snort. "Theater, sculpture, bards.' "

How about opera? Olive wondered. She held the parchment in front of her and read aloud: " 'Had a vision. Off to Zhentil Keep. Follow soon. Hugs, Alias?' "

"Are you certain? There don't seem to be that many words to me," Mist said, her eyebrows raised in suspicion.

"She uses a lot of abbreviations. Like scribes, you know,"

the halfling replied.

"Do your friends usually leave you behind just because you sleep late?" the dragon asked.

"Well, you see, they knew I was a little reluctant to go to Zhentil Keep. I would have preferred visiting another city, like Hillsfar. I guess they didn't feel like waiting for me to make up my mind to join them or not."

Mist raised up on her rear haunches, stretched, and yawned. Then she settled back down. "You have no idea the trouble I've gone to to find the two of you," she said. "Matter of honor and all that."

Olive couldn't have said what came over her, but some demon inside of her, tired of being pushed around and bullied, prompted her to ask rudely, "You mean you've brought us the chest of gold you promised us?"

Mist's eyes narrowed into slits. "Before I rush off to deal with the Zheeks for your friend's hide, I think a little late lunch would be in order."

The demon within vanished. "Oh," Olive said, "you wouldn't want to do that. Flying on a full stomach, you'll get cramps. Besides, you'll need someone to help you negotiate with the Keepers. They're a terribly bureaucratic bunch. Forms, red tape, memos. They could give you the runaround for days. I can be terribly useful in cutting through the paperwork, and you know how entertaining I am. Remember the good times we had together in the cave—er, lair, I mean, your home."

"I do," the dragon agreed with a smirk. "And I must confess that the desire to reclaim you, my little, lost trophy, motivated me almost as much as my desire for revenge." Mist paused a moment before asking, "You've heard of singing for your supper?"

With a gulp, the bard nodded.

"Well, with me, you must sing or become supper. I might just spare you . . . or not."

Ruskettle sighed. Repressing all the smart remarks that came to her head, she reached for her yarting.

❦ 20 ❦

Dragonbait's Feint of Honor

The smell of blood caught Dragonbait's attention a hundred yards before he entered camp. He dropped to all fours and crawled forward cautiously. By the campsite was a huge dark mound. The massive shape was easily ten times greater than the upended wagon that had shielded the whole party. As the lizard drew closer, he heard singing.

The voice was Ruskettle's, but it was unusually uneven. It rang out strong and sweet for a few lines, then wavered helplessly for a half dozen notes before regaining its tone. Olive sang the tune Alias had taught her way back in Cormyr, the song about the fall of Myth Drannor. Here on the battle-strewn plain, in the dark, with fear so obviously in her heart, the song took on a poignancy Olive might never have been able to give it before a human audience.

The lizard crept closer still, using the wagon as cover. Once he was crouched behind the wagonbed, he looked back toward Yulash. The eastern sky was developing the sickly glow of sunrise through fog, but Dragonbait didn't need the light to pick out the great hulk of Moander. To the lizard's sight, the Abomination stood out against the mist-chilled fields, warmed as it was with the fresh blood of its victims. It was heading south toward the Elven Wood.

Dragonbait turned his attention once more to the matter close at hand. He peeked around the edge of the wagonbed and instantly recognized the monster that crouched like a great cat at the bard's feet.

A lair-beast, a very big lair-beast, Dragonbait concluded, ducking back behind the wagon.

He sniffed at the air and recognized the monster's scent.

Alias had gone into this creature's den and brought out the halfling. Even from the back tunnel, his sensitive nose had been able to pick out the dragon's scent, and he had rankled at the swordswoman's order to stay outside while she went in to do battle.

Mist's great tail wrapped around the camp, trapping the halfling in a ring of crimson.

Dragonbait sighed inwardly. This was a very inconvenient time to have to fight a lair-beast, he thought. If he died, there would be no one left to help Alias, but he needed Olive's help. There simply wasn't time to find new allies.

He climbed to the top of the wagonbed so the halfling would be able to see him without alerting the dragon.

Olive's voice quivered with exhaustion. It wasn't easy being so frightened. When she spotted Dragonbait, she almost shouted out the next lyric, but years of training stepped in and she was able to repress her excitement before she gave away the lizard's presence.

Her voice grew in strength as she sang the final verse. A plan was beginning to form in the back of her head. She had seen the lizard in combat, and he wasn't bad. With her brains and his brawn, she might just have a chance. She finished the song with a flourish.

The dragon let out a great contented sigh, steam pouring from her nostrils. "That is a new one. You must have learned it since we last parted, or were you keeping this little gem hidden from me when you stayed as my guest?"

"A good bard is always picking up new pieces for her repertoire," the halfling replied evenly. She stretched and asked, "So, have you decided to eat me now or wait until you find Alias of Westgate?"

"I am of two minds," Mist answered, standing up to stretch herself. She turned around like a cat trying to decide the most comfortable position. Dragonbait dropped behind the wagon not a moment too soon. When the great wyrm had settled herself back down, in nearly the exact same spot as before, Dragonbait climbed back up the wagon to watch the proceedings.

"Two minds," Mist repeated. "On one hand, your talent would be a great loss to the world. On the other hand, artists don't usually become really famous until after their deaths. I would be doing you a favor by allowing you to satisfy this peckish feeling in my belly."

"But then I couldn't help you find Alias," the halfling pointed out calmly.

"No," the dragon admitted, "but then, neither could you escape to warn the foul-tongued wench. You see my problem." A long, lolling tongue slid out from between Mist's jaws and licked at her two protruding upper fangs.

"Yes," Olive admitted, her eyes riveted to the great, forked organ until it withdrew back into the dragon's mouth. "It sounds as if you've already made your decision."

"You're right," Mist said as rivers of drool began to slide down her chin hairs. "I think a light meal is definitely in order before I resume the hunt."

"Sounds appropriate to me," the halfling agreed, reaching into her shirt as if to scratch an indelicate itch. "I guess I have no choice, then."

"Not really."

From his perch atop the wagon, Dragonbait crouched forward, ready to leap on the dragon and save the strangely acquiescent bard.

Olive withdrew her hand from her shirt and presented a small, stoppered bottle. "Have you ever heard of peranox?" she asked.

"It's some human poison, isn't it? It's supposed to smell like cinnamon, I believe."

The halfling nodded and unstoppered the bottle. The scent of cinnamon immediately drifted to her nostrils. Mist sniffed and no doubt caught a whiff of it, too.

"Yes, a human poison." Olive nodded as beads of perspiration began rising on her forehead and cheeks. "And a halfling poison as well. Fast acting. Deadly. What I have here will kill me. It may kill you, too. Though of course I don't know the correct dosage for a beast your size."

"Such a desperate action."

"These are desperate times." Olive rose to her feet, using the tiny vial as a shield. Now, work up to this slowly, Olive-girl—you can't afford to miss any steps, she warned herself as she prepared to use the same legal arguments she'd learned from the swordswoman. "You don't think much of me, do you?" she asked the dragon.

"Beg pardon?" Mist replied in confusion, her eyes never leaving the bottle in the halfling's hands.

Dragonbait unsheathed his sword, but remained perched on top of the wagon. The poison stand-off could not last long. Eventually, the dragon would just decide she wasn't hungry enough to ingest a poison-laden bard and simply incinerate the halfling. Yet, Dragonbait could sense Olive was preparing some other cunning plan. It might be worth the risk to let the halfling play her hand before trying to battle this lair-beast myself, he decided.

"Were it Alias the human you found here with me, what would you have done? Sat down and demanded four or five songs as you tore apart her favorite horse?"

"I'm sorry," Mist said. She nodded toward the remains of Lady Killer. "Was this a friend of yours?"

"It was Alias's horse," Olive snapped. "But that's not my point, is it? You wouldn't have made her grovel before you."

"No," Mist admitted. She thought carefully for a moment. "I would have killed her directly, using flame and fangs and claws and every other weapon at my disposal."

"Ex-actly!" the halfling said. "You wouldn't waste your time while . . ." Olive caught herself. She'd been about to say, "while she waited frantically for reinforcements to arrive and rescue her," but that was too close to her own situation. Mist might sit up and look around, ruining the lizard's surprise. She gulped and then continued, "while the night passed, demanding more songs like a drunkard at an inn calling for more mead."

"Well, if you're offended by my sparing your life, I can correct that." The dragon's smile revealed nothing but sharp teeth, all the way back down her mouth.

"Offended," Olive mused. "Yes, that's the word. Offended. My honor, small though it be, has been besmirched. I see no remedy but a Feint of Honor."

"Feint of—" The dragon reared up, accidentally knocking the wagon with her shoulder. The upended wagon overturned, sending Dragonbait sprawling backward. The lizard landed on all fours and pressed himself tightly against the ground.

Meanwhile, Mist rocked back and forth, issuing a loud braying that Olive could only assume was laughter. The halfling shifted to the left somewhat to keep the dragon's attention away from Dragonbait's position.

How did he ever get a stupid name like Dragonbait? the bard wondered as she caught a glimpse of the lizard stalking forward. I just hope its not prophetic. When Mist had quieted some and fixed her gaze back on the halfling, Olive asked testily, "Are you quite through?"

"Dear child," the dragon chuckled, "do you take me for a fool? Being foiled once this year by a warrior schooled in the old ways is enough. To be taken in yet again, by a halfling, would be unforgivable."

"There you go insulting me again." Olive thrust out her chest and brought the bottle close to her, determined to spill it on herself. "I challenge you, O Mistinarperadnacles, to a Feint of Honor!"

Again the dragon brayed. "You have missed your calling, small one. Comedy, not music, is your vocation."

"We settle terms next," Olive persevered despite Mist's attitude. "I suggest three hits, no flames, no claws, little bitesies. Any friends that happen along are welcome to join in the fray."

Mist rose up on her hind haunches. Steam began to curl out from between her great fangs. "Little fool. There is one small portion of the Feint of Honor of which you are no doubt ignorant. It must be issued by a good fighter and true. You are no fighter, you are not good, and I doubt, little bard, that you are true. You are beginning to bore me, and so you must die."

Just then, the sun broke through the mists and the dragon became a great, dark shadow outlined with an aura of light. Olive was certain she had met her doom. She took a deep breath and closed her eyes tightly. She wondered if her end would be the agony of fire or, should Mist be willing to risk the effects of peranox, the pain of razor-sharp teeth.

When several heartbeats had passed without a violent attack on her person, the halfling, still holding her breath, popped open one eye. She was ready to close it at a moment's notice should the dragon attack.

But her view of the dragon was blocked by the body of Dragonbait. The lizard stood before Mist, brandishing his toothed, diamond-headed sword.

Olive could not believe her eyes. *He's going to defend me.* But Dragonbait remained motionless before the dragon. *What's he doing? Praying? It's too late for that,* she decided, crouching down and edging away from the lizard. Mist ignored her. The dragon's amber eyes were locked with the lizard's.

Why aren't they attacking? Olive wondered. Neither creature moved. Her curiosity overwhelmed her good sense, and Olive stood watching the two combatants.

Banks of steam evaporated off Dragonbait's neck and chest. Olive found herself suddenly thinking of baking bread. Then she realized it wasn't a stray thought; she smelled hot rolls, fresh from the oven, begging to be smeared with butter and jam. The halfling's mouth watered. It was, after all, time for breakfast.

As the dragon and lizard engaged in their battle of wills and the daylight grew brighter, Olive became aware of the additional damage Mist had wrought while the halfling slept. The ground about the campsite and where the horses had been staked was all torn up, plowed by the dragon's claws. "And I slept through it all," Olive muttered in a daze.

Then Mist rumbled, "Well challenged, noble warrior. What are your terms?"

Olive stared flabbergasted at Dragonbait. *Mist understands him? After all the foolishness I went through to try to communicate with him, he talks to a dragon first. That figures. They're both lizards.*

But even more astonishing to Olive was the polite manner in which Mist accepted the lizard's challenge. She treated him with a courtesy she hadn't bothered to use even when Alias fought her.

Mist continued to watch the lizard, nodding occasionally as though taking in some point or other, though the halfling could not hear a sound from Dragonbait. *Is he some sort of telepath?* she wondered. *No. Then he would have talked to us in our minds.*

Finally, Mist said, "An interesting tale. Yes, agreed. Maximum damage. If you win, I'll help you take on this abomination you describe. But after the beast is killed, our deal is ended. If I win, you shall tell me where to find Alias before I slay you and your ally."

"Brandobis!" cursed the halfling. His ally—that's me. Where does he get off forfeiting my life? She did not take into consideration that there was little else Dragonbait could do if he lost the battle.

Her first instinct was to flee. She reached down for her pack, but as she picked it up, that idea curdled like blood in her mind. The thin platinum coins in her pack clinked together, reminding Olive of her deal with Phalse. She wore the tracking ring on a chain around her neck, near the ring that detected magic. If she abandoned the lizard now, she might not be able to find the warrior woman, and Phalse's friends would believe she had reneged on her agreement and deal with her accordingly. But if Dragonbait won, he would take her right to Alias.

How do I get into these messes? Olive sighed. She wracked her mind for some means of helping the lizard battle the dragon.

"We start at three," the dragon explained. "One . . ."

Dragonbait went into a crouch. Olive wondered if she could loft the poison into the beast's mouth.

"Two . . ." Mist said, unfurling her wings. In the sunrise they were the color of human—and halfling—blood. The dragon flexed her rear legs and leaped into the air, hovering with a massive beat of mighty wings.

"Three!" Mist roared, as Dragonbait dodged beneath her.

Mist breathed fire—a short, spitting flame that divoted the earth where Dragonbait had been standing. The lizard was beneath the dragon, but Mist lashed out with her tail, batting him forward, once again in her sight.

She's playing with him, the halfling realized and began desperately searching through her pockets for something to help. The poison? No, she might need that for her own use later. Besides, she'd never get it up that high. The coins weren't enough to bribe a dragon. Her halfling short sword and daggers would be useless against that great hulk.

The blow of the dragon's whiplike tail separated Dragonbait from his weapon. He dodged another small spit of flame and leaped on the lost sword. As he did so, the hovering dragon swooped, snagging his shirt. The shirt ties were already torn off though, and the lizard managed to slip out of the garment. He fell to the ground with a thud, rolling back toward his weapon.

Mist landed with her paw on top of his leg before he could reach his blade. She moved her head very close to him and smiled broadly, gloating.

"What's this, little dragon-warrior?" the dragon mocked her prey. "I think I've seen these markings before on your mistress. Are you a matched set? A pity to break you up."

The bard gasped. Dragonbait was branded with the same blue sigils as Alias. Only his were set in a ring.

A ring! Olive thought excitedly. Brands just like Alias! Olive pulled the chain out from beneath her shirt and slipped on the magical detection ring. She ran toward the battle, twisting the ring and pointing her finger at Dragonbait.

The azure sigils that marked Dragonbait's chest exploded with a satisfyingly brilliant light.

Mist pitched backward as the sapphire fireworks exploded in her face. Reflexively, the dragon raised her front paws to her eyes, tossing her prisoner through the air. Dragonbait spun about like a trained acrobat, landed on his feet, and ran toward the dragon's rear haunches.

As Mist pawed at the motes of light dancing before her eyes, she flapped her wings desperately, churning up clouds of dust. The mighty breeze caused blankets and cloaks to flutter about like theater spirits and sent equipment packs rolling over, scattering their contents through the camp. Mist roared, and steam gushed from her mouth.

Dragonbait swung his sword two-handed, biting deep into the monster's thigh. Mist gave a shout and pitched forward. Olive sidestepped just in time to avoid being struck by the dragon's jaw as it hit the ground.

Raising her neck, the dragon fired blindly, torching the overturned wagon. Her neck snaked, spreading the flames in a wide swath. But Dragonbait had dodged beneath her head, preparing to attack her opposite flank.

The dragon began batting her wings again, trying to take off. Dragonbait jabbed his sword into her left wing. The backward curved teeth caught in the flesh and tore a huge, flapping gash in the membrane.

The red dragon crashed to the ground once again. Olive had been waiting for this chance, and she ran toward the huge head. Her sight now cleared, Mist opened her mouth, preparing to bite the brave but foolish halfling into two tidbits. The bard turned and dodged away from the beast's maw, but not before she managed to toss in, at point-blank range, the opened bottle of peranox.

The bottle cracked beneath the snapping jaws, sending shards of poisoned crystal deep into the dragon's mouth. Dragonbait struck Mist again, opening a third wound along her belly. The dragon spat and flamed, trying to drive the poison from her mouth.

Mist rolled over in the dust like a flea-bitten dog tormented by insignificant invaders. She flamed at the sky until nothing but heated air escaped her innards. Dragonbait made one last gash in her neck, then dashed away, scooping Olive up in his arm and running from the camp—ten, twenty, thirty yards before he stopped. Then he turned to watch the dragon as it tossed and twisted in agony.

After five minutes, the thrashing stopped and the huge, crimson monster lay still in the dirt. Dragonbait pushed Olive to the ground and pointed as though he were ordering her to stay. He crept warily back toward the dragon. Unwilling to miss this historic moment, Olive followed disobediently after him.

They halted a few feet from Mist's head. She was still breathing. Drooling sweat ran from the corners of Dragonbait's mouth, and Olive had a stitch in her side from her short attack-run. Still, there was no doubt they had won. She wondered if Mist would really obey Dragonbait now or try to deceive him the way she had Alias.

She turned to the lizard, touching his scaly arm shyly. "Thank you for saving me," she said.

Dragonbait bowed his head politely.

"You can talk, can't you?" Olive asked.

The lizard felt for his belt pockets, where he had put the talis deck Olive had given him. But the pouch he reached in was torn along the bottom seam and now completely empty. Dragonbait shrugged.

"Boogers," Olive said. "You know what happened to Alias, but you can't tell anyone."

"Nonsense. He's told me already," Mist said, popping one eye open, but remaining otherwise immobile.

Dragonbait raised his sword, and Olive caught a strong whiff of tar. Mist's eye closed and she whispered, "Yes, I surrender, dragonling. I apologize for judging you by your raiment. You win. I will honor our agreement." The dragon sighed and opened her eyes. "Bard, you don't have any more of that putrid-tasting potion, do you?"

"Oh," the halfling lied, "about six or seven more jars. Large jars. Why?"

The dragon closed her eyes. Dragonbait snarled, and the eyes opened again. "I said I give up. You win. Just keep that peranox away from me. I think I'm going to be sick."

Ruskettle suddenly realized she was shaking, though whether from aftershock of the battle or the thought of a violently ill dragon, she did not know.

Slowly, like a drunk recovering from her first hangover, Mist reared up her head, flexing the damaged leg and torn wing. "That tears it," she said. "Literally. I won't be able to fly for a year. Sorry, but I can't very well help you if I'm damaged. What say I just let you go and I trek my way home?"

Dragonbait snarled again. "Only a suggestion," Mist muttered, laying her head back down on the ground.

The lizard moved back toward the torn wing, grabbed a handful of it on both sides of the tear, and pulled it toward him like a seaman about to mend sailcloth. He ran his fingers along the tear, and the torn webbing began to mesh. A faint, yellow glow emanated from the wound as it healed. Olive caught the scent of woodsmoke. Dragonbait restored about half the damage along the trailing edge of the wing, leaving a few spotty holes.

"Thank you," Mist sighed without lifting her head, obviously relieved of some pain.

Ruskettle looked at the lizard in confusion. "How did you

do that?" she demanded. "Where is Alias? And who are you, anyway?"

Dragonbait jerked his head from Mist to Olive. Mist appeared to concentrate on the small lizard for a few moments and then began to "translate" his silence. As the dragon spoke for the opponent who had defeated her in combat, Olive's eyes widened and her jaw dropped.

"I don't believe you," she told Mist. "You're making this all up. It's impossible!"

"No one could make up so improbable a tale," Mist sniffed. "Not even you, bard."

Olive fixed her attention on Dragonbait. The lizard was already gathering the party's belongings that were still salvageable from the destruction Mist had wreaked on them.

Olive planted herself firmly before him and demanded to know. "It's not true what she said, is it? You can't be what she said. You're a lizard!"

Dragonbait looked down at the halfling without expression, holding her eyes with his own unblinking ones. Olive grew nervous beneath his gaze because she realized Mist had told her the truth. He really was one of them. Though he hadn't seemed like one of them before, there was no other explanation for all his actions.

"It's true." she squeaked.

Dragonbait nodded.

Boogers! Olive swore silently. How do I get into these messes? More importantly, how do I get out of this one?

☙ 21 ❧

Moander's Puppet and Mist's Pursuit

Alias stirred beneath the moss-stained roots, and her mind crawled back from the lands of darkness. She twisted once, then again, straining against her bonds.

She recalled the passage through the wall of enchanted masonry. It had felt like an immersion in a cold mountain lake, chilling her skin and knocking the wind out of her. When she had finally gasped for air, there was a spongy mat against her face—a fragrant glove of pungent, vegetable smells which had reminded Alias of mushrooms in butter sauce gone bad in the summer heat.

And then she knew nothing. It was like the dark emptiness that preceded her appearance at The Hidden Lady.

When Alias awoke, the exposed portions of her skin were chilled and slightly wet from the fog. She had no idea how long she had slept, or what had happened while she did, but her adventures in Cormyr and Shadow Gap, and the conversations at Shadowdale, all remained crisp and clear in her memory. If anything, they felt more real than the adventures she'd experienced before she had received the deadly, cursed tattoo.

Finally, she opened her eyes to glare at the curse scrawled across her arm, only to find it trapped in a blanket of green fibers. She tried to shake loose, but her arm was held fast. She tried to move her left arm, but that limb was also pinned down by the same sort of damp, slimy blanket.

Alias tried kicking. Her legs were trapped, too. She wriggled and thrashed and bucked, but a wet root, as thick as her arm, held her to the ground. Whenever she moved, the tendrils moved with her. She sensed one of the bonds tearing, but new shoots sprouted immediately to replace it.

Frustrated, she looked around. She lay on an odd collection of garbage, bog peat, sickly green vines, and large moldy roots. At the edge of her vision she spotted something clean and white jutting out from the greenery. Alias recognized it as a human bone.

She felt the pile of boggy vegetation shift as though it were moving on a great wagon. She was lying on a ledge at the leading edge of the pile, about fifteen feet from the ground, but she could see no horses or oxen ahead.

A pile of dead leaves shifted by the right side of her head. As she watched, a single, green tendril burst through the rotting vegetation. At the tendril's tip was a pumpkinlike pod. The tendril swiveled toward her, and the pumpkin pod opened like a flower. At its center was a great, weeping eye, trapped on all sides by jagged, spined teeth.

The sight touched some memory buried within Alias, a memory she wished had stayed buried. She screamed.

The pumpkin pod closed up, startled or frightened by her reaction. The tendril withdrew into the refuse pile.

Alias swallowed with some difficulty, keeping her eyes fixed on the spot where the tendril had sprouted. When it did not reappear, she began to look around again, though her eyes kept returning to that site every few seconds to make sure her ocular companion had not returned.

The mound was passing over terrain that resembled the plains about Yulash. The sun was on her left and there was a thick, dark line of green across the horizon straight ahead.

If that's the rising sun, we must be heading south out of Yulash, toward the Elven Wood, she thought. Unless I've slept for days again—then we could be anywhere.

The sound of something moving through the garbage made her realize she and the wretched tendrils were not alone. Three figures appeared at the corner of the mound— men, moving in a matching stride like soldiers. A vine trailed behind each man, attached somewhere to his back.

The man in the center cast a long shadow on her and blocked out the sun, so she could only make out his silhouette at first. The sun shone through the light robes he wore—revealing spindly legs, but a powerful torso. He wore some sort of helmet. She could not make out his features, but by his bearing she knew he was Akabar.

The men who flanked the mage were dressed in moldy, torn battle gear. They moved stiffly as they picked their way through the garbage.

"Akabar?" she said softly, but the figure did not respond. "Akabar? What's going on? Cut me out of this stuff."

"I'm afraid I must inform you," the lean figure began in the roundabout speech of the South, "that I am not your Akabar." He broke rank from the two soldiers and knelt beside her head.

He was Akabar. He had Akabar's face, marked with the three blue scholar-circles on his forehead, and Akabar's square-shovel beard, and the same sapphire earring which marked him as a married man. His dark eyes, though, were completely fogged over in gray and patches of listless white swirled through them. The thing Alias had mistaken for a helmet was a cap of vines that pressed suckers against the mage's forehead and into his ears. Dried blood flaked around the suckers.

Her breath came in short gasps as a scream tried to claw its way up her throat. She found the strength to ask, "Who are you?"

"I am Moander," said the thing that was Akabar, "the most important being in your world."

In a smooth, gentle motion he lowered his body into a cross-legged sitting position and waited for his prisoner to stop squirming. Having exhausted herself in a futile effort to pull away from the mound of garbage, Alias finally lay still. She turned her head away from Akabar's body and kept her eyes squeezed tight. "Oh, gods," she moaned.

"Just a god, singular," Moander replied. "The only one that matters. Hold on, you have something stuck to your chin. Let me get it."

Akabar used the sleeve of his robe to dab at a fleck of garbage near Alias's mouth. He used too much pressure and pushed her head backward into the spongy bed of compost. It was as though he were unaware of his own strength.

"There. Much better. Now we can talk."

"You're not Akabar," Alias whispered, still trying to convince herself, but not wanting to believe it.

"Not really, no, but I'm all the Akabar you're going to get for a while. Might as well make the best of him. By rights, he should have died of fear, being the first human in this millennium to behold my godliness. How he survived I'll never know. But that kind of luck shouldn't be tampered with, so I left his body in better shape than the others. Look."

Alias felt shambling footsteps through the boggy ground and looked past Akabar's body at his companions. One's neck was ripped open, and his face was pale and ghostly without its lifeblood. The other had no face at all, only a slab of pummeled, bloody meat. Both had tendrils rigged around their bodies, moving them like puppets.

Alias felt her stomach heave and twist, but it was overridden by a chill, clammy terror. Her body trembled and she began to hyperventilate.

"There, there," Moander said, using Akabar's hand to smooth her hair. "I just brought them as an example of what I could have done to your friend. I'll send them away now."

Moander gave no verbal command and made no physical gesture, but the shambling corpses retreated around the side of the hill of garbage. Alias stared at the passing plains. After a few moments, she grew calmer. "Who are you really?" she asked.

"As I said before, I am Moander. Though that is a lot like calling a newborn prince the king."

Alias swung her head and stared at the stranger in Akabar's body. He imitated the mage almost perfectly, his pose, his gestures, the tone and cadence of his voice. But the smile was wrong. It was an exaggerated, forced smile—as if someone had pinned the corners of his mouth.

"Are you . . . I mean, is he . . ."

"Dead? Not really. He's gone, for all intents and purposes, but his soul and mind are still around, locked away in some corner. Rather like a man poisoned by a Jit snake, who lies in fever dreams, not waking, for weeks. You still have Jit snakes around here?" He paused, tilting his head as if listening to an unheard speaker. "No, I guess you don't anymore."

He rested his milky gray eyes on Alias and sat quietly, as if waiting for her to ask him another question.

Alias only stared at the passing scenery, so Moander continued. "In this case, if I were to let the mage go, he would awaken. But he cannot break my control, and I will control him until he is no longer useful. And this one is so incredibly useful. I needed his mouth and mind to talk to you. Of course, I could have linked up with you, but you are far too valuable to risk that. Besides, he is so very amusing."

Moander giggled. "I can't begin to tell you all I'm finding in his mind. It's like being in a great mansion, with new surprises behind every door. Here are memories of his wives, and here is you calling him a greengrocer, and here is a good piece of history of the South. Gods below, so much has happened. I've been out of touch for too long!"

"Out of touch?" Alias taunted. "I thought gods were omniscient."

"Well, normally that would be true. Gods stretch through a number of different planes, with different levels of power in each. This part of me—" Akabar's hand motioned to the pile of garbage which towered over them— "you might call the Minion or Abomination of Moander. More than a thousand years ago, back when Myth Drannor was a major power, the cursed elves banned my spirit from this world by imprisoning this part of me in my own temple."

A weakness crept over Alias's spirit. This vast garbage heap was her enemy, and not only did it hold her prisoner, but it waved her friend before her eyes like a puppet.

"Soon, when this part of me arrives at the new temple my worshipers have prepared, and I gather even more worshipers to my fold, I will grow strong enough in this world to command the powers that gods are endowed with. Had I been in full control of my powers when my spirit was finally able to return to the Abomination, I would have left a pit where Yulash stood and ascended into the heavens to mete out punishment to those who banished me."

"But in the meantime, you're pretty weak. Relatively, I mean."

Moander cocked Akabar's head like a hanged man. "Relatively. But I have plenty of stored life-fluid in this form. More than enough to reach my worshipers, pop the heads off a few sacrifices, and make demands on the populace. I'm conserving my strength by traveling this slowly so that I can have enough energy to indulge a whim."

Alias stared at the approaching forest, wondering if the sludge mountain that was Moander would break up when it hit the trees or flow around them.

Moander gestured with Akabar's hands toward the trees which held Alias's attention. "My first stop is Myth Drannor. According to your friend's mind, all the elves have deserted their capital. I've got to make sure. If it's true, at least I can dance on the rubble. From there we'll continue south until we reach Sembia. I love the way your friend thinks in terms of maps and trade routes. He is so useful."

"And once we've reached Sembia?"

"Ah, curiosity, my servant. A good sign. We'll cut southwest through Sembia toward The Neck, between the Sea of Fallen Stars and the Lake of Dragons, and just hop in the water. Scum, like cream, floats. We shall sail triumphantly to our new home."

"Which is?" Alias asked. She already had a strong suspicion, but she had to know for sure.

"Westgate, of course. Where we built you."

* * * * *

The trio of non-humans climbed higher into the sky, keeping well above the range of the catapults of any surviving Keepers or Red Plumes.

"Why so high?" Olive bellowed in Mist's ear.

The dragon let out a puffing grumble, "What?"

"I said, what are we flying so high for?" The halfling grasped the ropes which Dragonbait had fashioned into an impromptu saddle.

The dragon rumbled between deep puffs of air. "Can either" (long breath) "fly or talk." (Long breath.) "Try singing" (long breath) "while you're running hard." (Long breath.) "Hang on."

The dragon ceased flapping, locked her wings in a gliding position, and began to circle the city, her wings catching the thermals rising from the mound. Olive looked back at the dragon's great batlike membranes. One wing still showed a pink line from the recently healed tear.

Dragonbait, who sat where the dragon's wings joined her body, had done the healing. According to Mist, the warrior lizard communicated with his scent glands, so he could not "speak" as they soared through the air. The wind would carry away the perfume of his words. But he made his desires known quite effectively by prodding the great wyrm with his sword.

"You were saying," Mist prompted the bard, now that she was able to breathe normally, her labors eased by the helpful warm air.

"Can't you fly any lower?" Olive asked.

"Do you want to catch a ballista-bolt in the crotch?"

When Olive did not answer immediately, Mist said, "Thought not. Trust me. I know what I'm doing. Besides the danger below, this is the best place to gain altitude. And I need altitude to soar after your lizard's Abomination. Flying, especially with passengers, isn't easy."

"Looks like they've made a ruin of it," the halfling commented on the city below.

"Human wars tend to do that," Mist replied curtly. "When I lived in this area, I heard of Yulash's destruction five, no, six times. Some group or another is always on a crusade or war of liberation. Merciless killing, cloaked by the niceties of civil tongues. They are a race of lawyers, these humans. I wonder how they survive."

"My people wonder the same thing."

An idea rose to the surface of the halfling's brain. "Say, O mighty Mist. I was wondering . . ." Olive trailed off, leaving the question hang for a moment. Based on what she knew about human and draconian nature, the halfling calculated some odds before continuing.

The dragon banked and, catching another updraft, began to rise again. "Yesssss?" she prompted.

"Once you've fulfilled your bargain with Dragonbait and freed Alias, you're going to attack her."

"Is that a question or a statement?" Mist's voice was low and guttural.

Olive glanced over her shoulder at Dragonbait, but the lizard was twenty feet away and couldn't possibly hear their conversation. His attention was focused on the ground below. "Well," Olive noted, "you haven't been very, uh, successful the last two times out of the paddock."

"If memory serves, you aided in my defeat both those times."

"My point exactly," Olive said. "And next time you'll have both Dragonbait and Alias to deal with. Now, if, my services were suddenly available on your side of the dispute . . ." Again she let her voice trail off.

For several moments, the only sound was the rush of the wind. Finally, Mist said, "Why the shift in loyalties?"

The halfling considered how much she wanted the dragon to know. The game I've been playing for Phalse has become too dangerous, Olive thought. I'd have no trouble fooling Alias. Dragonbait, however, is not so easily deceived.

To Mist Olive simply said, "Let's just say I do not trust our companion. He has misrepresented himself and that makes me uncomfortable. I'm not sure I want to continue traveling with him much longer."

"But you still want to rescue the woman."

The dragon was no dotard, Olive realized. "Yes," she admitted. "I want to rescue Alias. You might wish to reconsider which warrior has done the most to earn your vengeance. If you decide on the lizard rather than the woman, you will find yourself with an ally."

"I see."

"Besides," the halfling added, "Alias has a lot of enemies. She is bound to get her comeuppance sooner or later."

The dragon banked again, then spoke. "I'll take your suggestion under advisement. Speaking of His Righteousness, turn around and see what he wants."

The bard twisted in her makeshift saddle. Dragonbait was banging on the side of Mist's neck with the flat of his blade. Having caught the bard's attention, he pointed southward.

"I think he wants you to get on with the hunt. He's pointing south."

"Everyone thinks they're an expert."

"I imagine he thinks he's the boss," Olive replied slyly.

Mist's neck stiffened some, and she remained silent. She banked again and began to glide away from Yulash.

"Can you see the monster's trail from this height?" the

halfling asked.

"Bard, I can see field mice from this height."

"Um, I guess I meant, could I have a look?"

Mist turned her head ever so slightly so Olive could peer down at the ground. Yulash looked as though it would fit in the palm of her hand. Four roads stretched away from it, east, west, northeast, and northwest, but far wider than the roads was a path of crushed vegetation and broken copses of trees heading south by southeast.

"Just how wide is that trail?" Olive asked, unable to judge size from such a distance.

"About fifty feet. Though it seems to be growing the farther south we go," Mist mused.

"This Abomination must be huge," the halfling cautioned. "Think you can handle it?"

"Not handle a shambling mound with a gland problem?" Mist sniffed. "So far you've only seen me in action in Feints of Honor. Unfettered by conventions, I am a force to be reckoned with."

"You fight dirty," Olive translated.

"That walking garbage heap will want a bath when I'm through with it," Mist bragged.

The bard smiled. She turned to look at Dragonbait. He kept his eyes fixed on the plains.

"Does he have a name? Besides Dragonbait, I mean."

"Indeed," the dragon answered. "But it doesn't translate well. I much prefer Dragonbait. It's so appropriate."

Without the thermals rising from Yulash, Mist was forced to pump her wings to preserve her altitude. The conversation with the halfling ended as Mist conserved her breath for the exertion of flying.

Far in the distance, on the southern horizon, a line of green marked the Abomination's destination—the Elven Wood.

❧ 22 ❧

Moander's Revelation and the Rescue Attempt

"You really don't know, do you?" Moander asked with Akabar's tongue. Carefully it rearranged the merchant-mage's face. Placing a hand against his cheek, it dropped his jaw, mimicking a look of extreme shock.

"I don't know what?" Alias asked, but even as she spoke, some notion stirred deep within her consciousness like a serpent that had slumbered heavily and was only now rising, rising quickly to strike at unwary prey—her.

"You carry my sign," Moander said in Akabar's cheeriest voice. "And you have done me a great service, so I should return the favor. It will help pass the time, and, I think, upset you."

"First, understand this," Moander said, using the formal words of a southern scholar. It pointed one of Akabar's fingers at her face. "You are a made thing, no different than a clay pot or a forged sword or some creeping bit of gunk in an alchemist's lab. Is that clear?"

"I don't belie—" Alias began, but the serpent notion sank its fangs deep into her heart. Beneath the mossy blankets her branded sword arm responded with a sympathetic ache.

"Yes, you do believe me," Moander insisted. "Now that I have told you, you cannot resist the truth. Golem. Homonculous. Simulacrum. Clone. Automaton. All these things come close to describing what you are. But not completely. You are a new thing, for the moment unique. A fake human, but to all appearances the real thing. You are an abomination cloaked in the manner and dress of the everyday."

As a mage and scholar, Akabar would no doubt have recognized the words Moander used to describe her, but to Alias most of them were gibberish. She had a notion they involved arcane rituals of the type that made her not only non-born, but inhuman as well.

"Now, know this," it demanded. "Your spirit is enslaved in the prison of that body, and that body is a puppet. A puppet made of meat, you might say, in much the same way as is the body I use to speak with you." To dramatize its point, Moander lifted Akabar's elbow into the air, leaving his forearm and hand to droop, and slouching his other shoulder downward so he resembled a marionette supported only by a single invisible thread.

Alias's mouth opened and closed, but she could think of no retort. Moander continued its lecture without acknowledging her distress.

"Now, golems and automatons follow a set pattern, invested into their make-up at their creation. These patterns are usually very rigid, no more complicated than 'guard this room,' or 'kill the first man to enter.' Useless rot, entirely too limited. No creativity or resourcefulness or initiative.

"But you," his tone lowered with pride, "you were built differently. It took many hands to create you. My followers allied with mages, thieves and assassins, a daemon of great power, and . . . well, the other hardly matters. With your deceptive appearance you can allay suspicion and travel at will until you have fulfilled your patterns—traveled all the paths set before you."

"Paths?" said Alias. Her chest felt tight, as though she were being crushed by the mad god's words. Each claim it made struck a resonant chord inside her, leaving her unable to deny what the god said. She choked back her screams, determined not to show this monster her helpless rage.

"Yes, paths or patterns, whose eventual outcome will be the accomplishment of some goal set by each of your makers. Rather than simply issue you some rigid order, we set you on a course whereupon you would achieve these goals without knowing what they were, or even, once they were achieved, that you had done so. You could commit theft, espionage, sabotage, murder, and never know why or for whom, not always remembering, other times believing it to have been your own idea."

They've made me a damned thing, Alias thought, like the bowl that carries poison or the sword that deals a death blow. She pressed her nails into her palms and once again began breathing too fast.

"The goal set for you by my last few followers was to seek my prison and release my Abomination form so that my spirit could return to this world. It was my life energy, summoned and collected by my followers, that brought you to life, you see, so that you, the non-born child, could free me."

"I'm not a child," Alias snapped.

"But, of course you are. It was the first day of Mirtul when my followers summoned my life energy and you began breathing. Only a month and a few days. So you see, you are but a child. Yet even so, you are my greatest servant, my liberator, an honor many before you have died for.

"At first, when the lizard arrived, I nearly perished with despair. (Well, not really, just a figure of speech.) When I saw his markings and sensed his determination to pass through the wall, I thought he was you. I sucked his life energy nearly dry trying to pull him through the wall. But I suppose being hatched counted as being born to the cursed elves who imprisoned me. He could not pass through the wall, and hence he could not help me pass through it. I thought all my plans had failed utterly."

Akabar tilted his head, an action Alias suspected was Moander's way of sifting through the mage's mind. The gray swirls in his eyes thickened and circled more quickly.

"Of course. That's what the saurial was doing there. Omniscient gods, indeed. Your magical friend has figured it out for me. He really is so amazingly useful. The last step in your manufacture was never completed. It required the blood sacrifice of a pure soul to secure the shackles on your spirit. Those bumblers down in Westgate chose the saurial, got careless and let it escape, and it took you with it. You've been wandering around ever since, a great spell primed to explode, requiring only the last enabling component—the death of the saurial. Those incompetent idiots! I can tell mankind needs me desperately."

"Saurial?" Alias asked. She was not certain who Moander

meant, but she had an uncomfortable suspicion.

"The lizard your mage friend thinks of as Dragonbait. The creature was marked, just like you were. That explains what it was doing trying to pass through the elven wall that imprisoned my body. The saurial was following your patterns. And you've been able to draw on its independence, because the two of you are linked until its death. But don't worry, we'll take care of that shortly."

Another wave of anger swept over Alias, anger now mixed with anguish. Then I'll be damned for sure. Something created by the evil sacrifice of my friend. Of my friends, she amended, realizing that not only Dragonbait's life was forfeit. Akabar was almost as good as dead. I'm not even human, she thought. I had no right to their aid and friendship, and now I've doomed them.

"Oh, Akabar," she whispered to his body, hoping some part of his mind was aware of what she said. "I'm so sorry. I should never have let you get into this mess."

But if the mage could hear her, he gave no indication. Moander's control over him was complete, and at the moment Moander wasn't even paying attention to her. The god was using Akabar's form to stare at the line of trees that they were fast approaching. Already the mound of refuse, now quite dusty and grass covered from its passage through the plains, was pitching and weaving from running over small trees and bushes near the edge of the prairie. As it engulfed and absorbed this green matter, the Abomination grew into a small hill, already as high as the trees on the fringes of the Elven Wood.

Apparently satisfied that the Abomination could control the forest, Moander used Akabar to return his attention to his prisoner. "The most amazing thing is that, despite your premature debut into society, most of your patterns still held. You attacked a man who sounded like the king of Cormyr, no doubt a goal of the Fire Knives. And then you came all the way north, just to free me." Akabar's finger stroked her cheek. "When you are returned and fully tamed, you will be my perfect servant."

Alias kicked and struggled futilely in her bindings. She knew she could not escape, but like a bird beating against the bars of a cage, instinct made her frantic. What Moander suggested was worse than slavery. The god and its followers and allies would turn her into an unthinking mechanism, with only the illusion of life and the sketchy memories of some woman. Where had they gotten the history she thought had been hers? Fairy tales? Or was there an original Alias who lived her life before, then died to become her?

Alias stared at the vine-draped form of Akabar, and oddly enough, the crudeness of the god's method of control soothed her anguish and helped her regain her composure. Moander could never have created me, she thought. Neither could the blundering Fire Knives, not even with the help of the mages who created the kalmari and the crystal elemental. They're all quite powerful, but despite all their claims, none of them could have made my mind or my spirit or my personality. She shoved back the horrible weight of evidence. The Abomination is lying, she decided. After all, isn't that what abominations do best?

When she had ceased struggling again, Moander continued. "Telling you all this has been most amusing. The news makes you unhappy, doesn't it? Of course, the others will want to purge your memory of everything I've said. After all, the best assassin is one who does not know she is a weapon, since she, or you, could then withstand all manner of telepathic prying. You do not register as a constructed creature, and after the sacrifice of the saurial, the runes on your limb will be hidden from view so that no one, not even you, will ever suspect your . . . eh? What's that?"

They reached the tree line, and Moander's now fungous form began uprooting the nearest trees, plowing them under and adding their mass to its own. But what drew the attention of the god was the huge shadow that blocked the high-noon sun. Akabar's head jerked upward just as a bolt of fire shot from the heart of the darkness. The flame tore a huge gouge in the mound's side, instantly igniting the fresh timber Moander had recently accumulated.

Akabar screamed and pitched forward into muck next to Alias. His cry was joined by a chorus of hundreds of fanged mouths which suddenly opened in the mucky hillside, all piping the same horrendous scream. Alias gagged on the smell of the smoke from burning offal.

The shadow dove below the tree line for a moment and then circled back. Now able to watch it without the sun in her eyes, Alias could tell that the shadow was a dragon—one of the great red wyrms reputed to haunt the north country. As it closed in for its second attack, the swordswoman spotted two riders mounted atop the beast, one on its head, the other a greenish lump between its wings.

It can't be. Can it? Alias wondered, not daring to believe her eyes. But they saw true. Her friends rode atop the red dragon, and the red dragon looked strangely familiar.

"Here comes the rescue party!" shouted the high, childlike voice of Olive Ruskettle, as Mist dropped down to strafe the Abomination yet again.

Akabar stood up again and focused on the dragon. His eyes glowed a burning coal white, though his face wore a calm, deadened expression. From the mage's mouth came a low-pitched muttering interspersed with the sharp gutturals and clicks of magic words summoning power to the speaker. Alias tried to kick at Akabar's form, hoping to knock him from the mound or at least spoil his spell, but the Abomination had not been so wounded that it loosened its tight hold on her. Her struggles were useless.

The mage's body wheeled about, keeping the dragon in view just as she began making her second pass. A blinding flash of energy sprang from Akabar's fingertip and caught the wyrm in the belly. The dragon jerked her head back and bellowed, almost knocking Ruskettle from her head.

At the same time, great vines shot up from the surface of the Abomination, with great force as if fired from concealed ballistae. At the ends of the vines rode the decaying forms of the Red Plume mercenaries whom Moander had consumed. Some still wielded their weapons, while others tried to grapple the dragon's with their bare hands.

Most of the arching vines fell short of their mark, and the sickening thuds of dead flesh hitting hard ground sounded through the forest. Two vines succeeded in entangling the dragon, one in the middle of the neck, the other near the base of the right wing.

Akabar muttered another spell, and a trio of magic mis-

siles sizzled through the sky with unerring precision, striking the purplish plates over the beast's heart.

The former Red Plumes closed on the dragon's passengers
as the tendrils they had ridden upward spun about the
beast like spider's silk entrapping a fly. Dragonbait skewered the man approaching him.

The god-possessed corpse thrust itself farther onto the lizard's sword and grabbed at Dragonbait's shoulders,
attempting to knock him off balance. Dragonbait lashed out
with a powerful kick, removing his sword, and sending the
corpse spiraling down to the ground. The lizard chopped
loose the vine entangling the dragon's wing.

The dead man that had arrived on the vine about Mist's
neck crawled toward the halfling. The vine began dragging
the dragon closer to the mound of refuse.

Mist bucked, almost dislodging her passengers, but did
not succeed at tearing the binding about her throat. With
her wings she began sweeping the air before her in great
gusts. The loose matter atop Moander spun away in a whirlwind of stinking rot, and the puppet Akabar was driven to
his knees, the spell in his throat spoiled by the assault.

More tendrils trailed up the single, thick root that bound
the dragon like a hangman's noose.

Moander turned Akabar's body around to face Alias. "Say
good-bye to this puppet, servant," Akabar's voice instructed.
"I can afford to lose this tool, but not you."

The mossy ground began to rise around Alias, as the supporting roots beneath her withdrew. She struggled as she
sank into the heart of Moander. She screamed when the
leaves and rotting fungus began covering her, but another
porous, spongy mat of moss covered her mouth. She gasped
for air and pungently scented vapors flowed into her lungs.
Within moments she was asleep.

Dragonbait, alerted by the warrior woman's shout, and
seeing that she would soon be beyond reach, leaped from
the dragon's back.

Fifty feet separated the dragon from the oozing god, and a
number of fanged mouths at the end of tendrils had finished their snaking climb up the tether about the great
wyrm's neck. Olive was trying to fend off these horrid little

maws and dodge past the rotting soldier's corpse that blocked her attempts to cut the tether.

A fall from fifty feet to hard ground would have snapped even Dragonbait's legs, but where he landed on Moander, over the spot where Alias had disappeared, all was soft muck. Akabar turned to face him, but hesitated for a moment. Tendrils were already beginning to twist upward to ensnare the lizard-creature.

Akabar spat out the guttural words of another spell. Unaccountably the spell dissolved, but Moander did not waste energy registering its confusion on Akabar's face. The tendrils wrapping around the lizard hesitated, unsure about attacking the creature with the same markings as their valued prisoner. Without Moander's command, they were unable to come to any conclusion, and Moander's attention was elsewhere.

Meanwhile, the bard was losing her battle at the dragon's head. The mouths had succeeded in taking several little bites out of her, she could not get past the corpse of the Red Plume mercenary, and Moander continued drawing in the great flying wyrm with a slow, inexhaustible force. Already the distance between dragon and god had been halved, and white flecks of spittle dotted the dragon's lower whiskers.

Olive was reminded of halfling children fishing for bats with light, durable twine and live moths as bait. For some fool reason, this halfling is on the bat's side, she thought, even though the bat is losing.

Mist twisted her head so that her chin rested along the thickening vine. Opportunistic tendrils immediately laced themselves into the dragon's whiskers, then began trying to crawl into the wyrm's mouth to suffocate her.

Dragonbait faced the possessed Akabar. A sea of tendrils ebbed and flowed around the lizard, still waiting for Moander to direct them, but Moander's mind was fully occupied with controlling Akabar and dealing with the dragon.

Rivulets of sweat poured from the mage's face, and his robes were drenched and rotting from his contact with Moander's innards. His head tilted to the right as Moander sorted through his thoughts for a way the mage might deal with the lizard. But there was only one weapon left in Akabar's repertoire.

The mage's hand drew out his curved dagger. "Kill me, or die yourself," Moander challenged with Akabar's voice, now a gasping death-rattle. "You lose in either case, don't you, pure one?"

Dragonbait crouched, then leaped, using his overlong sword as a vaulting pole. As he sailed over the mage's head, Akabar's dagger caught in the side of his leg and remained there, twisting out of its wielder's hand.

Wounded, the lizard made a sloppy landing. The scaly flesh around his eyes crinkled in pain, but he spun his oddly shaped, toothed sword over his head and sliced at Akabar from behind.

The outer diamond tip of his sword struck at the back of the mage's neck right where the sucker-tendrils clustered in a main bundle before they trailed back in a thick vine to Moander's heart. Most of the cluster was severed neatly without a scratch on the mage's scalp. Dragonbait put his foot against Akabar's back to keep him in place and yanked the remaining vine-bundle from Akabar's head.

Just then, Mist breathed a mighty exhalation of flame and brimstone that caused her belly to flex deeply inward. The fire traveled down the side of the tether about her neck and turned the side of the god into a jungle inferno. The wet vegetable flesh alighted again, and the outer layers of the snare vine were reduced to ash.

Akabar's and Moander's mouths screamed, but their voices were no longer in hellish synchrony. They were separate entities. Akabar fell to his knees, gasping, his hands clutching the wounds made from the sucker that had been ripped away. The tendrils surrounding him and Dragonbait wavered and then closed in.

The lizard grabbed the mage by the arm and yanked him to his feet. He lopped off a few more tendrils on the living mound, tugged the mage with him, and jumped.

Warrior and Turmishman tumbled down the slope, resisting the impulse to stop their fall by grabbing hold of the overhanging vines and tree stumps that stood out from Moander's lower flanks. They fell in a heap at the base of the monster.

Moander burned and crackled. Plumes of acrid smoke billowed up from his body. Moander tired of this battle—it was dangerously exhausting his life energies. The Abomination desired a retreat, but if he loosed the dragon, the beast might yet find the strength to breathe again and destroy the god's earthly form. The tendril snaring the dragon was almost burned through. Moander had to damage the wyrm first, and damage her badly.

The god played out an additional length of the tether vine. Mist felt the line slacken and, believing in her exhaustion that the line had finally broken, pulled back with a frantic beat of her wings. She succeeded in snapping the line even more taut. Moander gave one last great pull, and the weakened vine snapped apart.

Mist, with the halfling clutching for dear life to her ears, pitched over backward and crashed among the trees.

The huge god-hill, burning and mostly blind, shifted one way then another before plunging deeper into the forest. Smaller trees were plowed underneath, but now Moander flowed between the larger trees, unable to snap them.

Dragonbait pulled Akabar from the Abomination's path. The mage oozed blood in scarlet ponds from half-a-dozen shallow head wounds. He moaned softly and began to cry.

Dragonbait pulled the mage's curved dagger from his scaly calf and examined the gash. His hands glowed softly in the dim woods, and the cut grew less deep but did not close completely. His healing ability exhausted, Dragonbait tore his ragged new shirt in two to use as bandages.

Akabar sat in a shocked silence as the lizard bound his head wounds. He did not respond to the warrior's touch or his tug on his robes or his prodding. He would not move. Dragonbait slung his sword over his shoulders, hefted the Turmishman in both his arms as if he were a child, and began moving in the direction of the dragon's crash. The time had come to regroup his forces, such as they were.

Akabar's Recovery, Moander's Offer, and the Second Rescue Attempt

When Akabar awoke it was dark, and the light of a nearby fire played across the ground. The firelight glittered on the scales of an immense dragon. The bulk of the beast lay in shadow, but Akabar could see Dragonbait napping, curled up on the great beast's snout. The rune-marked lizard had a green bandage tied about one of his legs. Between the mage and the fire loomed a huge shadow. The towering form knelt before him, holding out a huge silver flask.

"Drink this," Olive said, pushing the flask to his lips.

The draught tasted horrible, but Akabar let it slide down his throat. His mouth felt like he had been eating dirt, and his flesh crawled with a cold, clammy feeling, as if he had been immersed in water too long. He looked down and saw he was naked, save for a couple of halfling cloaks knotted around him for warmth.

"My . . . clothes?" the mage puzzled. His voice was reedy, as though he'd been singing or shouting for hours.

Olive motioned to the fire. "I'm afraid what was left wasn't worth keeping. Dragonbait thought you were dead, so we didn't bring any of your spare clothing." Her eyes brightened. "I emptied your pockets, though, and I brought your spell books." She pointed to a backpack near his feet.

"What happened—oh, gods," the mage moaned as his memory came rushing back. There'd been a fight in Yulash, then something hulking and oppressive had sat in his mind like a spider in a web. He wondered if this was how Alias felt after being forced to try to kill a priest and then the Wyvernspur noble.

"Take it easy," Olive said sharply. She was an impatient

ministering angel. She put both her hands on his shoulders to hold him down, though the mage had made no effort to rise. "The short version is, after your little adventure in Yulash, Dragonbait came back to camp to get my help. When you three had gone, I was left alone to deal with Mist, who chose that moment to drop in. You remember Mist from Cormyr? Right. Anyway, I subdued her by the old codes, and the three of us went after you and Its Ooziness."

Olive paused for breath and to let what she had said sink into the Turmish mage's fevered brain. Then she started again, "Unfortunately, Its Ooziness mopped up the floor with us. Misty got slammed around pretty bad, but with me at the helm the old girl managed to damage the Abomination. It ran away from us, not the other way around. Though we did get knocked out of the sky. However, the luck of the halflings was with me, and I managed to land on a Red Plume mercenary's corpse. You sliced up Dragonbait a little before he could rescue you." She paused and then concluded reluctantly, "We didn't get Alias."

"Alias," muttered Akabar, trying to rise against the pressure of the halfling's hands. "She's still prisoner!"

"Reign in your horses," the halfling ordered. "You've been out for about eight hours. Another few won't make that much difference in catching up to that slithering compost heap, but it will make us all stronger. Dragonbait needs his beauty sleep so he can finish healing you and Misty. She snapped some wing bones when she fell, and she needs to restoke her furnaces before going into battle again. You need to study your spells. Drink more."

Akabar took another swig of the drink Olive offered and made a face. "Is this a healing draught?"

Olive shook the flask and giggled. "Some call it that. It's spiked honey mead. Last of my stock, too."

Akabar felt his empty stomach rise, then settle. So much for the halfling's skill as a nurse. "You say Dragonbait healed us. He did that before, when we were running from the Abomination in Yulash."

Olive nodded. "Yes. Turns out the little sneak's a paladin among his own people. He's been keeping it secret, but healing us when we weren't looking. Seems I can't trust anyone these days."

"A paladin?" Akabar murmured. "How do you know?"

"He told me," Olive said. She dropped her voice to a whisper before going on. "Not only did he keep his profession secret all this time, but he can communicate. He doesn't use real words like you or me. He puts out scents, like a perfume shop. We can't understand him because our little noses aren't refined enough, but Mist can. He talks to her and she translates, and then he confirms what she's said by nodding his head. So you see, he does understand everything we've been saying."

Akabar shook his head to clear it. The halfling sounded angry, but the mage could not understand what had upset her. "So?" he asked.

"So!" Olive exclaimed, then dropped her voice to a whisper. "We have a lizard paladin who's too haughty to try communicating with us until an evil dragon comes along. This paladin has been traveling with us and spying on us for two rides. Doesn't that make you the least bit angry?"

"Saurial," Akabar mumbled suddenly, letting the word linger in his memory. A dark shadow hovered there, the residue of the Abomination's visit to his mind. "Moander said Dragonbait was a saurial."

"Moander—that's the creeping crud?" Olive asked.

Akabar hesitated like a swimmer hovering at the edge of cold water. He wanted to forget the evil that had been inside him and used him so vilely. But he needed the information Moander had inadvertently left in his mind. He plunged in.

"Moander is a god. Or a piece of god. An old piece, kept in storage beneath Yulash, until Alias let him out. He's taking her to Westgate, via Myth Drannor."

Akabar's body began to shake violently.

"What is it?" Olive demanded. "What's wrong?"

"Gods, it was like . . . like having some disease that rots everything but your mind and leaves your body shambling around. I was conscious, but I had no control. I couldn't speak. I couldn't see. I could hear things in my head, Moander's thoughts, and Alias speaking, but I was tied and gagged in the darkness. And . . . and . . ." He looked up at the halfling. "I stabbed Dragonbait, didn't I? You said I did. I remember. I was trying to kill him."

"Apparently, he doesn't hold it against you. He carried you back here and used the shirt off his back to bandage you."

Akabar felt along the bandage on his head, glancing at the lizard lying on the dragon's snout.

"I wounded the dragon, too, didn't I?" he whispered.

"Less said about that the better," Olive suggested. "It took all my eloquence to convince Mist you were included in the bargain for our protection until Alias was freed. She only relented because we need all the firepower we can muster.

"So Its Ooziness is a god, eh? Another thing our lizard friend neglected to mention."

"Saurial," Akabar corrected again. "Why are you suddenly so annoyed with him? He's saved our lives."

"No. He's saved your life. I can take care of myself." Olive did not bother to mention that she'd be digesting in Mist's stomach now if not for the lizard. "I don't need a sneaky, spying, goody-two-shoes wheedling his way into my trust."

"What makes you so sure he's a spy?"

"Use your brain, greengrocer," Olive snorted. "What else would a paladin be doing traveling with us? You're a merchant, and I'm halfling scum. And Alias—think! She tried to murder a priest and someone she thought was the king of Cormyr and then she let loose an evil god. Dragonbait sneaked off just when we were in the most trouble, and now he's dragging us along on a suicide mission. He says it's to rescue Alias, but suppose he's really just interested in killing Moander? His type doesn't really care about our problems."

"I suppose," Akabar replied. His eyes were looking a little glazed, and Olive could see that he wasn't really concentrating on her words.

"Akash, what is wrong with you? You aren't listening to me at all."

Akabar shook his head and spat. "Some mage I turn out to be. I can't get us the information we need, I don't even notice that a member of our party can heal, and I'm at my fighting best when I'm controlled by an insane abomination. You shouldn't have bothered to rescue me."

"Don't be stupid," Olive chided. "You have your health,

your mind, and your money—all the blessings, as we half-lings say. You can't blame yourself for what happened. It's not as though you were trained to fight old gods."

"Or anything else, for that matter," Akabar added. "You and Alias are right, I'm a greengrocer. This has been my first real adventure not tied to the logical, reasonable flow of trade and money and safe, secure routes, and I've botched everything. I thought that with all my learning I could take on the world, but I've failed. I'm useless."

"Look, Akash, adventuring isn't as logical as columns in an account ledger. You can't learn about it from books. You have to experience it to know what to do. You'll get the hang of it eventually. And you haven't been completely useless. If it weren't for you, Dimswart would not have known to send Alias after me, and she never would have met Mist, and then we'd be fighting this Moander alone."

"That is a rather tenuous recommendation of my talents."

"Well, then, consider the fact that you saved us all from being poisoned."

"What?"

Olive grinned slyly. "If I had to do the cooking, we all would have died from indigestion."

Akabar did not respond to her little joke, so the halfling rambled on. "Look, what I'm trying to say is that eventually you'll learn to think like an adventurer. Then you'll really be a force to be reckoned with. Who knows, you may even teach us a thing or two. Reason may make all the difference between our success or failure, and nobody else in this group has as much of it as you do."

Akabar remained silent, and Olive worried that the mead might have been too strong for him. "Anyway," she said with a shrug, "I sort of like having you around. I sort of like you."

A tiny smile played across the Turmishman's lips. He sighed deeply. "I sort of like you, too," he replied. "Do you have any more of that mead?"

While Akabar took a long pull on the flask, Olive asked, "So, what about him?" Ruskettle jerked her head in the direction of the sleeping reptiles. "Dragonbait the Cereal."

"Saurial," Akabar corrected, yet understanding how Olive felt. Guilty, no doubt. It was one thing for Alias and himself to recognize the halfling's pettiness, selfishness, and thievery, and overlook it in the interest of party unity. But it was quite another thing to have one's actions silently watched and, no doubt, judged by the likes of a paladin. Akabar himself wondered with acute embarrassment what the lizard thought of him and his constant failures.

"Saurial," Olive said, finally getting the pronunciation correct. "He's kept a couple of major secrets from us. He could be hiding a lot more."

Akabar caught the blue glimmer of the runes shining on Dragonbait's chest. Unbeknownst to Olive, she was late trying to raise Akabar's suspicions against the lizard. Since yesterday, the mage reflected, I've battled him twice, lost both times, and then discovered that he was trying to save my miserable hide. Something he's rather in the habit of doing. And though the halfling was right when she pointed out it was highly unusual for a paladin to travel with an adventuring group with their . . . character, the Turmishman found it impossible to believe that the saurial meant them any harm.

"After he helps us get Alias back," Olive said, ignoring Akabar's pensive look, "I think we should find a way to ditch him. Alias won't like it, but it'll be for her own good."

"No," the mage said. "If he keeps his own counsel, that's his business. If my account balances, then so does his."

In Olive's eyes Akabar saw the look of a merchant who had decided it would be in her best interest not to drive too hard a bargain. She shrugged. "You're probably right. There's nothing to worry about. You rest. We'll be moving out in the morning, and this time we'll squash Its Ooziness. I'll be tending the fire, not that difficult a job considering all the deadfall Big Mo left in its wake. Been a dry summer, too—wood catches easy."

"Ruskettle?"

"Yes, Akash?"

"Would you please hand me my books? I think I'd better start studying. Like you said, we'll need all the power we can get. Even mine."

* * * * *

Alias woke in a dim chamber deep beneath Moander's

surface. All around her, patches of slime gave off a sickly green light. The glow from her sigils was brighter and purer, and to study her prison she held her arm out as a lantern, for she was no longer bound by mossy shackles.

The chamber was round and lined mostly with moss, except where moisture ran down its surface, nourishing the patches of luminous slime. She dug into the side of the wall with her fingers, but beneath the spongy moss she discovered an impenetrable mesh of thick roots and tree branches. She tried pulling the moss away in other spots, but found no weaknesses in her cage. The air was close and heavy with the smell of rotting leaves but quite breathable.

She still wore her armor and her leather breeches, but her cloak had begun to disintegrate so badly that it could no longer be tied on. She had lost her sword somewhere in Yulash, and her shield and daggers were missing, probably stripped from her person by the tendrils while she slept— knocked unconscious by Moander's sponge mosses.

Trapped like an alchemist's mouse, she thought. Then she decided, no, more like a broken machine crated in a cushioned box for the journey back home. She remembered all that Moander had threatened would be done to her in Westgate. Her memories would be wiped out again, her spirit smothered somehow. She shuddered.

Then she snarled in defiance. But what could one do to a god? Spit in its eye before it crushed you?

The wall across from her rippled. Chunks of moss dropped away, and a huge hand, palm upward, thrust into the chamber. It was woven, like wicker, of tree limbs. In the center of the palm a ball of light glowed with a swirl of gray and white. Alias thought it was some sort of eye, and she wanted to back away and hide from it.

Then the ball spoke. Two voices blended, one the highest alto, the other the lowest bass, with no middle range between the two. The essence of Moander's voice.

Alias remembered the swirling gray and white that had covered Akabar's eyes when the god had possessed him. She wondered if this ball was the true face of Moander.

"Hungry?" asked the voice. "Eat."

The wall moss peeled in another spot, and a pair of tendrils thrust in her shield covered with half a dozen high-summer apples and a dead, uncooked yearling boar.

Taking a deep breath to steady her nerves, Alias walked over to the shield. The hole it had been pushed through was already rewoven shut. Her stomach rumbled, but she waited until the tendrils retracted through the wall before she reached for the apples. She backed away from the boar. It looked like it had been throttled to death.

She strolled back over to the palm and crunched into an apple. Without really expecting an answer, she asked the glowing ball, "How long have I been asleep?"

"A day," the ball replied, pulsing in rhythm with its words. "Going slow. Woods thicker than once were."

"That's a problem? Some god you are!" she mocked it.

"Only so much life energy. Must husband carefully. Could fly or teleport, but would hurt. Find more power Myth Drannor. Move slow till then."

"You're not as fluent," Alias noted aloud, "without Akabar. Where is he?"

"Dead. See?"

A hole opened by her shield, and a pile of bones was thrust into the chamber. Alias dropped her apple. The bones sank into the floor again.

"And the others?" the swordswoman whispered.

"All dead."

"Oh, gods." Alias dropped to her knees.

"Just one. Me," Moander's light reminded her. "Have offer."

Alias hugged her arms about her shoulders.

"If you slay other masters," the voice said, "their sigils will erode and you will work for me alone."

"Then I'll have to kill you all," Alias growled defiantly.

"Without me, no purpose, no life. Besides, cannot slay me. Have tried and failed. Think, I will help."

"Go to hell."

"Abode not hell—Abyss. Prefer it here."

Alias laughed at the creature's transparent bid for power. "Why should I help you get a monopoly on my . . . services?"

"You are now puppet of many. Can be servant of one. Serve me, greater rewards—wealth, freedom."

Alias held her hands over her ears to block out the Abomination's voice. The tips of her fingers touched the eagle-shaped barrette in her hair. Though muck-encrusted, the silver pin unsnapped without crumbling.

"Think. More freedom yours than others enjoy. Be my high priestess. Be my—" The voice stopped, and the chamber swayed, and the walls vibrated. "Will return," the voice promised. Again the chamber swayed. "Think about offer."

The woven wood palm began to retract into the wall.

Something's attacking it, Alias realized. For a brief moment, she considered Moander's claim that without her "masters" she could not exist. It didn't matter, she decided. Despite the Abomination's promise, she knew she would never be free while it lived, and her freedom was all she wanted. Better to be dead than its servant, and this could be my only chance to escape, she thought.

It was an outside chance, but having been held helpless and frustrated all through the last battle, she could not let the opportunity to injure the Abomination slip by. She plunged the pin of the barrette into the sphere.

The ball was as hot as a bonfire and singed Alias's fingers. She yanked her hand back, but Moander's "hand" lay still on the floor.

A high-pitched wail filled the chamber, followed by a deep rumbling. The swaying motion of the room turned to a severe rocking, like a ship in a storm. Alias, her shield, the apples, and the dead boar were tumbled from one side to the other. The swordswoman curled into a ball and wedged herself in tightly between the floor and the hand.

Spit in the god's eye, she thought, sucking on her fingers, for all the good it will do you. The sickly glow of the slime grew dimmer until it was finally extinguished. She was left alone in the glittering sapphire light of her cursed brands.

* * * * *

"I think it knows we're here," Akabar declared.

The lizard, seated in front of the mage on the back of the great wyrm, growled in agreement. Pressed close beside him, Akabar caught a whiff of fresh-baked bread. Now that Dragonbait's means of communication had been rubbed in his face, so to speak, the mage realized that he could catch the saurial's more excited outbursts. The lizard had to, in effect, shout with his scent glands for a human to notice the smells. Akabar was beginning to piece together some sort of pattern between scents and sense. He berated himself for not having figured it out before—but then he hadn't figured out anything else correctly either, so far.

Dragonbait had awakened them all before dawn. Previously clownish and servile, the saurial had been transformed by the crisis into a sergeant major. First he healed all the wounds about Akabar's head. The mage noticed the woodsmoke scent that had surrounded them the last time Dragonbait had cured him.

"That's the smell of your healing prayers, isn't it?" the Turmishman had asked.

The lizard had nodded and given him a friendly squeeze on the shoulder. With a stern look he prompted Akabar to study his spells by jabbing his fingers at the mage's tomes. He patted and pushed Olive into packing their meager gear, while he used his skill to reknit the cluster of bones that held Mist's wing splayed out in flight. Lastly, he'd closed the gash Akabar's dagger had put in his own leg.

Akabar watched guiltily as the saurial performed this last task—guilty both for having caused the damage, and for taking his concentration from his assigned task to watch it repaired. Dragonbait worked in the glow of the finder's stone Alias had dropped. It was hard to see the glow of his hands as he healed his flesh, but now that Akabar knew what to expect, he would never miss it again.

Now, as they rode the dragon toward battle, Dragonbait held the finder's stone in his lap, although the sun had already risen. He still wore a kilt of sorts about his loins and one of Alias's cloaks wrapped around to keep out the wind, but he no longer bothered with a shirt. He left the runes on his chest exposed for the world to see.

Akabar wore one of the lizard's shirts and the makeshift kilt the halfling had fastened together out of her own cloaks. Olive wore a bright yellow cloak and looked, seated on the dragon's head like a flashy helmet.

When Olive had shouted a warning and they'd first beheld the Abomination, the monster-god was deep in the heart of the Elven Wood and still moving, albeit slowly. It had grown considerably though. The midden mound that had exploded out of its Yulash prison now stood seventy or more feet in height—a hill towering over all but the most ancient gnarled oaks and duskwoods.

Its composition had changed as well. Human rot no longer figured prominently in its make-up. Instead, huge trees and crushed shrubbery were rolled into the hill. It still had an oozy, wet appearance, but now the ooze came from extruded sap and damp underbrush.

The mound seemed to become aware of them as soon as they spotted it, for it began to speed up.

Mist circled from a safe distance. The forward edge of the moving hill was a sharp angle, literally plowing its way through the forest.

As they flew toward the front of the Abomination, a volley of black-barked trees shot out from the hill, trailing long streamers of vines. The god was trying the same tricks as before, only now he was using fifty-foot duskwoods instead of zombie soldiers to weight his snare vines.

The larger size of the missiles and the redundancy of the attack made it easy for Mist to dodge the assault. The catapulted trees fell in the tangle of woods, smashing down other trees and carving huge divots where they landed.

"Any sign of Alias?" Akabar shouted to Dragonbait.

The saurial shook his head. Just as Akabar suspected. If Alias was in the mess, she was probably well hidden beneath the surface, something they had discussed before they left camp, with Mist translating.

The dragon continued to circle Moander without attacking. The mound fired another volley of tree missiles. Once again, Mist dodged them with ease, until a particularly large one passed in front of her face. She pulled up suddenly, as if alarmed, and plummeted toward the ground. Moander lost sight of her behind the tree line.

Moander chuckled with the arrogance of a god. It might have considered telling Alias of the failure of her friends if only it had not bragged of killing them earlier. It trained some of its eyes in the direction the dragon had gone down, while it continued its crawling march south. Myth Drannor, and the powers held within, awaited it.

Dragonbait exchanged positions with the halfling and sat on Mist's head. He kept the party waiting in the clearing where Mist had landed for a quarter of an hour. The lizard could sense the distance between them and the evil god. When he gave the signal, Mist rose and, skimming low over the trees, circled away until she had reached the tree break Moander had left behind. Along this trail she made her attack run, moving in on the god's rear.

"They're going to have to call this 'Moander's Road,'" Olive shouted to the mage as she took in the devastation.

Akabar nodded wordlessly, awed by the destruction around them. Moander apparently no longer needed to absorb more bulk; it just plowed up the great trees, pushing them aside and leaving them to die on the forest floor, half buried by the great mounds of dirt it also overturned.

The dragon flew on unfazed by the rape of the Elven Wood. She kept her eyes forward, ignoring the great trench beneath her and the shattered trees at her flanks.

The mage closed his eyes, trying to shut out the sound of the heavy wings beating, the rush of air on his face, and the rise and fall of the dragon's back as she flew. He concentrated on his magic.

Olive nudged him and pointed. Akabar opened his eyes. Mist was less than twenty yards from Moander. No duskwood bombards fired from the hill. The god was oblivious to the dragon's proximity. Akabar allowed himself a brief smile when he spied the mass of duskwood trees and deadwood woven into the Abomination's mass, the perfect materials for their plans. His spell was prepared; he awaited only Dragonbait's signal.

The lizard waved, and Mist rose above the hill, spouting a long, heavy stream of fire as she did so. Like an assassin's knife, flames ripped into the greenery where the creature's spine would be if it had one. Moander screamed just as Akabar triggered his pyrotechnic spell. The red streams of the dragon's breath exploded in a further cavalcade of twisting yellows, spiraling oranges, and lancing azure blues. In the process of transforming the dragon's fiery breath to explosive fireworks, Akabar's spell snuffed the upper flames issuing from her maw, but the fireworks pierced deeper into the heart of the hill.

New shoots cropped up immediately to cover the scarred area, but Mist was not through. As soon as she crested the top of the hill, she twisted and spun about, her passengers tied and braced. As she dropped along the back of the hill, she breathed again, sending more flames into the open wound she had carved.

Though his stomach had risen to his throat when he'd momentarily hung upside down, the mage did not lose his focus. Another pyrotechnic spell speared the god.

Moander burned. The hill, now composed more of harvested wood than refuse and slime, blazed. Even better, Ruskettle and Akabar could spot great flames shooting up through the coarse outer mesh of trees and brush, flames that originated nearer the heart of the monster.

In her plant prison, Alias felt the air grow stuffy. The walls began to weep thick, yellowish tears through the moss. She rose to her feet, but was knocked back to the ground by a sudden sideways jerk of her enclosure. It seemed as if Moander had decided to move her prison.

Moander halted and flattened out in an effort to draw more material into its mass, perhaps in an effort to smother the flames. But as the halfling had noted to Akabar the evening before, the forest was quite dry. Whatever the god drew into itself just fed the fires more. And the duskwoods were renowned for their fine burning resins.

Next the Abomination tried to contain the fire by creating a firebreak in its body, splitting itself in two and leaving half of its mass behind. The pyrotechnics had done their job, though. The fire was everywhere; there was no escape from it. Flames curled out of the heart of the moving half of the hill and, like a fire that's just been stirred, the blaze leaped higher and burned hotter.

Mist had retreated, circling high overhead to evade any return attacks, but when none seemed forthcoming, she swooped back to administer the final blow. Akabar felt the dragon's chest swell with a mighty intake of air.

Before Mist had a chance to exhale, though, the top of Moander popped off like a cork in a bottle. Startled, Mist pulled up sharply, wary of some new type of attack. A pod twice the size of the dragon, but less than a tenth the size of the god before they'd attacked it, shot out from the hill. Egg-shaped, the missile tumbled end over end as it rose into the air. At the zenith of its flight it righted itself and then swept southeastward in a blur of movement.

"Gold lions will get you good lunch that our woman is in that thing," Olive shouted.

Akabar nodded. "Along with whatever passes for the consciousness of Moander."

Dragonbait gave the dragon a sharp prod, and Mist took off after the pod.

Behind them on the ground below, the burning pile of trees that had once been the Abomination of Moander spewed out a black column of smoke high enough to be spotted in Shadowdale, Hillsfar, and Yulash.

Mist began to strain, flapping her wings faster to keep pace with the escape pod. Akabar concentrated, then barked the harsh syllables of another spell and pressed his hands against the back of the dragon. Summoned energies flowed from his hands into the great wyrm.

Mist lunged forward at twice the speed. Her wings beat the air as gracefully and as quickly as a bird's. The ground blurred in their vision, and they began closing the distance between them and the pod.

"What did you do?" Olive gasped, her words torn from her mouth by the wind.

"Haste," Akabar explained. "Dangerous for humans—ages them a year. Can't hurt this creature, though. She sleeps longer than that after a meal."

* * * * *

Moander spoke again to Alias, but now with just a bass voice, rumbling against a garbling background chatter that was almost unintelligible.

"Flying," he said after a garble. "Life energies low. Must gate." Another long garble, then the bass voice surfaced. "Prepare for transport. Damaged goods."

The last phrase struck Alias as something that Akabar might say, and she fancied that some part of the mage's mind must have entered into Moander's being and not just the other way around. Perhaps it was the mage's spirit warning her to keep herself safe. The further deterioration of Moander's communication skills gave her a burst of hope. Things apparently weren't going well for the god. Maybe an army had attacked it, or a horde of powerful adventurers.

The circular shell of her prison wall began to shrink. Mouths surfaced all over the walls. Alias feared that Moander had decided to eat her rather than see her rescued, but the walls began to spit out streams of thick, moist silken strands. She was being cocooned.

Instinctively, she tried to beat back the rising mass, afraid it would suffocate her. Would her "masters" find a way to make her breathe again, she wondered. She was soon overwhelmed by the fiber. Covered from head to toe, she could still breathe through the wrapping, but the air was stuffy, and she felt as though she'd been buried alive.

The egg-shaped pod flattened till it looked more like a giant pumpkin seed. It tore through the sky. Along its trailing edge, half a hundred eyes opened at once to watch the advancing dragon. Moander had husbanded its energies carefully. But either the god had miscalculated or dragons had become faster during its imprisonment. Moander weighed its options. Its last desperate bid for escape was to use magic—the most costly method of travel.

They were still far from the ruins of Myth Drannor, but Moander could sense the siren song of the old city's dormant power, still humming away deep beneath toppled buildings and battle-scarred halls. With its godly abilities, Moander reached out and began syphoning off the magical energies of the dead elven kingdom.

The god channeled this energy directly into its spell. At the forward point of the pumpkin seed a blur of purple appeared, then stretched about the seed like a thin mist.

Mist, the dragon, was close enough for her passengers to make out the crawling glow that began to envelop the pod carrying Alias. Akabar was trying to figure out what it could be. A protection device, perhaps? Or—

He never finished his thought, for once the glow completely covered the pod, it began to shrink. Like a street magician's trick, there was nothing left in the purple cloak Moander had wrapped itself in, nothing to keep the cloak from collapsing in on itself.

A Turmish curse escaped Akabar's lips before he explained, "That's a gate between worlds."

Olive looked around in a wild-eyed panic.

"We've got to pull up," the mage insisted. "If we pass through that cloud, we could end up anywhere."

Both halfling and mage began to thump the sides of the dragon, trying to get her attention. When she turned back to look at them, they mimed pulling back on imaginary reins to symbolize their need to halt.

Mist turned her head forward again. Dragonbait kept his head turned to watch Akabar and Olive signaling him to stop the dragon. Dragonbait shook his reptilian head. He leaned over Mist's forehead and made some motion Akabar and Olive could not see. When he sat back again, Dragonbait held the finder's stone over his head.

Mist sped toward the purple cloud that dotted the sky low over the Elven Wood and dove in. Like the god preceding them, they were obscured from view. The shouts of the mage and the bard died away. The cloud dissipated slowly, as though reluctant to give up its form.

✿ 24 ✿

Battle over Westgate

This is like riding up into a maelstrom, Olive thought as they plunged into the purplish fog that had swallowed Moander, though she could not honestly say she had ever done so. The purple fog became a long, gray tube—the oozing wake of the god's passage from the forest north of Myth Drannor to wherever it was heading.

Floating castles and statues danced along the edges of the tube. Ruskettle noticed that Alias's finder's stone, which Dragonbait now held high over his head, shone a beam before them that stretched all the way down the tube to illuminate the retreating rear of the mad god.

Moander disappeared in another purple fog. They plunged after it, were buffeted by a second stomach-churning whirlwind, and suddenly burst into bright sunshine in a clear blue sky.

Below them to the left was a bustling, walled city of some size—a sea port. The green-blue water told Olive that she was looking at the Inner Sea. The shape of the harbor and the seven peculiar hills outside of the city walls identified their destination as Westgate.

*   *   *   *   *

Giogioni Wyvernspur let out a deep sigh of relief as he topped the last rise on the road from Reddansyr and surveyed the city of Westgate and the land surrounding it. Since his narrow escape in Teziir from the sorceress who so resembled the sell-sword Alias, Giogi had been moving overland, first by carriage, then on horseback.

From his vantage point, the Cormyrian noble took in the plain, which ran along the sea coast. Covered with the same rich, slick grass as the hills bordering it, the greenery of the plain ran right to the stock and caravan yards scattered around the city wall. A ring of seven mounds lay south of the city just east of the road on which he traveled. All seven hillocks were crowned with old ruins—stone circles of druids and temples of more sinister cults.

"Now this," he informed the horse he now rode, Daisyeye II, "has been a much more pleasant experience than my last trip on horseback. That ended, you see, with the death of your namesake, the first Daisyeye, followed by a singularly unpleasant interview with a dragon—an incident that will stick in my mind as long as, if not longer than, the nasty affair of losing Aunt Dorath's pet land urchin."

Giogi sighed again. He had been expecting to be waylaid by any of the hundred thousand brigands, bandits, dark powers, and orc bands that were said to lie in wait just beyond the borders of the civilized world. Yet, despite all the expected awfulness, his trip overland had been relatively peaceful.

About time I had some good luck, he thought, pulling off his wide-brimmed hat and letting the wind rustle through his hair.

At that moment the crash of a powerful lightning strike echoed all around him. Daisyeye II reared on her hindquarters. Directly overhead a great rend appeared in the sky. Through this a huge rock jettisoned into the world.

Giogi reigned Daisyeye in tightly to avoid being spilled onto the road. He might have been better off patting the beast and whispering soothing words, but his eyes were glued on the rocketing projectile. It looked like a rotting basket, with masses of greenery hanging from all sides. Along its trailing edge it spurt out jets of blue flame.

With a piercing howl the gash in the sky began to close. Then a red dragon burst through the hole overhead, pursuing the "basket." The dragon's appearance was Giogioni's first indication of just how big the lump of decay really was.

The head of the dragon chasing the basket shone with a yellow light. Giogi squinted. The yellow light seemed to be coming from a figure riding between the dragon's ears. Then the Cormyrian noble noticed the dragon's color.

"No. It can't be," he whispered to himself. But his heart sank with the certainty that it was indeed Mist.

If Giogi had remained on the hilltop observing the dragon, he might have noticed the other figures on her back; he might even have heard the eerie chant that rose from one of the mounds just south of him, but Daisyeye II decided she'd had enough. She plunged uncontrollably down the hill into the high grass, taking the young Wyvernspur with her.

*　*　*　*　*

Akabar kept his eyes glued to Moander. Blue flames spurted from the god, but the mage recognized that the flames did not originate from the damaging fires they had set within the monster. They were some means of propulsion. Somehow the monster's temporary occupation of his mind had left the mage with more than just the memory of the words he'd been forced to say to Alias or the evil deeds he'd been maneuvered into performing. He understood the means of the Abomination's flight, and while he admired its cleverness, he shivered with horror at the reminder of what the god had done to him.

Moander's vast godly knowledge, however, was not going to aid in its escape. The dragon, under the effects of Akabar's spell of haste, was still gaining. The god arced downward toward the seven mounds outside the city walls. Then it halted, hovering over one of the hills. Great red stone plinths shaped like fangs curved inward about the crown of the hill. In their center burned a bonfire. Olive spotted tiny figures moving about the hilltop. From this distance the figures looked no bigger than ants.

Moander let a drop of slime fall away from its body. The slime oozed like a water drop slipping along a strand of spider silk, then it hung ten or so feet before splattering on the ground. The ant-sized figures were on it in a second.

"It's delivered Alias to its followers," Akabar shouted.

The halfling nodded. "We have to land and rescue her."

The mage shook his head in disagreement. "We have to finish our battle with the god first," he said.

"Are you crazy? We could be killed. I want off this ride, now," Olive insisted.

Akabar's eyes glittered with vengeance, and the halfling realized she wasn't going to get anywhere trying to convince him to help her down. Fortunately for her, it wasn't up to him. "Dragonbait!" she hollered. "Alias is down there! We have to land and help her!"

But Olive was not to discover whether the lizard paladin was more concerned with the warrior woman or destroying Moander. Moander took the decision out of his hands. Once it had unloaded its passenger, the god launched itself toward them.

Mist banked sharply, and the mass of fungus, slime, and forest rocketed past them. The sudden movement caused the halfling to lose her grip on the safety rope. She would have fallen to her death if Akabar had not seized the hem of her skirt and pulled her back. Olive suddenly was not feeling hungry—the human equivalent of feeling frightened out of her mind. Mist completed her banking maneuver by turning about to face Moander's return charge.

This time, however, dodging the god was not so easy. As it streaked toward them Moander increased in size. In its approaching side a great maw opened, lined with duskwood tree trunks sharpened to fanglike points.

The Jawed God it was sometimes called, Akabar remembered. But how did it grow without absorbing more mass? he puzzled. It was now four times Mist's size, and the open cavity could swallow the dragon whole.

Mist struggled to gain altitude. She managed to rise above the gaping mouth, but a tree-weighted vine shot out at her, entangling her neck and her wings. The dragon beat her wings furiously, but she was held fast. More red vines, pulsing like blood veins, snaked up the snarevine.

Cursing, Olive drew her dagger, preparing to cut any plants that came her way. She turned, thinking to offer Akabar her sword, but to her surprise he began chanting another spell. She thought he had exhausted the last of his magic on the enchantment to haste the dragon. Apparently he was getting better at the game. He looks worn, though, Olive thought, noticing the lines in his face, deeper and more plentiful than when they'd first met in Cormyr. He was beginning to look like a real wizard, she decided.

With furrowed brows, the Turmish mage completed the last sharp syllables and tossed a handful of iron powder over the dragon's scales. The metal filings sparkled in the air, causing Mist's whole body to glow.

The struggling dragon's scales shifted beneath them. The halfling grabbed at the safety ropes, but they snapped away, as did the majority of the vines tethering Mist to Moander's form. Olive gripped at a scale, but it was difficult to grasp as it grew in size. Akabar, she realized, had enlarged the dragon with his magic.

"Should even the odds," the Turmishman said.

Mist, using her back claws, slashed open Moander's side. A foul vapor burst from the god's wound, and it screamed. The air smelled like a swamp.

Mist jerked her head up, breaking the last cord holding her near the god. The suddenness of her movement sent Dragonbait bouncing high into the air. With a gasp Olive tugged on Akabar's kilt and pointed at the lizard.

Akabar was already aware of the saurial's plight. He stood up nimbly on Mist's shifting back and stretched out his arms. In each hand he held a single feather. He incanted fast and furious and then fell from the dragon's back. Reflexively Olive grabbed at the mage's ankles. She'd forgotten she was no longer anchored. The pair of them, mage and bard, plummeted toward the ground.

As Akabar pulled out of his dive and began to fly upward, he became aware of the halfling's weight. Would he be able to carry her and Dragonbait? he wondered.

The saurial had begun arcing downward. He'd lost his grip on the finder's stone, but still clutched at his sword. Akabar flew upward to intercept him.

Drat the halfling, the mage thought as he struggled to reach the saurial. He would not be able to cross the horizontal distance between himself and Dragonbait before the lizard fell past him. If Olive had not tagged a ride, he could have done so with ease. As it was, he was forced to angle down, arms forward like a diver.

Dragonbait fell with his arms spread open, presenting the most resistance to the air. Akabar did not think the saurial was the least panicked, but he was willing to bet the air around Dragonbait smelled of woodsmoke.

Behind the mage, Olive swore loudly and profusely. She had no idea how to present the smallest profile when flying, so she slowed the mage's movements even further with the resistance of her body in the wind. Akabar offered his own prayer that he would reach the saurial in time.

The flying mage's path intersected the free-falling lizard's about thirty yards from the ground. By then Dragonbait was plummeting like a comet, and Akabar's tackle hit him with so much force that something gave in the mage's shoulder and the saurial's ribs. The trio of wizard, halfling, and lizard was too heavy to remain in flight long. From their mid-air impact, they lofted in a very low arc, before they began to sink earthward.

They landed in a dell between hills. The ground was soft, but littered with boulders. The threesome rolled and slid, lost their grip on one another, and fell apart. Akabar kept flying after he lost the added weight. He pulled up and landed smoothly on a large rock. He touched his shoulder gingerly; the flesh dimpled inward and his wrist and arm buzzed with a thousand tiny needle-pricks. A dislocated shoulder, he realized, almost intrigued with the injury.

The halfling, with the luck endemic to her race, had skidded to a stop in a particularly soft, boggy area. She rose to her feet completely uninjured but quite slimy, smeared with mud and grass stains. Dragonbait needed to lean on his sword to rise to his feet.

Akabar turned his attention to the battle between the now-gigantic Mist and the monstrously swelled Moander. The Jawed God had increased its size once again and regained its hold on the red dragon. The two behemoths tumbled in midair, though why they did not crash was yet another mystery puzzling Akabar. Mist's wings were too entangled to fly, and the blue flames that had propelled the god through the sky were no longer apparent.

The air shimmered around them like heat rising from the desert sands. Beneath the tattered shards of the god's body, which Mist had ripped away with her claws, lay only great vacuities. The smell of fetid swamp Akabar had noticed aboard the dragon reached his nose even on the ground.

Along Moander's side, a second huge, duskwood-fanged mouth split open. So wide did the jaws part that the god resembled a giant clam.

Confronted with this new set of jaws, Mist began thrashing like a wild beast. She was a great wyrm, one of the most powerful of her race, and much enhanced by the Turmish mage's magic, yet, while her opponent seemed to be made of nothing but that great maw, she was still flesh and blood. Then she remembered she was also fire.

Mist breathed a long stream of flame from her bloody mouth and nostrils. The fire plunged deep into the god's mouth. With a sudden horrifying insight, Akabar understood the significance of the swampy smell, Moander's great but empty size, and its ability to hover. The mage squeezed his eyes shut and turned his head away from the battle.

A small star exploded in the sky over Westgate. The shell that was Moander the Darkbringer and the curved figure of the dragon were black pieces of ash against the blaze that consumed them. Mist's fire-resistant scales ignited, her flesh became translucent, and her skeleton visible to any eyes unfortunate enough to witness her demise.

A booming sound rolled across the plains. The three adventurers were knocked from their feet by the force of the blast. Ruskettle lay toppled in the mud with her fingers pressed into her ears. The mage fell from his rock.

When Akabar looked up again, the star had faded, leaving behind the falling, burning shards of the god Moander. The long, blackened body that had once been Mistinarperadnacles Hai Draco spiraled to the earth. From the small valley, the mage could not see where the dead beast landed, but he felt the ground shake from the impact.

Akabar felt very tired. He prayed he had been right in his assumption that the package Moander had dropped off on the hilltop had been Alias. A further fear crept over him and tightened his gut. If Moander were indeed a god, they had destroyed only its earthly incarnation—somewhere beyond the borders of reality, it still lived. Should the Darkbringer find a way to return to the Realms, the mage knew that he would be at the top of the god's list of enemies.

"So be it," the Turmishman muttered. The beast had invaded his mind and made him a puppet. Now it was no more, destroyed by his hand, for without his spells Mist would not have lasted ten minutes against the Jawed God.

A feeling of intense satisfaction washed over Akabar. The feeling blended with the knowledge that he had rescued Dragonbait and Olive from death by flying them to safety. For the first time he was sure that he was more than a greengrocer merchant who dabbled in spell-casting. He was truly a mage of the first water.

Smoke rose in the sky from the direction of Westgate, and Akabar realized that the dragon must have hit the city. He felt a twinge of sadness for the beast. Evil though Mist had been, her evil had been no worse than that of a selfish, monomaniacal old woman. Like a villain in a street panto-mime, she was all sneers and threats—her wickedness paled before the reality of the Darkbringer. She died honoring her agreement with the saurial paladin—battling and destroying a greater evil than herself.

Ruskettle should write a song, making Mist a hero, Akabar thought with a grin. The old wyrm would've hated that.

"You waiting for the moon to come up, Akash?" Olive snapped. "We have a swordswoman to rescue, in case you'd forgotten."

Akabar shook his head, clearing it of his self-congratulations and melancholy meanderings. Dragonbait, his hip bloody from their rough landing, and clutching his ribs where Akabar had intercepted him, stood beside him. The lizard was reaching for the mage's shoulder to heal it first. Akabar moved away from him, cradling his bad arm with his good. He clenched his teeth against the pain.

"No!" the Turmishman insisted. "I can walk at least. You should take care of yourself first."

Dragonbait paused in protest, but he was not about to argue with the mage's new determination. He used the last of his healing power on his injured side, then the three of them set out to find Alias.

♣ 25 ♣

Alías's Escape

While Alias's companions chased Moander over the Elven Wood, through the magical gate, and above the countryside surrounding Westgate, the swordswoman lay still in her dark cocoon. The cushioning about her did little to reassure her. Blood rushed in her ears as her prison rocked and swayed, spun, and finally turned over and over.

Alias's nostrils flared. The mossy smell of her prison blended with the scent of swamp gas. She gagged and coughed, but was unable to avoid breathing the noxious vapor. She began to feel weak. Perhaps Moander did not realize the gas would damage her. Perhaps it would kill her by accident and the other "masters" would not be able to resurrect her.

That idea brought a peculiar comfort to the warrior woman. Her isolation had accomplished what Moander's words had failed to do. Alias despaired. She'd caused the death of her friends. Her only real friends, as far as she knew, since her relationship with the Swanmays and the Black Hawks had been nothing but imaginary stories given her by her makers. She wasn't even human, had never had a mother, was non-born. And soon she would be nothing but a trinket for evil forces to fight and intrigue over. She would become their unknowing puppet, forced into actions she had not chosen—a mockery of life, like a skeleton or golem. Better to die, she decided without feeling, her heart numb.

She wondered, though, whether there would be an after-life for the likes of her. In the dark cocoon, she whispered, "Do I even have a soul?" She sighed. "What difference does it make?"

What difference *does* it make? she wondered. I'm alive. I enjoy being alive. She relished the satisfaction she'd felt when she'd defeated an enemy in combat, the contentment that settled about her when she sang, the camaraderie she'd shared with Dragonbait and the others. She'd made her own friends, real friends. She'd proven herself an adventuress, even if she was only a month old. And somehow, she had found the will to deny her would-be masters.

"Even if it isn't a natural one, I have a life of my own," she announced to the darkness—and to herself.

Heartened by her declaration, a new determination to live sprang up in Alias, coupled with an assurance that she would somehow defeat everyone who had branded her and reassert her free will.

"Moander!" she shouted uncertainly, not knowing if the god could hear her. "Moander!" she hollered louder. "You're killing me! I can't breathe! You have to let me out of here!"

Her prison made one more gut-wrenching turn. Her ears popped. Then the foul air in her lungs was driven out by a sudden impact against the bottom of her cocoon.

Her bindings were torn. She blinked in the sunlight. The air was fresh and warm. Half a dozen hands reached down to pull her from the moist, silky mass that entangled her. Despite her wooziness, Alias spotted the tattoos inscribed in all their palms: mouths full of jagged teeth.

Dizzy from her travel, her muscles atrophied from her imprisonment, and still weak from the effects of the gas, Alias could not resist as the people pulled her to her feet, no doubt prepared to transfer her to another prison, more conventional perhaps, yet equally inescapable.

Alias looked around. She stood by a bonfire in the center of a circle of giant, inwardly curved fangs carved of red stone. Around her were two dozen men and women, their faces hidden in the cowls of their robes. Their leader wore a mask of white with a single eye painted in the forehead and surrounded by teeth. A priest of Moander.

Alias gulped in deep breaths of air to fight her nausea and dizziness, though she did not know why she bothered. Even if she managed to escape from Moander's minions, she would still be a puppet. One of the minions snapped a band of metal around her sword arm. The band was attached to a long chain of cold iron.

Her legs gave way beneath her, and she sank to her knees on the dusty hilltop. They would drag her off to her other masters, and she hadn't the strength or the will to resist.

But instead, everyone ignored her. Their attention was fixed on the sky. Mutters passed through the crowd, then cheers.

Alias looked up with everyone else. At first, she did not understand what she saw. Moander, the oozing god, bobbed in the sky, a great, swollen balloon with jaws. Trapped in its tendrils was a red dragon. The beast flapped its wings vainly, but could not resist being drawn into the god's maw. The pair of monsters twisted and turned in the sky above a great walled city. The sea lay beyond them. "Westgate," Alias whispered.

Suddenly, Alias knew that the red dragon was Mist. The Abomination had not killed her. As a matter of fact, she looked bigger than ever beside Moander.

Alias's captors began chanting a prayer for their god's victory, though some less pious or more excitable, continued cheering as though they were watching two warriors wrestle in an arena.

Alias felt like cheering as well, though not exactly for the dragon. If Mist were still alive, the warrior woman realized, then so might Dragonbait, Akabar, and Olive be. Moander's failure to mention the dragon's survival gave Alias reason to suspect he had lied about her friends.

Fury and hope surged within her and gave her strength. She assessed the lanky man holding her chain. He was armed with a cudgel dotted with crude shards of crystal. She was weaponless. But they made me a weapon, she thought. She drew her feet up beneath her knees, remaining crouched near the ground, her eyes fixed on her guard, waiting for an opportunity to attack.

The man's body shielded her vision from the brilliant explosion that threw the landscape into highlights of white contrasted against shadows of the deepest black. Alias stood up, but was immediately knocked to the ground by a powerful, booming wind. All her captors fell as well, thrown like rag dolls by the wind that ripped over the top of the hill.

A sudden pain shot up Alias's sword arm, as though the cold iron that bound it had suddenly turned red hot. She ignored the ache and the burning star in the sky. Taking advantage of her guard's fall, she pulled the iron chain from his numb fingers. The man lay staring sightlessly at her, blinded by the death of his deity. Rising to her feet, she gave him a kick, knocking him out. Then she stole the sharded cudgel from his other hand.

Moander's minions went to pieces. Some stared blindly at the sky like statues, while many flung themselves on the ground and wept. Alias shot a glance skyward in time to see the last bits of Moander drift down over the city. A fell grin crept over her face. She spat good riddance to the god.

She slipped toward the far side of the hillock, but the priest in the white mask rushed forward to intercept her. He caught a cudgel in the face. Blood spattered from beneath the mask. The priest dropped to the ground.

Alias slid down the hill on the wet, slippery grass. At the bottom, she circled the mound and began to make for the road that led to the city gates.

No pursuit seemed imminent from Moander's worshipers, but Alias was sure that her respite was only temporary. If they did not hold her responsible for the destruction of their master's earthly form, they would still consider her part of their property. And without the power of their god behind them, they would fight for any scrap left to them.

Tired of carrying the weight of the chain, Alias held her arm forward to inspect the lock on the band. Perhaps she could smash or pick it open somehow. She smiled with glee as she spotted the cause of the earlier pain on her arm.

Moander's sigil was gone.

Just as Moander claimed, death destroyed the bond each master had on her. For Moander, that meant his material body in the Realms.

Death had cut the connection. But could she defeat the other four? Should she? She remembered Moander's threat that without the purpose of her masters she would not live. If she eliminated the rest, could she function without someone pulling her strings? She didn't feel lessened any by

Moander's death. Her heart felt lighter, but she most certainly was not lost without his godly guidance.

A man's voice interrupted her thoughts. The sound came from the plain stretched out before her.

"Now, Daisyeye," the man's voice said, "you've been a very naughty girl, though I was afraid, too, the first time I met a dragon."

A wizard addressing his familiar, perhaps, Alias guessed. Cautiously, he crept closer.

"But, you have nothing to worry about, even if that dragon was Mist. The nasty old beast is dead."

With a start, Alias recognized the gold, green, and black markings stitched onto the back of the man's cloak. The coat-of-arms of the Wyvernspurs. And the voice was familiar, though its tone was somewhat braver than it had been the last time she'd heard it. This was too great a coincidence. Yet, she could not be mistaken. It was the same voice that had desperately tried to excuse its faux pas of imitating Azoun IV. His name came easily to her memory, as though it were engraved there by the voice of that nagging woman who'd begged him to do the impersonation.

"Giogi?" Alias remembered, whispering the name aloud.

Giogi Wyvernspur leaped three feet, spinning around as he did so. A silver flask flew from his hand, and amber liquid arched through the air.

"You!" he gasped. "The madwoman! I mean, the bard's friend!" He dived behind his horse. "What are you doing here?"

"Just dropped in to borrow your horse," Alias replied with a grin. She advanced carefully, looking to each side to make sure the young noble was alone.

"My . . ." the young man's throat went dry, "horse?"

Alias nodded and swung the chain manacled to her arm. "Do you have a problem with that?"

"No! I mean, no problem. You probably have a good reason that I don't need to know. Honest!"

"Don't fret," said Alias. "I'm not dangerous, just in a hurry to get into the city." She patted the skittish Daisyeye's front haunch and slipped her foot into the stirrup. "Just out of curiosity, what brings you to Westgate?"

"Diplomatic mission," the Cormyrian noble lied. "Nothing important. Just trade agreements. That sort of thing."

The warrior woman swung herself into the saddle. "You want your gear?" she asked.

"No!" Giogi answered. "I mean, no thanks. If you're heading to Westgate, maybe you could . . . uh . . . drop off my things. At The Jolly Warrior. Just let me get . . ." He summoned all his courage to approach, then fumbled in a saddlebag. Pulling out a large, official-looking document bearing the purple dragon of Cormyr, he stepped back. "There," he said. "All yours."

Alias looked down at him. He wasn't really dressed for hiking. "You know," she said with a smile, trying to show no ill will, "two can ride as well on a horse as one."

Giogi gulped. "No. I mean . . . that is, you said you were in a hurry, and I need the exercise, anyway."

"As you wish." She couldn't blame him. "I'll drop your gear at The Jolly Warrior. I'll even make sure I don't stay there. Oh, and Giogi, thanks. I'll make it up to you when I get the chance." With that, she wheeled the horse around and set it trotting toward the road.

Giogi frowned after her. He'd come here at Azoun's request for the express purpose of finding her, but he'd panicked when actually confronted with her presence. Now I'll probably never see her again, he thought. Or poor Daisy-eye.

He sighed and cursed his bad luck. Giogi began walking, head down, kicking stones, and talking to himself.

"Yes, I'll let you ride with me, provided you behave. If you don't, I shall be very cross. That's what I should have said."

He kicked a particularly large rock, which glittered as it danced away. Curious, he chased after it. When it had stopped rolling, he lifted the great yellow gem out of the high grass and marveled at it. Maybe his luck was changing, he thought.

❦ 26 ❦

Reunion at
The Rising Raven

Alias reached Westgate well ahead of her friends and, of course, Giogi, only to find the city sealed. Persons without residence or official business within were turned away from the gates by squads of guards, backed by crossbowmen on the walls. She did manage to convince a guard to take Daiseyeye to The Jolly Warrior and board her for, as she explained it, "a warrior who will arrive from Cormyr on official business." She trusted the purple-sealed document would get the young Wyvernspur past the guards.

As she stood by the gate, Alias could see smoke rising from the northwestern section of the city. Other travelers told her that a dragon had crashed within the city, smashing into a portion of the city wall, damaging some buildings in the slums just outside the city and several of the Dhostar warehouses within. The Dhostars, one of the powerful merchant families that ruled the city, convinced the others to slam a seal down on the city's gates until the matter was cleaned up.

Alias considered circling around to survey the damage from the outside, but she was feeling worn from fighting and riding and dragging around the chain attached to her arm. Besides, the inns outside the city wall would soon be filling up with other travelers banned from the city. She decided she'd better get a place to stay.

She remembered an old inn near the south gate: The Rising Raven. Perhaps she could hock her eagle barrette as an artifact in order to pay for a room and a bath. Used in battle against a god, she thought, holding the slightly melted piece of silver up to the sun.

Her cheer faded some since she had no one with whom she could share her joke. Even if Moander had lied and her friends were still alive, they were still up north, hundreds of miles away—she would not see them for a long time, if ever again. Already she missed them and felt lonely.

She was rounding the merchant yards of the Guldar family, when a familiar but very hoarse voice bellowed her name. She turned and peered down the road behind her. Three mud-spattered, bedraggled figures were waving their arms to attract her attention.

"Akabar!" she shouted. The weariness dropped from her and she ran to them, hugging first the mage, then the lizard, and finally even the halfling. Olive bridled some, drawing back, more concerned with brushing hardened mud from the front of her outfit.

"You're alive!" Alias blurted, beaming at them. Olive looked as though she'd been swimming in a swamp, Akabar was dressed in a ragged kilt, and Dragonbait leaned heavily on his sword.

"You noticed," Olive grumbled. "We just chased you from one side of the Realms to the other. Now we can't even get in the gates. Damned forces of law and order."

"It's all right," Alias assured her. "I know a place outside the city walls. They . . ." She almost said, "They know me there," but she realized that they, like Jhaele of Shadowdale, would remember nothing about her. "They have good food," she finished.

"I don't care about eating," Olive retorted. "I just want to get clean. I feel like I've been swimming in a sewer."

Alias looked up at Akabar, wanting to apologize again for all the horror he'd gone through because of her.

As if reading her thoughts, the mage said, "We can talk when we get where we're going."

The swordswoman nodded. "Here, Dragonbait, give your sword a break and lean on me for a while," she insisted, slipping herself beneath one of the lizard's scaly arms and taking his sword in her other hand.

Akabar expected the proud saurial to refuse her help, but he accepted Alias's close proximity and fussing like a cheerful child. Is it only the identical markings that bond them together? Akabar wondered. Or something more?

Alias did not recognize the innkeeper from her previously "remembered" stays at The Rising Raven. The inn was packed with traders and adventurers. Even if it hadn't been so crowded, the innkeeper needed only one look at the ragtag crew before he began shaking his head vigorously, denying the existence of any vacancies.

Olive was the one who came to the rescue. Following the man across the tavern room, she whispered something to him that Alias and Akabar could not catch. Then she slipped him a coin. The innkeeper's hospitality brightened. He led them from the inn, past the stable, to a warehouse with a small apartment within. The quarters were cramped but clean, and the innkeeper promised to send them hot water as soon as possible. Then he left them.

Dragonbait began to lay a fire in the stove, and Olive sat down in a corner, resting her head on her knees, exhausted. Alias examined Akabar's shoulder and grimaced.

"You've dislocated it, all right. How'd you do it?"

"Ran into an old friend," Akabar joked and tried to shrug. He winced at the pain.

"I wonder what Olive said to the innkeep when she bribed him," Alias said softly.

"I wonder," Akabar replied in an equally soft voice, "where she got the platinum coin she bribed him with."

Olive moved over to the whisperers. "You want to wear that to bed tonight?" she asked Alias, nodding to the shackle about her arm. "Or do you want me to pick the lock?"

While Olive was working on the iron bracelet, two footboys arrived at their doorstep, one bearing a large copper tub, the other an ornate screen. They set these down, scurried out, and then returned with a pair of buckets and an oversized kettle. After setting the kettle on the stove and the buckets on the floor, they pointed out the location of the well, should the adventurers desire more water.

Olive declared the honor of the first bath and began setting up the screen to block the tub from view. "I'm sure I won't be able to reach into that well," she said to Alias. "Would you mind?"

"As soon as you get me out of this chain," the swordswoman insisted.

"Oh, bother," the halfling grumbled. She banged the manacle once with the end of the chain, and it sprang open.

"You have a really light touch," Alias teased. She grabbed the two pails and set out for the water. Akabar followed.

"You won't be much good for hauling with a bad arm," the swordswoman said as she poured water from the well bucket into one of the pails she had brought.

"I am good for other things," said Akabar, unsmiling. "I am a spell-caster as well as a merchant."

"We'll have to get a healer for that shoulder," she continued, not understanding that she'd offended him.

"We've developed our own methods in your absence," Akabar added, leaving Alias completely confused. His coolness hurt her. She realized that even though she'd come to terms with not being human, accepted it, and was now prepared to go on living, Akabar might not feel the same way about her. And if her friends didn't accept her, who would?

An awkward silence fell between them.

Finally, Akabar overcame his pride—his usefulness was no longer at issue, and they had more important things to discuss. "Alias, what Moander said, what it made me tell you, what it made me do, the way it used me—I think I understand how you must feel."

Alias finished filling the second pail and set it down beside the first. She shook her auburn hair and stared at the ground. "It told me you were all dead," she said, swallowing back the memory of the grief and horror that had accompanied that moment. "It was lying then. It could have been lying before."

Akabar was silent.

"What is it?" Alias asked. "Tell me," she demanded.

"I was in its mind, as well," the mage explained. "As far as it knew, it was telling the truth."

"I see." She looked down into the well. Her reflection in the water mocked her. Golem, homonculus, made-thing, that's how the mage saw her now.

"It changes nothing, though," the Turmishman said. "You are my friend, and I mean to help you, no matter how many gates we must pass through."

Alias stretched out a hand and laid it on his good right shoulder, prepared to tell him he must leave, that she would not have him facing any more danger on her behalf, for the very same reason: he was her friend.

Before she could open her mouth, though, Olive, wrapped in a towel, called out from the doorway, "Are you getting water or what out there? I'm getting chilled, and the kettle's already boiling."

Alias grabbed both bucket straps and duck-walked the full buckets back to their apartment. Akabar followed, cradling his bad arm and quietly cursing the small, dirty halfling. She had been a nuisance since the day they'd met.

Once the bard was settled in her bath, soaking, and half-humming, half-singing some obscene ditty to herself in the tub, Alias turned her attention to Dragonbait's wounds.

The sigil of Moander had faded from the lizard's tattoo just as it had from hers. Her glee at discovering this was soon squelched by the sight of his wounds. There was a bloody half-healed gash on his hip, and he flinched when she touched an ugly greenish bruise on his side, indicating a possible broken rib. She offered him some warm compresses for the pain.

"We're going to have to get a cleric," she said again. "I wonder if one will be available after the dragon's crash. Every time I turn around, Mist's victims seem to be sucking up all the available healers. This'll be the last time, though. How did you ever come to team up with her?"

Akabar sat down beside Dragonbait and gave him a gentle nudge with his good arm. "Do you want to tell her, or should I?" Dragonbait made an amused snorting sound.

"Listen closely. Mist followed us from Cormyr. She ambushed Ruskettle while we were in Yulash, but Dragonbait subdued the dragon and convinced her to work alongside them to rescue us. They rescued me first only because Moander thought me more expendable. The god opened some type of magical gate from the Elven Wood to here, and we followed the creature through it with the help of your finder's stone. I think we lost that, didn't we?"

Dragonbait nodded and looked down at the ground, apparently ashamed at having mislaid Alias's property.

"Then Mist shook us loose, whether intentionally or not I could not tell. She died fighting the old god."

Alias held up a hand. "You said Dragonbait subdued Mist and convinced her to help. You mean Olive . . ."

"Not the halfling. Dragonbait. He can talk, but not in ways that we can understand. He uses—"

"Smells," Alias guessed, remembering the heavy odor of violets she had detected in Moander's temple in Yulash.

Akabar nodded. "Mist understood him. And he has no trouble understanding us. You know from Moander, of course, that his people are called saurials."

"Yes," Alias said, remembering. "It also said something about him being a pure soul—he was intended as a sacrifice to enslave me somehow."

"He's more than that," Akabar explained. "He's a paladin in his own world, much like the ones you have up north. He can heal in the same fashion. So you see, we need only wait a few days and he can make both of us good as new."

Alias looked into the lizard's yellow eyes. "You healed me when I came out of Mist's cave with my chain mail fused?"

Dragonbait nodded without expression.

"And when I hurt my arm smashing the crystal elemental with your sword?"

Again the saurial nodded.

"You sneaky devil," Alias said with a grin.

My feelings precisely, Olive thought behind the screen, but she did not give away her eavesdropping.

Alias, however, meant the words as a compliment. Dragonbait hung his head, though, ashamed of his deception.

"You had no idea, did you?" Akabar asked.

"No."

"You don't seem very surprised."

Alias shrugged. "I have evil assassins, evil mages, evil gods, and evil who-knows-what-all chasing me. Why shouldn't I have a guardian paladin?"

Then it occurred to her why not. So far, Moander's words were a secret between her and Akabar. She did not think Dragonbait knew. Akabar would not give her away, but it would not be right to keep Dragonbait with her, risking his life for her. She was just a thing. She was fully intent on sending her companions away, out of danger, and now she had the means of driving the faithful lizard from her side.

The idea of losing Dragonbait's tender concern left an ache in her heart, and the thought of losing his protection left her more than a little afraid. Don't be stupid, she tried to convince herself. You've taken care of yourself all of your life. You can do it.

Then she remembered that that just wasn't true. She'd only been born last month, and all that time she'd had the lizard as a nanny. How could he not know? But if he knew, why did he stay? No doubt he'd been fooled like Akabar into having pity for her.

I'll have to leave them, and I'll have to leave without telling them, she thought. She ran her hand down the smooth, pebbly scales of Dragonbait's arm. Aloud, she said, "I just want you to know how much I appreciate you. Everything you've done." She could not resist—she hugged the lizard again and then turned and hugged Akabar. "Both of you."

"Well," Olive said, stepping out from behind the screen. "Nice to know you're safe and appreciated, isn't it?" The bard was dressed in a pink robe, with scarlet pants beneath. Her yarting was strung across her back, and a pouch hung on her belt. The expression on her face was a mixture of jealousy and disapproval.

"I appreciate your friendship, too, Olive," Alias assured her as she walked toward the screen. She knelt before the halfling and reached out to hug her as well.

The bard stepped backward, almost toppling the iron tools stacked by the stove. "Please, don't," she snarled, holding up a hand. "You're filthy dirty, and this is my last clean outfit. And halflings don't hug. Hugging is a problem when you're the size of most human children. So no hugs."

"I'm sorry, Olive," Alias whispered.

Ruskettle glared at her for a moment, then announced, "I'm going to try to get into town. Get some gear for us, see what rumors I can pick up about Moander's people and all your other 'pals' down here."

Akabar broke in, "I've been to Westgate before. I think I might have better luck getting past the gate guards."

"You're decked out in borrowed halfling gear," countered

Ruskettle. "They won't take you seriously. I'll get something suitable for you to wear. And, no," she waved aside Alias and Dragonbait, "I work better alone. Especially considering you two are probably wanted by someone or something in Westgate." She strode to the door and then turned back, looking at Akabar.

"One more thing. If I can get a healer to come out here, I will. There's no sense in you living with the pain until he gets enough beauty sleep to fix you up."

She left the room, slamming the door behind her.

"Was it something I said?" Alias asked Akabar. "What's gotten into her?"

Akabar remembered how annoyed Ruskettle had been by the saurial's deception. Apparently, it would take the halfling longer to overcome her anxiety.

Dragonbait hissed at the closed door, and the scent of freshly baked bread wafted from his body.

* * * * *

Ruskettle strode east from The Rising Raven, her short legs still complaining about the earlier long walk to the city. If the dragon had crashed to the north and west, then the guards would be at their weakest at the south and east. The river gate would be her best bet.

The halfling's ears burned, and she was positive that her "friends" were talking about her in the warmth of their warehouse apartment. She had been the one to provide their shelter, yet everyone still fawned over Alias, fought for Alias, and chased through the nine hells for Alias, while she, Olive, had been abandoned with a dragon. And for what? It wasn't like they got any money for what they did.

And to top it off, Alias was so bloody perfect. Like a doll. You wound her up and she rescued people or slew monsters or sang perfectly beautiful songs. And her luck was incredible. Not even a halfling had that kind of luck. She'd been kidnapped by a god— a god, for god's sake!—and she'd escaped, and Akabar and Dragonbait and the dragon had slain the god for her.

The lizard-paladin was another problem completely. The halfling's thoughts wandered back a number of years to an ugly incident in the Living City. She'd been at a bar when some holy fighter, a human paladin, rose unsteadily to his feet, pointed a worn knuckle at her, and shouted, "Thief!" No one doubted him; no one believed her. The fact that she had another's purse in her hands did not help her situation, but she had managed to escape. Since then, she walked carefully around such beings, beings who could look into a person's soul and tell if he was good or evil. That scared Ruskettle. It wasn't fair. And now it turned out that one of these snooty law-and-order types was a member of their party. She felt the saurial's eyes on her all the time, judging her and weighing her worth.

Olive ground her teeth. Now she was going shopping for the warrior-woman, her pet paladin, and the mage. Even Akabar had a tendency to treat her like a child or a thief. He was the hero of Alias's rescue, his spells made the difference, while it had been the lizard's skill in battle that had recruited Mist in the first place. But she, Olive, had been useless. And Akabar would have left her on Mist's back, left her to die, when he flew off to rescue the paladin.

Part of her mind refused this interpretation, knowing full well that everyone had good reasons for doing what they did. But the small part of her mind was easily ignored. What difference does it make? she thought. Sooner or later, Phalse's friends were going to show up and take Alias away.

"I could use a drink," she muttered. "Better yet, several drinks."

She was just passing the Vhammos yards, its paddocks jammed with horses and caravan oxen, when suddenly someone addressed her. "Hello, Lady Olive."

Ruskettle was startled. Perched on a fence post was a short, familiar figure. He was dressed in sunburst yellow taffeta, fashioned into the costume of a Vilhon Reach merchant. His smile stretched nearly ear to ear in an inhuman mockery of the humanoid form.

"Phalse!" Olive wondered if the pseudo-halfling could read minds. "A Fortune. Well met."

"A fortune and well met to you, dear lady. You've surprised me. I did not know you were bound for Westgate. May I accompany you into the city?"

Ruskettle nodded, and Phalse hopped down from his perch. He paced the halfling as she walked. "The river gate?" he asked.

"However did you know?" Olive grinned pleasantly.

"Thinking like a halfling, my lady," he answered. "I must repeat, I am astonished to see you here so soon. Were you involved with the sky display earlier?" He waved an arm toward the seven mounds south of the city.

Olive's eyes narrowed. "Maybe," she replied coyly, but she wondered how he could possibly know that.

"Maybe—that's a straight answer from a halfling. I take it the human woman is with you?"

Ruskettle shrugged her shoulders. "Maybe." She had the uncomfortable feeling that her time with Alias was going to end much sooner than she'd expected.

Phalse smiled. "I see. Will 'maybe' be the answer to my inquiries about your other traveling companions, the mage and the lizard?"

"Maybe." She wondered what the pseudo-halfling's interest was in Akabar and Dragonbait.

"I think you and I should have a drink," he said. "Several drinks."

The small couple approached the gates, where a squad of soldiers was posted, checking credentials. Phalse took Ruskettle's arm gently, and they strolled through gates, into the city, completely unchallenged.

"I'm impressed," the bard said, jerking her head back at the gate guard. "What's your secret?"

Phalse winked one of his peculiar blue eyes. "Clean living. Let's find a nice, quiet bar with private booths and low ceilings. I have a deal that I am certain will interest you."

"As long as you're buying, I'm all ears." Olive moved a little closer to Phalse, and he tightened his grip on her arms.

* * * * *

"Well?" Alias said, pursing her lips.

"Gone," Akabar replied. He'd been peering at the swordswoman's arm and the saurial's chest with a tiny magnifying glass. "The surrounding pattern hasn't just covered up its sigil, the sigil has disappeared completely."

"Do you think the sigil might return if Moander gets another body in the Realms?"

"I'm afraid that's a possibility," the mage sighed.

They were all cleaned up now, wrapped in towels and blankets while their clothes dried in the late afternoon sunshine. Dragonbait had played nurse, helping Akabar with his bath, a service that had made the Turmishman mildly uncomfortable, but which he had accepted gratefully since his only alternative was Alias's help. In the meantime, Alias had fashioned him a cushioned sling to cradle his arm until Dragonbait could repair it properly.

Akabar leaned back on the room's lower bunk. "So where does this development lead us?"

"Into more hot water. We're just outside the city where Cassana and the Fire Knives are supposed to reside. I have a hunch that our mystery bull's eye sigil owner resides here as well. And now that we've exploded a very large calling card over their city, odds are they know we're in the area."

"Maybe they'll reconsider their actions and leave us alone. We destroyed one of their partners already—the god."

Alias shook her head. "No. They'll just become more ruthless. Akabar, I want you to go home to Turmish—take Olive and Dragonbait with you. Being near me is too dangerous."

Akabar asked, "What good do you think you can accomplish alone?"

"Find these people," said Alias, "Talk to them. They need Dragonbait to put their plans into motion, so they won't be able to control me as long as he's safely hidden somewhere."

"They could always just brand another victim to sacrifice."

Alias shook her head again. "I don't think that would work. Remember, Moander said I drew my independence from Dragonbait, that we're linked until his death. They won't kill me; they've even taken precautions to see that I'm not injured. But all the rest of you are targets."

Akabar harumphed. "They haven't shown a tendency to talk before. Bully, threaten, and battle, yes, but never talk. They won't negotiate with you. As far as they're concerned, you're no better than a horse, to be owned and ridden and slain as need be. If they already have you in their sights, it will be that much easier for them to accomplish their ends.

All they'll have to do is search out Dragonbait. Running and hiding won't do us any good."

"Maybe not, but if you stay here you're at risk. Please, Akabar," Alias pleaded. "I don't want to see you killed."

"There are worse fates. You and I both know that."

Dragonbait knocked on the side of the bed, summoning their attention. Using a charred stick, he drew on the flag-stones the four sigils he and Alias both wore and also the unholy symbol of Moander.

"Yes?" Alias prompted.

Dragonbait pointed to Alias and himself and then scuffed out the flaming dagger—the mark of the Fire Knives.

"Yes, we beat the assassins," Alias agreed. "They weren't very tough, were they?"

He pointed to Alias and himself and Akabar and then scuffed out the sigil that might or might not still belong to Zrie Prakis, the sigil of interlocking circles. Then he pointed again to himself and Alias, drew an inverted tear drop with a mouth and scuffed it out along with the insect-squiggle of Cassana's mark.

"We beat the crystal elemental and the kalmari. The kalmari belonged to Cassana?" the mage asked.

Alias nodded. "She told me in a dream. You dreamed the same thing, didn't you?" she asked the saurial.

Dragonbait nodded. He pointed to Akabar and rubbed out the unholy symbol of Moander like he was squishing a bug. Alias noted that the paladin gave all the credit for the god's death to the mage. Then he pointed at the three of them and splashed water from the kettle onto the flagstone.

Akabar laughed. "He's right, you know. Between the four of us we've defeated everything your would-be masters have thrown at us. If we remain together, we can defeat the lot of them."

"Only if you continue to cooperate," a sharp female voice said from the doorway, "and if we do not. But your little demonstration this afternoon persuaded us to unite."

Alias, Akabar, and Dragonbait leaped to their feet, their eyes fixed on four people who had entered their cottage apartment. Three men, dressed in black leather, and the woman from Alias's dream in Shadow Gap.

"Cassana," Alias breathed.

The woman lowered her hood. Her chin was sharper, her features older, her hair longer and better tended, but her features were Alias's. She might have been her mother. "Yes, Cassana. I've come to take you home, Puppet."

Favoring his good leg, Dragonbait sprang for the upper bunk bed for his sword, and Akabar began chanting a spell. Alias grabbed a poker from the stove tools.

Cassana laughed.

Akabar's spell was disrupted as the floorboards beneath him erupted and skeletal hands grabbed him from the hole and pulled him through the floor. He disappeared with a scream.

A trio of daggers arched from the black-clad assassins, embedding themselves unerringly in Dragonbait's hide. The weapons could not have caused much damage—they were small and had struck only his shoulder, his arm, and his tail—yet the saurial dropped like a sack of laundry. Poison blades! the swordswoman realized.

With a cry of anguish, Alias charged the Fire Knives. She cracked one assassin in the head with the handle of the poker, then rammed the tip into the throat of a second. Snatching the sword from the scabbard of the third one, she turned it on him instantly. He fell over the bodies of his brothers, staining them with his blood.

Only Cassana stood between Alias and the doorway. She muttered no spell, nor did she look alarmed. Alias hesitated uncertainly. Cassana applauded the swordswoman's performance briefly.

"Very good, Puppet. Welcome home," the sorceress said, slipping a slender, blue wand from her sleeve into her hand. "Now sleep."

Alias lunged at her foe. Cassana, the puppeteer, waved the wand, and Alias collapsed at her feet.

♣ 27 ♣

Alias's Masters

When Alias awoke, her head felt as though molten lead had been poured behind her eyes, and her mouth was as dry as the sands of Anauroch. She blinked in the dim candlelight that illuminated her room, a room in an inn like a hundred others at this end of the Sea of Fallen Stars.

A moment of panic seized her. Was she being forced by the gods to relive all her mistakes as some sort of punishment? No. This was not The Hidden Lady, nor any other place she'd ever been.

She found herself placed on a bed with her arms folded like the dead. She was not alone. Dragonbait had been unceremoniously dumped at the foot of the bed and was sprawled out on his stomach. Akabar had been propped up in an overstuffed chair across from the bed, his hands manacled by thick bands of cold iron to contain his magical ability. She and the mage were still wrapped in blankets, but Dragonbait was naked, like an animal.

Alias slid to the floor and knelt beside the saurial. He was still breathing. She sighed with relief, and tears welled in her eyes. The poison on the assassins' blades hadn't been deadly. Horrid red and violet bruises speckled the green scales along his legs and torso. Why had they been so vicious with him? she cried inwardly. She tugged the coverlet off the bed and draped it over him, then shook his shoulder gently. He did not stir.

They'd been much kinder to Akabar. His shoulder had been snapped back into place, though it still looked bruised and tender. A soft touch brought him fully awake. He took in her concerned features, Dragonbait's body, the room around him, all with a quick glance.

"What happened?"

"We lost," she replied. "They swept us up like dirt in no time at all."

The mage frowned. He tried to stand up, but something had drained away all his energy. He flopped back into the chair, clanking his chains. Pain radiated from his shoulder. He sucked in air, trying not to cry out.

"It looks like we'll be with you through the bitter end, whether you want us or not."

The despair in his voice twisted Alias's heart. Stubbornly, she tried to renew his hope. "We're not all captured yet," she pointed out, pacing the room. "Olive is still at large. We've gotten out of worse."

Alias tried the door. The knob did not turn, and an experimental slam with her shoulder indicated that it was barred on the far side, as well as locked. The window was not constructed to be opened and, being made of crown glass set in a lead frame, could not be smashed out. The circles of glass would have let in light, but it was dark outside. The prisoners had no clues as to their whereabouts.

Alias bit her lip and stood in the center of the room, wracking her brain for some way out. There was no chimney, the walls were brick, the floor and ceiling solid oak.

Akabar rose shakily from the chair and staggered over to Dragonbait. He tried to wake him first with gentle shakes and then, in frustration, with more violent ones. Akabar looked at Alias and shook his head.

"Okay, masters," Alias said. "It's your move."

Her words received an immediate reaction. A portion of the wall near the door became misty, then translucent, and finally transparent. Alias reached out and touched it. It was firm and cool, like glass in the autumn. Taking a gamble, she slammed into the clearing wall with her shoulder, hoping to break through. The wall may have looked like glass, but it still felt like bricks. Alias rubbed her aching shoulder.

Cruel laughter came from beyond the wall, and Alias caught sight of Cassana seated on a raised throne on the other side of the transparent barrier. It distressed Alias that the witch's features were so similar to her own. Will I look like that, sound like that, be like that, in a few years' time? the swordswoman wondered. She tore her thoughts away and concentrated on the two other figures beyond the wall.

A male halfling in a flashy yellow taffeta costume sat at Cassana's feet, playing with a wicked-looking knife. There was something bizarre about his eyes—they had no whites around the irises, yet the pupils looked white. The halfling smiled far too broadly, reminding Alias of the kalmari.

A skeletal figure in a brown cloak stood beside the throne, leaning on a twisted staff. His face was hidden beneath the hood of his cloak.

"Hello, Puppet," Cassana greeted her. She was dressed in a rich, flowing gown, worn off one shoulder. The white cloth glittered in the candlelight like woven diamonds. A band of matching material circled her brow, holding her auburn hair in place. She turned the slim, blue wand over and over in her hands.

Alias's spine stiffened at the sorceress's address. The voice was so familiar, but not because it was her own. Alias recognized the harsh, bitter tones. She had listened to the voice before, and she had hated it then as she did now.

An old, lost memory surfaced. She was rising out of a pool of silver streaked with crimson. Cassana stood over her with that wand, laughing in low, rich tones—the laughter of a vain woman, delighted to see herself replicated.

Alias bared her teeth in a tight smile. "Hello, Cassana. Or should I call you Mother?"

Akabar now stood beside the swordswoman, his jaw slack, amazed at the resemblance Alias bore to the sorceress.

Cassana gave a guttural laugh and shattered her illusion of being an older Alias. Such a laugh could never come from Alias. It was a cruel, heartless laugh, and Alias was neither of those things.

Akabar pointed at the tall form beside the throne. "That's the one who grabbed me."

Cassana motioned lazily, and the skeletal figure reached up with age-rotted hands and flipped back the hood of its cloak. Beneath lay a skull covered with translucent, jaundiced flesh stretched like a drum head. Its features consisted of a rictus-grin, a deteriorating nose, and ebony eye sockets in which sharp points of light danced.

"Yesss," the undead creature hissed. "I reached up and snared you tight, stopping your blood and freezing your muscles." The creature flexed a skeletal hand, each finger bone sharp as a knife. "Yet you live, petty wizard. But only because the Lady Cassana craves unblemished fruit on occasion." The undead creature laughed, too—a hoarse, wheezing laugh disturbingly familiar to Akabar. Try as he could, however, the Turmishman could not place it.

Alias did, though. She remembered the laugh in concert with Cassana's, for this thing had also been present when Alias had been "born." It had laughed at the swordswoman's nakedness and helplessness—the same laugh that had emanated from the maw of the crystal elemental summoned by the undead thing.

"Zrie Prakis," Alias whispered.

"Yes. I believe introductions are called for," Cassana said, her tone as proper as a society matron's. "I am Cassana. This male child is called Phalse." The halfling looked up, and his too-wide smile grew even wider. "And this, as you have guessed, is Zrie Prakis, formerly a mage, now a lich. You've already heard, so I understand, of the grand passion he and I shared that nearly ended in a fiery blaze. But I never let go of things that are mine." She grasped the blue wand tightly to emphasize her point.

"Gentlemen," she addressed Phalse and Zrie Prakis, "you already know our dear Puppet and the thing on the floor. The handsome mage," and with that description her eyes seized on the Turmishman like the talons of a hawk about a hare, "is Akabar Bel Akash, powerful in both magic and cooking. Your peppered lamb is notorious even here, Akabar."

Akabar furrowed his brow in puzzlement.

For a third time Cassana laughed. "Come now, mageling," she mocked. "Surely you did not expect us all to be as out-of-date and foolish as the moldy old god you so amusingly destroyed? We have followed your journey, at first in bits and pieces, but more steadily since Shadowdale.

"We decided to let you continue on to Yulash and free

Moander. Once the Abomination was loosed, it was only a matter of time before the old fool met its fate—humankind has grown much in power since that garbage pile last reigned here. The sooner we got it out of the way, the better. And with its demise we need no longer worry about the bizarre schemes its followers had for you, Puppet."

Alias wondered if Cassana had any inkling that Moander had planned the same double-cross for her.

"Once Moander dropped you off in our back yard, it was child's play to track you down and pick you up."

"You can track me," Alias said in a flat, emotionless tone.

"Well, to be honest, no. We were too clever by half. You see, your very being is impregnated with a powerful spell of misdirection. You cannot be detected by scrying, nor can anyone who travels with you. Since we did not expect you to slip from our grasp, we never thought the misdirection spell would pose any problem for us. A serious miscalculation on our part. One of many, I'm afraid. But you can't create art without a few mistakes. The best we can do is correct them in the future.

"Fortunately for us you were intelligent enough to wonder about your brands. Whenever magic is detected on your arm it acts as a beacon to locate you. We relied on our black-leathered allies to capture you in Suzail. Their failure was almost our undoing. But by some stroke of luck you stumbled upon an old haunt of Zrie's and revealed yourself to us again by displaying the magic content of your brand. But, alas, you were also more than a match for the heavy-handed methods of my love here."

At this, Zrie Prakis bowed deeply, and Alias could hear the skin stretching and popping over his bones.

"And then, even more luckily, my kalmari spotted you coming through Shadow Gap. It could be no coincidence that you continually alerted us of your whereabouts. I knew you wished to come home to us, Puppet. So we made it easier to keep an eye on you. We contacted one of your followers and planted a tracking device on her. And, as I said before, once you came to Westgate, finding you and defeating you was easy. A halfling's trick."

Alias felt as though the chilling fist of a frost giant had

closed about her heart. "No," she whispered.

Phalse motioned to a hidden figure, who edged cautiously into view. She was decked out with the finest robes, glittering imitations of those worn by Cassana. She looked like a little princess, a child-bride from the east. She smiled sheepishly at Akabar and Alias.

Olive Ruskettle.

"Hullo, everyone," Olive said, nervous sweat beading beneath her headband. "If I'd known you were in trouble—"

"Hush, child," Cassana interrupted. "You jumped at the opportunity to help us, as any good halfling would." Cassana smiled at the prisoners. "Gold coins weigh more than friendships. Now, mageling, I'll give you the same chance that we gave the child here. You've been misled by the false charm of this puppet. Forsake the slave and join its masters. I'm sure we can find a use for you." Prakis put a possessive skeletal hand on Cassana's bare shoulder, and the sorceress squeezed it affectionately to underscore her point.

The fury building in Akabar's gut spilled out. "I'd rather roast in the lowest hell—"

Cassana, with an angry frown, muttered something and motioned with her wand. Alias backhanded Akabar in the jaw. Backhanded him hard with all her warrior's strength.

The mage toppled backward, staring at the swordswoman. Her legs were rigid; her fists clenched and unclenched in sharp, fast spasms. The remaining runes on her arm writhed and glowed. Cassana's insect-squiggle shone the brightest of all.

"Alias?" Akabar gasped as he rose to his feet.

"One chance is all you get," Cassana said, "for now. Hit him until he is unconscious, Puppet." She motioned with the wand again.

Alias spun in place like a sentry and caught Akabar in the belly with her foot. The air rushed from his lungs, and he collapsed. He tried to rise again, but the woman warrior brought both fists down on the back of his neck, knocking him from his knees so he sprawled out on the floor. The mage rolled on his back, trying to ward off the rain of blows and kicks with his chains.

He froze when he caught sight of Alias's face. Her eyes

burned with a wild anger, and tears ran freely down her cheeks.

Gods! Akabar thought, Cassana is doing to her what Moander did to me. She has no control of her actions, and she is even more aware of the evil she does than I was. Pity for the swordswoman overwhelmed him, and he dropped his guard completely.

A kick to his jaw plunged him into a spiraling blackness.

Cassana laughed as her puppet stood poised over the helpless body of the Turmishman. "Look, Zrie," the sorceress said, "she's crying. I bet I know who taught her that trick." With a second wave of the wand, the sorceress returned Alias to unconsciousness. The swordswoman collapsed on top of Akabar.

With a lazy wave of her free hand, Cassana signaled the lich. Zrie Prakis let his spell elapse, and the transparent wall turned back into stone and mortar.

Cassana applauded her little play. Olive sat in shock. Every hair on the back of her neck, no, every hair on her body, had stiffened as she watched the beating. The sorceress slid out of her throne and, beckoning the lich, headed down the hallway. Phalse and Ruskettle fell in behind them, but dropped back to confer in private.

"Did she have to . . ." Olive let the question dangle.

"She's a human," Phalse replied. "Humans tend to be cruel, as we both know." He paused for several paces, then added, "You know she did that for your benefit, as well as his."

"Oh?" The bard was certain that beating up mages had never been on her list of entertaining events.

"Sure. She wanted to point out how lucky you are to be joining our little family. Eventually, the mage will get the same message."

"And if he doesn't?"

"Sorceress Cassana is loath to use magic to get her way with a man," Phalse explained. "But she will use it rather than damage this Akash fellow beyond repair. I think she likes him."

Olive shuddered inwardly at the thought of what Cassana might have done to Akabar if she hated him.

"She could have made the One kill Akash," Phalse pointed

out, as if reading the halfling's mind. "But she didn't."

Olive felt the return of the nervous sweat beneath her headband. She forced the idea of money, lots of it, to the forward part of her mind. "You all have different names for . . . for her."

"The One? Yes, I suppose we do. Another mistake to be corrected. Cassana calls her Puppet. Moander's priest called her The Servant. The Fire Knives called her Weapon. The lich calls her Little One, as if he were her grandfather or something."

"Who called her Alias?"

"Not important," Phalse replied sharply. "Come, there's much to done."

They were in a simple, two-story merchant's house just inside the city wall. The cellar led to underground passages that delved under the wall and surfaced in an abandoned ruin beyond. Upstairs and down were long hallways with rooms jutting off them. The prisoners were being held in one of the upstairs rooms.

Nearing the top of the steps leading down to the first floor, Phalse and Olive heard Cassana's voice below. She spoke in Thieves' Cant, which Olive had no trouble translating.

"Grandfather, has the task been carried out?"

"All are cared for, milady," replied a thick, guttural voice.

"And you will take their place?"

"Aye."

"Morning, then, we'll complete the pact."

The sound of Cassana's gown swished off in one direction, while the cat-foot patter of the one called "Grandfather" faded away in another. Olive wondered where Prakis had got to. The undead magic-user could move more silently than the most graceful halfling.

Phalse flashed Olive an impish grin. "You understand the Argot?" He took the halfling's shrug as an admission of ignorance and explained, "He was the leader of the Fire Knives, reporting the death of Moander's surviving followers—all the ones that did not hurl themselves from tall places at the death of their god. The Fire Knives will take the place of Moander's minions at dawn when we seal the pact."

"When you make that final correction to the human

woman," Olive said.

"And when you receive final payment," Phalse added.

Yes, the halfling thought to herself. Try to keep your mind on the money, Olive-girl.

* * * * *

In Olive Ruskettle's estimation, the midnight dinner she was presently sitting through was one of the most frightening events in her life. For sheer terror, Olive thought, it rated somewhat above being discovered and accused by that pig paladin in the Living City, but just below being swept off a wagontop by Mist's dewclaw.

The dining room, a solemn, musty hall, was dominated by a huge oak table. The windows were covered with heavy, black velvet drapes. Hundreds of candles burned in candelabras, but the room was still dim.

Cassana, draped in scarlet satin that seemed to flame with brilliance, dominated one end of the table. Rubies dripped from the sorceress's throat, ears, and fingers. Prakis sat unmoving at the far end of the long table. He was dressed in yellow robes of equal finery. Before him had been placed the mounted bones of a goose, a haunting joke about his undead status.

Olive was seated midway down the table at Phalse's side. The halfling bard kept a firm grip on her mind, trying to channel her thoughts away from abstract ideas like cruelty, sadism, and perversion, and tried to focus on real objects, like the food laid out before her.

In the food department Phalse put even the most gluttonous of Ruskettle's race to shame. He wolfed down vast quantities of dark-roasted venison ringed with stuffed mushrooms and the pickled vegetables carved into the shapes of skulls. He also downed mug after mug of mead, motioning for refills by swaying his goblet. Table was waited by silent men and women in dark tabards. Fire Knives, was Olive's guess. Apprentice murderers.

Though Olive was quite hungry and the repast was delicious, the food sat like a brick in her stomach. As out of place as the bard had felt among her former companions— Alias with her perfect voice, Akabar with his learning, Dra-

gonbait with his virtue—here she knew she was the prover-
bial fifth wheel.

There's something else at this table, the bard thought,
something that outranks me. Power. That's why they've
seated me beside Phalse instead of opposite him. Olive imagined she could see the power rippling between her three
hosts—Cassana, the lich, and Phalse. The Fire Knives are
servants, Olive realized, nothing more. Phalse has his aura
of charisma, an almost tangible swirl of attraction. Prakis
exudes all the authority of dry, dusty, ancient tomes, and
Cassana sits like a spider in the center of her web, aware of
every movement within her realm—Mistress of Life and
Death. If these three ever get into a disagreement, the bard
decided, I don't want to be around to get caught in the middle. I don't even want to be close enough to watch.

"So, what do you think of our little group, small bard?" the
sorceress asked.

Olive almost choked on her meat, unable to resist the idea
that her new allies could read her mind. "Well," she held up
a finger as she chewed and swallowed and gulped mead
down to give herself time to phrase a suitable reply. "To tell
the truth, I was unaware of how successful your alliance
already was when Phalse offered me the chance to join. I
understand you were subduing my . . . traveling companions even as I was speaking with him." She chose her words
carefully, picking her way through the conversation as deli-
cately as she would pick the lock of a cleric's trunk.

"Yes, we broke into two groups," Cassana explained. "One
to check out The Rising Raven, the other to follow the lure
of your ring. Prakis or I would likely have relied on clumsy,
human means to keep track of Puppet, but Phalse, smart,
wise Phalse knew that a halfling would easily topple to the
lure of power and gold. And how better to reward your
faithful service."

Olive's mouth was dry, and she took another gulp of mead
before she nodded.

"And so we have another member of our band," concluded the sorceress. "A good thing, too, because our numbers
are rapidly dwindling. Moander is dead, the crafter useless
to us, the Fire Knives thinned in rank. We could use young

blood." She emphasized the last word just a little too much, leaving Olive with memories of the legends of vampires.

The silence hanging over the table was oppressive. Struggling to lift it, the bard began to ask, "Crafter? Who's—" but before she could finish Phalse gave her thigh a sharp squeeze. Olive almost jumped from her chair. She turned to glare at him for an explanation, but he was busy draining his goblet. Holding out his glass for a refill, he bestowed her with a wink from one of his peculiarly blue eyes.

"I'm sorry," Cassana prompted. "You were saying?"

"Nothing. I was too wrapped up in your tale."

"Of course," Cassana replied. She began nodding and murmuring to herself, and Olive wondered if Cassana had channeled too much of her power into keeping up her good looks and let her mind go a little mushy. The sorceress's head snapped up and she announced, "Now, the three of us will be very busy for the next few hours, preparing for the ceremony to be held at dawn. But you, Olive, were up very early this morning, before dawn. And since then you've been a very, very busy little girl. You must be exhausted. Take a nap, and Phalse will send for you."

Whether it was the suggestion, the food, or the long hours and miles between Yulash and Westgate, Olive suddenly felt very weary. She swayed in her chair, trying to shake the cobwebs from her brain. Phalse put a hand out to steady her, his grip like iron.

"Now that you mention it," the bard said, not bothering to stifle a yawn, "I'm dead on my feet."

"Good. Prakis my pet, why don't you take the small bard up to Phalse's room for her nap?"

"I would prefer—" Phalse began to protest, but Cassana cut him off with a motion of her hand.

"You and I have some private matters to discuss," the sorceress insisted.

"Just how private do you intend to get?" Phalse bantered.

The lich rose silently and stood behind the halfling's chair as she tumbled from it. She staggered from sudden exhaustion, then began weaving her way to the staircase.

Cassana laughed behind her, calling out, "Sleep tight, little one." When the lich had maneuvered the bard up the first flight of stairs, the sorceress turned her cold, hard eyes on Phalse. "Well?"

"She's scared witless, but that's understandable," Phalse replied in the halfling's defense. "But it's a rather delicious sort of terror, don't you think?"

"She seems a bit unstable. She'll sleep through the ceremony. When she wakes, her former allies will be dead or under our control. The choice will be easier for her once her options have been limited. I would prefer it, though, if you would use her and get rid of her tonight," said Cassana.

Phalse flashed his inhuman smile. "I'll slay her myself if you similarly dispose of your lovers, including the Turmite."

Cassana pouted "You'd deprive me of my pets?"

"You'd deprive me of mine."

The two glared at one another, locked in a contest of wills. Then slowly, both began to laugh.

* * * * *

When the halfling collapsed on the second landing, Prakis bundled the childlike bard in his yellow cape and cradled her in his arms, carrying her to Phalse's opulent bedroom. He lay the halfling woman on the satin coverlet and leaned in close to her face, muttering a few words. Then he touched her on the forehead and shoulders.

Olive sat bolt upright, her eyelids flying open like pigeons startled by a temple bell. "What!" she gasped, then cringed away immediately from the mockery of humankind hovering over her.

"Hush," the death's head rattled. "I've cast a spell on you to counteract the magical suggestion Cassana the Cruel used to make you sleep," Prakis explained. His voice sounded windier than before, as though suddenly it was a greater effort for him to speak. "How do you feel?"

"I feel . . . I feel like I've slept for a week. Did I miss the ceremony?"

"No, only a few minutes have passed since you left the table. But my counteractive spell will give you energy now for hours. I woke you to make you an offer. Have you killed?" the lich asked. The red points of light in his eye sockets were suddenly still like a magical light.

"Killed? Of course. Easy as falling off a log."

"Can you do it again?"

"Uh . . . sure. Who do you want killed?"

"Cassana." The red pinpoints in the skull's eye sockets danced again.

"Wait a minute. I thought you and she were . . ." The halfling groped for polite words. "Close, I guess."

"I am Cassana's tool, her pet, much like you are—or will be—Phalse's pet, if he gets his way. The wand that controls the Little One also controls me. The farther I am from the wand, the more dead I become. Cassana keeps the wand on her person at all times, and when she travels too far away, I die entirely, only to come back as a shambling form when she returns. She is literally the sun my world revolves around."

"But your symbol is on Al—the Little One."

"My power over death was needed to bring the Little One to life, so I was allowed a small measure of control over her, but Cassana is the ultimate puppet master, pulling both our strings."

Up close to Prakis, Olive could see the deep blue stitchery of long-dead blood vessels and smell the fetid stink of the corpse's breath. He did not need to breathe, save to work his speech organs, which gave his voice an odd, mechanical quality.

"But why do you need me?" Olive asked. "Couldn't you just strangle her or something and take the wand?"

"No. That would not work. Cassana the Cruel is very clever. She has bound up her life energies into the wand so that, as long as she holds it, nothing the Little One or I do can harm her. She knows my hate; she knows the wand is all that stands between her and death by my hands. She loves knowing this—it thrills her."

"So you want me to steal the wand?"

"Yes. Then I will kill her."

"Um, just out of curiosity, how?"

"With this!" the lich thrust forward his staff of dark wood. "I am still permitted to wield this. It is a staff of power. Do you know what it can do?"

Olive nodded, remembering the lay written in honor of

Sylune. The river witch had used the same kind of staff to blow herself and a marauding dragon to kingdom come. The halfling didn't want to be anywhere near Prakis and Cassana when they finally ended their "lover's quarrel."

"No offense, Prakis, old bones, but what's in this for me?"

"Your freedom and your life."

"Oh?"

"Phalse considers you his property now. Surely you must realize that, as charming as he appears, he is no halfling."

"What is he?"

"I don't know. Not even Cassana knows, and that is not a good sign. Furthermore, Cassana does not like you. She never could stand any competition, no matter how small. And she is superstitious about halfling luck. She really sent Phalse after you to make sure you did not interfere with our capture of the prisoners. When Phalse's back is turned, she will slay you, gut you, and use your body as a vessel for her kalmari. Once you've helped me take care of Cassana, I will rid you of Phalse's company."

Olive gulped. "These are good reasons, but, um . . . I don't suppose you might offer me any other incentives?" She was terrified of angering the lich, but how much could it hurt to ask? she wondered.

Prakis laughed, genuinely amused. "I can see why Phalse kept you. You have a greed for life that must astound even him."

"Well, life is short, as you discovered, and it makes sense to get all you can out of it. The best things in life aren't free, you know."

"I did know that once. Cassana has amassed a great deal of wealth hidden in the cellars beneath this house. Besides selling and leasing her monsters, she skimmed a good deal off the top from the funds the Fire Knives poured into the project of making the Little One. Whatever you can carry away on a pony is yours, unless—perhaps you could remain here with me and the Little One, a member of our family."

The thought of living in the same house with a zombie Alias revolted Olive, but quite a bit of gold could be loaded onto a pony.

"You have a deal, but first, as a gesture of trust—tell me,

who is the crafter?"

Zrie Prakis's red eyes stabbed at the halfling for several moments. He must have decided the knowledge could do him no harm, because he told her. "He is—he has no true name. He gave the Little One a mind, a life, the name Alias. But he feels he's been damned for it."

"But he's still alive?"

The lich nodded with a crack of his neck bones. "Cassana the Cruel hates to cast aside her pets. He is prisoner in the cellars. But he is quite mad."

Olive decided to agree with the lich for now. Glibly she asked, "When do we start this revolution?"

"Use the time when we're at the ceremony to lace the house with traps. Lay in wait and ambush. Now, mime your sleep while I prepare the prisoners. And do not give yourself away, or I will be forced to slay you myself." The skin over his forehead wrinkled the slightest bit as he made an attempt to threateningly raise eyebrows he did not possess.

Then he drifted from the room, silent except for the creaking of his bones.

Olive leaned back in the bed and closed her eyes, and the energy the lich had channeled into her did indeed keep her from falling asleep. Unfortunately, it also made her restless. Her mind kept flipping through her quickly diminishing options.

She turned on her side, away from the door, and thought harder. Though she'd been wishing for Phalse's friends to show up and take Alias, she'd felt a pang of disappointment when she'd learned they'd already captured the swordswoman. Her second meeting with Phalse had not left the bard with as charming an impression of the pseudo-halfling as their first had. Strangers always looked friendlier sitting behind a stack of coins, Olive realized. His offer of great power had sounded amusing accompanied by fine Luiren ale, but Olive had never really been interested in power.

Especially not if it meant watching people getting beaten to a pulp.

While she'd been drinking with Phalse, Olive had formed some half-baked scheme of joining the alliance in order to discover by her own means—stealth and cunning—the identities and intentions of Alias's foes. In her mind, she would then have reported back to Alias, revealing how she had succeeded where the book-laden mage would not and the scaly paladin could not. That would have impressed them.

But the plan had backfired drastically, and now she was trapped, a little spider in a larger spider's web. She could think of only three options: Escape somehow and flee, living in fear of retribution; find a way to free the others and fight; or join the alliance for real, submitting herself to whatever Phalse and Cassana had in store for her.

She did not consider the lich's plan. It was entirely too dangerous. Cassana would fry me like a banana, Olive realized, if I came within twelve inches of her wand.

Olive didn't much care for the idea of sticking around. Besides disliking her role of low woman on the totem pole, an alliance with these people was very risky business. Their partners had a habit of dying off.

Olive granted that she was greedy and ambitious, but these people were cruel and hateful and perverse—no act of hers could ever bring her to their level of perdition.

Still, despite herself, and despite Prakis's warnings, she felt drawn to Phalse. He had treated her with courtesy and rewarded her with more cash than anyone else had in a long time. He understood her halfling heart.

The door creaked open behind her and then closed. Someone tiptoed over to the bed. The bard snapped her eyes shut, and began breathing shallowly with a melodic semi-snore.

A small hand touched her knee, and Olive shifted slightly to cover her startled movement. Small fingers danced up her thigh and then cupped her breasts. After a moment or two they withdrew. It wasn't until the door opened and closed again that Olive realized she'd been holding her breath.

She sat bolt upright after Phalse's retreat, gritting her teeth against a scream. She scratched one option from her list. She couldn't stay here. She would escape—with or without the others.

❧ 28 ❧

The Crafter

Olive crept about the room, slipping some of the more pawnable and valuable items into her backpack and her pockets: ivory combs, a silver mirror, crystal perfume vials, a gold wine goblet. After scavenging for half an hour she noticed sounds of greater activity in the hallway.

Olive crept over to the door and pressed her ear against it. She could hear men in the hallway, panting as if from strenuous labor, accompanied by a dragging sound. Olive peeked out the keyhole. Two Fire Knives were hauling something behind them. Olive caught sight of a scaly, green arm—Dragonbait. A thumping noise came from the staircase—they were being none too gentle with the saurial.

Two more assassins flicked by the keyhole, carrying Akabar by the arms and legs. Cassana's new toy, he was given preferential treatment. He was not thumped down the steps. Olive heard Phalse say, "Leave him in the cell next to the crafter's."

Last of all, Zrie Prakis floated by with Alias cradled in his arms. He paused by Olive's door, blocking her view. Olive heard a bolt sliding across the door.

She waited until all noise in the hall had ceased and no sounds came from the stairway. Then she tried the door.

Prakis had unlocked it for her. The bard poked her head out of the doorway. The house was silent. After closing and bolting the door to Phalse's room behind her, she crept down the hallway and tiptoed down the stairs. She dashed through the entry hall. The front door beckoned her. She twisted the knob, but it was locked.

Olive reached into her hair and drew out a pick, but

before she began working on the bolt, she noticed a blue line drawn across the threshold, with three interlocking circles sketched above it. A magical ward—one of Prakis's. Was it the type that warned the designer something had crossed over it, or the kind that disintegrated into dust whatever crossed over it? There was no way for Olive to tell.

"Boogers," Olive muttered. "What's the matter? Don't you trust me, Prakis, old bones?"

Dodging into the dining room, the halfling slipped behind the heavy curtains. The lock on the large windows was easily unfastened, but another blue mark was scrawled along the window sills. Grinding her teeth in annoyance, Olive dashed back into the entry hall and up the steps. There was a window in the upstairs hallway, but it, too, was warded.

Zrie Prakis had made sure she would stick to her side of the bargain. He'd unlocked her cell door, but he was not going to let her escape from the prison. As she saw it, she had one chance. Unlocking the door to Phalse's room and slipping back inside, she examined the window within. Unguarded. The wards must have been a last-minute thought on the lich's part, and he had neglected to come back to Phalse's room to set one there.

Olive climbed out onto the window sill. The roof sloped away gently. She would have an easy time slipping down to the gutter—a perfect halfling's footpath—and walking along that until she found a rain spout to slide down. But what then? she wondered as she sat with her feet dangling over the roof tiles.

She'd have to find another adventuring group to travel with, one that could help protect her from Phalse and family should they decide she was worth chasing.

Finding a new party wouldn't be easy. Alias and Dragonbait were perhaps the finest sword wielders she'd ever seen, and Akabar had helped destroy a god, and the three of them had been defeated. Of course, she hadn't been there to help them out, she consoled herself. She wondered idly if her presence would really have made a difference. According to Prakis, Cassana had been concerned that it might have. Is it possible, Olive wondered, that Cassana put me to sleep because she was afraid I might interfere somehow in this ceremony to remove Alias's will?

Although Phalse had not told her, Olive knew the ceremony would involve the sacrifice of Dragonbait. Alias had said something about it to Akabar the day before, back at The Rising Raven. The loss of the paladin would not have made too much difference to the halfling before yesterday. Yet Olive had to admit, he hadn't done her any harm so far, and his death would seal the fates of Alias and Akabar.

Akabar would remain in Cassana's clutches, not something Olive would wish on anyone, certainly not on Akabar, whom she liked a little.

Alias was another matter. Olive found it difficult to like someone so perfect, but she felt more guilt about abandoning the swordswoman. For one thing, Olive realized, I owe her for rescuing me from the dragon and saving my life. She let me join her party, and she shared her songs with me. She stole my audience once, but she'll never do that again. After the ceremony she'll probably never sing songs again. Without a will she'll be a zombie, and zombies don't sing. All those lovely melodies and haunting lyrics would be lost to the world. That would be a crime, Olive sighed.

Not that people like Cassana, who liked kidnapping, torture, and murder, would care about such a loss to the musical world. Of course, I'd be just as responsible if I didn't do anything to stop the witch and her merry band, Olive acknowledged.

Jump, Olive-girl, the halfling told herself, before you wind up doing something you may regret later. The halfling could not get out of her head the image of Akabar being beaten and the sound of Dragonbait's head hitting each step as the Fire Knives dragged him downstairs.

But the thought of Alias never singing again was even worse.

Olive swung her feet back into the building, jumped to the floor, and left the room. The upper hallway was still empty, but she heard men's voices coming from somewhere below. Pausing to listen, she noticed great drops of red dotting the steps below her. Blood. Akabar's or Dragonbait's? she wondered. She followed the red spatters down the stairs.

The voices were coming from the kitchen. The trail of

blood went through the entry hall in the opposite direction. Olive tracked it to an alcove that featured a particularly obscene statue of an overly endowed succubus.

The trail ended in a pool of blood at the base of the statue, as if the prisoner had been left there for a moment. Olive made a "tch" sound. Why didn't they tell the world there was a secret passage here somewhere? she scoffed.

Footsteps and voices approached from the dining room. Olive ducked behind the statue of the succubus.

"—unfair. That's all I'm saying," the first protested.

"Unfair doesn't mean a thing to Her Ladyship," the second voice argued. "We don't have the seniority, we don't have the clout. The rest get to play clerics and gods in a few hours. We don't rate. So what?" Here the speaker's words became incoherent as his mouth was occupied with chewing and swallowing. "—prefer raiding Her Ladyship's larder to standing outside in the cold and damp. What?"

"Something by the dungeon door. Watch."

Olive's intestines cramped uncomfortably. Of all the stupid things—I've chosen the exact spot they're heading for!

A soft footstep then a second crept closer to the alcove. If the situation hadn't been so serious, Olive would have giggled at the picture of a burly human trying to creep like a halfling across the floor. She didn't even need to guess how close he was, she could feel the floorboards shift slightly under his weight. Pressing her back against the wall, she thrust against the statue's pedestal with her feet.

The top-heavy statue rocked, then toppled from its pedestal. The crash of stone against stone blended with the sickening thunk of flesh and bone being crushed by a great weight, as the succubus claimed the life of the first Fire Knife. The stonework ran with fresh blood.

The other Fire Knife, a grossly overweight human with a stubby short sword in one hand and half of a melon in the other, had been standing ten feet away when his partner had met his demise. His eyes were wide with shock, but he approached the pedestal. Olive slipped out of the alcove to face her attacker.

"Murr," muttered the Fire Knife. Whether this was the name of some god or his late companion, Olive did not know. "Ya just a girl. C'mon, kid, I'll make it fast. We'll just lock ya up until . . ."

The halfling didn't wait to find out how long she'd be locked up. She dropped to one knee, grabbed a piece of the broken statue, and threw it. Clunked square in the forehead with a succubus breast, the assassin rocked back on his heels. Olive grabbed the sword from his dead partner's hand and charged.

The Fire Knife dropped the melon and swung his blade downward. Olive dove to the right, and the steel blade sparked off the stonework, sending a ringing peal of doom through the hall and up the stairs. The assassin whirled and slashed in a cross-cut. Olive dipped her head slightly, and the blade swiped over her. The man's reflexes were trained in battling opponents his own size.

Olive slipped inside his guard and thrust his partner's short sword upward in the all-too-ample space between his leather jerkin and his belt. The blade sank deep into the flesh. Blood welled from the wound. The Fire Knife stepped backward, but Olive moved with him like a bulldog, wriggling and twisting the sword.

The assassin grabbed at her hair with his left hand, but before he could take advantage of his grip, he gurgled and collapsed on top of his enemy. It was several moments before Olive could get any air into her lungs and wriggle out from beneath her vanquished foe.

Blood stained the entire length of her gown.

"Like falling off a log," she muttered to herself. "Nothing to it. Done it lots of times." She tried to pant more quietly, listening for others. If anyone else was still in the house, they would have heard the fight.

There was no other sound but her labored breathing.

She returned to the pedestal and began exploring its carved edges for a catch to open the secret door. Badly rattled, her fingers ran over the surface for almost three minutes before she managed to press just the right bit of fluting. The wall in the back of the alcove slid open, revealing a spiral stairway leading down.

Stealing a torch from a wall sconce and the obese assassin's short sword, the bard pattered down the steps. The air grew chill and damp as she descended. At the bottom, a passage was cut deeply into the bedrock. The passage was lighted by a magical glow issuing from statues of demons mounted on the walls—magical light that did not flicker, but shone in steady red beams from the red glass eyes and in white fans from the tops of their heads. Along the right side of the passage were three archways blocked by cage bars. The passage continued on, lit by a pearl-like string of red and white lights.

Beyond the first archway lay an empty cell, clean but for a dark red smear streaking the back wall. The second cell caged a mass of rotting cloaks and blankets. Akabar hung in the third cell, the chains of his manacles attached to a hook in the ceiling. The Turmishman's toes dangled three inches from the floor. The assassins had left him in the cold and damp with nothing but a sheet wrapped around his waist. His face was puffy and discolored. Blood trickled from his mouth and welled in the troughs of four-fingered scratches across his right cheek and chest. Ruskettle could not remember Cassana's nails being particularly long. Then she recalled the sharpened finger bones of Zrie Prakis, and shuddered.

"Akabar," she hissed, wondering if there were any other Fire Knives left behind to guard the prisoners. She searched the bars for a door or a lock, but they ran from ceiling to floor without a break.

"Akabar!" she said louder.

In the cell next door the mound of furs and cloaks stirred. Olive started and watched the pile closely. A man's head poked out. His hair and beard were shaggy and black, with splotches of gray and white. His eyes were blue and rheumy. His face was lined with cracks of old age and cold. Cocking his head he chirped, "Hullo."

Olive cast a glance back at Akabar, but the mage had not moved. "Uh, greetings. You must be the crafter. Are we alone here?" she whispered.

"No," the crafter said, shaking loose the furs and cloaks. He rose slowly to his feet, and his legs wobbled as if he'd been bedridden for a long time. He wore a tattered tabard that must have once been purple and green, but was now faded to gray and yellow. "There's a new prisoner next door," he replied, pointing toward Akabar's cell.

"I mean, are there any guards?"

"Let me check. GUARDS!"

Olive toppled backward in shock. Scrambling to her feet, she sought desperately for a bolt hole. She could run farther down the corridor or back up it. The crafter's cry echoed back to her from both directions, but the sound of human feet did not follow it.

"Sorry. No guards. I think they're away. That way." The graying crafter pointed farther down the passage.

Prakis warned you the fellow was mad, Olive-girl, she berated herself. Obviously, he wasn't joking.

"Where are the locks?" she demanded.

The crafter's eyes became sharp points. "There are no locks here."

"How did they put you in there?"

"Through the bars."

Olive cursed. She didn't have time to play riddles with crazy people. "Must you be so cryptic?"

"As long as I'm here, yes. Otherwise, I'd shed light on the subject for you."

Olive considered continuing down the passage to search for Cassana's hoard and then leave when she'd found enough treasure to keep her in flight for a year. But the hoard might be similarly barred, and who knew how many Fire Knives were stationed to guard the end of the tunnel?

The light from her torch, dropped when the madman had bellowed, fizzled out and died. Only the magic light of the demon statues illuminated the corridor now. Light. Shed some light on the subject, she thought. What was the subject? The bars. Of course!

It took the halfling several tries to climb up the smooth walls. Reaching behind the head of one of the demon figures, she found a glass sphere, cold as ice, but with a magical light that shone with more brilliance than any candle or torch. Olive withdrew it gently and jumped down.

She held the light in front of Akabar's cell. "Nothing's happening," she growled, putting the sphere down to retrieve her sword.

"Why should anything happen?" the madman shrugged. "You're just standing there."

"So I am," Olive nodded. She stepped forward—and passed right through the bars.

"Hey, that's great. Thanks," she called back to the crafter. She set the sword on the floor and checked on the mage's condition. He was still breathing, but she would never be able to lift him off the hook. She might have tried climbing up the mage's body and picking the locks on his manacles, but the wrist bindings had been welded, not snapped on.

"Need some help?" a voice beside her asked. Olive whirled around and would have skewered the speaker if he had not so agilely sidestepped her attack.

The halfling gasped. The crafter stood next to her in Akabar's cell. She had set the glowing sphere down in such a position that it had shed light on the bars of his prison as well. He held the globe now in one hand.

"Keep back," Olive ordered, brandishing her sword.

The crafter's lips curled up in a wry smile. His eyes were now clear and piercing. He stood straighter and looked stronger. "If I keep back, how are we going to get your friend down?" His voice was now firm and reasonable.

Olive wrinkled her brow in puzzlement. "You're not mad."

The crafter harumphed. "So I have always maintained."

"I mean . . . well, you're different than you were a moment ago."

"The cell I was in works a spell of enfeeblement on its occupants."

"Oh." Suddenly remembering that the crafter was still one of Alias's would-be masters, Olive took another step backward and held out her sword. "Why should you want to help?"

"Look, are you going to stand there all day demonstrating your incompetence with a short sword, or climb up on my shoulders and unhook this unfortunate southerner?"

The halfling frowned at the insult, but the crafter had a point. She sighed and set her sword down behind her, then approached him cautiously.

The crafter stooped, set the sphere of light on the ground, and made a foothold for her with his hands. Olive put her hand on his shoulder and stepped up. He was a big man, as tall as Akabar, and even broader at the chest. She climbed nimbly to his shoulders, and he stood up smoothly.

"When I lift him, you detach the chain," he said.

Once Akabar had been released, Olive scrambled down the crafter's back. Cradling the mage in his arms, he carried him from the cell and set him on the ground outside. Olive followed with her sword and the sphere of light.

The man frowned at the mage's wounds. "Can you heal?" he asked Olive.

"What do I look like? A paladin?"

"Upstairs there's a bureau in the dining room. It's trapped, but there's a small button along the base that deactivates it. Unless Cassana has changed, there will be a number of potions there. Fetch them and some clothing for this one and come right back. Oh—and leave the sword."

Olive obeyed without question, suddenly relieved to not be making all the decisions. She was back within fifteen minutes, laden with the potions, Akabar's spellbooks— which had also been in the cabinet—one of Zrie Prakis's robes, two kitchen knives, and a sack of food.

The crafter was seated by Akabar's side, using the sword to scrape away his ratty beard. His face was deeply care-worn, like a general who'd been at war too long or a king's wisest but least heeded adviser.

He rummaged through the tablecloth that served as a sack, pulled out two potions, and mixed them together to form a gummy poultice, which he smeared over the cuts on Akabar's chest and face. Akabar moaned, but the wounds began to close. The crafter slipped the rest of the potions into his tabard pockets.

"His wounds will take about an hour to heal," the crafter said. He turned a stern eye on Olive. "Now, who is he, and who are you, and how did you come to be in this foul place?"

"He's Akabar Bel Akash, a mage. I'm Olive Ruskettle the Bard. I'm trying to rescue Alias the Swordswoman from Cassana, who is trying to enslave her—"

"I know all about Cassana's business with Alias," the crafter interrupted. "Who are you really?"

"I told you. This is Akabar Bel—"

"I mean you, halfling. You cannot be a bard."

"I beg your pardon?"

"I said, you cannot be a bard. You might use it as a cover for your other activities, but you cannot be one. There are no halfling bards."

"Well, you are very much mistaken," Olive huffed. "I am a halfling, and I am a bard. I sing, play the yarting and the tantan, compose music and poetry, and weave tales."

"That makes you a troubadour or a minstrel. Your skill may be such that you can impress and entertain people, but to be a bard you must be trained. Without training, the power of the calling will never be yours. And I know, better than any three of my colleagues and better than any sage, that no halfling has ever been trained."

"And how would you know?"

"Because I am a bard. The Nameless Bard."

"The Nameless Bard? Just what's that supposed to mean?"

"It means they took away my name. In much the same way that barbarian kings wipe out the wives and children of their enemies, they banned my songs and erased my name from history—and from my own mind."

"You mean Cassana?"

The Nameless Bard laughed. "Hardly. It would take a power far greater than hers to overcome even a single melody of mine."

A flash of inspiration struck Olive. "You wrote the songs Alias sings. You're her Harper friend."

The Nameless Bard turned a piercing look on the halfling. Olive grew uncomfortable beneath his gaze and turned away. "Didn't mean to pry," she mumbled.

"I remember a bard, a true bard, named Ruskettle. Olav Ruskettle. Had a bad gambling habit. Would have staked his own mother on the roll of a die. I suppose by the time you ran into him, he had nothing left but his name."

Olive glared at the Nameless Bard. "He was situated very comfortably as a tavernkeeper in Procampur. He couldn't gamble away the tavern—his wife held the title."

"So he offered you his name."

Olive shrugged. "He couldn't play anymore—lost his right hand. His voice was beginning to fade."

"So you accepted. Loaded dice?"

"No!"

"Very well. You won the name fair and square. But all the rights, privileges, and immunities thereunto appertaining, you never earned."

"Just because humans don't recognize a halfling's talents doesn't mean they don't exist."

"Did you even try applying to a barding college?"

The halfling was silent for a moment. "No," she admitted.

"Why not? No, don't answer me. I'm really not interested in your excuses. Answer to yourself. Now, tell me, would-be bard, how did you come to be a companion to the swords-woman, Alias?"

Olive bridled some at the title, but she needed the Name-less Bard's help to free Alias. She began with Mist's abduction of her from the caravan in Cormyr, then explained how Dimswart had come to hire Alias. She described their battle with the crystal elemental, the disastrous brawl at the wedding, all that Dimswart had discovered about the sigils, and the destruction of the kalmari. She began slowly and nervously, like a schoolchild asked to recite, but she was not naturally a taciturn person, and her tale flowed smooth and clear by the time she described the events in Shadowdale.

To her own astonishment, she told the truth about her dealings with Phalse. She knew the story would not make much sense if she left out crucial elements. She related all Akabar had told her about the events in Yulash, how Dragonbait had subdued Mist, the battle with Moander, and finally how all of them came to be captured by Alias's enemies, the others by force, she by stupidity.

Olive had never had such a polite and riveted audience in her life. He interrupted her tale only once, when she was describing how Cassana had made Alias batter Akabar.

"You say she wept?" the true bard asked.

"Of course she wept," Olive said. "Akabar is her friend, and the witch was using her to pulp his flesh. I could see the streaks her tears left on her cheeks and the dark spots where they landed on the floor. Cassana thought it was pretty funny and made a stupid joke about it. She said, 'Look Zrie, she's crying. I'll bet I know who taught her that trick.'

Then she used her wand to knock Alias out."

The true bard's lower lip quivered for a moment. He clamped it shut. "Finish. Quickly. Your friend is coming around."

Olive told how Cassana had put her to sleep, and the deal Zrie had offered her. "He unbolted the door for me. There were only two guards upstairs. I killed them and came down here looking for Akabar."

Akabar awoke slowly. Though weak, he was still strong enough to grab Ruskettle by the throat and throttle her. The Nameless Bard pulled the mage's hands away with his own sure grip.

"You've signed her death warrant, you greedy, little bitch!" Akabar shouted.

"I think there has been a misunderstanding," the Nameless Bard said calmly. "Your friend was using a ruse to win your enemy's trust."

Akabar's eyes squinted with disbelief, but he could not fight the strength of the true bard's hands.

Olive felt a rush of gratitude toward the bard. She had told him the whole truth, that her reasons for accepting Phalse's offer had been as much for greed as for a desire to play at espionage, but he had given her the benefit of the doubt.

"Look, Akash. I came down here to get your help to rescue Alias." That much was half true. "If you'd rather go back to your cell and wait for Cassana . . ."

Akabar spat on the halfling's gown.

"He's very emotional," she explained to the crafter.

"Look at me, Akabar Bel Akash," the Nameless Bard said. The power of his voice drew Akabar's eyes unwillingly from Olive.

"Do you want to rescue Alias?"

Akabar took a deep breath, almost a sob. "Yes."

"So does this creature. So do I. Contain your anger. It is a waste of your energies. You should know that."

Akabar took another deep, slow breath. He relaxed his muscles. The true bard released his wrists.

"Who are you?" Akabar asked.

"The Nameless Bard."

"Nameless? No one is nameless."

"They took his name away," Olive explained.

"Who?" Akabar asked.

The Nameless Bard sighed. "Eat," he said, motioning toward the food that Olive had taken from Cassana's larder. "You'll need your strength very soon. I will tell you my story while you dine."

Akabar noticed his books in Olive's bundle and motioned for them. Olive slid them to his side. She remembered how he had asked for them after being freed from Moander and took this as a sign that he was prepared to carry on—and put the past behind him—at least for now.

"You have no doubt heard of the Harpers," the Nameless Bard began. "They were established in the north long before you were born. Their members are primarily bards and rangers, though not limited to such. All are good and true men and women devoted to preserving the balance of life, opposing all that threatens the peace of the Realms, protecting the weak and innocent. You might recognize them by their small silver pin of a harp and a moon.

"One of their number was a bard, a master of his craft, with a voice and a memory like polished ice. A creator of songs that could move people to action, or calm them to slumber. None heard his music but that they were impressed. The bard himself was often astonished by his own skill and wished for all his works to be preserved for eternity.

"Yet songs are so easily changed, their lyrics tampered with, their melodies maligned. The bard's own colleagues had done this to his works, substituting a phrase to suit a particular audience, quickening the tempo to end an evening's entertainment sooner. Or simply forgetting a line. And though such things are only natural, the bard was obsessed with preserving his works as he'd intended them to be sung."

"Prickly sort, wasn't he?" Olive asked with a tiny grin.

The corner of the true bard's mouth turned up in a half-smile. "We all have our faults.

"Rejecting human singers as the preservers of his art, he turned to mechanical means. Paper and stone would not suffice—the written word could not convey the meaning as well as spoken words, and written notes describe only the melody, not the spirit of the music. And paper and stone can be destroyed. Even magical attempts to reproduce his music dissatisfied him. They could not demonstrate the full interaction of the bard with his audience.

"Finally, he determined a mixture of these methods that would fulfill his requirements. A human shell, unwilling, even unable, to stray from the original rendition, a repository for his tales and music that could render them unto generations."

"Alias," Akabar said.

"Alias?" Olive chirped.

"Alias," the true bard said. "The price to make such a creature, however, was very great, involving dealing with powerful mages and extra-planar powers. The price was also horrible. It would cost the life of a noble innocent, both pure and true, by brutal means.

"The master bard, with his apprentices, men and women of lesser power but great talent, tried to create this shell on their own. The attempt failed, costing one assistant his life and another her voice, so that she was silent for the rest of her shortened, painful days.

"Many men and women of the Realms might have shrugged off such a tragedy. But the Harpers considered themselves better men and women and were horrified by what the bard had done. They summoned him to judgement.

They stripped him of his name, stole it from his memory. His name being a given thing, this was easy to do. But knowledge discovered is like an efreet let out of a bottle: it cannot be forced back in. The struggle to discover it makes it part of the discoverer's soul. They could not destroy the knowledge in him. They feared he would try again, or pass the knowledge to another. So they could not let him go free, yet they would not slay him, for he was one of their own, and they did not want his blood on their hands.

"They decided he would have to be imprisoned, but no ordinary prison would do. They could not risk his ever passing on the method he had developed. So they shackled and exiled him beyond the bounds of the Realms, in the lands where reason fails and the gods roll like storm fronts across the sky. All his songs, his words, and his ideas were expunged in a sweeping attempt to cover up what he had achieved. Those who knew his songs were told to sing them no more, and such was the respect and fear of the Harpers in those days that many complied.

"So that which the master bard feared most came to pass: the songs he sought to preserve were dead things, unremembered in the Realms. The Harpers had been thorough, indeed. The newer members know nothing of the story. Only the old remember the tale."

"So how did you escape?" Akabar asked.

"Some vestige of the tale survived. A scrap of a letter I'd written to an apprentice fell into Cassana's hands—something about how my human shell could be made indistinguishable from the real thing. Cassana went to great lengths to track me down. She put a bounty out on an old Harper and tortured him for the information on my whereabouts. I hear he did not submit until she began torturing other creatures as well.

"I knew none of this when her allies completed a bridge to my place of exile. If I had not been half mad with loneliness and grief for the death of my songs, I might have seen through Cassana's unholy alliance immediately. But Cassana used her sweetest manner, and Phalse played on my desire for retribution. Zrie cloaked himself in the illusion of a living mage. I was not told of the Fire Knives or Moander or Phalse's master.

"I gave up all my secrets, and they helped me build Alias. Later, I learned that the money for the project came from the Fire Knives, and that Moander provided the life energy needed to start Alias breathing. Cassana provided the body, Zrie the power to keep death from her, and Phalse's master the power to bind a soul in her."

"Dragonbait's soul," Akabar breathed.

"The saurial, yes."

"And you taught her to sing," Olive said.

"Oh, more than that. I spun her entire history, her thoughts, her feelings, her beliefs. A full personality that could interact with others. She was to be my redemption, my justification, of all I had done. I wanted to be sure that no one could see the beauty of my achievement without forgiving the evil means I used to accomplish it.

"But my allies had their own purposes, something I should have realized when each gave her a different name. I named her Alias because I could not give her my own. All I wanted was for her to live in peace and sing my songs.

"Then they branded her and the saurial, which Phalse's master had provided as sacrifice to give her a soul, and I understood they intended her to be a slave.

"I argued with Cassana, and for the first time she showed me her true nature. She'd left the empty space in the brand to represent me—another of her cruel jokes. I walked out on her and came down here, for this is where Alias and Dragonbait were being kept. I tried to convince myself to destroy Alias rather than bring her into this world bonded to so much evil."

The former Harper looked in the cell where Akabar had hung as though he still saw someone there. Tears welled in his eyes. "I am too reasonable a man to believe in miracles, but I suppose they must occur in spite of what I believe. When we'd left her in the cell that evening she was breathing but unconscious. Our calculations said she would not awaken until the saurial was slain. He was very near death already. He had killed many Fire Knives in one attempt to escape, and they beat him every chance they got. They'd left him hanging by the same hook you occupied, mage.

"When I returned here that night, the lizard was lying on the straw, wrapped in Alias's cloak. She had taken him down and was tending his wounds, singing him a lullaby, like a child with a doll.

"I sneaked upstairs to fetch the sword I had bought for Alias and some healing potions for the saurial. I also sought his sword, which Cassana had given to me because I was the only one who could pick it up without pain. I wasn't certain I could trust Alias with the swords. She was like a very little child. So I gave her the potions and told her what to do with them. When the saurial regained consciousness, I told him I would free him if he would help Alias escape—that he must take her as far from Westgate as possible. He readily agreed.

"I had to remain behind to cover their escape. An hour before dawn, when we were all preparing to leave for the sacrifice of the saurial, Cassana realized what I had done. She would have destroyed me that moment, but Phalse ordered that I be spared. He thought I might know where they had gone, and he interrogated me in his own fashion. I thought I was safe because I had given the lizard no specific instructions, but I planted in Alias a great nostalgia for Shadowdale. I wanted her to sing there. Phalse learned this, and that is how he knew where to wait for you."

"That's where you met him," Akabar accused Olive.

The halfling shrugged. "You knew Alias wasn't human, but you never told me." She turned back to the true bard. "Phalse let you live then?"

"That was Cassana's decision. She changed her mind about destroying me. She left me in this chamber, where my thoughts would wander and my strength fade so I would grow more pliable. She wanted my help on other projects and . . . my company."

"Piggish, isn't she?" Olive said. "Just think, Akash, you could have been co-concubine with an ex-Harper."

Akabar fixed the halfling with a cold stare.

"Well," Olive Ruskettle said with a grin, "she may be a witch, but I can't knock her taste in men—living ones that is. Shouldn't we be leaving soon if we're going to stop this saurial sacrifice?"

"We wait only until moonset," the true bard explained. "To avoid the patrols of Fire Knives."

"You've been babbling away in that cell for a month now. How do you know when moonset is?" Olive asked.

The crafter picked up a drumstick and took a bite of the meat, chewed, and swallowed before he smiled sweetly at her. "You forget, Mistress Ruskettle, a bard never loses count of the measure."

✤ 29 ✤

The Sacrifice

When Dragonbait woke, he was tethered face up on a cold, stone slab with his tail flattened uncomfortably beneath him. He flexed his claws, trying to cut at the bindings that pulled his limbs toward the four corners of the stone, but little metallic twanging noises told him the bindings were not hemp or leather, but thin, steel wires. A dull ache warned him that the wire was slicing through his scales whenever he moved.

He opened his eyes and, through the great fangs carved of stone that ringed the hillock, saw that the sky was beginning to redden. Just beside the stone slab, in the center of the fanged maw, was a large fire circle filled with day-old ash. He had seen it from the air yesterday—the mound outside Westgate where the worshipers of Moander had waited to receive Alias from their god. The ancient and worn stone they had tied him to was lined with blood-gutters, leaving him no doubt as to the stone's purpose.

Concentrating, he summoned his *shen*. Mist had come as close as she could when she described him to the others as a paladin. From what he had gathered in his short time on this world, he and his brothers had much in common with that breed of fighter, and they had many of the same gods-given powers. But *shen* was not quite the same as a Realms paladin's ability to detect evil. With it, Dragonbait could determine all the myriad types of evil that preyed on the soul, the absence of evil, and the grace that nourished the soul. He was also able to judge the strength of a spirit.

The human mage's spirit had begun as an orb of dull yellow—weak, but without malice or arrogance; a little greed, but not much. The change in him had been astounding. His battle with Moander had strengthened his spirit a hundredfold. His soul grew cleaner, though grace was something he had yet to reach for.

The halfling had changed little—a wavering spirit, colored with avarice and ambition, heightened by pinpricks of petty, but deeper, nastiness. Her music helped keep these things at bay, but recently not even that had halted a growing smear of jealousy.

He would not ordinarily have searched two such as these, but the human swordswoman had decided to travel with them, and he took his oath to protect her very seriously. Her spirit was often so weak it frightened him. He was afraid her spirit would falter, not only because he was duty bound to her, but because her soul was touched with a midsummer sky blue of grace. He wanted to preserve that.

Now, though, he admitted to himself that he had failed. The hill around him ebbed and pulsed with an evil light. Soon, he would be killed, the swordswoman's spirit would be quenched, and she would be turned to evil.

Evil climbed the hill in many bodies. Weak and strong spirits mingled. A double file of cloaked and hooded men and women entered the circle of stone fangs. They split their ranks upon stepping into the circle and surrounded him. Their dress marked them as followers of Moander and their leader bore the faceless mask common to evil masters, even in the saurial's world.

But the worshipers handled their long robes clumsily and their voices faltered as they sang, occasionally missing notes or forgetting the cadence, only to pick it up again several beats later. Could they be imposters? Dragonbait wondered. They all had the feel of the assassins Cassana worked with—The Fire Knives.

When the pseudo-worshipers of Moander, numbering two dozen, had formed a circle about the perimeter of the hilltop, four figures in gaudy array stepped into their midst.

First came the small, grinning form of Phalse. He was all in blue—a sickening blue of decaying meat. His blue-on-blue-on-blue eyes shone with anticipation. Dragonbait hissed, and Phalse smirked. Phalse had found the saurial roaming the plane of Tarterus stalking demons. The pseudo-halfling had captured the paladin and brought him to this plane so he could be slain to enslave another.

Zrie Prakis entered second, decked in red robes the color of blood, trimmed with dirty, bone-white edgings. He bore his staff of power like a ceremonial weapon, ready to strike down any who failed to obey him. His movements were filled with energy, though his atrophied muscles stretched and popped over his bones.

The lich's liveliness was due to the proximity of his mistress, Cassana, who strode in behind him. She was dressed in a strapless gown of shimmering green, slit up the side. In her hands she turned the small, slender wand she used to control her pets. She had a wicked, cruel smile.

Last of all, Alias entered the circle, moving more like the undead that Prakis was than a living being. The puppet's body was under control of her mistress. She was garbed in leathers split up the sides, the bare flesh cross-tied with thongs which looped about silver button-hooks. Long, shiny black boots with incredibly high heels covered her feet and calves. She wore an ornate girdle at her waist, with the skull of some creature etched in silver at the front. She had been given a chain shirt split open at the middle, baring the flesh between her breasts and offering any sword an easy target. Shoulder plates of lacquered black, a red velvet cape, and a collar of black and silver completed the showy, but impractical, ensemble.

In her hands she gripped Dragonbait's diamond-headed sword so tightly her knuckles were white. Her face was drawn into a tight mask, the lines and vessels of her neck standing out. Along her sword arm, the runes glowed with a hellish light, creating a false blue dawn around her.

Dragonbait pulled at his metallic bonds, trying not to give his captors the pleasure of seeing him thrash. The wires were too well mounted to give way, though, and his wrists grew wet with blood.

Zrie Prakis stood at one end of the stone, near Dragonbait's head, and Phalse stood at the lizard's feet. Cassana took one side, and Alias, fighting the pull of the runes, lurched to a position directly across from her. The saurial understood all that was to happen. They would use Hill Cleaver, his own sword, to slay him. If only he'd been able to reach the blade back at The Rising Raven, he could have negated all of Cassana's magic and turned the tide of the battle. Now the blade would shatter upon tasting his innocent blood and two good things would be destroyed in a single blow. Three, counting Alias. If all of this was not evil enough, Cassana was forcing Alias to perform the deed. It was completely unnecessary to the ritual. The witch did it only to bring pain and grief to her puppet.

Dragonbait looked deep into Cassana's eyes. She would permit no flower to grow without her permission, and before Alias could bloom, the sorceress would encase her in amber. A perverse curiosity prompted him to use his *shen* sight on her before he died, just to know what such evil looked like. The heat of her soul caused him to flinch. Within was a black wall riddled with flaming red cracks. Hatred burned deep in her and crackled between her, Zrie Prakis, and Phalse. The lich, like a void, sucked up emotions, and beside Cassana he was a vortex of hatred and fear. Phalse glowed like a city put to the torch by invaders. His maliciousness ran the gamut of yellow greed, red hatred, and a sickly green jealousy.

Cassana grinned, as if she guessed what the saurial was doing. She looked at the sky behind Alias. The sun had almost cleared the horizon. The tops of the sharp, tooth-shaped plinths looked as if they had bitten into something bloody.

The sorceress motioned to Phalse, who turned his back on Dragonbait. The small servant motioned with his hands in an arcane fashion that seemed to deny the existence of bones in his arms. They swayed back and forth like snakes. Beyond him, a pinprick of light appeared, then grew. It began as a sphere of multicolored magical force, then flattened, turning into a swirling pattern of silver and red.

Dragonbait had seen this gate before. It was the passage to the Citadel of White Exile, where he and Alias had been branded. Now, that passage had to be opened again to draw power from the domain of Phalse's master. With it, they would seal control over Alias at the moment of Dragonbait's death.

Dragonbait finally looked up at Alias; he did not want to grieve her, but he could not help himself. Their eyes locked like pieces in a magical puzzle. Her eyes were red-rimmed from exhaustion and evaporated tears. He used his *shen* sight. If he was going to die, he wanted to do so with his eyes fixed on the brilliant blue of her soul.

Her spirit's glow was as slender as the flame from a single candle. It flickered like a living sapphire. Yet on all sides rose a tide of darkness, crackling with energy, forcing itself upward to smother the flame. The flame blazed for a moment, but the forces surrounding it rose as well.

The chanting increased as Phalse worked his spells to control the spinning disk that reached between the planes. The first tendrils of dawn caught Alias's hair from behind and set it on fire, a glory of bright red against the newborn sky. "Prepare to sacrifice the innocent!" the sorceress bellowed. "Raise the blade!"

Alias hesitated and Dragonbait saw the candle's flame burn hotter. Cassana made a pass with her wand, and the sapphire flame dimmed as if a smoked glass chimney had been dropped over it. Alias raised her hands, clasping Hill Cleaver's hilt, the blade pointed down at the saurial's chest. His own sigils were now answering the dark siren call of their masters, and Dragonbait thought his hearts would burst from the strain.

Through eye contact, he tried to plead with the swordswoman to fight, to strengthen her will. He wished desperately to add his own inner strength to hers and fight off the darkness. However, while his skill allowed him to see her spirit, he could not encourage it. Silently he cursed his inability to communicate with her.

Blue sparks arced between the sigils on his chest, and the runes on Alias's arm responded in kind. The Abomination had told her that she drew strength from him, but Dragonbait had not discovered how. Maybe, the saurial suddenly realized, he had denied the evil brands for too long. Perhaps they could yet be turned to good.

Deliberately, he channeled his will through the runes, trying to force the light to arc higher. The sparks showered upward like water in a fountain, their display mirrored on Alias's arm. Finally, sparks touched and interwove, bridging the gap between sacrificer and sacrifice.

Cassana's voice sounded far off as she shouted, "Seal the pact!" The darkness in Alias rose like bile, and the candle flame of her spirit faltered. Then, feeding at last on the saurial's own, her flame strengthened and grew in intensity.

Dragonbait shuddered. He felt as if he had just rolled a massive stone up to and over the crest of a hill. Every muscle in his body spasmed. Now that the stone had been given one last push, however, it rolled of its own accord. Alias's flame grew hotter and brighter with each passing second. The well of darkness began to harden and then crumble like drying mud. New surges of the surrounding mass of evil rose, but they were repelled by the increasing blue fire.

Alias hovered over Dragonbait, her muscles locked, her face almost serene. Phalse and the Fire Knives impersonating Moander worshipers held their breath, as would have Prakis, had he any breath to hold.

Cassana screwed her comely face into a twisted mask of rage—rage mixed with a hint of fear that the made-creature should reveal a newfound strength. Clenching her wand in her fist, she brought her hand up in a sweeping gesture, yanking hard on the strings of her rebellious puppet in an attempt to force her will on Alias.

Like an old leather thong stretched to breaking, something within Alias snapped. She drove the blade down hard, but she leaped forward as she did so, plunging Hill Cleaver not into Dragonbait, but straight through Cassana. The diamond-headed tip protruded out of the witch's back, but there was no blood on it.

The sorceress staggered backward, a look of shock on her face. Both Phalse and Prakis stepped toward her, but she waved them off. Still clutching her wand in one hand, she reached up to draw the blade from her body. Blue sparks danced from Hill Cleaver where she grasped it. Sorcery kept her alive despite her fatal wound, yet nothing could negate the power of the saurial's sword to defend itself from the touch of evil. Cassana screamed and ripped the blade from her. Very slowly, blood began to well up from the gash in her chest.

Her face contorted with pain, Cassana whirled the blade at Alias's throat. The swordswoman fell backward, dodging the weapon, as Prakis and Phalse lunged at her. She rolled from the lich's chilling touch. Phalse came at her with a dagger as she rose to her feet. The pseudo-halfling caught one of Alias's boots in the face and the Fire Knives at the edges of the circle began to converge, prepared to bring Alias down by force of numbers.

There was a shattering explosion to Dragonbait's right, behind the kneeling form of Cassana. A pillar of fire shot up from the base of one of the sharp-toothed plinths, catching two Fire Knives. The great tower of stone rocked, then toppled sideways.

A second and a third explosion followed, as screaming fanfares of fireworks and smoke struck two more of the stone fangs, blinding anyone looking at them. Dragonbait at once recognized the handiwork of Akabar Bel Akash, as the southerner proved he was indeed a mage of no small water.

Then the saurial felt small hands creep across his body. He turned his head, intent on biting them if he could. He caught himself when he spotted Olive Ruskettle moving alongside him. The halfling carried a glass vial, from which she poured a thick, greenish mixture on his metal tethers. The wires smoked and gave off a deadly, acrid stench, but weakened immediately, as if suddenly rusted through.

Dragonbait yanked at his bonds, snapping them in half as the halfling moved to free his legs. Still caught up in the mild trance of his *shen* sight, the saurial could not help but notice that the halfling was purged of much of her bitterness and her vacillating spirit burned with a strength of purpose.

A Fire Knife charged at Olive with a blade tipped with the yellow ichor that had felled Dragonbait in Westgate. The halfling dodged, and Dragonbait swung his free foot with claws extended. His sharp, natural weapons sank deep into the assassin's belly, and she fell backward, spurting a fountain of blood.

Dragonbait searched the circle for Alias. She was surrounded by Fire Knives, but she had acquired one of their swords and two of the assassins already lay at her feet. He looked in the other direction for Cassana, but she had disappeared. The saurial slid off the sacrificial stone and moved to regain Hill Cleaver.

Cold, bony fingers closed around Dragonbait's throat from behind, and an icy chill flowed into his veins and crept through his body. Prakis laughed hoarsely as his paralyzing touch began draining the saurial paladin's strength. On a human, the lich's grip might have been impossible to break, but taking a saurial from behind was not so easy. Dragonbait threaded his tail between himself and the lich and used it as a lever to pry Prakis away from him. The lich staggered back a few paces, then lowered his staff's tip at the saurial and muttered something.

Prakis burst into a pillar of fire.

That was hardly the reaction Dragonbait had expected. He whirled around to see who might have aided him. Standing atop the stone was a graying, clean-shaven man in ragged garb. He pulled a small vial from his cloak and flung it at Phalse, who was trying to take Alias from behind. Phalse saw the missile and dodged. A Fire Knife behind him was not so lucky and became a human pyre.

Dragonbait recognized the man. He had been the one who had demanded the saurial protect Alias in exchange for his freedom. Dragonbait had seen him only once since then, in Alias's dream in Shadow Gap—Nameless. Now he fought openly on their side. The saurial took the briefest moment to study Nameless with his *shen* sight, but all he detected was a gray mountain against a gray sky. Neither evil, nor good, but very, very proud.

Prakis laughed with the horrible mechanical vocal sounds of the undead and walked out of the pyre that Nameless's potion had lighted around him. The lich's clothes were ash, and his remaining skin a blackened ruin, crumbling from the bones. Yet the pinpricks of light still danced in his eyes, and he still carried his staff.

Alias had felled two more assassins, but they had tightened their ring around her. She was closed in on all sides. One blade was deflected by the tightly knit chain shirt, but another came perilously close to her head, clipping some of her hair.

A bolt of lightning struck at Alias's feet, knocking her to the ground. Action froze on the battlefield. Blackened Prakis grinned through fire-stained teeth, swaying his staff of power back and forth, aiming it at Dragonbait, then Ruskettle, then Nameless, making it quite clear that any sudden moves would result in instant destruction. The remaining assassins stood guard around the fallen swordswoman.

A red light shot up from one of the remaining stone plinths. Cassana stood atop the pillar, one hand clutching her wand, the other gripping shut the skin of her chest, as a modest woman would hold closed the front of a torn gown. Dragonbait twitched, debating whether he could lunge for Hill Cleaver and put an end to the mages' threats before they fried him to a cinder.

"Let this be ended," the sorceress shouted from her perch. "Nameless, your little play is over. Phalse, take a sword and slay the saurial and Nameless. I will keep Puppet occupied." She raised the wand over her head. Dragonbait could feel a sympathetic ache as Cassana used the blue wand to rack Alias's body with pain.

A shadow rose behind Cassana, snatching the wand and kicking the sorceress off the stone. Cassana screamed a curse as she fell and landed hard on her side. Zrie Prakis whirled with his staff, trying to set his sights on his mistress's attacker. Akabar's flying form appeared for a moment above the stone pillar, the wand grasped tightly in his hand, then he dodged back and forth in an erratic pattern. Long lances of energy spat from the tip of Prakis's staff, exploding just behind the mage in huge fireballs, but Akabar stayed just ahead of their swelling blossoms of flame.

Dragonbait finally managed to grab his sword, but with Akabar in flight he couldn't risk using Hill Cleaver to dispel magic in the area. Instead, he used the sword to bite deeply into the lich, pulling ribs from the burned chest. Prakis's fighting ability was still unaffected, though. He backhanded Dragonbait with a swipe of his wickedly sharpened finger bones.

"Akabar!" Nameless shouted. "Throw the wand into the disk!"

Dragonbait whirled about anxiously. It made the best tactical sense to remove the wand from their enemies' reach, but would it ultimately prove their undoing? What effect would it have on Alias?

Akabar swooped low to evade the lancing bolts of the staff of power. One caught him in the leg, and he almost lost concentration and flight. He reached his goal, however, pulling up at the last moment and flinging the wand into the silver and red disk.

Three screams went up at once. Phalse shouted and barreled toward the disk. Olive stood blocking his path, but he leaped over her and tumbled into the vertical pool. He was swallowed without a ripple.

Zrie Prakis screamed and in screaming fell apart. With the wand thrust into another plane of being, he could not tap the energy bound up in it that kept him from death. He crumbled to dust. But in the moment before his spirit fled from the bones that Cassana had "cherished," the lich cried out, "Die, Cassana!" His hideous laughter was carried away on the breeze.

His staff of power fell to the ground. Dragonbait felt a sharp pain in his chest, just as he had when Moander had died. Without checking, he knew that a sigil had disappeared. He glanced at Alias, who was wielding a sword two-handed, but if she felt Zrie Prakis's mark burn away from her arm, she did not let it disrupt her combat.

Lastly, Cassana shrieked, for much of her own magic was locked up in that wand. She, too, began to decay—her shoulders stooped, her skin became more torn and ragged, so that she looked dressed in the tatters of her own dead flesh. The sorceress's chest wound began spurting blood.

Akabar swooped down and plucked the staff of power from the battlefield. Some of the Fire Knives, uncertain whether or not the mage could wield it, began to move toward the perimeter of the circle. Dragonbait stood guarding the rear, as Olive and Alias backed toward him. The saurial paladin now bid Hill Cleaver to swallow any magic cast.

And not a moment too soon. The hag form of Cassana pointed toward the saurial paladin and muttered. A bolt of zigzag lightning shot from her finger, only to dissipate into a harmless shower of sparks.

"Kill them!" the sorceress shrieked to the remaining assassins, as she struggled to her feet.

The Fire Knives regrouped and began driving the party back. Akabar could only use the staff of power to strike their foes. Alias had lost her weapon, and Olive stumbled as she moved. In the chaos and frenzy of the sword fight, no more of the assassins had chosen to poison their blades. That was fortunate for the adventurers; Alias was bleeding from half a dozen cuts, and Olive was clutching at a jagged wound running down her side. Dragonbait risked taking his attention from parrying a sword thrust long enough to look for Nameless. The graying man dove into the silver pool. Like Phalse, he disappeared without a trace.

The saurial felled an assassin closing on their left flank and chirped to gain the swordswoman's attention. When Alias met his eyes, he jerked his head toward the silver pool. She jerked her head back indicating he must go first. He growled. If he went first, Cassana could again use her magic to attack them, but he couldn't explain this to Alias. He jerked his head indicating again that she must go before him, but she shook her head seconds before she launched a kick at an assassin's chin with her boot.

Minutes ago, she had no will power of her own, he thought with grim amusement. Why does she pick now to be so stubborn? He caught her attention with another chirp before he spun Hill Cleaver about and tossed it to her.

Alias caught the weapon, reclasped her hands about the grip, and spun to decapitate an assassin who had lunged forward when her attention was focused on the saurial. Dragonbait snatched up the halfling and loped to the planar disk.

The silver pool had already shrunk to half its original size. The swirls had become solid rings and the portal now resembled the bull's eye sigil of Phalse's master.

Dragonbait plunged in, taking Olive with him. Alias and Akabar blocked the portal. The Turmish mage brought the end of the staff up hard, cracking the jaw of an assassin.

Then two withered hands, strong as steel, closed around

the staff. The aged face of Cassana, drooling and twisted beyond the limits of humanity, confronted the mage. "You use it as a club," she lisped. "Now feel its full force."

Alias slew another assassin with Hill Cleaver, but there were more than a dozen left, and the effects of her wounds were taking their toll on her reaction time. "Into the portal!" she ordered the mage.

"But the witch," Akabar protested, as Cassana began to intone words of power.

"In!" the swordswoman cried.

Alias put her foot on Akabar's stomach and shoved the mage through the disk. Akabar would not loosen his hold on the staff, and Cassana was dragged toward the bull's eye. Akabar was lost to sight beyond the silvery glow of the portal, but the haggish sorceress managed to plant her feet firmly on the ground and hold her position. With the tendons of her arms popping from the strain, Cassana began to pull the staff back from the portal.

Alias stepped halfway into the portal, straddling it with one foot on each side of the planar gate. She brought Hill Cleaver down on the half of the staff of power that jutted out from the disc hovering over the Hill of Fangs.

The blade cut through the ancient wood like an axe, and a multicolored fireball blossomed out from the broken staff. Alias felt heat wash over her body as the force of the explosion pushed her through the gateway, into the lands that lay beyond. The shock wave caught the last pieces of Cassana's body and the fire-ravaged forms of the remaining assassins, carrying them from the top of the Hill of Fangs. The last curved and pointed stones toppled from their moorings, and, for the second day in a row, a new star burned over Westgate.

❧ 30 ❧

The Citadel
of White Exile

"Alias, are you all right?" Olive asked, bending over the swordswoman.

"I feel like I've been taken apart and put back together, with lots of pieces missing," Alias moaned.

"That's a pretty sick joke," Olive chided. "Apt, but sick."

"What do you expect?" A throbbing pain had filled her head, her flesh stung from half a dozen cuts, and she felt badly sunburned. She opened her eyes, then shut them instantly, growling, "Well, that was a mistake."

A bright white light seared her eyeballs, leaving blue dots dancing before her mind even after she'd squeezed her eyes shut and covered them with her hands. This was not the icy white of sun on snow or the ivory white of silk, but the hot, burning white of coals in the center of a forge.

Shielding her eyes, she ventured another look. The sky above was convoluted whirls of white-whites and off-whites—hot matter and even hotter matter swirling and twisting in a vain attempt to combine.

"This is where the gods roll across the sky like storm fronts," she muttered.

"What?" Olive asked.

"Nothing. Just a line from an old tale."

"Right," the halfling said, realizing just who must have told her the tale. "You going to lay there all day?" she asked.

Alias sighed and sat up. Beneath her were gray flagstones shimmering in the light of the white-on-white sky overhead.

Olive knelt beside her. The halfling's glittering white dress, a copy of the one Cassana had worn to last evening's midnight dinner, was covered in mud and blood.

To Alias's right, Akabar and Dragonbait were kneeling over a fifth figure—the stranger who'd helped them fight the battle on the Hill of Fangs. Alias felt a momentary twinge of jealousy that they were looking after the stranger before they did so for her.

Don't be a fool, she told herself. For someone who's just fought two dozen assassins, a witch, and a lich, and who's broken a staff of power, you're in pretty good shape. You got off easier than Sylune did in Shadowdale. A pang of grief went through her, though, as she remembered how the river witch had met her end.

Is there a difference, she wondered, between the sadness that real people feel and the sadness I was made to feel? What reason would any of my makers have to make me grieve for someone like Sylune? None, she decided. I can think for myself, and I can feel for myself. The "masters" don't have anything to do with it.

Remembering the recent deaths of all but one of the masters, she looked down to examine her sword arm. The limb still ached from the disappearance of the top three sigils—Cassana's, Zrie Prakis's, and the Fire Knives'. All remaining members of the assassins must have been wiped out by the explosion of Zrie's staff of power. The arm that the sigils occupied had been overgrown with the waving serpent pattern, but only the concentric rings of Phalse's master remained. And the blank space that's left, Alias thought, remembering with a shudder Olive's prediction that something might now grow there.

Alias tried to stand and stumbled to one knee. She was tired and battered. She leaned on Dragonbait's sword, stood up, and looked around. They were atop a very tall tower that thrust into the shining white sky. The crenelations of the wall about them were curved and pointed like the stones about the Hill of Fangs had been.

She looked down from the tower. It rose from a plain of shining, gray stone that spread out in all directions as far as the eye could see. In a circle about the tower's foundation, the stone was solid and unmoving, but just beyond, the ground was cracked and shifting like a mud or lava flow.

"You know, Olive, I don't think we're in the Realms anymore."

She limped over to Akabar and Dragonbait. The stranger's faded garb was a shredded mass of tatters, and his arms and legs were lacerated by a hundred bites the size of large coins. Larger gashes lay across his forehead, chest, and torso, and blood ran freely from his wounds. Olive came up beside Alias and whistled in a low tone.

Dragonbait had the man's head cradled in his claws, and small, bright arcs of yellow bridged the space between his hands and the man's face, visible even in the bright light of the white sky. The smell of woodsmoke filled the air. Before their eyes, the flow of blood ceased, and the wounds on the man's face began to heal. The stranger's grimace faded and his expression grew peaceful, the deeper wrinkles smoothed from his weather-worn face.

Akabar moved swiftly and surely, tending to the damage that remained when Dragonbait's healing powers were exhausted. The mage smeared a viscous, green paste over the wounds not yet closed and bound them with strips of his borrowed robe.

Alias knelt beside the mage and the saurial. "Who is he?" she asked.

Dragonbait turned a curious stare on her, and Akabar said, "You don't recognize him? Are you sure?"

Alias studied the face. He was familiar. Beneath the gray hair and the wrinkled flesh was a man who must once have been very handsome, with a well-formed figure. "Nameless!" Alias whispered.

She turned to explain to the others. "He was in my dream in Shadow Gap, only much, much younger. Unless this is his grandfather or someone."

"You don't remember him from anywhere else?" Akabar prompted.

Alias screwed up her face trying to think, but she couldn't recall him. He wasn't in her pseudo-memory and there was no other time that she could have known him.

"Of course she can't remember him," Olive said with a sniff. "She was just a baby then."

"What are you talking about?" Alias asked.

"You were just born—so to speak. He set you loose with

Dragonbait to look after you. You might say he's your father." Olive reached down to touch her on her right wrist where the tattoo wound about the empty space. "He's the Nameless Bard. Ring a bell?"

"The Nameless Bard," Alias echoed as she leaned back and thought deeply. She knew that story, but hadn't associated it with Nameless from her dream. She rocked back and forth as she recalled the tale in full and began to really understand for the first time what she was meant to be and what she had actually turned out to be.

Nameless opened his eyes, and, though his sight was mostly shielded from the bright sky by the four adventurers surrounding him, he raised his hands to shield his eyes. He scowled deeply and muttered, "Home again, home again, jiggidy-jig."

Akabar and Olive exchanged glances. The halfling shrugged. Alias moved closer to the old man.

When Nameless caught sight of the swordswoman, he tried to sit up, but his remaining wounds caused him too much pain to do so. Dragonbait moved to support his back, but Nameless waved him away. With some effort, he pulled himself to a seated position, facing Alias.

He gazed at her bloodied, disheveled form and sighed. "You are everything I intended—and more."

"You're the Nameless Bard," Alias replied, her tone even and emotionless.

"Yes. Do you remember my tale? I did not put it in you, as I did the other tales, but told it to you the hour you first woke, while we waited for the potions to heal Dragonbait so you could run away with him."

Alias shook her head. "I don't remember hearing it. I only remember it."

"What do you remember?" Nameless prompted her.

"It's the tale of a man with overweening vanity who betrayed his scruples trying to complete a task he knew very well had the potential for tremendous abuse."

Olive gasped and Akabar bit on his lower lip.

The color drained from Nameless's face.

"Am I wrong?" Alias asked.

A long moment passed. The cloudless sky flashed and

crashed as a lightning storm erupted overhead. The energy discharges cast sharp shadows of the party on the tower roof's gray flagstones.

"How can you say that?" Nameless whispered.

"Sounds to me like she put her own interpretation on the story," Olive said smugly. "What do want to bet she tinkers with your songs, too?"

In a defeated tone, the true bard said, "I've failed."

Akabar grinned. "True. You tried to make a thing, and instead you created a daughter. In Turmish, we'd say you were blessed by the gods."

Alias smiled at the mage gratefully.

"Might even outdo her old man as a bard," Olive predicted.

Nameless looked up in surprise at the halfling. Obviously it had never occurred to him that his creation might improve on his work. He was too proud and too vain. "I gave you everything I could," he said.

"A false history, your songs, and no true name," Alias said.

"I gave you a past so you would not feel alone and removed from those you would live among, and my songs were all I had left. I set you free at the price of my own freedom. When Cassana dragged me from my cell to distract you in a dream, I tried to warn you. She controlled most of my words and actions, but I did tell you how to defeat her kalmari."

"Yes. You did those things," Alias admitted flatly.

The true bard looked anguished. "But you still hate me."

"I didn't say that," Alias replied. A grin broke through her grim expression. "Don't human children often disagree with their parents without hating them?"

"Do you think of me as your father then?"

The swordswoman shrugged. "I don't know. You hardly gave me anything in the way of a family in my memories. I'm not very practiced at feeling filial affection. Do you think of me as a daughter?"

Nameless looked down at the flagstones for a moment before meeting her eyes again. "To be honest, no. At least . . . not until now."

"That's all right." She leaned forward and brushed her lips against his wrinkled cheek. "I found myself two good friends, and you gave me a brother."

"A brother—" Nameless did not understand at first. "Oh, yes. You share the saurial's soul."

Dragonbait shook his head.

"You do. Phalse divided your soul," Nameless told the paladin. "You have half a soul each."

Dragonbait's eyes squinted with displeasure. He extended two claws, pointed at Alias and retracted one, pointed at himself and retracted the second.

"He should know," Olive said. "He's the expert on souls."

The lizard nodded.

"You can't split a soul and get two souls," Nameless argued.

"Why not?" the halfling demanded. "They're infinite things. If you break them up, you still have two infinite things."

Akabar stared in amazement at the short bard.

"What?" Olive asked, uncomfortable in his case. "Am I wrong?"

"No," the Turmish mage replied. "I'm simply surprised at the firmness of your theological argument."

"Halflings go to church, too, you know . . . sometimes."

Alias yawned. The exertions of the past month, the first month of her life, were beginning to catch up with her. "This is all very interesting," she lied, "but what I'd really like to do is catch Phalse and his master and take care of this last blasted sigil."

"But don't you see what this means?" Nameless said. "You really could be human."

"So?"

"So?" the true bard exclaimed. "Doesn't that matter to you?"

Alias shrugged again. "Dragonbait says I have a soul, and that means I'm not a thing. I've already decided that the rest doesn't matter much. Most adventurers aren't particularly fussy about whether you're human or halfling, mage or fighter, and all the rest, just so you pull your own weight and remain loyal to your party. Isn't that what you taught me?"

Nameless nodded, a little astounded that she had come to all these conclusions on her own without guidance. Perhaps, as Akabar had said, his endeavor had been blessed by the gods—better gods than Moander.

"So," Alias said, trying to steer the conversation to more practical matters, "this is the Citadel of White Exile. It used to be your home. Do you have any idea where Phalse could be?"

"I abandoned the citadel to Phalse. Before I left, Phalse's master built a bridge from here to his own realm, which Phalse uses to report to him. It's in the courtyard below. Unless the little monster hides in one of the tower rooms, there is no place else for him to go."

"Why not? Where does that plain lead?" Alias asked, pointing across the monotonous expanse of gray below them.

"This place was built to be completely secure. Heft a rock into the sky."

Dragonbait broke off a piece of flagstone and did as the bard had instructed. The stone went up smoothly about fifty feet before it exploded in a rainbow of fireworks against the background of the white sky.

Nameless explained, "Above us is the Plane of Life, called the Positive Material Plane by sages. Any unprotected thing that enters explodes as every bit of matter within it achieves its full potential and becomes a star. There is no escape that way."

He motioned toward the gray expanse beyond. "We sit on the border between the Plane of Life and the Plane of Gems, which sages call the Para-elemental Plane of Minerals. Wordy lot, sages. Out on the Plane of Gems, all unprotected living things are relentlessly turned into crystals of stunning beauty and complete lifelessness. Phalse, as far as I know, has no protection against either of these effects. The only way to this place are the two bridges built by Phalse's master, one to his domain and one to the Hill of Fangs.

"You must be very cautious looking for Phalse. When I arrived, I was attacked by one of his master's guard beasts— all mouths and teeth. And Phalse still has Cassana's wand, which still has power over you."

Alias nodded. "What about Phalse's master?"

"None of us has ever seen him. Cassana sent someone through the portal to his domain to find out about him. Her agent was returned in pieces. The saurial can lead you to the other portal. Phalse brought him out of it. Your . . . shell and his body were branded in the courtyard, then brought up here and taken to the Hill of Fangs, and from there into Westgate."

"Will you be all right here alone?" Alias asked.

"Yes. The energy-wrought sky has certain healing properties. I will wait here until I feel strong enough to walk. Then I will follow you."

"Perhaps, Alias, you should remain here, too," Akabar suggested, "so that Phalse cannot use the wand on you."

"Look, Akash, whose battle is this, anyway? Phalse might try to use the wand, but I've already beaten its power once. I'm not about to cringe from it now." Then, in a more gentle tone, she asked Nameless, "Are you sure you wouldn't prefer that we waited for you to heal?"

Nameless shook his head. "You don't want to give Phalse a chance to call in reinforcements from the lower planes. If you defeat Phalse, you can force him to call his master from his domain through the portal and deal with him." He looked up at the saurial. "You remember the way?"

The lizard nodded.

Alias frowned a little, still dissatisfied with leaving Nameless alone. Akabar thought to himself, she must care about him more than she knows.

"All right, Dragonbait. Which way?"

The saurial led them to a gap in the crenelations. A single set of stairs, steep, narrow, and without a railing, wound along the outside of the tower. Alias's frown grew deeper when she saw they would have to go down in single file.

"I'm going to go first until we reach a door," Alias said. "May I borrow your sword just a little while longer, Dragonbait?"

The saurial cocked his head in the manner that Alias usually assumed meant he hadn't understood the question. Now she was beginning to believe it simply meant he didn't want to answer the question. The fragrance of violets filled the air. She held the strange weapon out, thinking he might be uncomfortable allowing someone else to wield it.

"If you'd rather have it back, I'll understand," she said, but the lizard shook his head and pushed her hand away gently, indicating she should keep the blade.

When this is over, we're going to learn to talk together, she promised herself. She started down the stairs, Dragonbait behind her, followed by Akabar. Olive brought up the rear. The halfling sighed at the steepness of the stairs, though their narrowness did not disturb her in the least. She trotted down them casually. Akabar, however, pressed himself against the wall of the tower and kept his eyes on his feet.

Nameless waited until Olive's head disappeared below the level of the wall, then counted to twenty before limping to the staircase, gripping his wounded side. Half concealed by a large, fanged crenelation, he watched them descend. When they'd entered the first door, the true bard started down the stairs himself. He reached the first door and passed by it, continuing farther down the staircase. His only hope lay in the possibility that the tower had not given up all its secrets to its new owner.

On the ground far below, outside the tower's protective shell, a cloaked figure lowered the hand that had been shielding his eyes from the sky's light. Carefully, he removed the eye-cusps that gave him the sight of an eagle and replaced them in the small egg that was their home. He sighed, and his breath circled like fog through the transparent envelope that surrounded him. Then he took up his staff and made his way over the broken terrain of gemstones to the Citadel of White Exile.

When the companions had passed through the door, and Dragonbait had pushed past Alias to scout ahead, he had left Hill Cleaver still in her grasp. Without a weapon, the swordswoman was only a human of soft flesh and tool-using hands, while the saurial felt quite confident with his claws and powerful jaws.

The passages were lighted by the stones of the wall, which shone from within—a benefit of the citadel's position. Akabar was reminded of the light that had come from behind the elven wall that had imprisoned the Abomination of Moander, but these walls glowed with a rosy light that gave them all a ruddy hue.

They passed through one chamber, then another. Both had held some furniture, but recently had been stripped bare. The dust on the floor was disturbed as though several heavy objects had been dragged across it. The small prints of the pseudo-halfling crossed the rooms, as well as a set of large, heavier boots, nearly giant size.

They came to a pair of doors made of crystal that, like the the walls, glowed from within. The doors opened at a touch.

A large hall lay beyond. Dragonbait froze upon entering the room. It was not arranged the way it had been more than a month ago when he'd been dragged through it. There had been a long feasting table, and the walls had been covered with banners of some of the Realms' older nations. The table and banners were gone, replaced by twelve biers. Each funeral stand was occupied by a body.

Alias's first guess was that the citadel's new inhabitants had turned this room into a morgue, or maybe even a meat locker.

Dragonbait, already standing in the center of the room, spun about in obvious confusion. A brimstone stench emanated from his body.

"Brandobas's Beard!" Olive exclaimed, already near enough to see what useful things might be left on the corpses. "They're you!"

Uneasily, Alias walked closer to the bodies. They were all as similar as a batch of bowls a potter might throw in a day. Each face had the same features, some were thinner, some wider, but they all had her features. Each face was framed with hair some shade of red, from reddish black to strawberry blonde. Their skin tones covered the spectrum from the pale flesh of the north to the swarthy complexions of the south.

Their dress was more varied. A body in the heavy armor of Mulhorand lay beside one in wolfhide robes and the headpiece of the far north. The sultry slitted dress of a Waterdeep courtesan—something perhaps from Cassana's closet—adorned a body one bier over from another dressed in the conservative robes of a Moonshae druid. A weapon lay beside each, a mace or sword or sickle or dagger. One figure, wrapped in black, was equipped with eastern weapons whose uses were unfamiliar to Alias.

Yet they were all her. Earlier models? Alias wondered.

Then she shook her head grimly. No, later improvements. How foolish to think that they would stop at just one. A few minutes ago, when she'd thought herself unique, she'd been certain she could prove her worth, justify her own existence. But what if she was just one of a pack, a herd of Aliases to be unleashed on the unsuspecting worlds?

She forced herself to stand closer to one of the bodies—one dressed as a cleric of Tymora in robes of white trimmed with blue, with her holy symbol—a silver disk—hanging on a chain about her neck. Alias fought back the queasiness in her stomach and touched the body, grabbing the right wrist and turning it to reveal the underside of the arm.

The pattern of serpents and waves was there, as motionless as a tattoo placed on a piece of dead flesh. The only sigil in the pattern was the bull's eye of Phalse's master. There was no blank spot at the wrist for Nameless. The flesh was clammy, like clay.

Akabar came up behind her and put a hand on her shoulder. "Dead?" he asked.

"Dead," she echoed, "or at least not alive. Or less alive than me." She shook with anger. "This is all I was to them. A thing to be copied over and over."

"Easy now," Akabar said, squeezing her shoulder gently. "They're no more like you than a painting of you would be. If you want, we can destroy them."

"No!" Alias snapped. "Whatever they are, I will not see them destroyed. They're no more . . . evil than I am. I'm going to kill the last master and lay them to rest that way."

Akabar stood silent for a moment, then nodded. "As you wish."

Alias could tell he was trying to determine if her reaction was a natural one or another pattern, like her obsession to reach Yulash had been.

Olive shook her head, disapproving of Akabar's tone. Just like a mage. Thinking too much with the head, not enough with the heart. Wonder how he'd feel if we offered to burn up his brothers?

Dragonbait snapped out of his *shen* state. He could not understand what his senses were telling him about the women laid out before him. Each body possessed a living soul, but the saurial could not sense a trace of a spirit in any of them. Is that all that separates them from death—or birth? he wondered.

"Is the courtyard over there, Dragonbait?" Alias asked, pointing to a second pair of crystal doors at the far end of the hall.

The saurial nodded.

Alias approached these doors and inspected them. They glowed in the same fashion, but there was something different about them. They made her uneasy. Then she realized why.

They drew her. As with the elven wall in Yulash, she could not resist moving toward them. She wanted to open them. What she sought lay beyond them in the courtyard.

She glanced at the others. Akabar pulled a small bundle from his belt, fishing out spell components. Dragonbait took a two-handed sword from one of the biers. Olive placed an ear against one of the doors. She pulled back, rubbing her ear. "No noise, but it's very warm."

Alias took a deep breath as she reached for the door. She wanted to be prepared to slam it shut in an instant or dodge aside if some horrible beast came lunging out.

The door pushed open at a touch, revealing a large, open courtyard. To the right and left, passages wove farther into the mazework of the tower. Directly across from them, a balcony opened onto the splendor of the shimmering Plane of Life. In the center of the court was a large pool filled with swirling patterns of silver and red, like the portal on the Hill of Fangs. This pool was set into the floor, though, and ringed with bluish stones.

A small form, dressed in shades of red and brown was seated on the stones. He smiled a smile wider than any human or halfling could manage, and his blue-on-blue-on-blue eyes glinted wickedly. In his hands he passed back and forth Cassana's slender, blue wand.

"Welcome home, One," Phalse said. "I take it you have met Two through Thirteen."

❧ 31 ❧

Phalse

Alias strode into the court, casting a glance to the right, to the left, overhead. No assassins were hidden behind the crystal doors, no cage hung suspended above. Olive moved to the right, Dragonbait to the left. Akabar held back, slightly behind Alias, ready to cast in a moment.

Phalse remained seated on the portal stones, swinging his short legs back and forth, playing with the wand like a child with a stick.

"Where is your master?" Alias demanded.

"Where is yours?" Phalse asked with a giggle.

From the rear, Akabar began to cast a spell.

Phalse pointed a finger at one of the blue stones near the pool. The stone rose, hovered for a moment, then flew, as if propelled by an invisible sling, across the room. Alias ducked instinctively and raised Dragonbait's sword to deflect the stone, but she was not its target. It circled around the saurial's blade and streaked past the swordswoman. Alias heard the brutal impact of stone cracking bone. She half-turned. Akabar was kneeling on the floor, clutching his forehead. Blood oozed between his fingers.

"None of that, now." Phalse waggled a finger at the mage reproachfully. "Not fair at all to attack a poor, defenseless halfling."

"Zero for three," Olive said. "You're none of those things."

"Something wrong, One?" Phalse addressed Alias, ignoring Olive completely. "I thought you didn't like others doing your talking for you."

"My name is Alias," the woman warrior retorted, striding toward the little creature.

"You are One," Phalse said. "Two, Three, and Four are behind the door. As well as Five through Thirteen. While I worked with the other members of the now-defunct alliance, I was very careful to always refer to you as the One, instead of just One. I couldn't let them suspect that I only thought of you as the beginning of something far grander. Why make just one weapon when you can make several? Especially if you have as many enemies as I have."

Alias took a step forward, and Phalse waved Cassana's wand.

Alias stopped in mid-stride, as though she had walked into an invisible spider web. Unlike Cassana's taut bonds, these were gummy. Phalse could wield the wand differently than the witch had.

"Problems, One?" Phalse mocked her. "Cassana's toy still has effects you haven't learned yet. She built for variability, you know. When you were within her area of command, the wand made you her puppet, much like that poor, undead fool, Prakis."

Olive and Dragonbait began to close on the small form, but Alias growled at them through clenched teeth, "Back away. He's mine!"

Phalse laughed. "No, One, you have that backward. You are mine. If I want you, that is. I think I prefer Two. She'll be much more tractable."

The shorter strands of Alias's hair were rising like serpents as she fought the controlling force of the wand. Dragonbait remained in position, respecting Alias's desire to resist the wand without help.

Olive was not so amenable to the idea. She drew out her daggers, but she remained even with the saurial.

Alias felt as though she were pressing hard against a membrane, like the skin of some gelatinous monster. She strained and the muscles in her legs bunched, but she did not move.

"Now Prakis, he wanted you," Phalse said. "He really loved Cassana—devils knew why. She put him through hell. When you came along, though, I think he realized he could have his cake and eat it, too. You had all of Cassana's charm, not to mention her once-youthful looks, and after the sacrifice was made, you'd be pliable, too. Not one of Cassana's characteristics."

Alias looked like a medusa, with the longer strands of her hair standing out from her head. The strain of fighting the grip of the web was evident in her face. Her forehead beaded with perspiration, her teeth clenched together, and her eyes squinted—fixated on the pseudo-halfling's form.

Dragonbait gritted his teeth as he felt the familiar tug within his chest, the call of Alias's sigils to his own. No stranger to discipline, he remained in place.

He turned to look at the mage. He was still clutching his head, but the bleeding had stopped. Akabar staggered to his feet. The saurial sensed nervousness in the halfling and wondered if it would overwhelm her caution and she would attack. Or bolt.

A movement along the wall behind and above the halfling caught Dragonbait's eye. Two banners hanging along the sides of the courtyard parted ever so slightly. Another player had arrived on the scene. Slipping into his *shen* state, the lizard caught the familiar feel of the intruder. He turned his attention back on Alias's struggle.

"It's amazing, though, that all of them failed. Moander got you to free it, but it was so enfeebled that a laughably small group brought it down. The Fire Knives played their hand so badly that you only succeeded in throttling some Wyvernspur fop. Zrie was never going to get you to love him. Only Cassana was perverse enough to feel anything for him. And Cassana only used you to taunt and bash her lovers. She had no concept of the forces she was unleashing by trying to get you to kill your little lizard brother."

Phalse turned the wand over in his hands, batting his blue eyes. "They all thought so small. Once they left me this citadel, I quickly duplicated their work on a much larger scale. I needed their expertise to make you, One. Creation is so very difficult. But duplication, that's another matter entirely. It was child's play smuggling out the equipment used to create you, coaxing Cassana out of a piece of her flesh, syphoning off a portion of the life energies Moander contributed. That's why I chose this particular form. Halflings make such good thieves."

Alias watched his eyes. Blue within blue eyes. Bull's eyes. "The last sigil is yours," she said. "You have no hidden master, do you?"

Phalse broke into one of his widened grins, the corners of his mouth almost touching in the back. "Very good, One. I led Cassana to believe that I was just a servant. The ploy had its inconveniences, but it was much safer letting her believe someone even more powerful backed me. I couldn't risk letting Moander know we were partners. The old god and I are . . . rivals. As to the sigil on your arm, don't think of it as the last sigil. As far as you should be concerned, it's the only sigil—the only one that matters." Phalse stood up, moved to the side of the circle, and waved the wand.

Alias felt her muscles bunch up against their will, trying to march her straight ahead—into the pool of silver and red.

"Now, I have a small job for you. Pass through this portal and take care of it. I wouldn't be stubborn about it, if I were you."

"Why not?" Alias growled, fighting the pull toward the bridge into Phalse's domain. Along her arm, the single mark of the last master shone like a beacon.

"Because then I shall be forced to sacrifice you and the saurial and use Two in your stead. Two will be much more accommodating, anyway."

"I'll bet you made that same assumption about me," Alias said. "You can't be sure, though, which is why you're trying to persuade me instead of just forcing me."

"Oh, I'm sure. I've determined why you are flawed, and I know how to prevent it in other models. You see, when we made you, we hadn't taken into account the strength of the saurial's will. We needed a soul and a spirit for you. The soul was easy to divide, but a spirit is supposed to have limits. We assumed you would not come to life until we slayed the saurial so his spirit could transfer into you, enthralled by our will, of course. Somehow, the saurial found a way to create a spirit for you, broke off a shard, so to speak, from his own spirit. You were able to draw on his stronger spirit whenever you needed to. When I kill the two of you, I will take care that only enough spirit flows into Two through Thirteen to animate them, without making them unruly."

"I still think you're bluffing," Alias said. "I won't obey your commands willingly."

"Oh, but you can't refuse, One. It's not just the wand that controls you. You want to jump into the portal. You were made to jump into the portal. Don't you sense how right it would feel?"

Alias gasped. The portal was what had called her into the room. Its siren call was as subtle as Yulash had been, yet much stronger, like the compunction to kill Winefiddle and Giogi. The patterns compelled her to find what lay beyond.

"You see," Phalse explained, "through this portal lies a second portal which leads to the Abyss. As you may know, my former partner, Moander, resides there in its true form. Once you step into a plane where it exists, its sigil will return to your arm. Because you bear its mark and are known to its minions as its servant, you will pass through to its domain unharmed. Once there you will kill it. You will not be able to stop yourself. You will rid the world of a great evil, a noble purpose. Just right for you."

"How would you know what's right for me, you monster?" A raging fire ignited in her, hot enough to burn away the power that held her. "I will not be controlled! I am my own master."

The wand exploded in Phalse's hand, and the cloud of shattered blue crystals mixed with the blood spurting from his wrist. The last master screamed, opening his mouth wide like the kalmari. Alias felt the invisible web dissolve; she was free. She crossed the last few feet separating her from her foe, swung with Dragonbait's sword, and severed Phalse's head neatly from his body.

The head flew two feet away, toppling in a bloodless arch, while the body collapsed like an empty skin. Alias circled warily. She wondered if it was only a coincidence that Phalse's smile resembled the kalmari's, but no smoking monster rose from the two halves.

Olive shivered, suddenly exhausted.

"Finally," Akabar said. "It's over."

Dragonbait shook his head.

"No," Alias said in a quiet, angry voice. "It's not. Look." She held up her arm. It still bore Phalse's sigil.

Laughter rose from the floor, Phalse's laughter, loud and strong, issued from the severed head.

"Foolish, foolish, One. You shouldn't make me angry." Phalse's face leered at her from the disembodied head, and as it spoke it began to change. The head expanded, puffing up like a balloon and rising several feet off the ground, the laughter growing deeper and more malicious. Phalse's two blue eyes merged into a single orb above his over-large mouth. Thick worms snaked from his hair, and each worm ended with a fanged mouth shaped like a lamprey's. Phalse had become a huge beholder, only with jaws instead of eyes.

This was the creature that had attacked Nameless, Alias realized, recalling the multiple bites in the bard's body. It was Phalse all along.

The body's empty skin also began to inflate, turning into the naked form of a large, sexless humanoid. The skin darkened to a shiny, reflective black. The creature had only a sharp stump where the right hand had been blown off by the exploding wand, but the left appendage sported a set of pincers.

Olive lunged at the beastly head with her daggers. A worm-appendage snaked around her slender waist, lifted her from the ground, and sent her skittering across the floor like a ball. She hit the far wall with a bone-wrenching crack and did not get up again.

Akabar made a movement toward the halfling, but he was blocked by the headless, shining black body. It caught the mage firmly in its viselike pincers and squeezed. Akabar screamed.

Dragonbait had started toward the beholder, but now spun about to rescue Akabar. Using the sword he had borrowed from one of the Aliases, he hacked at the beast. Chips of dark crystal flew from the monstrous torso, and it stopped squeezing Akabar and began using him as a shield. The beholder used the pointy stump of its right arm to spear at the saurial, driving him back.

"One," the head announced with its largest mouth, the rest of them hissing as it spoke, "enter the portal now or die."

"Make me."

The beholder launched itself at her.

Alias put a foot on the well's rim and brought Dragonbait's sword up with a sweeping cut, shearing off the mouth-tipped worms along one side. The head turned and charged her again.

Alias dodged to the right, twisting and turning as she did so. Moander had taught her that the best way to fight tend-rils was to avoid them. She shifted the sword to her right hand and drew a dagger from her left boot.

Phalse began his third charge at Alias's head. At the last moment he swooped down and slammed into her knees. The swordswoman crashed to the floor, losing her grip on Dragonbait's sword and her dagger. Three of the lamprey jaws clamped tightly on her thigh, while the oozing stumps of two others wrapped around her leg. The beast began drawing her into its huge, central maw.

Alias grabbed at the stonework surrounding the portal and kicked at the beholder with her free leg.

* * * * *

Far above the fray, the figure behind the banner shook his head and reached for the crossbow he'd retrieved from the citadel's depths. The tower's new owner had not found the cache of magical items, scavenged during his exile.

Nameless drew a single quarrel from a slim case of dark wood. The bolt shone in the dimness of the secret passage, illuminating his careworn face. With his foot in the cross-bow's stirrup, he wound back the weapon's spring until the crosswire clicked into position. He loaded the shining bolt into the groove, tight against the wire. Sighting along the top of the weapon, Nameless chose the blue-in-blue-in-blue major eye as his target.

He hesitated as Alias pulled against the strength of Phalse's mouth-stalks. Had he believed the gods still favored him, he would have prayed.

A hand jostled his shoulder, and Nameless accidentally set off the trigger. The bolt sizzled as it left the crossbow but it flew wide of its mark, smashing deep into the far wall, unnoticed by the combatants below.

Nameless turned in rage, expecting some dire beast.

Instead, his blue eyes met those of an old man dressed in dirty brown robes, and sporting a voluminous beard which spilled out over his cloak.

"Elminster," Nameless growled.

"She must finish this battle alone, Nameless."

"So Phalse can kill her and do your dirty work for you?"

"So she can prove to herself, and to thee, that she is her own master."

"She could die!"

A smile played across Elminster's lips. "I thought she was thy immortal vessel, who could not be killed. Ye made her a powerful fighter. Will ye follow her around until the end of thy days, rescuing her from every danger? What good is she to ye as an eternal monument if she cannot defend herself from the forces of the world?"

"But she's human. I . . ."

"Care for her?"

"Of course."

"That's a first," Elminster said. "Now show it. Let her go free."

*　　*　　*　　*　　*

The deadly tug of war between Alias and Phalse continued. Alias felt as if the monster was tearing her arms from her sockets. Her fingers were white from gripping the rock, and her hold was slipping. The time had come to risk a new strategy. She pushed hard against the wall, toward the mouth-beholder.

Phalse tumbled backward with Alias on top of him. She kicked at the head, but it was not like kicking a balloon, as she had expected. The head was as hard as armor, and a numbing shock rang up Alias's leg, but Phalse's grip on her slackened. She took advantage of the moment to draw her other boot dagger. She slashed off the stalks that bit into her, leaving long trails of misty blood in the air. She fell to the ground as Phalse floated back a few yards and hovered.

Alias rose without taking her eyes from the head, brandishing her bloody dagger. Dragonbait's sword lay on her right. She spoke, trying to cover her movement as she edged slowly toward it.

"You're awfully quiet now, Phalse. Run out of threats and taunts?" She noticed that her kick had dimpled its side.

"I'm listening—to the portal. Can't you hear it calling to you? Don't you feel drawn into it?"

"You wish, Phalse," Alias said with a laugh. "You don't think my sisters out there can do it, so you want me to believe I'm expendable. None of them ever received the mark of Moander, did they? They can't get to Moander the way I can, can they?"

"Not as easily as you, One, but they will try. I will send them, one at a time, until one of them succeeds. You could spare them all of that pain and agony. How can you resist the challenge?"

"Forget it, Phalse. You're not going to talk me into it."

Phalse's words, though, managed to split her attention between the beholder and the portal, so she didn't notice Phalse's ebony body behind her until it was too late. It struck her with a hard, powerful swing of its handless arm.

Alias fell to the ground like a sack, only a few feet from Dragonbait's sword. The giant torso loomed over her with Akabar dangling from its claw like a rag doll. Dragonbait lay motionless on the floor. Olive was still out cold.

Phalse's head laughed as it drifted until it fitted itself securely in the depression between the ebony form's shoulders. "This torso was also a prototype of sorts, both part and not part of me, useful as a carrier and warrior. But not as good as you."

The united Phalse, body and head, bent over her, the sucker mouths opening and closing in anticipation. Alias reached for Dragonbait's sword, grasped its hilt in both hands, and swung it low, near the floor. The sword passed cleanly through one of Phalse's ankles and chopped into the other. The body toppled over, and Alias rolled away as Phalse separated himself from the fallen ebony torso.

"You spoil all my fun," said the huge, bloated head. "Now we must end this." He charged at her.

Alias faked a stumble to one knee, and the head swooped lower, still moving quickly. Alias leaped to her feet, stabbing with Dragonbait's sword as if it were a dagger—right into the central blue eye.

Phalse hissed from all his remaining mouths, and Alias thought she had beaten him, when suddenly several more mouth-stalks sprang from the head and engulfed her. The large, lower mouth tried to bite her. She placed her free arm in the space between the skewered eye and the mouth, trying to remove Dragonbait's sword, but the blade was stuck. She succeeded only in keeping the awful main maw from snapping at her flesh.

* * * * *

Dragonbait recovered his senses as Alias was grappling with Phalse's head. This was her battle; she had asked him not to interfere.

The saurial staggered from the courtyard and into the former feast hall to stand between the rows of bodies. He agreed with Alias that her copies should not be destroyed.

The saurial thought back to the evening when he and Alias had been branded, when his soul had been stretched and torn until Alias had suddenly become possessed of life and a soul, and, unexpectedly, a spirit.

Just how did I do it? he asked himself. Was it my prayers, my stubborn defiance of the evil around me, my acceptance that death was near?

* * * * *

The forest of mouths encircled Alias, blocking her vision, and she and Phalse spun about dizzily. Alias became suddenly aware that they stood on the balcony.

Catching her foot against the wall, Alias twisted at the waist, slinging the head about by Dragonbait's sword. She let go of the sword's hilt.

The torque created by her spin was enough to rip the mouths from her body. Phalse's head went spinning from the tower with the sword still embedded in it.

Thirty feet from the balcony, Phalse and Dragonbait's sword achieved maximum potential and burst into a ball of white light as bright as the recent detonations near Westgate.

Alias shielded her eyes from the explosion with her arms and backed away from the balcony. She felt a familiar burning pain on her arm. A welcome pain. Phalse's sigil flared and vanished from her arm.

* * * * *

A sharp pain on Dragonbait's chest broke his concentration. The air filled with the scent of violets as the saurial realized the source of the pain. Phalse was dead.

Suddenly, the twelve figures before him faded to shimmering, glassy outlines and then vanished completely.

A last trick of Phalse's? the saurial wondered. He hadn't had time to learn if he'd succeeded. Now he might never know.

* * * * *

Alias swayed unsteadily and put her hand against a wall. Dragonbait stood in the doorway between the feast hall and the courtyard. He looked disturbed but uninjured.

Then Alias saw two figures bent over the bodies of her companions and she leaped toward them. One of them turned toward her, and she paused.

It was Nameless, and he and his companion were smearing healing ointment over Akabar's body. The other man moved toward Olive and told Alias, "She's alive, too."

There was something familiar about the figure and voice, but Alias was too weak to place it. She sank to her knees, chiding Nameless, "About time you showed up." Then she allowed herself the luxury of collapsing.

❧ 32 ❧

The Tale Told

Elminster and Nameless smeared Alias with foul-smelling ointments and bound her wounds. When she came to, Dragonbait was using his power to heal Akabar, who had been the most grievously hurt. Olive had a nasty gash on her forehead, but the old man who worked beside Nameless assured the halfling that if she would only keep her mouth shut, her headache would go away.

Alias felt no pain, courtesy of the ointments, but she was bone-weary. Akabar, who sat beside her, gave her a nudge and pointed to the old man. "That one was talking to Dragonbait in Shadowdale," the mage told her.

Elminster crouched beside Akabar. "I understand ye wanted to see me on a matter of grave importance."

Akabar flushed with sudden understanding. "Elminster?"

"Really?" Alias said. "And I thought you were just a goatherd who knew more than was good for me." She realized now that Akabar had never actually spoken with Elminster. "He's nothing at all like you described him, Akabar," she teased. "For one thing, he talks funny."

"Have you ever considered keeping an appointment calendar?" Akabar asked the old sage angrily.

"Yes," Elminster replied. "They make excellent tinder."

"You knew all about Nameless," Alias accused him. "You knew what I was, didn't you?"

"I knew about Nameless," Elminster confessed sadly. "But I was not sure about thee. Ye seemed too human to be the made thing he had envisioned. In disbelief, I put off coming here to ascertain if the bard was still safe in his prison. As they say, the wise aren't always."

"Aren't always what?" Olive chirped.

"Wise," supplied Alias.

Elminster nodded. "Got off my hindquarters fast enough when Moander was unleashed, though. Took me two days to trek out here. I watched thy arrival on the roof. New portal—must remember it."

"But you tried to get me to give up the songs, and I refused. You let me go. You knew it was wrong to try to squelch Nameless's songs."

"Let's say I was uncertain. I was prepared to sacrifice them to a greater good. Thy vehemence made me rethink the greater good. It was hard to argue with a soul so pure."

Alias looked shyly at Dragonbait. If they'd given me a piece of someone else's soul, she wondered, would I have succeeded in freeing myself?

"What will happen to Nameless?" she asked. "It's a little late to keep him locked up to protect his secret. And you most certainly aren't going to lock me up."

Elminster looked startled momentarily. "No," he agreed. "That would be unjustifiable. What he did may have been wrong, but what we did may not have been right. The time has come, I think, to review the matter."

"A second trial?" asked Nameless.

"Perhaps," said Elminster. "If so, I will speak in thy defense."

"As will I," Alias said.

Nameless smiled at her. "You really refused to give up my songs?"

"It was wrong to abandon them, and I knew it."

Something tickled the base of her wrist, and Alias held her arm up. In the once-empty space a blue rose blossomed, shimmering among the stiller pattern of waves and serpents.

Dragonbait clutched at his chest and looked down. The snaking pattern on his green scales was replaced by a wreath of blue ivy.

"A sign of the gods' favor?" Nameless asked the sage.

"It would appear so," Elminster agreed. He turned to Alias. "I have closed the portal leading to Phalse's domain, so ye will be safe here."

Alias could see that there was only water where the portal had been. The sight of her reflection brought to mind the copies of her Phalse had created. Struggling to her feet, she limped to the feast hall door.

"They're gone!" she cried. "What happened to them?"

Dragonbait shrugged his shoulders. The smell of brimstone rose from his body.

"You hoped to lay them to rest by destroying Phalse," Akabar reminded her. "It appears your wish was granted."

"Maybe they were never really there," Olive conjectured. "Maybe they were just an illusion Phalse conjured up to use against you. They must have vanished when you killed him."

"Perhaps," Alias whispered sadly. She could not believe either explanation.

Elminster, detecting the scent of lemon and ham from the saurial's body, cocked an eyebrow but said nothing.

"I think it's time to check the larder and see what goodies Phalse left behind," Olive suggested.

"In the cellars of this place," Nameless said to Dragonbait, "you will find a sword. I would be honored if you would accept it in place of the one you lost."

Dragonbait nodded graciously.

Nameless knelt by the injured halfling, who still cradled her head in her hands. "There's something I'd like you to have, too, Mistress Ruskettle."

The halfling's eyes shone as she held her hand out. In it Nameless placed a small, silver harp and crescent moon pin, the symbol of a Harper. She smiled up at Nameless. "Really? For me?" She pinnned the gift to her tattered gown. "Thank you."

"That's going to raise some hackles," said Elminster quietly.

"Let it," Nameless said.

Elminster smiled at Akabar. "I have a gift for ye, Akabar Bel Akash, a piece of advice perhaps more valuable than any magic item. It takes less time to solve thy own riddles than to wait in Lhaeo's office."

Akabar grinned and nodded.

Nameless looked uncertainly at Alias. "I have no more gifts to give you, yet I would ask for something from you."

Uncertainty gripped the swordswoman, a fear that Nameless would ask for something she could not give him, or something she would not wish to. "What is it?" she asked.

"I know of your birth," her 'father' said, "and Mistress Ruskettle has told me something of your travels. But I wish to hear you tell your tale."

Alias laughed with relief. Moving to the edge of the pool, she sat down and beckoned her audience to draw close. Olive perked up attentively, eager to hear the tale that would bring her fame throughout the Realms when she began telling it herself.

"I woke in Suzail, in the land of Cormyr, to the sound of two dogs barking. . . ."

As the three men and the saurial listened to Alias's beautiful voice, Olive leaned back and promptly fell asleep.

ABOUT THE AUTHORS

KATE NOVAK grew up in Pittsburgh, where she received a B.S. in Chemistry from the University of Pittsburgh. After getting married, she gave up laboratories; her husband Jeff keeps her from starving while she pursues her writing career. Her works published by TSR include pick-a-path, adventure gamebooks and game modules. She is a Girl Scout leader and a fussy cat owner.

JEFF GRUBB, also a Pittsburgh native, was a civil engineer before being kidnapped by Wisconsin leprechauns and put to work designing games and fantasy worlds for TSR, Inc. His writing credits include *Manual of the Planes*, an AD&D® Hardbound supplement, and the FORGOTTEN REALMS™ Boxed Set. He is currently serving as authoritative source, guardian spirit, and traffic cop for the ever-growing Forgotten Realms. His wife Kate keeps him sane in all this.

60 Years of the Best Science Fiction

©JANET AULISIO 1986.

AMAZING® STORIES

That's right. For over sixty years, **AMAZING**® Stories has offered fascinating and thought-provoking science fiction and fantasy by some of the genre's best-known authors. Continuing in this proud tradition, we publish works from among the best writers, including John Barnes, Ron Goulart, Sandra Miesel, Rebecca Ore, Robert J. Sawyer, Jack Williamson, and George Zebrowski.

Enhancing the fiction are book and movie reviews by guest authors, interviews, science articles, and other features, plus stunning artwork by some of the field's best artists—Janet Aulisio, George Barr, Bob Eggleton, Stephen E. Fabian, Hank Jankus, and John Lakey.

TSR, Inc.

Subscriptions rate for 6 bimonthly issues: $9.00

TSR Inc. POB 756
Lake Geneva, WI 53147